# THE LAST BELIEVER

A NOVEL BY

## JEROME KOMISAR

THE LAST BELIEVER
a novel by Jerome Komisar

First Edition, September 2012

Copyright © 2012 by Jerome Komisar

Author Services by Pedernales Publishing LLC
www.pedernalespublishing.com

Hillel-Tzeporah Press
Washington, D.C.
hiltzepress@gmail.com

Library of Congress Control Number: 2012912403

ISBN: 978-0-9858584-0-7

*For My Sister*
*Roslyn Komisar Mayer*
*She walked me to the public library in Borough Park*
*and gave me the world.*

# THE LAST BELIEVER

# Chapter 1

Benjamin Palmer's dream had misled him. He expected to wake up in his own bed with Caitlin in his arms, her soft hair brushing his chest, her breathing tender, her lips almost touching his skin. A radio was to be playing in the background with comfortable voices talking about the weather and traffic and yesterday's stock market advance. And he was happy.

But he didn't wake in a dream. He woke to the sound of Ilya's fierce snoring, now like a train screeching off its tracks, then like a garbage truck swallowing a week's trash. In other places and other times, it would have been comical, Benjamin thought, but here it was exasperating and unnerving. It was a metaphor for his isolation and imprisonment.

He pressed a tattered pillow against his ears to shield himself from the infuriating clamor, but it only made him more sensitive to the noise. He turned his face to the cracked plaster wall and pulled his knees towards his chest. Instinctively, he closed his eyelids tighter as if shutting out light would stifle his hearing. Nothing helped. He turned around and leaned on one elbow. "Shut up," he shouted although he knew it would have no effect. He glared at his captor. Almost every morning was the same, Ilya looking half-crazed, his heavy-lidded gray eyes partially open, his disheveled beard coated with spittle. Ilya's body shuddered, jerking the rifle barrel that he clutched between his arms. The snoring momentarily stopped and Slavic words rattled from his mouth, frenetic declarations full of harsh consonants, sounding like remnants of a bitter argument or a declaration of contempt. Russian, Benjamin knew, but to his unlearned ears, it could have been Ukrainian or Polish or Bulgarian.

"Do you understand what he's saying?" he yelled to Marya.

"Only the words."

"And?"

"Not important," she answered without emotion.

Benjamin tossed the rough blanket to the foot of the thin mattress, picked up his ill-fitting pants from the floor, and pulled them on. Marya turned away.

"Can I use the outhouse?" Benjamin asked, his voice louder than necessary, his tone sarcastic.

She did not answer. It was unnecessary. Benjamin knew she understood the game he was playing, constantly reminding her that he was a prisoner by asking permission for all the things he knew he could freely do. He refused to let her believe that her courtesies detracted from his sense of internment.

As Benjamin exited the dilapidated split-log cabin he smelled Ilya's foul breath, a mixture of vodka and garlic and rotten teeth.

All mornings were bad, but this one promised to be worse than most. It was his dream, he decided, that made it impossible for him to accept the schizoid nature of his imprisonment. He wanted his unfocused anger to smolder, his self-pity to percolate. He forced himself to deny that the cool morning air thrilled his skin; that the early sunlight, still too angled to yield warmth, made the countryside beautiful. He tried not to hear the birds, to notice the rustling leaves.

Benjamin Palmer put his hand over his mouth and looked at the ground when he passed the outhouse—a narrow, rectangular structure, its wood exterior stained black by time, its timbers oddly angled, its porous roof covered by tangled weeds. When the wind blew from the east, the structure's fetid stench floated over the vegetable garden Marya carefully tended and slipped into the cabin. At first, he thought he would get used to the smell, but he never did. Instead, he fought the stink by waiting until he reached the patch of woods that separated the cabin from the river before taking a deep breath. Evergreen trees, mostly, surrounded him, their branches filtering the sun, their fallen pine needles scenting the cool air. It was a treasured remnant, Benjamin had realized during the first days of his captivity, of the vast forest that had covered this land through most of human history. Once a dark and forbidding place where generations of hunters stalked deer and wild boar, the great forest had been felled by the myriad of people who came through this land—Poles and Lithuanians, Ruthenian peasants and Cossack warriors—and was now mostly fertile farmland covered by acres of grain and small vegetable gardens. Chickens ran free around the one house Benjamin could see from the edge of the woods, and a lonely cow grazed lazily in the large backyard.

Benjamin unzipped his pants in front of an old Linden tree, but the sweet aroma of its flowers caused him to turn away, and he spent his urine on the thick underbrush. He ran his fingers along the base of his penis searching for the small scar, and was relieved that the wound was no longer tender. But he was still afraid that he had been permanently diminished if no longer evidently damaged. He carefully zipped his pants and continued through the woods until he reached the narrow river that cut along its western edge. He let the cold water run over his hands, washed his face, and wet his hair. Then, to his surprise, he gave expression to his despair by letting out a loud and bitter scream.

The unnerving squeal startled the three children who were washing clothes on the other side of the slowly moving water. Their heads snapped up, their faces filled with incomprehension. Finally, the oldest, already a young woman at fourteen, broke the silence and yelled a few words he did not understand. Embarrassed by his outburst, Benjamin waved his arms over his head and smiled broadly. He chuckled to himself. His friends, as Benjamin had begun to think of them, were concerned about him. They were evidently all from the same seed, with identical sun-bleached yellow hair and broad faces, their legs long, their hips narrow, their eyes a light and brilliant blue. Ilya had laid down the law while pointing the decrepit rifle at Benjamin's head, "Never cross the stream. It is your western wall. Touch the other side and you will drown. Understand? The fruit trees, to you they are solid stone—the apples to the left, the pears to the right. Go beyond them and a rope will fall around your neck. And the dirt road, you can go to the other side, but not too far. A black bear will eat you and rats will chew on your carcass. Understand, my brother?" Benjamin understood.

"Good morning," the captive yelled over the stream and waved his hands over his head.

"Good morning," the boy yelled back with great pride.

"Good morning, Kostya," Benjamin echoed.

"Good morning, Benya," the small boy responded, showing all his teeth.

Benjamin sat on the dew-covered embankment and leaned against an ancient willow tree, its trunk encircled by thick green vines. The stark contrasts of his world overwhelmed him. The gray, threatening cabin commanded by Ilya and his rifle—a place where life was fragile and extinguishable, where drunken laughter instantly twisted into blazing outrages—contrasted harshly with the surrounding countryside, the green of the rolling hills, the yellow of the sinuous fields, the brilliant sunlight, the vibrant air, the voices of birds and children, of brook and wind. It was bewildering and eternally sad, Benjamin thought, this constant battle between ugliness and beauty.

Benjamin stretched out his legs and watched the children go about their morning chores. Marya had shared their names with him. The boy was Konstantin, but was called Kostya. He was ten or eleven, Marya thought but was uncertain. The older girl was Ludmila, but was called Mila by her siblings. Darya was the youngest, and in many ways the cutest. "Dasha," Mila would yell out whenever the child tested her older sister's patience. She looked no older than five, but Marya had told him she was seven, the one age of which she was certain. "I talk with Dasha," Marya had told the prisoner. To Benjamin they were company. They were cheer and energy. Simply knowing their names eased his captivity. Their knowing his name, however they pronounced it, proclaimed that he was alive, that he still existed.

The children threw the wet clothing into a wicker basket and turned to walk back to the small farmhouse that lay at a distance from the river. Two young goats were following Dasha, butting their heads together, and then butting her. After climbing up the rocky bank, the children stopped, their bodies half-hidden in the tall grass, and talked among themselves. Kostya, carrying a tin plate, ran downstream to a spot where widely separated flat rocks formed a precarious bridge across the water, and, hopping barefoot from one stone to another, effortlessly made the journey to the opposite bank. Benjamin struggled to his feet fearing that the young boy was breaking some secret code, that his crossing was an infraction that could bring severe punishment to both of them. He looked around to see if anyone was watching, but the dense foliage limited his vision. He was ready to retreat when Kostya's soprano called out his name. "Benya," he shouted, "Benya."

With an enormous smile on his face and his blue eyes sparkling, the boy motioned to Benjamin to cup his hands. His happy expression turned into intense concentration as Kostya poured the dozen strawberries that lay at the bottom of the pan into the man's hands. When the last strawberry fell, the young boy broke into laughter.

"Thank you," Benjamin said in a voice filled with surprised delight.

"Hello," the boy said in a thick accent while continuing to laugh. He turned quickly and headed back to the other side. Dasha yelled something cheerful to her brother. Mila waved to Benjamin.

Then they left. He could only see their heads as they ran through the field of wheat and made their way home, but he imagined their tanned skins glimmering in the sunlight, their hand-me-down clothes blowing behind them.

Benjamin settled under the willow tree and carefully placed the unexpected treat of strawberries on a nearby rock. He leaned his head back and closed his eyes so that he could feel the sun's rays upon his face. He listened to the comforting sound of the river as it slowly meandered south and then bent to the east. It had become part of his daily routine if the weather allowed, walking down to the river, sitting under the willow, waiting until the sun was high enough in the horizon for the branches of the tree to shadow on his body before returning to the cabin. It was one of the habits that allowed him to tolerate the strange prison in which he found himself, and push to the back of his mind the fear, the pain, the unbearable anxieties of his first days of captivity. Benjamin's physical strength was returning; his emotional balance, as far as he could tell, had been restored. Ilya, he had learned, had no desire to hurt him, and Marya—he had begun to think of her as more of a fellow inmate and less as a guard.

It was the river itself, Benjamin realized, that put him most at ease, the music made by its rushing water, the laughter of children that floated from the opposite bank. He often daydreamed about following its course, expecting that soon he would come upon another homestead, or a riverside village, or even a small city. He could leave at dawn, he mused, long before the sunlight seeped into the cabin and woke Marya, and be miles away before Ilya was informed of his disappearance, before his captors could organize themselves to find him. Yes, it would be easy to start a run for freedom, but what would happen then? He had no single answer. On bright days, when the morning air was dry and cool, and his spirits were high, he saw himself discovered by sympathetic people, by men and women who despite difficulties of language would understand his plight and happily help him get back to America. On other days, when the air was heavy, the morning hot, and his spirits low, he found himself following the river to isolated farms worked by friends of Ilya who would recapture him and drag him back to the cabin. Ilya's trust would disappear, and he'd find himself tied to his bed at night and shackled in the barn during the day, no longer free to walk down to the river and see the children, no longer free to help Marya in her garden. If he avoided the farmhouses and wandered along the river until he came upon a village or a city, would he become prey to thugs and bastards who looked just like his kidnappers in Kyiv? He imagined himself once again rotting away in a damp, dark, earthen basement, tied to a rickety chair, a filthy gag stuffed in his mouth.

The sweetness of the first strawberry pushed him to eat another and then another. He smiled when he recalled Kostya yelling "Benya," and saying a thickly accented "hello." Unexpectedly, he found himself feeling sorry that he had no children, believing—in an irrational twist of mind—that having sons and daughters would somehow protect him. But there were no children awaiting his liberation. There was only an estranged wife, a ruined reputation, a life without a clear future. There was no rush to run away, Benjamin told himself as he finished the last of the berries. He would wait for his strength to come back before he attempted to escape, and wait to see how the string played out, his patience, he realized, made possible by knowing that if his captivity became insufferable there was always the river, there was always the possibility of freedom downstream.

# Chapter 2

A tall, heavyset man in his early fifties met her at the reception desk. "Mrs. Palmer, I'm Ernest Hockney," he said. He instructed her to hang the visitor's pass around her neck and led her through the metal detectors.

She corrected him as they stepped onto an elevator. "I'm Caitlin McCoy."

"Your maiden name?" he asked.

His gaze made her uncomfortable. "My only name. I never gave it up. Benjamin Palmer is my husband."

He led her through a dimly lit corridor and into his windowless office. "Coffee?" he asked over his shoulder.

"Please," she answered without thinking. It was a little past nine. If it were a normal morning she'd be at home chewing on a toasted English muffin spread thinly with orange marmalade, a third cup of coffee in her other hand. But it wasn't a normal morning.

"Could you tell me what this is about?" she said before taking the armed chair in front of Hockney's desk.

"Let me get the coffee first. I can use some," he said. "Would you like milk and sugar? I'm afraid I can't offer you any cream."

"Just black," she said, annoyed by his substituting courtesy for communication. It was the State Department, she reminded herself. Posturing had to be expected.

He kicked the office door closed when he returned with the coffee. Georgetown University read the white mugs.

"Well?" she said as soon as Hocking had sat down behind the desk. She was not going to hide her anxiety.

"Do you know where your husband is?"

"Has something happened to him?" she asked as her hand began to shake. She put the coffee down on Hockney's desk.

"We don't know. That's why I asked you here. Where is he supposed to be?"

"Is he dead?" she blurted out and began to tremble.

"No, Ms. McCoy. We have no reason to think that he is in any way hurt. I know this seems very abrupt, but try to be patient. For all we know he's sunbathing on the Riviera. Please. Just follow me for a minute if you can."

His forced smile did nothing to dispel her fears. She had to stop herself from yelling at him. "So why all this mystery?" she asked.

"Where is your husband?" he repeated.

Caitlin closed her eyes for a second and breathed deeply through her nose, a handy relaxation technique she had learned while studying acting at the College at Purchase, and which she used whenever she was to appear on the evening news.

"Are you alright," Hockney asked in a subdued voice.

"I'm not sunbathing on the Riviera," she answered.

Hockney didn't seem to find her answer clever. He put the mug down on the desk, leaned back in his chair—the florescent ceiling light reflecting off his ebony complexion—and waited.

"We've been separated for over a year. We don't keep in daily touch,"

"I'm sorry," he said. He sounded sincere, although she didn't know if his sorrow was owing to her being separated or that she wasn't in daily contact with her husband.

"He was going on a peculiar quest. To find a village, once in Poland but now, he believed, somewhere in western Ukraine," she said. She surprised herself and recalled something she had thought she didn't know, "Peczenizyn, or something like that, near the Carpathian Mountains."

"Can you spell that for me?" Hockney asked as he lifted his pen.

"That was the same question I asked Benjamin," Caitlin noted before struggling to remember what her husband had told her.

~

Benjamin moved out of their townhouse after they split and into a one bedroom, third floor apartment on New Hampshire Avenue, with a balcony that overlooked the tops of deciduous trees and into the windows of once grand houses. But he rarely sat outside. The street below was too noisy, the air too cold in winter and too hot in summer. The address had no architectural distinction, nor could the building claim a list of famous past occupants—senators or congressmen or presidential aspirants—like so many neighboring apartment houses in Washington. But it was a relatively safe building, and just blocks from his townhouse. Its convenience to Capitol Hill and the law firms on K Street appealed to the young and single aspirants who had found employment in the nation's capital, twentysomethings who were unlikely to recognize his name, who were indifferent to recently past Wall Street scandals. It was only after he had moved in that he realized the location's drawbacks. At thirty-eight, his neighbors made him feel like an old man. Kids, he called them under his breath, and thought of them as being at once narcissistic and full of self-doubt. He avoided using the elevator in the morning, jealous of the young men in dark business suits and white shirts, uncomfortable with the women in high heels and conservative dresses, their breasts firm, their legs appealing, their bodies thin. At night, his neighbors metamorphosed into jeans and polo shirts, the women's thin and revealing tops making them look too hungry for attention to be attractive. But the neighborhood was home, its bookstores and restaurants places that he and Caitlin had enjoyed during the six years of their marriage. "Name the cuisine and it's within walking distance," he had told Caitlin when they first looked for a place to live. "Thai, Indian, Italian, Russian, you name it, and it's within a ten minute walk. You can even get a hamburger if you search long enough."

After the separation he continued their habit of eating out, a once necessary accommodation to both of them working long hours and hating to cook. Even eating alone was not new to him, but where it was once due to Caitlin's evening news obligations, it was now due to his being single. When his loneliness became insufferable he'd invite a woman he had met at a Phillips Collection Thursday night gathering or at an evening lecture at the Smithsonian to join him. Sometimes he'd bump into someone he had once worked with and persuade him or her to share a meal. But dining with former colleagues was often awkward.

After a month of living alone he lost interest in varying cuisines and settled down to just a handful of restaurants. Most often, he ate at a simple Greek restaurant where you picked up your food at the counter and carried your tray to a table.

It was there that he met him, the man with the faded beard, his eyes magnified by thick glasses, his bulbous nose darkly veined. They were both sitting outside on the restaurant's patio. The old man was half-hidden behind a copy of the Washington Post. A glass of ice tea was pushed to the center of his table.

Benjamin could feel the old man's eyes studying him. When he looked up, the man raised the paper to hide his face.

Benjamin went back to his food and to the used copy of Isaiah Berlin's *The Hedgehog and the Fox* he had just picked up at a bookstore on P Street. Again, he felt the stranger's eyes. Again, the paper quickly covered his face. Benjamin returned to his lamb on rice.

The stranger was there again a week later. A wrinkled newspaper printed in Cyrillic shielding his face. Benjamin sat down as far away as possible, his back to the stocky, bearded man.

He heard the stranger's chair scrape against the concrete patio floor. He listened for his footsteps, but the noise coming off Connecticut Avenue smothered his approach. Still, Benjamin knew he was coming.

"Neuman, is that your name?" the stranger asked in a Slavic accent.

"Are you speaking to me?" Benjamin said abruptly.

"Please excuse me, but you have such a familiar face. Neuman was the family name—from Poland. That's why I ask."

He looked much older than Benjamin had originally thought, his gray hair thin, his beard yellowed by time, his lips covered with black spots. Yet his blue eyes were bright, his voice strong. "I apologize," he said in response to Benjamin's bewildered expression. He attempted to walk briskly back to his table, but his gate was unsteady and he seemed to totter before he sat down.

Benjamin thought he might skip the restaurant. There were countless places where he could dine in private, places where he could relish his loneliness as if it were an appropriate penitence for a soiled career and a failed marriage. Yet his curiosity had been triggered. "Neuman," he said to himself, "from Poland." Two weeks later he went back to the Greek cafe, loading his tray with lamb and rice, with a cup of hot coffee. He was disappointed that the old man was not there.

He ate at the restaurant the next night and the night after that. A few days later the old man reappeared, sitting with his tea, with a newspaper that looked as if it had passed through numerous hands. Benjamin carried his tray over to the stranger's table. "May I join you?" he asked.

There were multiple gaps in his teeth when he smiled. "Please," he said. He made the word sound Russian.

"Benjamin," he said after he took his seat. "Benjamin Palmer."

"Abramowitz," the old man said, "Martin Abramowitz."

"From Poland?"

"Poland then, now Ukraine; when I was born, the Austro-Hungarian Empire. My mother thought Franz Joseph was blessed by God—you know, the Emperor."

Benjamin nodded, amused that Abramowitz would think that he wasn't familiar with Franz Joseph. "Neuman, you said?"

"Neuman. A family of rabbis from Kolomyja and Peczenizyn. You look just like them."

"Were they clones?"

It took a second for Abramowitz to realize that the younger man had made a feeble jest. He let out a hesitant laugh to be polite and pulled a battered black folder from a breast pocket, the type of wallet used to hold credentials and foreign currencies. Benjamin could see the edge of a passport. "Let me show you," Abramowitz said, his fingers fumbling through the thickly packed folder. He pulled out a faded black and white photograph and gently pushed it along the table to Benjamin. "See," he said.

It was a school photograph, five rows of boys, the youngest students, age seven or eight, sitting cross-legged on the ground. The other children stood in rows, the older behind the younger, the ranks thinning out when you got to the fifteen and sixteen year olds. They were all similarly dressed, with white shirts and dark ties and poorly fitting jackets. The young were wearing brimmed caps; some of the older boys wore fedoras. All heads were covered.

"Look at the last row, and look at the teacher," Abramowitz insisted and pointed his finger at the images.

Benjamin let out a nervous laugh. "If I had a magnifying glass ... ." he began to say.

"Please," Abramowitz pleaded.

The teacher's heavy beard made complete identification difficult, but his nose and forehead appeared in Benjamin's mirror every time he shaved. The face of the young boy standing in the last row—his wavy hair light and thick, his curly side locks combed behind his ears—looked much like Benjamin at the same age. He was stunned. He put on his reading glasses and lifted the picture.

"You're not Jewish, are you?"

"No. I come from a long line of non-Jews," Benjamin said, amused, and a little bit honored.

"It matters not. The winds of love blow seeds far and wide." Abramowitz's tone made the sentence sound lascivious.

"Sex, you mean."

"Rabbi Neuman would have said love."

"Well, there's your proof that we're not related. I know it is sex."

Abramowitz plucked the picture from Benjamin's hand and began to return it to the wallet, but then stopped himself and began to study the photograph. "Now you understand my mistake. The picture is close to 80 years old. I treasure it. The boy standing next to young Neuman is me. We were great friends. We were the same age, but Neuman was my teacher. From the day after his bar mitzvah, everyone called him Reb Neuman, although he wasn't Hassidic. It began to sound like one name, RebNeuman. The teacher was a rabbi, young Neuman's father. See how alike they look. Clones they could be."

Benjamin thought he saw Abramowitz's eyes water. "I wish I could be of help," he said.

The old man nodded. "Eat before your dinner gets cold," he said. There was a trace of resignation in his voice.

~

Hocking looked disappointed in Caitlin's responses when he finished the last of his coffee and placed the cup on the edge of the desk. "Our embassy in Kyiv received telephone calls from someone claiming to have kidnapped a Benjamin Palmer." He paused for a second, trying to judge her reaction. She could feel her face pale. "We thought it a hoax, a call from some drunken Russian or Ukrainian who picked your husband's pocket and learned his name from his passport; a petty thief who thought he could make a quick buck. Maybe it was someone who just wanted to pull our chain? We don't know. We gave them our official response, we don't pay ransom."

She sat in disbelief, her mind incapable of absorbing the situation. She wished there was a friend sitting next to her, someone to share what Hocking was saying, someone to attest to this actually happening. "Is he hurt?" she asked.

"I have no reason to think he's injured."

"But if he's been kidnapped—what do they do to the people they kidnap?"

"Let's not get ahead of ourselves," Hocking said holding his hands up, their palms facing her.

"That's not easy to do. How much did they ask for his return?"

"They didn't. 'Make us an offer,' was the message."

"Is that usual?" Caitlin asked, deciding to try to play reporter and not victim.

"The first in my experience," Hocking said, his body again leaning back in the metallic desk chair. He looked relieved, Caitlin thought, glad that he wasn't dealing with a half-crazed wife pulling at her hair. "There were a number of things that seemed different. He didn't name the group he was with by either a fake or a real name. He spoke English proficiently, I was told, his accent a mix of Eastern Europe and Britain. We've concluded he must have studied in England or Australia or New Zealand. The Brits are the most probable. They get a lot of foreign students from Eastern Europe."

"A Ukrainian? A Russian?"

"We don't know. But the accent was evidently from that section of the world."

"Terrorists?" Caitlin asked nervously.

"There is no reason to think so. There is no reason to think he's been kidnapped other than the calls. That's why I asked to see you and to find out where your husband was supposed to be."

"There is more than one Benjamin Palmer in the world. It could be someone else entirely," she said.

"There may be many Benjamin Palmers, but not many who have recently flown to Kyiv."

The conversation was moving too fast. She was beginning to panic, her husband of seven years disappeared in a foreign country. A ransom demand received from an unknown criminal, most probably a sadistic terrorist who doesn't give a damn if her husband lives or dies. She nervously shifted in her chair and altered the way her long legs were crossed. Then she shifted her body again, put her feet flat on the floor, and leaned forward. She felt her heart race; her throat turn dry. "Could I have some more coffee? I'm sure you'd like some more to drink, too," she said in a play for time.

"How can you be certain it is Benjamin?" she asked after he handed her the refilled mug.

"The second phone call convinced us that it was your husband he was talking about, although we are still not certain he is actually being held hostage. The caller asked if we had come up with a figure, and then, disappointed that we wouldn't, said he was holding a rich American who had run afoul of the law but got away with it."

"I see," she said sadly. Hocking had done his homework. "So how can you still consider that it might be a ruse?"

"That is always a possibility," he said without emotion. "Are there other relatives he may have been in contact with?" Hocking lifted a pen from his desk as if preparing to take notes.

"No. His parents died a number of years ago—they were in their forties when they had him. There are no siblings. He has a few cousins, but we haven't seen much of them since our wedding."

"Close friends that he may be in contact with."

"Perhaps, but I don't know of any. When he was indicted his friends abandoned him. There were never many. He's a private person. My friends became his friends. I'd know if they were in contact with him."

"Girlfriends?"

Caitlin gave out a dry laugh. "How would I know?" But she did know. There was no one serious. He was still in love with her, or so he kept saying. It was suddenly important to her, this fidelity. It tied her to his welfare.

~

Abramowitz had chosen an outdoor table close to the restaurant's entrance before Benjamin arrived. A large, checkerboard umbrella protected him from a cool drizzle.

"Do you always eat lamb and rice?" the old man asked after Benjamin had settled down.

"Not always, but it is my favorite."

"Variety is good."

"I know."

"Good for the stomach and the soul. Not many things are good for both," Abramowitz continued.

"How about scotch?"

"I'm not convinced about the stomach," Abramowitz said with a wink.

He had had a haircut since the previous night and his beard was trimmed. Unkemptness no longer protected him from looking old. "How old are you?" Benjamin asked rudely.

"Ninety-three last month. And you?"

"Thirty-eight."

"You look younger, but in my eyes everyone is younger."

"So there is a half century between us."

"More like a century and a half," Abramowitz chuckled.

Benjamin answered with a smile.

The old man took the beaten wallet from his an inside jacket pocket and pulled out two pictures. Solemnly, he handed them to his companion. "Neuman's wedding picture, and a picture he took with me a few years later. He was a rabbi when he got married."

It was Benjamin's nose and eyes, his forehead, his thick lips and solid chin. Even the body build was the same, slender, with narrow shoulders, the torso and legs perfectly proportioned. In both pictures he was shaven. Abramowitz had a full dark beard. The bride was too overdressed to be glamorous, and her eyes were too close together for beauty, her chin too small. But happiness was written across her face.

A shiver went up Benjamin's spine. His hand shook when he picked up his fork.

"Strange, is it not?" Abramowitz said. "The likeness is unmistakable."

"I can't deny it."

"Why would you want to?"

"Was he always clean shaven? You look more the rabbi than Neuman. What was his first name, by the way?

"Yaakov. He shaved when he turned twenty and never grew a beard again. When the Jews in the study hall asked him why he shaved, he'd answer, with a wink of the eye, that his wife didn't like the feel of facial hair. They enjoyed the answer. It made them laugh. But he had a deeper reason for his appearance. He wanted to be able to bridge the worlds of his time, the old world of the Talmud and the Cabala with the new world of science and engineering, to tie the worship of God to the age of free thinking.

"And what happened to him?" Benjamin asked.

"He was swallowed up in the Holocaust by the children of darkness. I lived and Neuman died. God plays his tricks. When I saw you, I said to myself, maybe he escaped. Maybe Gabriel's chariot carried my best friend over the ocean and to the new land, stealing his memory for compensation—that his holiness lives on in you. You lifted an old man's spirit."

"You're a romantic, Martin, a 19th century romantic. I have the kind of face that people think they know. That's all. I'm not the child of lost nobility."

"Perhaps, Benjamin, perhaps. You were reading Isaiah Berlin's *Russian Thinkers* when I got carried away. Two signs, I thought, the face and the book."

"I had just picked up a used copy. I hadn't gotten very far."

"See, there are things for you to explore."

# Chapter 3

Marya was pulling weeds out of her small vegetable garden when Benjamin got back from the small river, her dark hair tinted by the sunlight.

"You've been gone a long time," she said. There was no question in her comment, no admonition, and no accusation. It was a simple comment, a way to say good morning.

"The children gave me strawberries."

"They must like you."

"Do you know their parents?"

"Nice people," she said before bending down and continuing to weed.

There was cheerfulness in her voice and a lightness of spirit. There usually was. When they met on the first day of his life in the cabin, when Ilya was still binding him to an oak chair with rough, thick ropes that tore at his skin, he had found Marya's voice grating. He thought she was a simpleton, totally unsympathetic to his plight, incapable of empathy or pity. He had been wrong, very wrong. What he first thought was stupidity was an innate ability to see beyond the ugly, to peel back Ilya's anger and find kindness, to recognize a light breeze when those around her felt only the hot, humid air. Or so he wanted to imagine. He needed her to be clever. He wanted her to be kind.

Her gray skirt rose above her knees. Her large breasts pressed against a darkly colored blouse. It was the outfit she wore most often, her legs uncovered, her black hair combed back in a bun. Twenty-nine, or at least that's what she told him, but to Benjamin she looked older, older than the women he knew in Washington who claimed to be close to thirty, women who controlled their diets and jogged three times a week. "Russian women have two ages," Marya had told him. "We are young until we are thirty—sometimes only twenty-five. We are old at thirty-one. Russia doesn't allow women to age gracefully."

"And men?" he had questioned. "Do they age gracefully?"

"They don't age at all," she had answered amiably. She had a sweet, shy giggle, usually delivered with her eyes cast down and a small smile on her robust lips. It was a chuckle, Benjamin thought, which belonged to a teenager on her first date or a peasant girl with a first suitor. He couldn't imagine Marya ever turning truly old.

"Is he up?" Benjamin asked.

"He went down to the water and already came back. You didn't see him?"

"I didn't. How is he?"

"Cheerful. Very cheerful. He was singing when he left."

"Even after such a fitful sleep? He must have gotten lucky," Benjamin said.

Marya laughed at his minor indecency, but it was a half-hearted laugh. "He's pixilated, Benjamin. What else can it be?"

"Pixilated? You don't hear that word very often."

Marya stopped what she was doing to look at him. "I used it correctly, no?"

"It's the perfect word."

This time her laugh was robust. "Make yourself some tea. Ilya brought some jam for the bread. Cut yourself some cheese. More will come tomorrow."

She was not attractive in the way his wife was attractive. She didn't have the perfect figure, the small, slightly upturned nose, the cheekbones that cameras love, the fair skin, the startling blue eyes, the small and shapely ass. Marya was too tall and too solid to be a fantasized mistress. Her round face, no matter how pretty he found it, would be cruelly treated by television cameras. She was designed to be a mother, Benjamin had thought after getting to know her. Mother, he knew, was the wrong word, but he hadn't yet found another.

Caught up by their voices, Ilya came out of the cabin, a basket swinging from one hand, an almost empty bottle of vodka in the other, the rifle hanging over a shoulder. "Come, Benjamin, have some breakfast with me. Nothing but the best, bread, cheese, a little vodka, and a piece of herring I caught last night. It was swimming in the restaurant's refrigerator." He placed the basket on the weathered wooden table, under the shade of a thickly leafed oak tree, and quickly removed its contents.

They had fed Benjamin well over the last three weeks. His plate crowded with foods he had never noticed in the markets of America and certainly never bought. Soups made from beetroot or cabbage, main dishes of mushrooms and sour cream, and herring mixed with boiled potatoes, beets, and carrots, and overcooked lamb and beef, and chicken drowned in paprika. Yet he was tiring of it, bored with the repetition, with the limited variety of fruit. What had been refreshingly new to his palate now seemed unrefined, almost tasteless. Paprika, sugar, and salt—lots of salt—seemed to be their only spices. There was an endless supply of vodka and a fair amount of Russian brandy. The label called it Cognac. He found the beer tasteless, but the wine from Georgia, which only appeared on the table after Ilya had spent a night brawling at some distant tavern, was drinkable, sometimes it was even good.

"Don't you want to eat with an old man?" Ilya barked. "Is my English too fancy for you?"

He had used that line often, but Benjamin could never resist responding with a snigger. Ilya was proud of his command of English. Three years in the English speaking west—two at the University of St. Andrews in Scotland studying engineering and a year at the London School of Economics—had convinced Ilya, at least when he was sober, that he sounded like Tony Blair. When Ilya was drunk, he thought he spoke like Winston Churchill. But he sounded like neither. Every word was full of Slavic vowels and consonants, every sentence bore the cadence of Russian. Marya Ivanova had the better ear for languages. Her accent added sweetness to English.

"Something to eat?" Benjamin yelled out to Marya.

"I've eaten twice already. If I eat more, I'll never get an American figure."

"Good," shouted Ilya. "American women look like twigs."

Benjamin sat across from his host on a bench that tilted to his right—as did the wooden table—shifted over time, Benjamin thought, by the rainstorms that pounded the ground in summer, by the melting snows that left the countryside coated with mud during early spring. But the table may have just been made unevenly, as unevenly as everything seemed to be built in this corner of the world. Floors tilted. The edges of roofs were unleveled. Walls didn't meet in right angles. To Benjamin, everything in this hamlet, this outpost of farmhouses and barns and a blacksmith shop, seemed thrown together with little attention, with no carpenter's measurements or plumb line, with no belief that they would still be used in five years or ten. And yet, these buildings, always ready to fall, always ready to be abandoned, must have served and sheltered countless generations. When it rained, which it often did, Benjamin found the enclave endlessly depressing, but when the sun shone, it was something else.

"Do you know why Lenin failed, Benjamin? Because he fought religion, that's why. Communism could never replace the belief in an omnipotent God, a God who holds souls in his hands, who controls fate. People need illusions to survive this world. They need to believe in a benevolent force. They need to believe in just reckonings. They need to worship. How long can you worship a little man with a sharp beard? How long can you worship a tyrant with a huge mustache and a pipe hanging from his lips? There are constants in the world, Benya, the sunset, the winter cold, birds nesting in a thatched roof, and the prayer of man. Even Lenin couldn't change that. Can you imagine Lenin dressed as Ded Moroz—your Santa Claus, I believe—and traveling across the continent behind a troika?"

Benjamin remained silent. It was far too early in the morning to contend with Ilya the philosopher.

"Have you no thoughts about important things, my American? Are you too rich to think about what makes us human?"

Ilya's question struck a nerve. "I care very much about being human," Benjamin answered hotly. "But being human is not talking about it, but acting it. How can you talk about being human when you hold me here like an animal? Is this what you think human is, isolating me from everything I know, keeping me in fear of tomorrow, threatening my life."

Ilya's lips tightened and his eyes flamed. He banged a callused hand on the wooden table and growled. The noise reverberated through the forest, startling Marya upright and frightening the horse that was tethered near the barn. The other Ilya was coming out, the prophet of vengeance. "Like an animal? I treat you like an animal? Do you have chains on your legs? Do you live in darkness with no one to talk to, with nothing but stale bread and water, with rats scurrying across your legs?" He turned his head and looked sideways at Benjamin. "My American fool, you do not know what it is to be treated like an animal." He let out a threatening laugh. "If you want to learn how to be treated like an animal, I can show you."

"You know what I mean, Ilya," Benjamin said in a softer voice, trying to stay firm and back away at the same time. "What is happening? Have you heard from the embassy? At least tell me that."

"They hear from me, Benya. I do not hear from them. They have made no offer. I asked them how much you are worth and plan to ask three times their price. All they do is lie and tell me they don't pay kidnappers. I said, 'don't pay me; just give me money.' They refused to so much as chortle. Your embassy people have no sense of humor."

"Maybe they don't think you're being funny?" Benjamin said in a tight voice.

"The attaché at the British Embassy would have laughed."

"So what's next?"

"I'll tell them the truth. You are willing to give up all your earthly possessions for your freedom. Since you have no wife and no children, we will concentrate on the money. The newspapers said you are worth at least five million. I'll settle for that."

"Newspapers exaggerate, Ilya. There are things I'd have to do to make any amount accessible. You know that. The government can't simply liquidate my assets and spend my money."

Ilya's eyes turned boyish. "Benya, Benya, Benya. I have done the physics. The rest is engineering. I have faith your government will work it out. They might even add a little to what you are worth."

Marya placed a basket of freshly picked pea pods on the table. "Faith to do what?" Marya asked.

"My faith that his government can get me my money."

"You mean his money," she said.

"Butchers, both of you," Ilya let out with a smirk. Then he shifted into Russian.

Marya's cast-iron expression began to break. The deep dimple on the left side of her face appeared as she giggled, but her smile was not wide enough to expose her two gold teeth. She saved her broad, infectious smiles for the late afternoon, when the sun was sinking below the Carpathian Mountains and she had come in from the forest, her dark skin shimmering under a thin layer of sweat. Topping a glass of water off with a dash of vodka, she would sit on the steps that led to the cabin's front door and lean back, her body luxuriating in the sunset's breeze. She'd pull her skirt high over her knees, her thighs cooling in the evening air. "Benya," she would call out. "Where shall we dine tonight, the Pushkin Cafe on Teverskay Boulevard? Or should we try the Korchna near the Gallery? We haven't been there for a while."

"How about less touristy places," Benjamin would answer.

"If you're homesick for American food we can try the Starlite Diner. I can wait for you outside," she'd joke.

"Why would that be less touristy?"

"Well, if you want to avoid tourists, why don't we just stay home? I can cook something fast, nothing fancy, but basic food designed to make you fat."

"I bet it's the best prison food in the world."

She didn't laugh whenever he referred to her cooking as prison food. "I hope you never find out what prison food is really like," she would say if she said anything.

Benjamin cut a slice of cheese and a thick piece of black bread, wondering what they could be talking about when Marya said something that forced Ilya to roar in laughter.

"What's so funny?" Benjamin asked.

Ilya answered in a loud voice as if Benjamin's lack of understanding was due to deafness. "I asked Marya if you had tried to seduce her. She told me you thought penises were only good for peeing."

Marya smiled shyly and blushed. Her dark eyes grabbed hold of Benjamin's, but he didn't know what they were telling him.

~

Benjamin could not shake Abramowitz's photographs from his mind. Eerie, he told himself, how familiar the face, the look in the young boy's eyes, the mischievousness of his lips, his nose solid, his body wiry. In the wedding picture, Neuman's complexion was darker, his face young yet mature, his hair as thick as Benjamin's own, his build as slender. Even the joyous expression on his face reminded Benjamin of himself, of his own wedding picture, Caitlin in a flowing white gown leaning against his side, a good head shorter than he was—slight, petite, radiant. Was it chance or genes? Was fate teasing him by bringing Abramowitz into his life, a sorcerer playing faded photographs like a deck of cards?

When he thought about the photographs rationally, Benjamin was certain that Neuman looked no more like him than half the men he passed on the street. We all look alike. No one looks like a dog. No one is a sheep. With the same number of eyes, with a single nose, with two ears, we are distinguished by little things. No, he had no more family ties to the Neumans than he had to all the families of man. Then rational thinking would slip away, and he would find himself intrigued by the idea of a lost family, of a line of learned men. But it was not the secret genealogy that most attracted him; it was something metaphysical, even superstitious. Abramowitz was a messenger of fate,

Benjamin would joke to himself, a guardian angel, not from Heaven but from chance. He was a bearded prophet, sitting in the temple of a Greek restaurant, waiting to set a younger man on a quest not for the family but for the self.

"The prophet Elijah will guide you, Benjamin," the old man said after listening to Benjamin whine about his wife and his indictment. "He will not let you linger longer than is necessary."

"And what determines the length of necessary?" Benjamin asked cynically.

"Long enough for you to be able to recognize your destiny."

Abramowitz's earnestness caused Benjamin to break into laughter.

"He had two wives, Benjamin. Neuman had two wives and a young woman who would help him translate works into Russian," Abramowitz whispered in a conspiratorial tone.

"Divorced or widowed?" Benjamin asked wondering where Abramowitz was going. He no longer believed much of what the old man told him about Neuman. As the days moved into weeks, he realized that Abramowitz used Neuman as a vehicle for tales about the old country he only half remembered, and for stories described by his father, by his uncles, by all those he knew who had made it to Canada before the gates of the old world locked Jews in and the gates of the new world locked them out.

"No, no, no, he had them all at once. He didn't bury any of them, at least not when we were living near him. The youngest wife lived in Lublin, a baker's daughter I understand, who stood no more than so high off the floor." Abramowitz raised his hand to touch the top of an imaginary dwarf. "He saw her only a few times a year but with exquisite timing. They had four children in five years. The oldest wife was our neighbor in Kolomyja. A big, healthy woman who ran a dry goods business and kept Neuman well fed and smartly dressed. She had two daughters from a prior marriage, and two sons by Neuman."

"And the girlfriend," Benjamin asked out of politeness. He didn't believe a word.

"She lived in Peczenizyn with her widowed mother. Her father had been a forester. They had enough money to keep their daughter from marrying young. She was very beautiful and sprightly—the daughter that is. The widow was miserable."

"How did he keep his wives and his girlfriend from learning of each other?" Benjamin asked with a chuckle.

"Of course they knew about each other, Benjamin," Abramowitz said indignantly. "Neuman was an honorable man. But it didn't matter. He loved them all, and they all loved him. He had too much love to have only one woman. There were other women as well. I was jealous. I had only one wife and no girlfriends."

"I thought Neuman was a holy man."

Abramowitz looked as if there was no hope for Benjamin. "He was, but he wasn't without sin. The devil teases us all, but I don't think it was Satan that drove Neuman to love many women. He was not doing evil but spreading happiness."

"And which marriage was the photograph from?"

"The first, of course. I never saw the others."

"A great story, Abramowitz, but one with no wings. Are you pulling my chain?"

Abramowitz cackled. "Maybe and maybe not."

"But why would you make up such a story?"

"So you'd know Rabbi Neuman as a man. So you'd want to know if his blood flows through your veins. Maybe it is wishful thinking, but who knows, maybe Neuman met a beautiful Anglican tourist and momentarily forgot his marriage vows and here you are?"

The old man peeled the wireframe glasses from his face and rubbed his eyes with a paper napkin. "Rabbi Neuman would rise early and go to the study hall just as the first rays of the sun broke over the horizon. He would knock on the door before he entered so that the souls of the dead who prayed there at night would know he was coming. Then he'd study the holy books and pray."

"I thought it was behavior and not prayer that made you holy." Benjamin argued.

Abramowitz looked affronted. "My friend was a very honorable man. He gave charity. He taught the children of the poor. He did not steal, or murder, or lie."

"It's hard to imagine a polygamist with a girlfriend not lying."

"Sex doesn't count."

"Isn't that the fundamental purpose of religion, to structure our sexual appetites and keep us from killing each other over bedmates?"

"To show appreciation to God, Benjamin, that is the center of faith."

"Only if you think of religion is the invention of God and not of man."

Abramowitz shrugged his shoulders, lifted his glass of tea, and looked out on the street. "I love this time of the night, Benjamin, the hours when people begin to walk more slowly, when the young hold hands. The women are all handsome and graceful. The men are awkward, trying to look innocent when all they care about are breasts, and legs, and the movement of hips. It is a wonderful hour, a romantic hour."

"I thought you said you were ninety-three."

"But I'm not dead. It is all memory, memory. But still … " his voice wandered off.

"Would you want to be young again?" Benjamin asked Abramowitz, disguising within the words "young again" the dilemma that he was facing, how do you find the energy to start life anew. Where on your vita do you put down that you're a felon, and when do you tell a prospective employer that your two-year probation was nearly over? How do you find the courage to seek companionship, to enter the universe of bar stool flirtations and Internet websites, of weekend trysts and singles cruises? He had no answers. Benjamin had only enough strength to brood and feel old.

Abramowitz didn't grasp his younger companion's thinking. "One life is all we get," he said. "And one life is enough. As Neuman would say, if you could count on having more than one life, you would never appreciate the full glory of being alive."

~

In the middle of the night, Benjamin was awakened by a blurry and confused dream. He turned on his back and tried to recall what it was about, but its content eluded him. All he could remember was that he was outdoors, mesmerized by the gigantic flames emanating from a blazing barn, with mountains looming in the background, and a scattering of restaurant tables and chairs. Frightening, Benjamin thought, and wondered if a disturbance on the sidewalk below his window had triggered his subconscious, a car backfiring, a pistol shot, someone screaming for help, but when he peeked out of his bedroom window all he could see were parked cars and streetlights. All was silent. He leaned over the kitchen sink and rinsed the sweat off his neck with cold water, then he dropped an ice cube into a small glass, covered it with scotch, and sank into his living room's single upholstered chair. Was it something Abramowitz had said, Benjamin wondered, some offhand remark that roused something black in his imagination, a comment about marriage, about success, about money? All he could remember was the old man's observation about having one life, and that having but a single life made it all the more precious. It was not the words, Benjamin realized, that had burnt into his memory, but the way they were said, the broad smile on Abramowitz's face, the exuberance in his voice. Yes, it had to be Abramowitz who had destroyed his sleep, Abramowitz, he now remembered, dancing around the tables, his legs strutting to an unheard tune, his mouth filled with laughter, his eyes flaming with joy, his arms appealing to Benjamin to join in the dance, his wrinkled hands beckoning the younger man to life.

What a stupid dream, Benjamin thought before taking a sip of scotch. But he knew it wasn't stupid. It was revealing. He was envious of Abramowitz, envious that this old man with a heavily veined nose cherished life more than he did, that this ancient with watery eyes and arthritic limbs treated each breath as a gift, each day as an unexpected prize. He was jealous as well, jealous that Abramowitz had Peczenizyn, that he had a village that he loved, a place—however fictional, however ill-used—that was recalled with adoration. What place did he, Benjamin Palmer, have? To where did he want to return? To where did he want to go? He didn't bother to answer. He just finished his drink.

~

Hocking rode the elevator with her and waited until a cab pulled up to the entrance of the State Department. "Let's keep in touch," he said like a casual friend.

She sat in the backseat, hot air blowing on her face through the half-opened window, annoyed that the taxi driver thought he was saving on gas by turning off the air conditioner, annoyed that she wasn't going to tell him to put it on, annoyed that she had sat in Hocking's office, cold, unemotional, with only superficial questions, her skirt bright and short, her hair too well-combed, her makeup perfect. Annoyed, also, that she hadn't taken notes, that she couldn't remember the exact words Hocking used, his tone of voice, what she saw in his eyes. How long had she been with him? An hour? Fifteen minutes? She looked at her watch. How little time had passed since she had left her apartment to meet Hocking, an hour and a half she calculated, and in so short of a time, her world had been made bleak. She glanced out the window as the taxi turned up 17th Street, disappointed that the sun's reflection off the Corcoran Museum's facade did not ease the tension that gripped her body, that the massive Old Executive Office Building, still covered in morning shadows, did not make her feel solid and indestructible. She remembered that the White House was only a short distance away and wondered for a moment if anyone on the President's staff knew her husband was missing. No, he was not important enough for that, she decided. The realization deepened her despondency. She closed her eyes when the cab stopped for a red light. Images from old newsreels invaded her mind, hostages pleading for help, roadside corpses, their bodies dismembered, their heads partially separated from their necks.

Her hands shook as she fumbled through her Coach pocketbook to find the keys to the townhouse. Her body trembled when she opened the door.

"How does he know it's not terrorists?" she heard her mother ask over the phone.

"He says terrorists act differently. That's all. It's a guess, Mom. It's all a guess."

"Would you like your Dad and me to come to Washington? Or would you like to come here?"

Caitlin had expected the offers and was determined to turn them down, but when the words were actually said, she hesitated. She didn't want to be alone. She wanted to lean on a shoulder, to hold a hand, to have someone share her worry. But her parents had failed to understand why she and Benjamin were heading for a divorce, and she was afraid their company would only bring endless hours of talk about the marriage, about her career, about all the things they had never understood about her.

"Not now, Mom, but maybe soon."

"Do you want to talk to your father?"

"Please," she said.

Her father's practical approach gave her some comfort. "Don't jump to conclusions, Cat. Your imagination can run away with itself. You'll learn more over the next few days. It may all be a mistake. If things are as dire as you think, there will be time enough to do what has to be done."

Speaking to her parents had not been enough. She continued to want to reveal her panic, to spread the burden of worry and concern. Names ran through Caitlin's mind, names of friends, of acquaintances, of former colleagues and former colleagues of her husband. One by one, she cancelled them out. Her friends were all in the media, columnists and reporters, editors and broadcasters, people whose pledge to secrecy would be imperfect, whose desire for a story would grind against the demands of friendship. It would be unfair and ultimately futile to demand they remain silent. As for Benjamin's former colleagues and friends, she didn't know them well enough to trust them.

A cup of freshly brewed coffee and a jam coated slice of toasted multigrain bread failed to ease Caitlin's headache. She downed a couple Advil and 5-grams of Valium left over from a prescription gotten a year before when she had pulled a muscle in her back. She lay down on the living room couch, covered herself with a thin cotton blanket, and waited for her headache to subside. Random thoughts filled her mind. It had been her decision to end the marriage. It was her future that demanded distance from his indictment, from his bad name. He had become persona non grata to people who counted, to financiers, to investment brokers, to hedge fund managers, to newspaper editors, to the people in Washington who meticulously kept up with published news and unwritten gossip. She had been caught in the wake of his disgrace, proven or not, convicted or set free, she had paid a price. The professional use of her maiden name offered only minor protection. For months her producers kept her from handling Wall Street news, from covering criminal investigations. For a time they removed her as anchor of the evening news and sent her back to reporting on local fires, windstorms, and police actions. All that had been put behind her, or so she thought, but would it happen again if Benjamin Palmer's name returned to the headlines?

Caitlin turned on her side and pulled the blanket to her chin. She tried to empty her mind of all thoughts, hoping to renew herself through sleep, but the more she wished for rest, the more it eluded her.

She had loved Benjamin, deeply, she remembered, but that was before he was accused of pumping up stock values; before he was accused of insider trading; before he turned state's witness and got off with a hefty fine and community service. At first she had stood by him out of that love, and later out of loyalty and decorum. By the time his short probation was over so was the marriage. It was his secrecy that ended it, or so she had convinced herself, not the infamy, not the damage to her, but his failure as a husband, as a trusted partner, to tell her what he had been doing.

Since the split, she had filled her hours reigniting her career. She regenerated musty professional friendships; she threw herself into every assignment no matter how small, how insignificant. Opportunities trickled in, a political analysis here, an interview with a foreign dignitary there, a special on a cultural exchange. It proved successful. She was back as anchor on the local evening news; she was once again considered a hot property, someone who might yet make it to the national scene.

Her success had its price. There had been little time for friends outside of the media; there was no time to cultivate acquaintances. So now, lying on the couch with a cotton blanket for warmth, Caitlin felt desperately alone. Hocking had asked her to keep their interview a secret and she would do anything that might help Benjamin stay safe. She would only talk to herself.

~

"Tell me more about your wife," Marya asked as she leaned over the large sink and rinsed a couple of glasses for morning tea.

"Oh, I think I've said it all, Marya. I haven't left much out. Why are you so curious?"

"Because I wonder what my life would have been like if I was born somewhere else, at a different time, with a different face. That's why."

"You never say much about your husband. I don't even know his name," Benjamin asked in turn.

"We were never officially married. Not like you. We just called each other husband and wife."

"Is that the reason, you're not officially married so you don't have to talk about him?"

"He was a louse. There is not much to say about a louse."

Ilya had left early in the morning. "On a mission," he said, but avoided describing it. "Only for the day," he said to Benjamin. He said more to Marya, but he said it in Russian. "He's planning to call your embassy again. That's what I know," was all Benjamin could get out of her.

"I can't imagine your husband being that bad. You were attracted to him, and you have a head on your shoulders."

Marya took a quick step back, her chestnut hair brushing the back of her tan blouse, and burst into laughter. When she turned toward Benjamin, her two gold teeth were showing. She looked younger when she smiled, her dark skin taut and without blemish, her nose attractive, her lips thick and sensual. He averted his eyes to keep her from feeling uncomfortable, and to prevent him from embarrassing himself.

"And what do you find so funny?" Benjamin asked. He tried to modulate his tone so that he'd sound serious. But Marya's gaiety proved infectious. A smile conquered his face.

"Was it your head that got you married, Benya? Do Americans marry with their heads?"

"I was thirty when I met Caitlin. I knew what I was doing."

"Louse was led by his erection," she giggled.

"And you?"

Her smile disappeared. "By the same six inches, Benya. Men and women are not so different. He wanted to put it somewhere, and my somewhere wanted it put. I wrapped the truth in dreams. There would be companionship, camaraderie, love, a child or two. And there was joy for a couple of years."

Marya turned back to the simple wooden counter on which she cut meat and vegetables. "Black bread and herring," she announced over her shoulder.

Benjamin rose to help her and together they brought silver forks and knives to the table and two glasses of tea. He invited her to sit before he stepped back to the counter to pick up the bread and herring. "And what happened after a couple of years?"

"The six inches wilted," Marya answered without humor.

"That's hard to believe," he said with a sly smile, a flirtatious hum in his voice.

"Ha! You're all alike, you men," she said haughtily. "He became a louse, that's what happened. He was from Vladivostok. I met him when he was studying law in Moscow. After we had decided to live together we went back east. His father had once been a big shot. He ran a collective farm during Soviet days and entered politics when the Soviet Union crumbled. Louse went back to work with him. Corruption was a family business. When they were caught, what is your phrase, with their hands in the cake drawer ... ?"

"In the cookie jar is what you're looking for."

"*Da, Da, Da,* in the cookie jar. Our apartment was searched. In the back of my closet, built into the wall, they found a safe full of gold coins and yen and dollars. I didn't know anything about it. Not a word. But no one believed me. I ran away. The louse, he ran too, somewhere. So I am hiding here, as much a prisoner as you are. There is no money on its way to buy me out. So there, my sad tale." She emitted an unconvincing laugh.

Benjamin drank some of his tea, feeling a little guilty about leading the conversation to hurtful memories. But he was not sorry.

"Did you hide money in your wife's closet?" Marya asked after a long moment of silence.

"Worse. My troubles shamed her, or so she felt. It hurt her career. It separated her from people who could help her become a celebrity."

"And that was what she wants to be, a celebrity?"

"She wanted to be a personage. It was much more important to her than I was."

"Losing a wife can be a high price to pay for corruption," Marya said innocently.

Benjamin bristled. "Corruption, is that what you call it?"

Marya looked astonished. "What would you call it?" she asked. There was no sarcasm in her voice. It was a simple question about English usage.

"We were all trying to make money. It was a bunch of rich people stealing from other rich people. We didn't think we were corrupt. We thought we were doing something that would pay off—to a lot of people. We just took our share first."

"But the captain is supposed to leave the sinking ship last, is he not?"

Benjamin didn't want to argue. He sat silently and then changed the subject. "My wife, Caitlin, is very beautiful. She studied to be an actress and had some success in small theaters. But she is strangely ungraceful, shaped like a photographer's model, with golden hair and a symmetrical face, but with no music in her movement. I used to think it was because her legs weren't long enough, but it had more to do with nerve endings and internal timing. She looked awkward on stage, and would have faced difficulties in movies. She is perfect for television. Her energy dominates the screen. Her animated face moves easily from laughter to contemplation to sadness. She writes well, very well, and is remarkably charming. So she became a television reporter and eventually an anchor. She was doing well until my indictment, went into a slump, but is doing well again."

"You must have loved her very much," Marya said.

"I think so. I fell in love with her in bed. Not before. So it may have been the six inches and nothing more."

"You men are all alike," Marya exclaimed again, but this time without humor.

"I hate how that sounds, Marya. It so diminishes me. I am I. I don't want to be a classification."

"Even if it is true?"

Benjamin watched the light dim in Marya's dark Gypsy eyes. He couldn't argue with her, not when spring was in the cabin. "Particularly, if it's true," he answered.

# Chapter 4

The strikingly attractive woman at the Ukrainian embassy forced herself to be helpful to Benjamin. "May I ask, why Peczenizyn and Kolomyja? Why not Kyiv and Odessa and Yalta? There is much to see there."

"I plan to spend a couple of days in Kyiv, but Peczenizyn is my primary goal."

She was tall and slim, with the long auburn hair and high cheekbones he had seen in Internet advertisements for Ukrainian romance tours. When she begrudgingly smiled, her large teeth glistened.

"Are you Jewish?" she asked.

It was a question Benjamin expected to roll around in her mind, but he had expected her to keep her suspicion private. "No. Why do you ask?"

"I mean nothing by it," she replied, and gave him a belated smile. "It's just usually Jews looking for ancestral villages, for the gravestones of their grandparents or great grandparents who want to go to that section of my country. There are a number of Jewish organizations that conduct tours to the Carpathian region."

"I have no Ukrainian relatives," Benjamin insisted.

"Then I repeat myself, why Peczenizyn?"

It was predictable question and Benjamin had prepared what he thought was a useful if dishonest answer. "Curiosity," he said. "It is the birthplace of Oleksa Dovbush, isn't it? The 18th century freedom fighter often called the Ukrainian Robin Hood. By the end of the summer my friends will be returning from Paris and London, the adventurous ones from Prague and Budapest. I'll be able to say I went to Peczenizyn, the birthplace of the Ukrainian hero Oleksa Dovbush. It will go over well at cocktail parties."

She didn't look as if she believed him. "Folklore," she said with a smile. "You have done your research. Do you speak Ukrainian or Russian? If you don't, that is a difficult place to get around."

"Is it still dangerous?

Her tone didn't change but her face tensed. "We have been a civilized country for a long time. Oleksa Dovbush and his men are long gone." She gave a self-satisfied smile before continuing. "The dangers of traveling in the rural parts of Eastern Europe have always been exaggerated. But without familiarity with the language travel can be uncomfortable."

"I plan a short stay and I won't be doing anything illicit, so it should go well."

"I'm convinced it will," she said salting her voice with confidence. "So let's talk about a plan."

He would fly to Kyiv, she suggested, and from there take the train to Kolomyja. In Kolomyja, she was certain, he could arrange for a guide to drive him to Peczenizyn. He might not be able to find accommodation in the village, but his guide would know best how to visit the town. "There are many tourist agencies that can help you," she informed him as he was leaving.

Washington's weather had turned pleasant by the time he left the embassy. A western wind had blown away the clouds, and a warm spring sunlight had replaced the intermittent showers of the morning. Benjamin felt an unexpected lightness in his step and a smile on his face when he strolled along M Street on his way to Dupont Circle. What was only a thought was now a plan, and, after a call or two, the plan would take on the gravity of a roundtrip ticket and a hotel reservation. It would do him good, he thought, just to get on a plane, to see a landscape he had never seen, to taste a different cuisine, to flirt with women whose language he didn't understand. "Why are you going to Peczenizyn?" she had asked. "To hunt down Oleksa Dovbush," he had answered. How stupid that must have sounded, he laughed to himself, how ridiculous he must have seemed to try to promote that fable. But what else could he have told her, that he was going to travel halfway around the world in search of a durable adult persona? Would that have sounded any the wiser? The truth sounded no saner than searching for Oleksa Dovbush. He had been bewitched by a man named Abramowitz, convinced that somehow he would be reborn in a ramshackle village that history had all but forgotten. And now Benjamin yearned to get off a 747 and onto a horse-drawn wagon, to bounce along rutted dirt roads, sweaty and dirty, a pilgrim searching for a distant century. The bizarre nature of it all amused him.

He bought airline tickets that day, but waited a week before making hotel accommodations. Just to be sure, he told himself.

~

It was in Kyiv that they kidnapped him, two burly men in sweatshirts and dungarees grabbed him on the second evening, three blocks from his hotel, their bodies smelling of sweat, their breaths laced with alcohol and cigarette smoke.

Dusk was just beginning as Benjamin made his way back from the Ukrainian Orthodox Caves Monastery. He hadn't planned to visit the holy place on his only full day in Kyiv, but the cab driver from Boryspil Airport convinced

him that it was the place to begin his visit if he truly wanted
to learn about this foreign land. Benjamin picked up a tourist
guidebook from the hotel desk before he went to sleep, and
grabbed a cab outside his hotel in the morning. Kyiv's traffic
congestion made the short drive seem endless, and by the time
he got to the main entrance to the complex, his sinuses were
irritated by exhaust fumes and his ears were full of blaring
horns and squealing brakes. Naively, he had expected to get
through the entire monastery before his energy ran out, but
the exalting majesty of the architecture overpowered him. He
found himself envying the carpenters and bricklayers who
constructed such beauty; he coveted the medieval lives that
found glory in faith and purpose in exalting God. Without
his notice his pace slowed while his attentiveness increased.
Ageless icons and crucifixes and textiles lifted his spirits, the
vaulted ceilings pulled him out of himself.

He made it to the Dormition Cathedral and the Great
Bell Tower, as he had planned, and to the Baroque All-Saints'
Church, but he gave in before he could explore the caves
where generations of monks were buried and for which the
monastery was named. "Someday," he told himself, but he
knew it was unlikely.

The route downhill toward the Dnieper River was
longer than the city map had led him to expect, the air
more polluted than he anticipated, the streets noisier. Kyiv
was three cities in one, he decided, the Kyiv of beautiful
churches and 19th century architecture, the Kyiv of Stalin-
style concrete apartment houses, of a decaying and polluted
waterfront, and the contemporary city fighting for a place
in the 21st century, stuffed with putrid smelling buses and
trucks and automobiles.

He never realized that they were following him or noticed
the worn-down Lada that was trailing them. He stopped to
look into a small cafe thinking, for a moment, that he might

take a cup of coffee. It caused his stalkers to pass by him, their reflections in the window, the taller man walking on the street, the shorter, stockier man moving hesitantly along the sidewalk. Drunks, he thought when he noticed their reflections, full of cheap beer and vodka. It was an expected sight. Only minutes later did he realize what little note he had made of them and by then it was much too late.

The cafe looked uninviting, at least to an American tourist, so Benjamin continued his walk, following at a distance the staggering strangers. When they abruptly stopped he prepared to push by them, but the shorter man jumped in front of him and blocked his progress. The taller man moved quickly behind Benjamin, fixed his large, powerful hand over Benjamin's mouth and painfully twisted his prey's arm behind his back. Benjamin fought back. He thrust his elbow into the taller man's ribs and tried to kick the smaller man in the face when the thug bent over to grab his victim's legs. They were stronger than they looked, and, as if trained for mayhem, had little difficulty restraining him.

In seconds, Benjamin was crammed on the rear floor of the Lada, a gag swelling in his mouth. Threatening words in a language he didn't know filled his ears. His face was pressed against the filthy carpet, his hands locked in tightly fitting handcuffs. One of his captors placed what felt like the barrel of a gun against his neck. Terror overwhelmed him. His bladder gave in first, then his bowels. Someone smacked him on the back of the head and shouted something ugly to the driver. Then he struck Benjamin on the head again. This time it was harder.

~

His telephone call upset her. Abramowitz was his name, Martin Abramowitz, he had told her, his accent heavy, his breathing unsteady and nervous. "You don't know me," he

46

began. "I'm a friend of your husband. I'd like to have a chance to talk to you."

"He's never mentioned you." She was standing in the kitchen, holding the wall receiver in her hand. Instinctively, she pulled a pad and pen from the drawer closest to the stove to jot down notes.

"I'm a new friend. We talked about his trip to Eastern Europe. I hadn't heard from him for a month and wondered if he was all right. I saw you on television last night and I knew I had to call."

"And how did you get my number?"

"Benjamin left it with me. Just in case," he had said. "It took me a while to find it."

Her suspicions mounted. It had been a week since she met with Ernest Hocking. Twice she had called him, but he offered no news. This was the first true contact about her missing husband. Who else could it be but the kidnappers? Clever, she thought, how he was trying to find out if she were aware of Benjamin's plight. Next he would try to discover if she was prepared to pay for Benjamin's freedom. "We're separated. You may know more about what he is doing than I do."

"I'm sorry to have bothered you," he said in a mournful tone. "I don't want you to worry. I'm certain he is fine. He is most probably just having difficulty sending e-mails."

Her reportorial instincts went into play. "Do you know why he decided to go to Eastern Europe?" she quickly asked.

"It's a long story. I don't think I could convince you over the phone. Could we possibly meet? I'd be honored to buy you lunch."

"Is it that complex?"

"It is a little complicated."

"I have to check my calendar. Where can I reach you?"

Abramowitz gave her his telephone number, and again told her he was sorry to have disturbed her, and that he had no reason to think her husband was in difficulty. "I'm an old man. I'm prone to worry," he said in a frail voice.

Caitlin waited ten minutes before calling back, worried that she might have lost a good lead, expecting that the telephone number was phony, hoping that if he were involved with the kidnapping he would call again, or someone else would. She thought of calling Hocking, but expected that he would want Abramowitz's number so that he could have professionals follow up. She was not ready for that.

Abramowitz answered the phone, his voice surprisingly strong. "So fast," he said after she announced herself.

They decided to meet at the Starbucks at Connecticut Avenue and Dupont Circle, at 10:00 a.m. the next morning. "You will have no difficulty recognizing me. I will be far older than the others, with thinning gray hair and spectacles."

He was sitting on a stool near the window and reading a newspaper when she walked by, his age written on his face. She walked by again before entering, but could not see far enough into the cafe to be sure he was alone. As she entered, a young man folded his laptop and got up from one of the few small tables. She tapped Abramowitz on the shoulder, bid him follow her as she moved to the vacated spot, and put her bag down on one of the chairs.

Abramowitz put down his paper cup of tea, and asked if he could get something for her. She told him to sit and went up to the counter to order a latte. They know what they are doing, Caitlin decided as she stood in line, using an old, lonely looking man as a contact. Everything projected innocence, his crumbled dark suit, his open shirt, his aged skin. When she turned her head around, she caught him looking at her, an approving smile on his face.

He pulled an old leather passport folder from his jacket pocket after she had settled down and formally introduced herself. He placed two faded photographs in front of her. "This is how it all began, with Rabbi Neuman," he said. He told her about his first meeting with Benjamin, and quietly spoke about how they had gotten to know each other.

How she could have ever suspected him of criminality, she asked herself midway through their conversation. The photographs, the tale of Neuman, the things he knew about Benjamin's life, no kidnapper could be that cunning. Abramowitz was as innocent as he looked. Caitlin relaxed enough to begin to like this shriveled old Jew who missed her husband, and she began to understand why Benjamin had befriended him.

"Peczenizyn," Caitlin said when he was done. "He told me he was going there, but I couldn't imagine why. I still don't understand it. His family has been in this country for generations, and originally came from England. His mother belonged to the Daughters of the American Revolution. They were Episcopalians."

"He wasn't searching for ancestors although he was awestruck by the similarity of the boy and man in the picture."

"Then why?" she asked impatiently.

"A spiritual quest, I think, although he never used the word. He wanted to be reborn and my stories made him think he could be reborn in the old world."

"But why not where his roots are, in England?"

"Because he wanted to grow into someone he had never been."

When Caitlin finished her drink Abramowitz asked if she wanted another. "And you?" she answered. She insisted on making the purchase. By the time she returned with a tea and latte, the photographs and wallet had disappeared into his pocket. She surprised herself by asking, "Did he ever talk of me?"

Abramowitz took off his wire rim glasses and rubbed his eyes.

Thinking she had made him uncomfortable, she said, "It's an unfair question. I'm sorry I raised it."

"It's a human question. I'm just thinking of an answer, that's all. He said you were very beautiful," Abramowitz looked away before finishing the sentence with, "which you are. He was sorry that he had done you a great disservice."

"He did himself the disservice. I was just collateral damage, to use that heartless term."

"He thought you were more punished for his transgressions than he was. He was very sorry to have damaged you so."

"I feel so guilty," she said. "None of this would have happened if I hadn't left him. He'd still be in Washington, not lost in Ukraine."

Abramowitz's face turned into a question mark. Her comment had shocked him. "Lost in the Ukraine?" he blurted.

She tried to catch herself. "Well, you don't know where he is."

"A strange thing for you to say, don't you think? Do you know things you are not sharing?"

Caitlin eyes began to tear. The paper cup shook when she raised it to her mouth.

"What have I said?" Abramowitz exclaimed when he saw her tears.

His gentleness made secrets impossible. "Benjamin is being held for ransom, somewhere in Ukraine they think, but no one knows," she said while cupping her mouth with her hand to prevent her voice from traveling. She told him about the call from the State Department, about the ransom request, about the appeal for secrecy. She purposely omitted any mention of Hocking's name.

Abramowitz seemed to grow older in front of her eyes. His pasty complexion paled. His thick lower lip quivered. "My God," he exclaimed. "My God." He pushed his fingers against his tightly closed mouth as if to prevent himself from screaming.

"Don't tell anyone," she repeated. "It could make things worse."

"How worse could they be?"

"I don't know," she said. Tears began to stream down Caitlin's face.

He reached into a pants pocket and pulled out a gray handkerchief. She refused and used a paper napkin to wipe her face. "I didn't mean to cry," she said.

"I'm the one who is guilty, not you. I talked him into going with my foolish stories, with my old photographs and my ridiculous imagination. I am the one."

"How could we have known," she said. She reached out and took his hand. It was moist.

"If only I was younger," he said.

"And what would you do?"

"I'd go to the Ukraine to find him, that's what I'd do."

"The government is doing that."

"And what good will they do? Governments are afraid of their own shadow. Whom will they irritate? Whom will they anger? That's how they think."

Caitlin played with the edges of her long blond hair. "Are you suggesting I go to Ukraine to look for him?"

Abramowitz looked startled. "No. Absolutely not," he insisted. "It's just an old Jew wishing he were superman. Don't listen to him."

~

They were far from any city lights when the Lada finally stopped. The sky was filled with ancient brilliance and an almost full moon cast a ghastly light over the surrounding farmland. The driver helped drag him out of the car and onto the earthen driveway. He exchanged what Benjamin thought was a weapon with the taller man, backed up the car, and drove toward a ramshackle barn that was not far from the house. His kidnappers forced Benjamin to his feet, and, painfully gripping his arms, forced him into a farmhouse with a steeply pitched roof. They used a large flashlight to illuminate the way.

They made Benjamin stand against the basement's damp earthen wall, his arms pulled over his head by a rope that was tied to his handcuffs and strung over a rough ceiling beam. The short, stocky man, called Boyko by his partner, cut Benjamin's jacket and shirt off, inflicting two painful scratches across his chest and one down his back. He sliced Benjamin's soiled pants and pulled them off. Holding his nose with one hand, he danced the fetid garments to the far end of the basement and dropped them on the dirt floor. The taller man, called Taras, laughed at Boyko's antics, grabbed a tin pail, and splashed cold water over Benjamin's genitals. He shouted something harsh at Benjamin, his teeth black, his large head shaking with emotion.

"Don't hurt me," Benjamin tried to plead through the gag. "Don't hurt me."

If his captors were interested in what he wanted to say, they gave no sign of it.

Taras poured the contents of Benjamin's wallet on a wooden table and slowly counted out the money. His face turned fierce when he realized how little cash Benjamin was carrying; he frowned when he discovered only one credit card. Benjamin's passport was of more interest, as was his business cards, his health insurance identifier, his driver's license. He examined the small photograph of Caitlin.

Boyko lit the two oil lamps that stood on the table next to the contents of Benjamin's wallet. He left one on the table and used the other to light his way up the stone staircase. In a few minutes, he returned with a couple of glasses and a bottle of vodka. A small, elderly women, her back severely hunched, her long dress blowing dirt up from the floor, followed behind him. A black pot swung from one of her hands, a rag and soap was in the other. A towel hung around her neck. She made some wet and sad sounds with her lips as she approached Benjamin, her eyes focused on his naked genitals. He could smell the harsh soap as she washed him with the rag and cold water, moving her hand gently over his penis and testicles, but more abrasively when she washed the shit from his ass and the top of his thighs. She avoided looking at him—as if not seeing him might make her invisible—and she accompanied her work with sounds of regret and pity. When the old woman was done with the washing, she took the towel that was draped over her shoulder and softly dried his skin. A dark blue kerchief covered most of her hair but the ends that Benjamin could see were a dirty gray. When she had finished with him, she said something unfriendly to the two men, and made her way up the stairs in the dark. They laughed as she left. Boyko imitated her hunched back, and Taras, glass in hand, let out a raucous laugh. They sat down on small wooden benches, the bottle on the table, and emptied glass after glass of the drink until their postures altered and their movements became awkward.

His captors chatted without stop, their voices often overlapping. To Benjamin, they sounded as if they were holding separate conversations, deaf to what the other was saying, just pouring out happy words, obviously pleased with their crime, almost giddy. As time went by, the vodka affected them differently. Boyko's complexion reddened, his grin grew more pronounced and his dark-blue eyes danced. Taras's face turned somber and his dark eyes became more menacing. Benjamin desperately wished to understand them, but the foreign words just ran into one another. Eventually his captors' conversation became background noise, and he began to listen to his own breathing, afraid that the swelling gag would eventually prevent any breath from exciting his mouth, that his nostrils would clog and stop him from pulling air up through his nose. He was certain he was going to suffocate to death. He closed his eyes and prayed that someone or something would rescue him. It had happened in daylight. There must have been witnesses to his abduction. How was it possible that no one had followed him? Hadn't someone informed the police? Benjamin felt his heartbeat. His stomach turned. He could taste the rancid gag in his mouth.

When the bottle was empty, Boyko picked up the lamp and went up the stairs. Taras stayed behind, moving his chair further from the table, his eyes riveted on his prisoner, his mouth in a lopsided grin. Benjamin shifted his weight from one foot to the other, his shoulders pained and exhausted by the unnatural position, his wrists irritated by the pitiless handcuffs. He felt humiliated and vulnerable, his body naked except for an undershirt, his genitals moving ever so slightly as he shifted positions. All of his senses were alive. He thought he could smell Taras's sweat, the vodka on his breath, the crushed cigarettes smashed against a chipped plate. He heard rats scurrying in a distant corner of the earthen cellar. He heard his captor pull the damp and foul air through his enormous nose.

Taras rose awkwardly from his chair and staggered towards Benjamin. For a moment he looked as if he were going to fall, but he grabbed hold of the side of the table with his free hand and reclaimed his balance. With guttural sounding Slavic words pouring from his mouth, he grabbed the vodka bottle with a tight fist and waved it threateningly. Benjamin didn't take his eyes off him, as if being a witness to Taras's barbarity would somehow pacify his tormentor. A cold sweat formed on the prisoner's brow and along his neck. He found himself hoping that Boyko would hurry back, that the old woman would return and dress him, that something, anything, would happen to protect him.

Taras dropped the empty bottle on the dirt floor and watched it roll away unbroken. Then he pulled Benjamin's undershirt up and leered at his captive's penis. Benjamin instinctively pulled his body back. "Boyko," Taras yelled when he heard his comrade's footsteps. "Boyko," he yelled again and then slurred some words. Boyko put a full bottle of vodka on the table and joined Taras. He peered at his prisoner's genitals, his eyes magnified by thick eyeglass lenses. His drunken laugh was mixed with foreign words, his complexion rosy, his thick, dark-brown hair unwashed. Boyko surrounded Benjamin's penis with his fist, pulled it up, and laughed at the circumcised tip. He looked into the eyes of his prisoner who couldn't fail to understand his captor's thinking. "No," Benjamin tried to shout, "I'm not Jewish," but the gag stifled his words. It didn't matter. They wouldn't have understood him. Boyko repeated himself over and over again until his words formed a drunken chant. Taras picked up the empty bottle and smashed it against the wooden table. The jagged edge of glass ominously reflected the flame in the kerosene lamp. When Taras approached Benjamin pulled up his legs and kicked out. His right foot hammered Taras's hip, forcing his tormentor to skip awkwardly to maintain his balance. Boyko stopped laughing and tried to hold Taras back. They screamed at each other for a moment before

Taras pushed by his comrade and grabbed his hysterical prisoner's cock. Benjamin could feel the glass nick the base of his penis and scratch a testicle. He drew his legs up defensively, determined to hold the position as long as his stomach muscles held out.

Taras staggered back as if he were assaulted by what he had done. Boyko once again yelled at him. Benjamin thought he could feel his blood drip to the floor. He prayed to die fast, without torture, without pain.

He heard the old woman shriek, a burst of inflamed language pouring out of her, a harsh, condemning tone full of outrage. The three voices formed a vicious and violent chorus. He shut his eyes, glad that he didn't understand. Someone banged on the wooden table. Benjamin thought he heard a chair being thrown against a wall but he couldn't bring himself to look.

When he finally opened his eyes the old woman was taking the kerchief from her head. She tied it around his penis while muttering under her breath. Curse words, Benjamin thought, directed at the two drunken men who had moved away from him. After another sharp exchange with the old lady they came toward Benjamin again. Boyko held him up so that Taras could slacken the rope and untie the handcuffs, and then they sat Benjamin on a wooden chair. The woman, her fingers smelling of cooking oil, struggled to get the gag out of his mouth. He gasped for breath as the cloth fell to the dirt floor. She kicked it under the table and put her fingers up to her lips to warn him against speaking. Taras staggered toward the table and took a drink from the bottle. Boyko went upstairs. He returned with some clothing and a bottle of water that the woman held up to the captive's mouth, carefully tipping it so he could drink. After he had taken a few swallows she put the bottle aside so that she could slip a pair of stained slacks over his legs and his waist. Then she threw a black knit shawl over the prisoner's shoulders. After Boyko had tied Benjamin to the chair, his hands behind his back, his ankles laced together with a thick rope, the woman again served the prisoner water. "Thank you," Benjamin whispered. "Thank you." She danced a couple of fingers over the back of his neck as if she appreciated the sentiment.

In a calm voice, she said a few things to Boyko and Taras, picked up one of the lanterns—Boyko took the other—and led the two bandits up the stairs.

Benjamin could see nothing. Not the table or the earthen walls, not even his lap. The blackness took on a physical presence, a dense blanket, he first thought, but as the minutes mounted, he imagined it a casket buried deep in the earth, his body shrouded in an old woman's shawl. never again to feel the sun or see light. A rustling in the far corner caught his attention, but he couldn't tell if it came from within the space or intruded from outside. Rats he thought, and prayed that they were outside the farmhouse, that they couldn't reach him. He twisted his head in one direction and then the other and then back again, desperate to see, to hear, to sense his surroundings. He listened for the rustling to return, but only silence. He strained to hear footsteps above his head, to hear a telephone ring, a radio play, but nothing. Had they left him? Had they taken the few dollars from his wallet and his credit card and decided that was enough? Was he going to rot, tied to the chair, slowly starving to death? The taste of the gag was still in his mouth, the base of his penis stung, and his heart was racing.

Benjamin wanted them back. He wanted to see Boyko bring a lamp down the stairs, to have the old lady hold a bottle up to his lips. He wanted to see Taras standing at the top of the stairs coldly eyeing the scene and plotting next steps, promising by his actions that there would be a tomorrow.

"Is anyone here?" Benjamin yelled into the darkness. "Is anyone here?"

Silence greeted his cries. So he yelled out again and again, rocking on his chair, trying to wrestle the twine off his wrists, to stretch the rope that bound his ankles, to loosen the thick cord that pulled him tightly into the hard backed wooden chair. The futility of his shouting finally overwhelmed his fear and he sat silent for a long time, convincing himself that there was a growing separation between his tethered hands, that there was some give in the cord that coiled around his legs. He pitched his seat with renewed urgency, first forward and then back, then from side to side, then back and forth, until he lost all sense of what he was doing and lost his balance. His body careened to the floor. "Fuck," he shouted in exasperation, and rolled over until his knees were on the ground, his forehead on the earth and dirt in his mouth.

No rope had loosened. No bond felt more forgiving. He prayed that he would die quickly, that he would die painlessly, that he wouldn't be butchered or brutalized, that his body would still be whole when and if anyone ever found him. Somehow he found the strength to turn on his side. He saw Abramowitz sitting down at the table and saying a prayer over his food. He heard his own voice in his head pleading.

*Hear my prayer, O God.*

*For strangers are risen up against me,*

*And oppressors seek after my soul…*

Then he heard himself laugh, the laugh of a crazed man. If he had fallen asleep, and he wasn't sure he had, it was only to allow him to dream that he was a captive in a dark hole, without light, without bread, without hope.

Hours seemed to pass before Benjamin saw the old woman clumsily descend the stairs swinging a kerosene lantern in one hand and a basket in the other. Boyko walked a distance behind her with a lamp of his own. Morning, Benjamin assumed, but it was just an assumption. It could have been noon or the next day or eternity. Boyko seemed to be cursing as he righted the chair, his eyes bloodshot, his clothes in disarray. He looked angrily at the old lady who was directing him.

The woman said something caustic. Boyko drew a pistol from his belt, sat stubbornly on the table, and scrutinized both of them. The woman struggled to free Benjamin's hands but the knots were too tight for her. She insisted that Boyko help her. The thug's clumsy movements revealed his mood. The ropes cut more deeply into Benjamin as Boyko fumbled with the knots, as Boyko pulled on the cord that tied the prisoner to the chair. He freed only one foot, forcing Benjamin to drag a rope across the floor when he walked.

The old woman pointed to the tin pail tucked into one corner of the basement and made believe she was defecating. When she moved away, Benjamin urinated into the dry pail. His stench rose to the wooden ceiling.

She moved Benjamin's chair to the end of the table and motioned for him to sit. Out of the basket came a bottle of orange colored soda, a large piece of black bread, and a hunk of nondescript cheese. He hadn't realized that he was thirsty until he had finished the watery carbonated drink. He pointed to the bottle in the hope of getting more. Boyko laughed. The woman, her thinning white hair held in place by a dark kerchief, shook her head and shrugged her shoulders. The prisoner broke off a piece of bread and, with his fingers, dug out a piece of cheese. He chewed them carefully.

Boyko, who had seated himself on the opposite end of the table, played with the pistol, every so often pointing it at

Benjamin and giving out a joyless chuckle. When Benjamin begged for more to drink, Boyko shouted something mean at the woman and she went upstairs. Taras was with her when she returned with more soda and some additional rope. When the two goons tied Benjamin back into the chair, the smell of vodka and cigarette smoke mixed with the stink of their unwashed bodies.

Night again, Benjamin thought after they left, although he knew it could be a different time of day. So he was to be kept alive, waiting to be traded for dollars. The thought gave him a sliver of hope. He prayed that Boyko and Taras were bright enough to pull off a kidnapping scheme, that behind their drunken pose, they knew more than how to roll drunks and steal handbags. He hoped that combined they had at least half a brain and were capable of contacting the American embassy and extracting ransom. Sorrowfully, nothing he had experienced evidenced any competence. In the movies the old woman would have been the mastermind. But this wasn't the movies.

There was a transcendent irony to his predicament, he decided, as he sat alone in the dark, his throat dry, and his sinuses rebelling against the mold spores that filled the basement. Once again he was a captive of greed, but this time it was the greed of others and not his own that brought him to despair. He could not escape by turning state's evidence. He could not live off hidden spoils. A first rate lawyer and publicity seeking prosecutors would not bring him absolution. So who would be his rescuers, the State Department, the CIA, or some Middle Eastern terrorists who wanted a hostage to exchange for one of their own? He searched his mind for the comfort of the Psalms he once recited in the small Episcopal church his parents took him to, but they came in snatches and he mixed lines from one into another.

*O God, why hast thou cast us off forever?*

*Why doth thine anger smoke against the sheep of thy pasture?*

*The sorrows of death compassed me, and the floods of ungodly men made me afraid.*

And when he couldn't find comfort in the psalms, he prayed that his weight wouldn't shift, that he wouldn't break a bone when he fell; that he wouldn't crack open his head against the table.

The next time they came, all three of them, he made fuller use of the pail. Boyko held his nose and Taras let out a long stream of expletives. They didn't need to cut any of the cords when they released one foot and one arm, when they removed the rope that fastened his body to the chair. She had brought two bottles of water, a smaller slice of black bread, and, to Benjamin's delight, a couple of slices of ham to go with the cheese. The old woman gave him a small smile when he thanked her.

# Chapter 5

Ilya pulled the hard peak of his leather cap further down his forehead, threw on a black weatherproof jacket, and tossed the rifle over his right shoulder. "Are you ready, Benya? The rain won't wash us away."

"I'm always ready to get out," Benjamin answered as he finished tying a leather boot. Like all of the clothing Ilya provided him, the boot was a piece of military attire manufactured somewhere in the old Soviet Union. Liberated from a warehouse that was half-forgotten when the empire collapsed, Benjamin mused, or stolen by an underpaid factory worker who was too poor to be honest. The same warehouse, Benjamin imagined, that supplied the gray-brown hat that protected him from the rain, the military jacket with wide labels and unadorned shoulder boards that kept him warm. Ilya had offered to decorate him with replicas of the metals once pinned on the defenders of Moscow and Stalingrad, but Benjamin had resisted. "I already look like a Latin American revolutionary, and besides, it would be vulgar to wear tributes designed for deserving men and women."

"There is hope for you yet, Benya," the Russian had said, "You understand honor."

"Where to?" Benjamin asked.

"Not far, my American, just over the rivulet to see our neighbors."

It had been raining on and off for several days, drenching rains that kept the three of them imprisoned in the cabin. They had grown ever more tired of each other's company, numbed by boredom, itchy to move beyond the four plaster walls and the smoking wood-fired stove. When the rain slowed down Marya would throw a heavy poncho over her thick sweater and visit the woods and her garden. Her clothing was soaked when she'd return, a basket of fresh vegetables, wild flowers, and mushrooms swinging from her arm.

Ilya rarely left the cabin. He escaped boredom by diving into his vodka at lunchtime, telling stories to Marya in Russian, arguing politics and philosophy with his two companions in English, his mind alert, his laughter in full force. By evening the vodka would take control and what had been conversation became a series of drunken discourses, unintelligible and unending, delivered in a mixture of Russian and English, tears often pouring down his cheeks, and then, a minute later, his eyes would rage.

"See, the rain is letting up," Ilya said over his shoulder as they exited the cabin. "Maybe Noah won't have to build an ark ."

The two men moved rapidly through the wet woods, kicking at the undergrowth, brushing low hanging branches aside, swatting at the ubiquitous mosquitoes. The heavy rains had caused the slim river to swell, hiding the rocks that normally allowed an easy crossing to the other side. The depth of the flow forced them to wade cautiously into the water and feel their way with the toes of their boots.

Kostya was watching them from the other side of the river, a small straw basket full of eggs in one hand, a cap similar to Ilya's protecting his head. He greeted his Russian neighbor with a shout and smile. He proudly yelled "Good Morning, Benya."

"Good Morning," Benjamin answered. "And what brings you out on such a wet day? Did your sisters throw you out?"

The boy gave him a blank look. Ilya chuckled. He exchanged some questions and answers with the young boy and then translated for Benjamin.

"He was sent out to collect chicken eggs. He thought he spotted an eagle across the rivulet so he wandered down to see better. That's what he's doing out."

"And was it an eagle?"

"We diverted him," Ilya said. "So we will never know. The story of mankind, isn't it Benya, always to be ignorant?"

"Not knowing is not being ignorant," Benjamin argued. "Ignorant is not seeking."

"You are beginning to sound like me," Ilya laughed. He steadied the boy's hand and took an egg out of the basket. He said something to Kostya that caused the boy to shrivel up his face and squeeze his eyes shut. Ilya placed the raw egg over one eye and chanted in Russian. He repeated the chant when he pressed the egg over the other eye. When the rite was over, Ilya placed the egg back in the basket. He said something in Russian and the boy ran off toward the farmhouse.

"And what was all that about?" Benjamin asked.

"You've never seen that done, Benya, have you? It's an old ritual. I place the egg over his closed eyes and say some words. It protects him from the evil eye or so we believe."

"Speaking of ignorance," Benjamin said irreverently.

"Do you know enough to say it doesn't work, my cultured friend?" Ilya asked with a laugh. "I don't believe it and neither does Kostya—or at least he won't. But doing it somehow makes the world seem gentler and more forgiving. Saying prayers is always comforting. You don't have to believe God is listening. If the Bolsheviks knew that they'd still own the country."

Benjamin had handled their being weathered in much the same way he survived every day of his captivity, with mindless physical tasks, splitting logs for the fire, sweat covering his back and running down his arms, patching the roof of the outhouse, a kerchief covering his nose and mouth, and helping Marya weed her garden or dig up potatoes. He'd pick mushrooms with her, questioning their edibility, wary when she sautéed them in rich butter, ever nervous when he ate them at dinner. And when the rain was too heavy or the hour too late, he would delve into a couple of the books Ilya had collected during his days in London, English translations of 19th century Russian political philosophy, Constance Garnett's translation of Alexander Herzen's, *My Past and Thoughts*, and Mikhael Bakunin's *God and the State*—an anarchist classic Ilya told him—printed by the Mother Earth Publishing Association in America early in the 20th century. Benjamin found the books as anachronistic as the hamlet in which he was imprisoned, as old fashioned as the well from which he drew water. But they helped put him to sleep.

Kostya was nowhere in sight, but the children's father was waiting at the door when his two visitors arrived. His dark, deeply set eyes glistened when Ilya yelled out a greeting, but they grew suspicious when Ilya turned his face toward Benjamin. He was about the same height as the Russian, perhaps 5'9", but his extraordinary thinness made him look taller and fragile. His high cheekbones looked as if they were going to pop out of his tanned and wrinkled skin.

"Dmitri," Ilya said pointing to the farmer. "Benya," he said pointing to the American.

The farmer gave a reluctant smile. His few remaining teeth were deeply stained.

"He wants to know if you are the stranger his children talk about. I told him you were and that you indeed were an

American. He thought his children had to be wrong. They told him they liked you but that you smiled a lot."

"An American habit," Benjamin said.

They followed the farmer into the central hallway that separated the two rooms of the whitewashed house, and settled down in the room on the left that served as kitchen, living room, and master bedroom. Mila was lifting a large wrought iron kettle from the stone stove when they entered, a brilliantly colored shawl covering her shoulders and draping over her budding breasts. She gave Benjamin a bashful smile before turning her head away. An older woman, as thin as the man but looking a decade younger—wife and mother, Benjamin assumed—was pulling out some glasses for tea. A plate of deep-fried bow-tie cookies, sprinkled lightly with sugar, sat in the middle of a wooden table. Mila poured the hot water into a large teapot. Her mother brought it to the table. Only the men sat down.

Whatever Dmitri said caused Ilya to laugh, but he did not translate for Benjamin.

"Tell Dmitri that he has beautiful children," Benjamin said. "And they're smart and kind."

Ilya's translation caused the mother to say something that brought laughter from the two men and the young girl. "Alena said they are her children, too. That's why they are smart."

Kostya came out of nowhere and took two cookies. "Good Morning, Benya," he said again.

The two Slavs drank their tea slowly, noisily sucking it through cubes of sugar held between their teeth. At first they didn't include Benjamin in the conversation, but rattled on for five minutes or so somberly exchanging thoughts, only rarely trading a smile or chuckle. Alena picked up the plate of cookies and held it in front of Benjamin until he took his third helping. Mila and Kostya disappeared into the other room.

The house was in far better shape than Ilya's cabin, Benjamin observed. Its wooden floors were smooth and waxed, its window glass clear, its shelves full of plates and pots. The double bed was neatly covered with a multicolored quilt. A large, unpainted wooden relief of a saint whom Benjamin did not recognize hung on the wall next to the door, a more familiar icon—an image of Christ as priest—stood on the bureau next to the bed. From a distance it looked like a traditional egg tempura painting, but Benjamin suspected it was a lithograph that had been glued to a rustic piece of wood and then coated with heavy shellac. A peasant's icon, affordable to the poor but bearing the beauty and artistry of the masterpieces owned by the wealthy. Ilya's cabin held no icons, no hints of religion, and no relics of belief other than manuscripts of forgotten revolutionaries. This house was a home; the cabin was a hideaway.

Ilya's question drew Benjamin out of his thoughts. "Dmitri wants to know why you came to the Carpathians. Did you come to steal its timber, to steal his land, or to steal its women?"

"Are those my only choices, Ilya? He doesn't think much of Americans. Tell him the truth, I came to learn, to discover. I have enough income to support myself. I don't need to steal."

"He won't believe me, Benya. He knows that rich people are never content, they always want more."

"Tell him, Ilya. Let's see what he believes."

Some words and laughter were exchanged before Ilya turned back to his captive. "He says that Mila is too young. Come back in a few years and maybe a deal can be struck."

Benjamin grew annoyed. "Did you tell him I'm looking for a wife?"

"I told him that you said you didn't steal. He doesn't believe you. All capitalists steal, and politicians. But if it were true that you were here to find a wife he would think you were smart. He said Ukrainian women make the best wives, although I'm not sure he would have thrown that in if his wife were not listening."

"He thinks I'm a thief, but I should come back for his oldest daughter? He's very accepting."

"Better to be in the house of the thief than in the home of the robbed, Benya," Ilya said. Then he slapped his thighs and broke into laughter.

Benjamin didn't share the humor. "Tell him Mila will be a beautiful woman and will deserve a younger and better man."

Ilya was gleeful when he translated Dmitri's answer. "She may want a younger man, but her parents want an old son-in-law who can support them."

Benjamin turned somber. "Does Dmitri realize I'm a prisoner?"

"I doubt it. He sees that your hands are free, that there are no chains around your legs, that you remember how to laugh, and that you look well fed. For the rest, he will think I have some business deal going with you, but he will be wise enough not to ask what."

Dmitri said something to Ilya, and the two men laughed.

"What did I miss?" Benjamin asked.

"He wants to know if you are running away from a wife and a dozen children or are you gay. I told him why not both."

Alena, too, enjoyed the joke. When she stopped laughing she walked over to the table and refilled her husband's glass. Ilya put his hand up to keep her from pouring more tea for her visitors. "Ready, Benya?" he asked.

"May I take a couple of cookies back for Marya?"

Ilya gave a sharp laugh, and then conveyed the question to Alena. Before there was an answer he picked up a handful of cookies and handed them to Benjamin. "She'd prefer flowers and chocolates," Ilya said snidely.

"Then you should get some for her," Benjamin hissed.

Ilya's laugh almost shook the plates off a shelf.

Alena yelled out something to the other room and the children came in to say goodbye, their faces covered with smiles and expectations. Ilya responded by reaching into his pocket and slowly distributing colorfully wrapped pieces of sucking candy, three pieces to each. He touched Mila's cheek and, to Benjamin's ears, said something charming. Dasha and Kostya exchanged a couple of words of gratitude. Mila curtsied—a deep and graceful genuflection fit for a Czar. Once outside the house Ilya slipped Dmitri a roll of rubles held tightly together by a rubber band. No words were exchanged but the farmer smiled reservedly.

The rain had stopped and sunlight was coloring the western horizon a robin egg blue. Birdcalls and insect chatter filled the clean air.

"The weather will improve," Ilya said as he threw the rifle over his shoulder. "In a day or two, when the heat is oppressive, we will be wishing for the rain to return."

Benjamin followed Ilya through the wheat field and across the river, wondering what the Russian had bought with the rubles—loyalty, service, both. Or was he buying silence. Silence about Benjamin's presence, about an American captive, about kidnapping and ransom.

"Marya will enjoy the cookies," Ilya commented when they entered the forest, "and will be happy that you remembered her. Do you like her?"

"She has been very kind to me."

"Kind is the right word, Benya. She is very kind. But that was not my question." Ilya stopped and waited for Benjamin to catch up. He shifted the rifle from one shoulder to the other, took Benjamin by the elbow, and leaned toward his ear as if to share a precious secret. "She should have been my daughter, Benya. I loved her mother intensely, but was too foolish to stay with her. I love Marya as much as if she were my child. She is the only life that I consider more valuable than my own. Do you have anyone whose life you consider more valuable than your own, Benya?"

Ilya didn't wait for an answer. He removed his hand from his companion and began to lead the way. "Do you?" he asked over his shoulder. "I can't imagine how narrow life would be if I didn't have someone whose life was that important to me."

"Of course," Benjamin said thinking of his wife. But as soon as the answer was out of his mouth, he began to question it. Was she still that important to him? His capture, he realized, had focused him on himself. His survival, his health, his rescue, or escape, were the only things that mattered.

"I hope the two of you can become friends. She needs friends. I am an old man. She is still young."

Benjamin brushed a low hanging branch aside and hurled his voice at his captor's back. "I'm not looking for friendship, Ilya. I'm a prisoner, not a vacationer. Or did you forget?"

"Even a prisoner deserves a friend," Ilya said as he continued to push ahead. "Do you find her unattractive?"

"And why did you slip money into Dmitri's palm? Were you buying his silence or his loyalty?"

"I don't need to purchase loyalty. It is freely given." Ilya shouted irately.

"Then what were you buying?"

Ilya turned around and, once more, shifted the rifle to his other shoulder. He looked sad. "Benya, sometimes I lose hope. You think like a capitalist. Maybe I gave him the money because he needs it? Wouldn't that be reason enough?"

Cynicism drove Benjamin to silence.

Ilya continued, "Need I quote Marx to you, Benya, 'From each according to his abilities, to each according to his needs.' I have the ability, he has the need. Is there anything wrong with that?"

"Nothing is wrong with it, Ilya, but history has proven you can't build a society on philanthropic shibboleths."

"That is the great Bolshevik tragedy, Benya. History gave them a chance to prove what you now think is impossible. Remember, Marx said that history is nothing, it has no riches, it fights no battles. Real men do it all. There were not enough real men, or real women. Tragic, Benya, tragic. History doesn't give you many chances. Mankind may never again have a chance to show that society can be built on generosity."

Benjamin shrugged his shoulders, dismayed, as he always was, by Ilya's loyalty to 19th century idealism.

~

It was after the evening news, but hours before a local jazz group was to begin to play, when Caitlin and Peter Johnson met at a restaurant in the Adams Morgan section of Washington. They chose the privacy of a small table in the rear of the dark bistro and spent the early part of their reunion reminding each other about their previous encounters. When they tired of the past, Caitlin talked about her growing newsroom responsibilities; Peter discussed the additional material he was preparing for the second edition of his popular textbook. With her voice in a near whisper, Caitlin brought him up to date on Benjamin's indictment and the disintegration of the marriage. Peter asked if she knew about his battle with alcoholism. She admitted to hearing the gossip but had learned that he had moved on. Finally the time came, or so Caitlin thought, to say goodnight or include her companion in her half-finished plans.

"I want to tell you something important, Peter, but I need to know you will keep it between us. Secrecy is imperative," Caitlin said.

"I'm paid to reveal secrets not keep them undercover," Peter said with a lilt in his voice.

"I need a writer, a sound technician, and a camera man all rolled into one…and a friend. You're the only one I know that fits the bill."

"And someone who can keep secrets?"

"That most of all."

Peter let out a quick laugh, picked up his glass of orange juice, and took a long swallow. The gossip was right, Caitlin thought. He was back on the wagon. Had been, he claimed, for over a year. And he looked it. Slim and broad shouldered, he burst with athletic energy, his light African American complexion vibrant, his grayish-blue eyes clear, his black crew cut dotted with gray.

"I have an opportunity that's made to order for you, Peter," she said with gravity, her face immobile, her eyes penetrating.

He was cautious. "I'm off for the summer and will be on a sabbatical next semester, but I'm not looking for anything, Cat. I'm content."

She wasn't certain. The grapevine had told her that Peter Johnson was restless, that he had tired of teaching and wanted to get back to the work that had distinguished him, making documentaries about distant conflicts and cultures. He was in his early thirties when he made his name covering the First Gulf War, but had left journalism soon afterwards to join the faculty of a small college in Pennsylvania, and every so often offer paid advice to television broadcasters and reporters. That's how Caitlin met him, almost nine years before, when she was working on a documentary about the gangs in Los Angeles and sought Peter's advice. Stale celebrity must be a sarcophagus, Caitlin thought as she watched Peter drink some juice.

"I know you don't need the work, Peter. This isn't an act of charity. I need help. If you want a new and compelling story we'll both win. If you don't, it was nice seeing you again. You do look terrific."

"Well, tell me the story. I promise to seal my lips."

His ebullient smile disappeared as she told him about her meeting with Hocking and the subsequent telephone calls. He formed a steeple with his fingers and put it under his chin when she talked about getting in touch with journalists in London, hoping they could lead her to Russian expatriates who had ties to the underworld in Moscow and Kyiv.

"Why me?" he finally asked.

"I can't go with a crew, Peter. I need one other person who can do it all, film, script, interviews. There aren't many with your range of skills. You're much more experienced than I am. I don't think I can manage it without having someone I can lean on."

"I'm flattered, Cat, but let me think about it. If it doesn't work for me maybe I can come up with someone who can help you. But I must say it does sound a bit dangerous."

"Doesn't every good story have its risks?"

Peter didn't smile.

"Would you be able to get the equipment we'll need?" Caitlin asked. "It has to be light but effective"

"That's not a problem. What I don't have I can get. Standard rates, Cat, or could I squeeze you for my lecture fees?"

"It's a speculative project, Peter, which I'll be financing. I'd like you to come on as a partner without a cash investment. I'd like to offer more, but God knows what I'll be asked to pay for information or ransom."

Peter reached over, picked up a napkin, and wiped some liquid from the table. "Will we have to share a room?" he asked.

"I'm serious," Caitlin blurted out. She emphasized her resoluteness by emptying her glass of scotch.

~

Hocking warned her not to go, but he had no way of stopping her. "You'll be dealing with bandits, Ms. McCoy, and endanger yourself and your husband. It's bad enough that I have to worry about him; I don't want to fret about you. They'll take your money and you'll get nothing in return, let me assure you, except, perhaps, something horrid. Don't do it."

"It's been over a month since we first talked. What have you done? You don't even know where he is being held or if he's alive. How can you expect me to do nothing?"

"We've been in contact with Kyiv and Moscow. They are fully aware of the circumstance and are doing their best to find him. We have our own people working. What do you think you can learn that the professionals cannot?"

"How do you know they're doing their best? How do you know they're even trying?"

"You have to have faith, Ms. McCoy. Do I have to pull your passport?"

"And how the fuck would you like to see that on the evening news?"

She took Hocking seriously. She didn't want to play the fool. She didn't want to come off as a crazed wife who was going to get her husband murdered. But how could she not try to find him? Abramowitz was right, of what moment was Benjamin's captivity to the government? What would the worst produce, a minor article in the New York Times about a financial manipulator being lost in the Ukraine? No, Benjamin was unimportant to the State Department, even less important to the Ukrainians and Russians. She was not going to be cast as the impotent wife, twirling her thumbs five thousand miles away, waiting patiently for someone to find Benjamin's body floating in the Dnieper or Volga or Moskva. She couldn't just sit on the sidelines. She was stronger and wiser than that.

Stealthily, she sought advice from friends and acquaintances by fabricating a story that she had been offered a job assisting in a television investigation of the Russian demimonde in New York and London, in Tel Aviv and Moscow. "If you wear a miniskirt with cash sticking out of your bra, you'll learn more than you want, Caitlin. If you have a press badge hanging from your neck and stick to those who want to talk, and don't go alone, well, it will still be more risky than doing the weather report but it shouldn't be daunting," was the advice she got from an a retired CIA operative. It was the very sentiment she wanted.

"It might prove dangerous," Peter said over the phone.

"I can't let fear cripple me. I have to do something. No one else will," Caitlin answered. She had placed the early morning call. Sleep was still in his voice.

"But they said they were working on it."

"Come Peter, you know what that's worth. I can't go alone. It's a chauvinistic world over there. I need a male escort. I want a journalist like you. We can send messages and photographs back as we go along, telling people what we did, who we expect to see, and where we plan to go. It will protect us."

There was a long pause. She imagined him sitting on the side of a bed and trying to sharpen his thoughts. "Do you know Selby Hughes? You may have bumped into her over the years."

"She was an instructor in a summer program I did at Oxford years ago. We've kept in sporadic contact. But why, Peter?"

"She's still in London and might be able to clue us into the Russian expatriate community. She was always good at networking."

Caitlin immediately e-mailed London, gave her telephone number, and asked Selby to call. But before sending it she replaced "it's a matter of life and death" with "it's very important." Selby called a few hours later. Caitlin didn't hold back.

"I'm sorry," Selby said. "You must be tormented. But I write restaurant reviews and cookbooks, Cat. I know nothing about international intrigues. I know this means a great deal to you so I'll give it a try. Maybe a friend of a friend knows something that will be helpful."

"I'd appreciate it more than I can say," Caitlin said.

Selby called back in two days. "I haven't found out much, Cat, but I do have the name of someone who might be helpful, Georgi Koslov. They tell me he's a middle rung player, not very high up on the food chain, but high enough to reach into Kyiv. If there is any chance of locating your husband, Koslov seems as likely as anyone I can discover to be the right person. He's a disreputable character, I'm told."

"How disreputable?"

"I wouldn't invite him for dinner."

"Is he Russian mafia?"

"If you're thinking of the characters in *Eastern Promises* he's not one of them. None of my contacts thinks he imports fourteen-year-old girls for prostitution. He doesn't break knees or slice throats. He's a middleman is what I hear. If he dealt in antiquities, you would describe him as the guy that stood between the gravedigger and the tourist."

"That doesn't sound very attractive."

"I never said he was although he does think he's a dandy, fancy clothes, a big apartment, a classy car, diamond rings on his fingers, you know the type. He seems to do all of this without a discernible source of money. They say he is always in debt to higher ups. He will try to extract every possible penny out of you, but it is unlikely that you will be in any personal danger—at least not in London."

"That's good to hear. I am concerned."

"You should be but not from him. The Russian community has had enough bad publicity. If you do decide to come over to meet him, you can stay with me Cat. I would enjoy the company."

"That's very kind of you, but I won't be traveling alone. I'll be bringing a photojournalist and reporter with me. Do you have room for two?"

"Oh," Selby said. Caitlin thought the expression contained a hint of suspicion.

"He's a business colleague, not a friend. And he's African American," Caitlin said. She recognized the manipulative part of her personality before throwing race into the mix. Selby wouldn't want to come off as a racist.

There was a laugh in Selby's voice when she asked, "Peter Johnson?"

"How did you know?"

"It wasn't a wild guess. He e-mailed me about your likely call. By the time his message reached me, you and I had already talked. But I didn't suspect he was on this venture with you."

"I didn't know you knew him."

"It's a small world, Cat. He will have to sleep on a couch in my library…because of the space not because of his color. I was hoping to see him on his next trip to London, although not so close up."

"That's very kind of you."

"It will be fun to catch up with both of you."

~

Ilya was right about the weather. High winds had pushed the clouds east, and the hot summer sun felt soft and luxurious when Benjamin exited the dense forest and made his way to the banks of the river looking for Marya. She was kneeling by the swollen stream and washing clothes.

"Blissful," she said over her shoulder, somehow sensing that he was approaching. "There is nothing like days of rain to make you love the sun."

"But soon we'll be complaining that it's too hot," he answered, consciously echoing Ilya's premonition.

She did not turn around. "Is that your mood, Mr. Benya, the world is never good."

He let out a gentle laugh. "I've always worried about tomorrow."

"It robs the day of its joy, does it not? You can always find black clouds in the future."

He looked for a spot to sit down, but the grass was still damp, and the rocks along the edge of the stream too uncomfortable. Impulsively, he touched her neck and rubbed her shoulders. Her muscles tensed for a moment, but only for a moment.

"That feels good," she said a minute later. "Come next to me. The work will be done faster if you help."

He moved some of the sand with his shoe, rolled up his sleeves, and kneeled down beside her. She was rubbing one of Ilya's shirts against an old-fashioned scrub board, the suds coming from a large cake of brown soap. She handed the shirt to Benjamin. "You rinse and I'll scrub."

The water was cold and the current swift, but there was something tender and enjoyable about being on his knees next to Marya, feeling his shoulder touch her shoulder, smelling her hair, picking up the soft odor of her body. Domesticity, he thought, thankful for the moment that there was no washing machine in the cabin. Her brisk motions revealed the definition of her muscles; the dampness of her blouse glued it to her brassiere. He felt his penis harden, and futilely dipped his hands deeper into the rushing water to dampen his desire.

"How was your visit this morning," she asked. "They are a nice family. Did you meet Dmitri and Alena? I don't know him well, but I am fond of her. She's a strong, independent woman. She teaches me how to cook."

"Didn't your mother do that?"

"Ha! My mother was a schoolteacher. She didn't like to cook. But she did like to bake."

"So you were raised on cake and not bread."

She burst into laughter. "Alena taught me how to do the laundry. Where did you think I learned the scrub board, in Moscow?"

"I never thought about it."

"See all the new skills you will bring home with you, Benya. You can scrub clothes in a stream, use an outhouse, drink vodka at breakfast."

He knew she meant to be funny, but he couldn't bring himself to laugh. "Are you that certain that I'm going to get home, or are you just being kind?"

"Ilya is a prosperous scoundrel. He will figure a way to make a small fortune with you. And that will mean your freedom."

"Ilya slipped Dmitri some money, Marya. What was he buying? His silence? Or was he ensuring that I couldn't easily escape across Dmitri's land?"

"Ilya doesn't buy people. He helps them. Poor people live here, Benya, people who start their work at sunrise and never stop. The land is good and the weather kind. But it doesn't buy medicine, it doesn't pay for the hospital, it can't get you a television or a computer. With luck you can buy cigarettes and Chinese made clothes. Ilya gives them money, not much, but enough to make a difference between being healthy and being sick."

"So he buys people. How can you call it anything else?"

Marya pulled a pair of Benjamin's pants from the basket and ran over it with the soap bar. Then she chuckled. "Ilya is right, you are a capitalist. He is not buying their silence. He gave them money long before you came here, or me. He doesn't give them money because you are here. He gives them money because they are here. He doesn't have to keep you in a cellar because his neighbors help him. He doesn't pay them to avoid having to keep you in a cellar. He is not that benevolent."

She handed the soapy pants to Benjamin, stood up, and stretched her arms over her head. The sunlight penetrated her thin skirt and revealed the strength of her thighs, the shape of her legs. His hormones screamed when he studied her body, when he stood up and lightly touched her face, her hair full of sunlight, her voice tender, her smile giving. If it were any other place he would have tried to bed her, to learn those things about her that could not be learned through words, or laughter, or working side by side. But he was afraid, afraid that his advances would drive her away, that the warmth she offered freely would be withheld because he had foolishly pursued more. He feared that he would end up tied to a chair, with foul air filling his nostrils, his chest full of phlegm.

"The world is changing, Benya. The land doesn't hold the young. It doesn't pay for cell phones. It doesn't get you to the Internet. The children will not be able to stay here. Few will. Mila is very smart. Ilya wants her to go to university. It doesn't make him happy. He loves this rural life. He thinks it keeps the soul clean. But he knows it will not last. The future is elsewhere."

She hummed before she continued. "Ilya sings to his own music. You should have more trust in him, Benya. Where are we if we do not trust?" She locked her hands behind her back, her firm breasts pressing against her blouse. "Ilya does not want to hurt you."

Benjamin carried the basket of wet clothes back to the cabin and helped Marya hang them up in the sun. She took his arm and held it tightly as they walked toward the cabin. "It's turned out to be a beautiful day," he said to her.

# Chapter 6

Peter was not prepared to spend his nights on Selby's couch, uncomfortably chaperoned by Caitlin's innocence. He had spent too many passionate hours sharing Selby's bed, making her breakfast, waiting for her to come home at night, cold bottles of beer in the refrigerator.

He arranged to stay at what was, before he met Selby and after they parted, his favorite London retreat, The Duke, a small upscale hotel hidden on a narrow street just a few blocks from the famous Ritz. It was perfectly located. London's National Gallery and theater district were a short stroll away; a longer but enjoyable walk got him to the Victoria and Albert Museum and the Royal Albert Hall. If shopping were on his mind, the exclusive shops on Jermyn Street were just outside the door, as was Berry Bros & Rudd, the London wine dealer that stored a small collection of Burgundies and Bordeaux for him somewhere in the countryside. The wine shop's claim to having been established in 1698 added historical spice to the shopping, a place made all the more affecting by Peter's assumption that early in its history the firm had assisted in the transportation of slaves to the Americas and rum to the homeland. Whenever he entered Berry Bros and glanced at the giant coffee scales on which Napoleon III and Lord Byron had once weighed themselves, he recorded the irony of a descendent of African slaves being served by the descendants of slave traders. At first his purchases were tinged with a sense of guilt. Why was he slipping money into the palms of an historic oppressor? But that emotion was quickly suppressed by a sense of survival and pride. How surprised the founders of the shop would be—and perhaps horrified—to know that the business was catering to the whims of a child of slavery.

The Duke did not date back 300 years, or so he believed, but it no less conveyed the feel of privilege. The concierge made certain his junior suite was ready for his early arrival, and that a basket of fresh fruit and a plate of handmade chocolates were on the table in the spacious sitting area. He took a light lunch in his room and made calls to the people he had informed about his visit to assure them that he had arrived in one piece. Then he settled back for a long nap.

It was still early in the evening when he went down to The Duke's bar, sat at a corner table, ordered a bottle of Kaliber, his favorite non-alcoholic beer, and took out his notebook. The place was almost empty, he noticed, as he began to jot down notes about the crowd at Heathrow, the expense of taxi rides, the excitement Caitlin exhibited when the plane touched down, when the taxi let her off at Selby's townhouse. Caitlin's attire had fascinated him. She had forsaken personal comfort for fashion, her skirt tight fitting, her blouse a shimmering white. She carefully handed her linen jacket to the steward to be hung up, and slipped off her high heel shoes after she was comfortably seated in a business class seat. Anticipatory socialization, Peter decided—a term he loved to use with his students when he invited them to a formal dinner at his house—dressing as if she were going to be met by a swarm of fans and reporters, a rehearsal for the time she expected when such crowds would indeed be greeting her.

The bar had begun to fill up by the time he was ready to order a second Kaliber. The usual suspects, Peter mused as he glanced around looking for his waiter, well-dressed men, mostly, but a few women, speaking with foreign accents and in foreign languages. There were a few Englishmen drawn from neighboring businesses, a couple of Americans, a French couple, and a group of Germans, four men and a young woman, who seemed to be rehashing their day's experience.

His attention was drawn to a thin man in his early forties whose monochromatic outfit separated him from the other patrons, his oddly cut jacket a black, shimmering leather, his black shirt—the top two buttons undone—a cheap rayon, his black pants tight and creaseless. He kept looking at himself in the mirror behind the bar, first full-faced, then one profile before the other. Pulling a small comb from his pocket, he ran it quickly through his dirty-blond hair and gazed into the mirror once again. From Central or Eastern Europe, Peter concluded, his taste in clothes left over from socialist days. Peter was tempted to record the stranger's appearance in his Moleskine notepad, but the Kaliber arrived and his thoughts drifted.

The stranger was examining his reflection in the highly polished elevator door when Peter made his way to the registration desk to see if there were any messages for him. A boring character, the American decided, wondering why such a seemingly low-life narcissist would take his drinks in one of London's boutique establishments. Perhaps he just didn't know how out of place he was.

Peter walked under the neon lights of Piccadilly Circus and along Shaftesbury Avenue, noting what was playing at the Gielgud Theater, at the Apollo, at the Lyric Shaftesbury. The youthfulness of the crowd made him feel old, and memories rekindled by the bright lights sobered his mood. He pictured the women with whom he had traveled, and estimated the length of time they had played couple. He thought of Selby and wondered if she would tell Caitlin about their affair, about his running away. Before he realized it the sun had set and the air had developed a chill. He had walked further than he had planned, all the way to the intersection of Charing Cross Road and Tottenham Court. So he decided to turn back to see if he could find the small restaurant that he had stumbled upon the last time he was in the city, one of the many precious restaurants that had replaced the plush grillrooms he used to patronize. He didn't think it was an improvement. Selby furiously disagreed.

To Peter's great surprise, there he was, the stranger, looking at his reflection in the window of a south Asian restaurant, the leather jacket buttoned, the gold chain around his neck shimmering. Peter walked by him perplexed at having twice seen this peculiar looking person, and at different ends of this crowded, bustling section of London. Up ahead was the restaurant Peter had been looking for, but he decided not to enter. No, he thought, go a few more blocks and then double back. He felt as if he were behaving ridiculously, a paranoid reaction to black leather and tight pants, he decided, but he kept walking. He turned sharply around the next corner, startling a young couple who were rushing somewhere. A green light on the next block got Peter to run across the street, automatically looking left as if he were crossing a street in Manhattan but getting away with it. He ducked into an antiquarian book dealer's shop, made it quickly into an interior room, and leaned against the edge of a bookcase to catch his breath. A twentysomething woman with long black hair looked at him suspiciously. He gave her a quick smile and took a deep breath.

He spent a few minutes reviewing his actions and concluded that he had overreacted to a chance meeting, that the atmosphere of intrigue that covered the entire mission to London had made him act silly. But he found comfort in the shop, as he always did when he found himself surrounded by books, and in time began to examine the titles on a stuffed bookshelf. He pulled out an early 20th century book on the Middle East and ran his eye over its table of contents. How little had changed, he said to himself, reading the titles of chapters that explored the politics and religion of that distant place. He put the book back and picked up another, and then another, momentarily losing track of why he had ducked into the shop to begin with.

A young woman in a thin sweater and tight white slacks slipped quietly into the room, her companion, a man in his thirties, Peter later recalled, followed her. They began to examine some of the books jammed into the opposite bookshelf. Peter turned back to what he was doing, but when he heard the thud of books hitting the wooden floor, he turned around to find the woman bending down to pick them up. The man bent down to help her, and so did Peter. She looked amused, her companion annoyed. When the books were restored, she gave Peter a neon smile, "Thank you," she said in a deep accent. Immigrants from Poland, Peter concluded when they left the room, and thought how mismatched they seemed. Her beauty stunning, his homeliness matched only by his growling disposition. "Life is not fair," he said under his breath.

Scores of volumes were exhibited in the bookstore's large window, severely limiting Peter's view when he tried to look out of the shop and onto the street. He was forced to go outside to look around. Much of the crowd had disappeared into their theater seats, allowing him to run his eyes up and down the street without obstruction. He saw no darkly appareled man watching the bookstore, no one in a leather jacket was milling around. He decided not to head to the restaurant on Frith, his original intent. Instead, he stuck to the wider and better-lighted streets like Shaftesbury and Piccadilly and headed in the direction of his hotel. He stopped every so often, acting as if he were examining a window display or reading a menu posted on a bulletin board, and glanced around to see if he were again being followed. No pursuer was obvious. The maître d' at a smart French restaurant said a table for one would be available in a quarter of an hour, but after waiting on a hallway seat for ten minutes, Peter left, annoyed with his own impatience but unable to push it aside.

The evening chill cut through his thin suit jacket as he rushed along Piccadilly on his way to The Duke. He hardly noticed the lighted billboards, but carefully followed the arrows painted on the road at the crosswalks and obeyed the traffic lights.

"Mr. Johnson," a clerk called out when Peter approached the registration desk. "This was left for you." The neatly outfitted, middle-aged woman handed Peter his billfold. "He said he found it in the bar."

"Thank you," Peter said, surprised and bewildered. He took hold of his wallet and quickly went through it. Nothing seemed to be missing, not any of the pounds he had picked up at the airport, not the credit cards, not the photograph of him and Selby that he had held on to for the last two years.

"What did he look like, the man who left this here?" Peter asked, assuming whoever it was had left it with this clerk.

"Different," she said. "I asked his name and told him you might want to contact him to thank him, but he didn't think that was necessary. The way he looked—a black leather jacket over a black shirt with pants to match—I thought he might want a reward, but he just turned around and left."

"And that was all?"

"That was all. Is everything all right? Are you missing anything?"

"Everything is fine, everything."

~

The children's voices floated into the distance as Benjamin followed Ilya along the banks of the river, walking further from the cabin than he had been allowed to go on his own. Forbidden territory, the American thought, excited by his thoughts of entering a village or the outskirts of a town that might offer refuge if he ever decided to run away. Why else would Ilya have warned him against walking east if it did not lead to a way out of his captivity? But if that were true, what had occurred to change Ilya's mind? Had he become so certain of his captive's fear of this alien land that he believed that Benjamin would never attempt to leave on his own? Or did Ilya think he had made his prisoner's life so comfortable that he would not want to leave? "Come," Ilya had insisted, "Come, it is too beautiful a day to stay cramped behind four walls."

The woods were still wet from the morning rain, but the long grass that covered most of the land had already dried and was now alive with butterflies and bumblebees. A flock of clattering jackdaws swept over the field hunting for grains and berry seeds. Marya touched Benjamin on his shoulder and pointed up to the sky where a white-tailed eagle was slowly gliding on the gentle wind.

They walked for close to an hour, mostly in silence, but now and then commenting about the landscape, or talking about the challenges of subsistence farming, lamenting the meager productivity of Ukrainian milk farms, and offering romantic remarks when they saw a horse-drawn plow or a gaggle of geese. They settled down on the grassy top of a small hill that overlooked a broad, fertile valley. The Carpathian Mountains stood in the distance. There had been no village, no town, no sign of refuge other than an isolated homestead, a lone shepherd. If there were telephone lines,

Benjamin had not seen them; if there were electric wires, they had to be buried deep in the earth, an economic impossibility. Benjamin put down the tattered blankets he had carried over his shoulders, and watched Marya empty the straw picnic basket she had packed before they left the cabin. Ilya opened a bottle of red wine and passed out three glasses. The drink helped ease Benjamin's disappointment.

"There was once a synagogue on this spot, Benya, or so they say, a grand wooden synagogue. Its exterior was described to me as simple, undistinguished, and boxy, with an outside staircase that led to the second floor. Its interior was supposed to have been elaborate, with a magnificent prayer center, different from the Christians, but just as ornate, with gold and silver ceremonial objects, some with fine jewels," Ilya said after they had lunched, and after he had opened a second bottle of wine. He was crouching down under a tree and examining a protruding rock. "But there are still a few people around who dispute that view, who say their grandparents helped build the place. They say there was no gold, not even silver. Brass was all they could afford to decorate their religious texts and protect handwritten scrolls. They, too, say it was beautiful inside, but there were no jewels and no precious metals. The artists worked in wood and copper, poor people's materials employed by the same artists that built wooden churches, who made fine furniture for nobility and landowners."

"Destroyed by the Germans in the Second World War?" Benjamin asked.

"Years before, Benya, during the war to end all wars, in 1917, but before the revolution. I don't know by whom. No one may know. It might have been accidental, the building too close to a battlefield; it might have been on purpose. It might have been lightning or a forest fire. By now, it doesn't matter. A fading memory, my American, hardly recorded."

Benjamin walked over to where Ilya was kicking at a rock. "Is that part of its foundation?" he asked.

"I doubt it. It's just a rock, nothing more. Actually, I've never seen anything up here that even hinted at any manmade structure leave alone a proud building. Not a brick, not a headstone, not a cement block. I think it is a tall tale. Synagogues like churches were built in towns, not in the countryside, places where people could walk to them, and by them, and look out their windows to see something holy. Sometimes, Benya, when I am drunk enough, I imagine that there was once a religious edifice up here overlooking this beautiful land and reaching up to heaven, but then I sober up and reality strikes, and I know that if there ever was a structure up here it was a fortress and not a church, a castle built for war and not a place designed for prayer."

"Do I hear something of a believer in your voice?" Marya asked humorously.

Ilya couldn't contain his laugh. "So you think you've spotted an internal contradiction, my beautiful one. How can anyone deny believing in religion, it is all around us? But do I believe in the teachings of religion? Not in the beliefs of any religion I know, not even in the religion of Marx and Lenin. But I believe in cathedrals, Marya, in buildings designed to lift the spirit, to make you think, if only for the length of a service, of larger questions, of goodness, of beauty." He took Marya by the arm and walked with her to stand closer to Benjamin. "My American friend, don't you think I would have made a terrific priest, my deep voice, my talent with language, my love of the people, my knowledge of right and wrong? So what if I didn't believe Jesus was the son of God, if I didn't believe in heaven and hell? Religion is an institution for the living, isn't it? It does nothing for the dead. I would have made life better for my parishioners. I would have made them righteous. But when I was a young man, Bolshevism smothered orthodoxy and commissars replaced clergy."

"You would have made a terrific priest. But I think your followers would have benefitted from an independent bookkeeper," Benjamin said without a smile.

"You are a scoundrel, Benya. I don't steal from my followers. I never have, not from my workers, not from my bosses. I am the essence of an honest man."

Benjamin forced himself to be silent. They had been over it too many times; Ilya's holding him captive, seeking a ransom for his release, and all the time thinking of himself as an honest prince, a gallant man. It was too beautiful a day to argue, their moods too buoyant, the air too bright, the sun too strong, and Marya too beautiful.

Ilya poured another round of drinks. He held the bottle up to the sun and to see how much wine was left and gave a despondent sigh when he realized little remained. After sitting down on a blanket, he waved to his companions to sit on the other.

"I don't understand you, Benya. You are an enigma to me," the Russian said quietly.

"And what brings this on?" Benjamin asked, surprised by the turn in the conversation.

"You are an honorable man, gracious, humorous, intelligent, and yet you don't seem to realize that you are a wound upon the world."

"A wound upon the world?" Benjamin questioned.

Marya came to Benjamin's aid. "That's a bit harsh, Ilya. Is it the wine talking?"

"You undermined your own belief. You corrupted the capital system. And you take no notice of it."

"I confessed my errors, Ilya, and I paid a price."

"A small price, Benya, you paid a small price. But you think your crime was stealing money."

"Stock market manipulation, Ilya, insider trading. I wasn't accused of stealing," Benya interrupted.

Ilya lay on his side, his head leaning on a bent arm. "That's what I mean; you don't even accept your minor crime, stealing. Even though you don't know the names or the faces of those you took from, it is still stealing. But that isn't your real crime. That's the crime in the law books. Your real crime is murder. You stabbed the very institution that fed you, you stabbed capitalism, you wounded your social order, your society. Just like the commissars corrupted the organizing principles of their society, you undermined your nation's ideology. You dug a tunnel under your cathedral, and when it collapses, and it will, you will be at fault, Benya. There won't be a trial; there will be no imprisonment, but you will be no less guilty."

"How much of a tunnel can one man dig, Ilya?" an annoyed Marya quibbled.

"That is where Americans are right, individual responsibility supports the world. Without it, all is lost."

"And where is America wrong?" Benjamin asked in a needling tone. He should have been angered by Ilya's condemning comments, but the Russian's voice was academic and not overly judgmental, he was once again playing the didactic social scientist and waiting for counter arguments to spur the debate.

"You use individualism as an excuse for excess, as a reason to make money, to accumulate, as Marx said, without a higher purpose. You dismiss your neighbor, you forget that the fabric of society is thin and fragile, that it can be easily made brittle and can break. If you had read Adam Smith more closely, you would have seen that the working of his market demands trust and honesty, that someone's word has to be his bond, as you would say. That is not Marx or Lenin, my friend; it is your philosopher Smith who laid down the basis of capitalism."

"You lived in Great Britain, Ilya, not America. I don't think you know either country very well. Your propaganda has blinded you from recognizing how generous and charitable Americans are," Benjamin retorted.

"An ad hominem argument, Benya. You know better. I read. I study."

"You read too much, Ilya. It prevents you from enjoying the beauty of a perfect afternoon," Marya said.

The Russian turned onto his back and allowed the sun to shine on his face. In minutes, he began to snore.

~

Ilya drove off after dark, heading, Benjamin assumed, to some distant tavern where he would meet some friends and drink until dawn. Marya carried a kerosene lamp to the outdoor table where she and Benjamin drank hot tea and ate chocolate covered cookies, where they waved away mosquitoes, and listened to the sounds of the night.

"What was your crime?" she asked as a cloud moved over a quarter moon.

"Nothing exceptional. No murders, no bomb explosions, just an ordinary white collar crime that usually goes undetected and is rarely prosecuted."

"I'm just curious, that's all. If you don't want me to know, I understand."

"No, it's nothing like that. Perhaps I should be more ashamed of what I did than I am. Certainly, Ilya thinks so. But I don't want to bore you."

"Oh, I have a great tolerance for boredom, Benya. I would not be able to live out here if I didn't. I'm sure your story will be of more interest than hearing Ilya tell of his exploits for the fifteenth time."

"You exaggerate," Benjamin laughed.

"I wish."

He was glad that she asked. The argument at the picnic had unsettled him. He felt unfairly attacked by Ilya, and made to look small and unattractive to Marya. "I worked for a relatively unknown investment banking firm that bought and sold small businesses, specializing in potentially profitable mergers. My training in finance and accounting got me in, but it was my ability to read people that got me promoted. I have a gift for smelling out executive talent, recognizing the creative from the lame."

"So you, too, are a psychologist," Marya interrupted.

Benjamin let out a quick laugh. "I'd like to think we were in the same business. You tried to help the lame get better; I tried to make sick organizations well. My firm would mold two or three unhealthy companies into one healthy business."

"That doesn't sound criminal to me."

"It wasn't, at least not at the beginning. But investment banking became more and more competitive and eventually it became difficult to find firms in which to invest. Money was all around, a lot more money than talent. So we extended ourselves and began not only to buy companies, but to sell short companies we thought were losers."

Marya frowned. "You've lost me."

"Oh, the intricacies aren't important. Our criminal act was greed. My colleagues began to make private bets on companies using the insider information dug up during merger talks, and when they felt they couldn't buy or sell under their own names, they told friends, and relatives, and colleagues from other firms what to buy and what to sell, which companies would be bought out and which would flounder, expecting some kickback from friends and family, and some useful insider information from the investment specialists we enriched by sharing our secrets."

"One hand washes the other, but was that enough to get you into serious legal trouble?"

"More than enough."

Marya poured some more tea. "Would you like something stronger," she asked.

"The tea is perfect."

"And then?" she asked.

"We were charged, tried, and convicted. Some of the firm's principles were sent to jail. I got off with a fine and probation."

"For testifying against the others. You must have many enemies."

"We were all ready to testify. The government chose me because I was small potatoes, lower down in the firm's hierarchy than the others. I had done a lot less than my colleagues and never involved family. My going to jail would not have made a headline. The other actors were much better catches. We were all ready to squeal. The industry knows that. I'm not a pariah."

"But you will find it difficult to get another job."

"Not really. I'm good at what I do. It's a very marketable skill."

Marya's confused look made him continue. "We were caught, but we weren't exceptions. Financial markets are always being manipulated. I know that sounds cynical and self-serving, but that doesn't make it untrue. I did feel shame, Marya, just not the shame that Ilya was talking about today. I don't think of myself as a wound upon the world. My shame was personal. My company disappeared. I was unemployed. Unflattering mentions appeared in the New York Times and the Wall Street Journal. But a wound upon the world, I just don't see myself that way. I don't feel like a criminal."

Marya picked up a cookie and dipped it in her tea.

"Do you see it the same way Ilya does, that I did something profoundly wrong?"

"Haven't we all," she answered. "It is easy to judge."

"And hard to be understanding."

Marya got up from the table and reached for Benjamin's empty glass. He took hold of her outstretched hand. "But you understand me, don't you?" he asked.

"I don't understand you, Benya, or what you did. It comes from a different culture, a different place. All I know is that if I had any money to invest and wanted an honest return, I might not seek your advice."

"Now that's harsh," he laughed.

Marya's voice remained nonjudgmental. "What did you want me to say, that I understand what you did , and it wasn't so bad? You would have liked hearing that, but you wouldn't have believed me. At least you didn't blame it all on your wife."

"If I could have figured out a way, maybe I would have," he joked.

She did not find it funny. Her smile disappeared, and her eyes darkened. "No, Benya, that much I do understand about you. You would have never blamed your wife."

# Chapter 7

Marya shook him awake, her hands on his shoulders, her face only inches from his. "Benya," she said in a soft and comforting voice. "Benya," she repeated.

Sweat covered his brow and the back of his neck when he broke free from the nightmare, unsure if the dream had ended or if the scene had shifted. As he struggled to sit up, she wrapped her arms around him and gently held his face against her breasts.

"A nightmare, Benya?" she asked. "A nightmare?" she repeated.

Marya rocked him like a worried mother and ran her hand through his hair. She assured him that in a moment, he would forget his torment, that he would find a comforting sleep. She put his head down on the feather pillow and brushed her lips on his forehead. "You have no fever," she said, "good. We don't want you to be sick."

Ilya turned over in his bed. He grunted something in Russian.

Marya shot back, "Mind your own business," followed by a few phrases in Russian.

Whatever she said worked. Ilya turned again, and in a minute he was snoring.

"Tomorrow you won't remember a thing Benya, not a thing," she said quietly as she got up.

He knew he would remember. The dream was meant to be remembered. He was back in the basement, kicking wildly into the air to fend off a shadowy molester, his wrists tied to a ceiling hook, his arms stretched far above his head, his shoulders screaming in pain. Taras was sitting behind a judicial bench, garbed in a black robe and shouting something in Russian or Ukrainian. He waved a huge gavel over the stacks of money that were piled on his desk. Caitlin was pacing in front of him, clutching a broken bottle with two hands. A man who looked like Benjamin—a twin, a doppelganger—pulled down Benjamin's pants and exposed his genitals to her. She was laughing when she approached him, a full-throated, joyful laugh. She slipped one hand from the bottle and used it to lift her skirt. Her pelvic hair danced in front of the hanging man as she began to slowly eviscerate him. Benjamin screamed.

The dream held little mystery, he told himself as he lay under the heavy blanket, afraid to close his eyes, afraid to return to the imagined courtroom, to the apparition of a vengeful wife. Only the doppelganger eluded interpretation. Why wasn't it Boyko that pulled down his pants? Why wasn't it Taras or Ilya?

"Thank you," he said to Marya the next morning as she prepared a glass of tea for him. Ilya had already left the cabin.

"For what, the tea?"

He was ready to say, "Yes, for tea," and leave unstated the evident reason for his gratefulness. But he couldn't bring himself to let her goodness disappear into silence. He wanted to remind her that she had put her arms around him, that she had comforted him with her breasts. "For being a decent human being, that's why."

"And does being a decent human deserve a thank you?" she answered with a sigh.

"In this day and age, it does."

"Sit," she commanded. He obeyed, and she handed him a glass of hot tea.

The first time she had done that, the glass was far too hot for him to hold. Now, he barely noticed the heat. How quickly we adapt, he thought.

"I'll bring the cheese and bread to the table. If you'd like, I can see if there are some fresh eggs," she continued.

"I'd rather you sat down and talked to me."

"About what, Benya?"

"About helping."

"You were keeping me awake, so I quieted you. I don't worry about you."

"Of course you don't," he said sarcastically. "Do you think I'm ashamed of what happened, and you don't want to embarrass me further? Or are you embarrassed by having held me so close, and are wondering if I thought you were making advances?"

"Advances?"

"Your English is perfect. You know what I mean."

She sat on the chair opposite him and mixed some honey in her tea. She did not look at him. "I'm the student of psychology, not you. Don't play Freud with me. I know him too well."

"I hear he was an old lecher."

"Yes, that's why I never missed one of his lectures,"

He raised the glass to his mouth to keep from laughing, but she had spoken with such sincerity that he couldn't contain himself. He spilled some hot tea over his shirt. It burned.

"It wasn't that funny," she said. "You laugh easily, Benya."

"I wasn't laughing because it was funny. I laughed because I can't find the words to tell you how much it meant to me, your holding me in your arms."

Marya hummed something in Russian and bashfully looked away. She got up from the table and threw another log into the stove. "Do you remember the nightmare?" she asked.

"Much of it."

"So, tell me what tormented you in the middle of the night."

"It is much too hazy to describe," he lied.

"So all you remember is my advances. You think of nothing but my flesh."

Abruptly, she threw on a thick woolen shawl over her wool sweater and left the cabin without eating.

Benjamin slammed his hand on the table surprised with her sudden departure, irritated that she left without a kind word. It had gone on too long, this artificial dance they had created, this behaving like distant cousins who were forced to share the summer at the family's retreat, two people afraid to discover if they had become friends or lovers. How long could he balance his unease with her complicity in his imprisonment and his desire for her tenderness, for her body?

By the time Benjamin reached Marya in the garden, tears were streaming down her face.

"You Americans smile easily," Marya said in a choked voice. "Russians cry easily. Do not mind me."

"How can I do that?" Benjamin said.

Ilya, who was just coming out of the forest, glared at Benjamin and shouted something in Russian to Marya. She answered quickly and shook her head. Ilya argued with her for a minute. When he turned toward Benjamin, he said, "You're a son-of-a-bitch. She is better than both of us."

"I didn't do anything to her," Benya shouted at Ilya's back as the older man walked toward the cabin.

"Bastard," Ilya yelled.

Marya knelt in her garden and wiped her eyes with the end of her long skirt.

After the cabin door closed behind Ilya, Benjamin said, "You held me in your arms last night. Does that embarrass you?"

"Don't think you can make a habit of it," she shot back.

"I dreamt that I was imprisoned in a cellar. I was strung up to the ceiling, my hands bound, my ankles tied, my feet unable to touch the floor. Some of the place looked like the cellar near Kyiv, but the rest was a bizarre courtroom. The judge looked like Taras, the prick who cut my prick. The prosecutor was my wife. And then there was a third person, a guard, or assistant, who could have been my twin."

Marya began to pull up some weeds.

"Are you listening?" Benjamin said insistently, irritated that she remained so far away, that she did not approach him and take his hand. He was tempted to bend down near her, to put his arms around her, to lift up her head so he could kiss her.

"To every word. Please, don't stop," she said. She sounded honest, but not sweet.

"That's most of it."

"Something more must have happened to make you scream. But you don't have to tell me."

A smile appeared on his face as he realized that Marya could never pick up a broken vodka bottle to threaten him. He was nervous, though, not by what he might say, but by what she might hear. He had to see her face.

"Please, Marya, stop what you are doing. Come sit down with me. Let me look into your eyes when I talk."

For a moment, she fondled the top of a potato plant, then brushed her hands on her gray skirt and stood up. "Would you like me to bring some tea outside?" she graciously asked.

"Just sit with me," he entreated.

She sat on the opposite side of the table and wiped her eyes.

"The judge glared at me, spewing out harsh words, and my wife, her words were harsher, her soprano voice cutting. My twin pulled down my pants exposing my genitals, and my wife grasped a broken bottle and threatened to mutilate me. Can you imagine—my wife?"

Marya reached across the table, her hand calling for his. It felt muscular and warm in his palm.

"My dream mixed my courtroom appearances with my kidnapping. The judge transformed into the kidnapper; my wife into the prosecutor. And when she left me, the broken glass and the castration sequence. But why was the guard a twin? Why was I both the torturer and the tortured?"

Marya smiled. "I don't know, Mr. Benya. Having your balls cut off is a very severe punishment. I doubt if you did anything deserving such a harsh act. A hand, maybe?" she said.

Benjamin couldn't contain his laughter.

She squeezed his hand. "Was the dream about your wife or about me, Benya? Have I not castrated you by helping Ilya keep you locked away from your home?"

"I don't understand."

"That's why I left you alone. I thought I was the nightmare, and you didn't want to tell me. That is why I cried."

"Nonsense. My wife chose to leave me. You are here because you have to be."

"But I have choices, Benya. I could help you run away, but I help Ilya. It is not something you can like."

"It is different," Benjamin argued.

"I hope so," she answered. "I don't want to hurt you."

~

"Have you fallen in love with her?" Ilya asked when they were alone in the barn later in the afternoon, Ilya polishing the Toyota, Benjamin watching.

The comment caught Benjamin off guard. It took him a moment to focus. "With Marya?" he asked foolishly.

"I wasn't thinking of Mila. She is a little too young for you."

"Don't you think that's getting a little too personal?"

"Were you playing chess the other night?" Ilya asked as he polished a door handle.

"I had a nightmare and my screaming woke her. She just came in to see if something was wrong?"

Ilya stood up and threw the rag he was using onto the SUV's roof. "So then comes the next question, Benya. Why haven't you fallen in love with her? Would you prefer me?"

Benjamin couldn't control his laughter. Here was his prison guard, the gray eminence who locked him away from his life, playing friend and confident and mentor. It was in Ilya's voice, in his smile, this audacious capacity to charm, to make a resistant stranger comfortable, to make a prisoner feel important and valued. He could be mayor of New York, Benjamin thought, or governor of California.

Ilya picked up the rag and resumed polishing the vehicle.

Benjamin waited a few minutes before speaking. "When am I going to get out of here?" he finally asked.

"A question deserves an answer, Benya, but I don't have one. Before the first snow, I hope. If it is much sooner, you will be sorry you didn't fall in love with Marya."

"Let's leave Marya out of this, Ilya. She might be horrified by any romantic attention. Have you considered that?"

"She is a good person. If I had had half a brain she would have been my daughter, but I was too stupid to value her mother. I was a young fool, although not that young. But Marya is lucky; she certainly wouldn't be as handsome as she is if she had inherited my nose, my forehead, my beard. But I've told you all that before. I am getting old. I hope that excuses my tiresome repetitiousness. Marya is a dear friend." He stopped abruptly and chuckled. "Don't get me wrong, Benya, the women I sleep with are friends too, but they don't live in the same cabin. Marya feels responsible for me and tries to change my bad habits. I love her dearly."

"She would want you to let me go free," Benjamin said softly.

"That too, Benya, that too. I also want you to go free, my American. I get no pleasure holding you against your will. But I want to get a good price. That's the difference between Marya and me. I have become a capitalist, and she has remained a woman."

"Shit," Benya said impatiently. "So tell me what's going on? Have you had any more contact with the American embassy?"

"I get the feeling you are tired of my company. It is a shame. If we had met in a pub in London, we would have liked each other. I am certain of it. But your embassy, they don't seem to like you as much as I do. I told them that if they didn't believe you were living in my cabin, I would send them a finger or an ear. They could do a DNA test. They said that wouldn't be necessary. But they still haven't offered a price. 'We don't negotiate with kidnappers,' they keep telling me. 'So send someone else,' I told him. 'Send a friend of his with a paper bag full of euros.' I'm willing to take dollars, Benya, but I wanted to get to them, to make a dig."

"Why don't you just ask for a quarter of a million dollars and get the process going?"

"Why so cheap? If I start with a quarter, they'll offer a tenth, and where will I be? It would hardly pay for my expenses. No, Benya, I'll start at three million and settle for two. I'm not greedy."

"It would have to be a large paper bag."

Ilya let out a boisterous laugh. "Good," he said, "let's go back to the important question. Why haven't you tried to seduce Marya? She would have you, you know. I can see it in her eyes, in the smile she gives you, in the way she keeps her nails clean and her hair washed."

"She has better taste than that, Ilya. But maybe I don't want to make you jealous?"

"Do you think I'll shoot you with my old rifle?" he said before pointing to the gun that was leaning against the rear bumper.

"I don't want to take the chance."

"For someone like Marya, you should be willing to take the chance. I will be jealous, but only of your youthful capacity to love, not because you have taken someone from me. You will not be here much longer, Benya. Things have dragged out long enough. If you cannot love her, it will be your loss."

~

There was no way to tell how many days had gone by. Eight he thought, estimating the movement of the calendar by the number of times the old woman had brought him black bread and tea, and by the length of the intervals between one visit and the next. All he knew for certain was that he was getting ill. His face felt flushed, his body often wracked with chills. He felt his forehead when his hands were free to see if he was running a fever, but there was simply no way of knowing. He ran his fingers over the base of his penis to see if it was so infected that his entire body was reacting. But he was healing.

He was shivering when they came down with what he assumed was a morning meal. The old woman brought down an ancient, hand knit wool sweater and placed it over his shoulders. She threw a blanket over his legs. He thanked her profusely but received only the small smile. He pleaded with Taras and Boyko, desperate to get them to understand how ill he felt, to declare that he would die if they didn't do something for him. If they understood, they didn't seem to care. Taras pushed him down on the chair; Boyko tied the ropes tighter.

When they left, he drifted in and out of sleep. His head ached. His breath grew short. He imagined his heart was racing wildly. He began to pray for death, but quickly stopped himself, his mind filled with Taras's mocking smile and Boyko's sickly indifference. No, he wanted life; he wanted time for revenge.

It was the light and not the noise that woke him. Two kerosene lamps stood on the table, another was held by the old woman, and a fourth, more lamps than he had ever seen at one time, was being swung in front of his face.

"Benjamin Palmer, Benjamin Palmer," the stranger said.

The light stung Benjamin's eyes. He closed them for a second. When he opened them, the light was closer. He could feel the heat emanating from the lamp. "Yes," he finally said, "Benjamin Palmer."

"Good. It would have left us in a quandary if you were traveling with a stolen passport and someone else's credit card," the stranger said in English.

The captive closed his eyes, thinking for a moment that he was hallucinating. He could feel the lamp being drawn away, and heard the man say something in a Slavic language. Boyko untied his wrists.

"Here," the stranger said. He handed Benjamin a small glass of vodka. "Drink it slowly," he warned.

Some Slavic words were exchanged, and Boyko pulled a chair closer to the table so that the man could sit down.

"They call me Ilya. It's the Russian name for the Old Testament prophet, Elijah. I am a prophet, but I don't communicate with God. You have an Old Testament name too, Benjamin. So we are historical soul mates, you might even say allies."

Benjamin was too disoriented to say anything. Just hearing the English language seemed delusive. The man was older than the other men, in his middle fifties or early sixties, with a full gray beard and piercing gray eyes, his large nose heavily veined, his face broad, his gray hair thick and long. He was wearing a well-tailored blue blazer and gray pants, his blue striped white shirt unbuttoned at the collar. Incongruously, an old rifle hung over a shoulder. The lamp's flame was reflected in the gun's highly polished wooden stock. His English puzzled the prisoner, a mixture, he thought, of a Russian upbringing and a lengthy stay in England. Or had he been trained by the Russian secret police to spy in the west? But what did it matter?

"Drink, Benjamin. I can assure you it is not poisoned. I am drinking some myself." He emptied his glass in one gulp.

Benjamin took a sip. It burnt his mouth and moved harshly down his throat. But it felt good. He paused for a moment and then swallowed the rest.

Ilya let out a boisterous laugh and shouted, "Salute." He slammed his four ounce, thick bottomed glass on the table. "Another," he said over his shoulder. The old woman refilled his glass a third of the way up, but not Benjamin's.

"Your friends want to sell you to me, but they are asking a very high price. Are you worth my investment, Benjamin Palmer?" When Benjamin didn't immediately answer, he continued. "Have they so mistreated you that you have lost your voice?"

"Who are you?" Benjamin blurted out.

"I am the man who will rescue you, if you are worth my while. Do you have enough money to make it worthwhile?"

"I'm worth enough," Benjamin insisted.

Ilya's laughter seemed uncontrollable.

So my savior is to be a drunken Russian, Benjamin thought. What would Abramowitz think of that? "Fortune and caprice," he would say, "they dominate life."

# Chapter 8

Peter was struggling with a large black umbrella when Caitlin found him at the entrance to the Victoria and Albert Museum. The thick morning fog had been replaced by a relentless rain that bounced off the sidewalk and ran down Cromwell Road. It promised to last until winter. After a brief glance out her window, Selby had insisted that Caitlin borrow a moderate sized red umbrella and a wide-brimmed explorer's rain hat. They failed to fully protect her. The bottoms of her brown slacks were soaked, and her low heeled shoes had become waterlogged by the time she had made it from the South Kensington underground station to the museum, but in her eagerness, she barely noticed how wet she was.

The travel companions nodded to each other and entered the building. "Is she here," Caitlin asked.

"She's wandering on the second floor, trying to figure out how best to cover the cafeteria. She'll set herself up once she knows where we will be sitting."

"Do you think she'll pull it off?" Caitlin asked nervously.

"Selby says she comes with terrific references. We have no choice. If you want to photograph our meeting, we have to rely on someone. I can't do it. Koslov told you he was not yet ready to consent to being filmed."

Caitlin shrugged her shoulders, took off the canvas hat, and slapped it against her thigh. Water spattered on the stone floor. They quickly made their way to the small cafeteria on the second floor. A handsome woman in an old-fashioned pillbox hat, a camera swinging from her neck, caught Caitlin's attention.

Peter took his companion's arm and turned her toward him. "Let's not look too interested in camera carrying tourists," he said sharply. "The man who followed me the other night is watching us."

He was leaning against a column in the open area outside the cafeteria, his black leather jacket unbuttoned, his black shirt and pants looking unchanged from the night he followed Peter. He bowed his head slightly and grinned.

"Please," he said as the couple approached him. "Take a big table. Koslov will join us."

He weaved around the glass-topped tables, most of them occupied, and settled on one in the far corner of the room. He touched the two chairs that faced the museum's interior and motioned to the Americans to take them. Caitlin resisted and moved toward one of the chairs that faced the wall, expecting that Peter would take the other and force the Russians to face the photographer.

"No joke, Mrs. McCoy," the stranger said insistently, and pointed to the chairs he had selected.

"Slava is the name," he said after they sat where they were told. "Mr. Johnson already knows me."

"But not by name."

"And you must be Mrs. McCoy."

Caitlin didn't correct him. "Is Mr. Koslov going to join us?"

Slava focused on her face for a long moment, his expression blank, and then ran his eyes down her body. Caitlin thought he looked disappointed, as if he had expected larger breasts, a low cut blouse, and a tighter fitting jacket. "Your camera," he insisted.

"We followed instructions and didn't bring one," Peter answered.

Slava turned to him. "Right," he said in a thick Slavic accent. "Right," he repeated, looking remarkably indifferent. "The coffee is good. They give you a pot and a cup. Why don't you get four?"

They left their raingear at the table and made their way to the small kitchen area. There were two people in line in front of them, but no staff seemed in a rush to serve.

"He looks like an extra in a James Bond movie, Peter," she said while they waited. "Grease pours out of him."

Peter gave her a quick smile and whispered, "He looks much more demonic at night when he's following you."

"I imagine. Do you think Koslov will show?"

"For all we know he is Koslov. Slava Koslov. I wouldn't be at all surprised," Peter murmured.

"God, I would be. And disappointed. Can you imagine him in a starring role? We'd be laughed out of the studio. The woman in the black coat and pillbox hat, do you think she is our photographer?"

Peter shrugged. "It doesn't much matter. With our Russians facing the wall, she won't get many useable shots," he said. Then he turned to the woman behind the counter.

They were served four small French presses, the freshly ground coffee beans already submerged under boiled water, and four ceramic cups.

Koslov was at the table when they returned, a diamond stud fixed in the center of his dark-blue tie, and a diamond pinky ring on his right hand. He was better dressed than Caitlin had anticipated. His checkered overcoat was made of fine gray worsted, his dark pinstripe suit sharply tailored. But no Bond Street haberdasher could conceal his thick neck, his black dyed hair, his sagging jowls, and small dark eyes.

"What exactly do you think I can do?" Koslov asked in a thickly accented and raspy voice.

"My friends tell me you're very well connected," Caitlin said. "If anyone can help, they said, it would be you."

"They exaggerate. I have connections, but I am not a magician."

"You know my dilemma. If you can't find out who is holding my husband, perhaps you know someone who can. I know information is not cheap."

Koslov's thumb played with his pinky ring. "What do you think?" he asked Peter.

"My friends think you know a great deal about what is going on, and what you don't know you know how to find out. But if you can't help us, we will just have to try our luck with someone else, or go home."

"Going home might be wise," Koslov said.

A chess player, Caitlin thought. She suspected that every gambit would raise his price. "I'm disappointed," she said, "but before we go home there are a few other people we can contact, in Paris as well as here."

Koslov smiled at Slava. "That might be wise. And why not Rome and Berlin? There are a lot of Russians there. I could give you some names, pro bono as you would say."

Caitlin looked down at her napkin and offered a small smile. She found the scene theatrical and thrilling, the black leather jacket, the diamond stud, the cat and mouse conversation, at once threatening and laughable. If only she could get it on film. But she would have to do with whatever photographs their hired help produced. The handsome woman in the pillbox hat was gone, but a teenage-looking girl, in dungarees and a gray sweatshirt, was taking shots of the two people working behind the cafeteria's serving counter. Caitlin was waiting to see her turn in their direction, but she caught Slava watching her eyes and decided to gaze at Koslov. It was too late. Slava turned around to see what Caitlin had been looking at. He said something in Russian to Koslov that did not sound pleasant.

"I do not have photographic features," Koslov said to Caitlin. "You will be very disappointed. Since you have done mischief, the next conversation will cost you two thousand British pounds."

~

Selby hadn't changed. Her auburn hair cut short, her wool and silk jacket conservatively cut, the gold eyeglass frames, the porcelain skin, the pale lipstick, all exactly as he remembered, as he would picture in the middle of the day when his mind needed to be rescued from boredom, as he would imagine in the middle of the night when he needed someone to love. He watched carefully as she lifted the teacup, as she spread clotted cream over a small scone and topped it with strawberry jam. She was forty-five, but time was a friend. It had not touched her since they had last met. There were no new lines on her face, no additional shadows under her eyes, no extra pounds. If anything, she had grown more handsome, her oval face, her large brown eyes, the slight break in her nose, the strong chin, the succulent lips. He felt his face light up when she entered the room. "You're as beautiful as ever," he heard himself say before he knew he was talking.

Peter pulled out a chair and held it until she was seated. Selby looked out of the window of The Duke's Drawing Room where they were taking an afternoon tea. "The garden is beautiful, isn't it?" she asked rhetorically.

He sat to her side as he always had, close enough to smell her delicate perfume, to put his hand on her lap if the occasion allowed.

"Thank you for not staying over," Selby said. "It would have been awkward to have you in the house. And with Caitlin there ... ." The sentence faded as she raised her eyes to look at him.

"I like staying at The Duke. You know that."

"I remember. I always wondered if you had a girlfriend on the side who visited you here." She did not smile. She allowed the lilt in her voice to underscore her teasing. "I reviewed this tea room a few months ago. I came with a friend and an armful of boxes from the stores on Jermyn Street so I wouldn't be recognized. Given that no one seems to notice me today, the disguise may have been overkill."

"The service is never rushed. It's English civilization at its best."

She smiled as a waiter appeared.

"How is the writing going?" he asked. It was not among the questions he really wanted answered, Are you seeing someone? Do you miss me? Is there any hope for us?

"I fear the string is running out, Peter. I've gotten too well known, if not here, at most places. The chefs come out of the kitchen to say hello; the staffs seem to know what I want to order before I know myself. My readers are beginning to predict my comments. Even my humor has gotten stale."

"I doubt it's that bad."

"It's worse. I've reviewed a couple of plays and have had some book reviews published just to test the water. The cookbooks are doing well, but I'm looking for a change. And you? Why are you here, Peter?"

The reappearance of their waiter caused a break in their conversation. "Could I prepare this one for you?" Selby asked as she pointed to one of the scones that had just arrived. She broke it in two and dressed each piece with clotted cream and strawberry jam. "So, Peter, why have you joined the hunt for Caitlin's husband?" Her smile disappeared. She picked up another scone and prepared it for herself.

"A hallway conversation, Selby, believe it or not. A couple of my studio course students were talking before class. 'What has he done recently?' a young man asked. The young woman he was talking to just shrugged her shoulders. I was glad he hadn't asked me the question. I would have had no answer. What I did have was a coming sabbatical. Caitlin caught me at a weak moment. But I'm glad I joined her, if just to have a proper tea with you."

His flattery didn't cause her expression to change. Her lips didn't automatically turn upwards, her teeth didn't immediately flash. There was nothing automatic in her smiles, in her laughter, nothing false and artificial. That's where they differed, the grin was his mask, laughter his shield. She chose the opposite expression, stoic and unyielding, but the purpose was the same. No one could read her thoughts on her face—except, he thought a second later, except when she laughed.

"Even after you were followed and mugged?'

"It has caused me to second guess. I thought there might be some danger, but not in London, in the Ukraine or Poland or wherever he is being held—but not here. It was done with such stealth; I have difficulty calling it a mugging. As I told Caitlin, I suspect they wanted to make sure I wasn't working with the CIA, or some other police organization. So they lifted my wallet to check my identification, as if I'd be carrying a badge with me. It must have been the couple in the bookstore. I didn't feel a thing. Still, if I'd been carrying a gun, they would have noticed, unless I had it around my ankle."

"Are you certain you didn't drop the wallet in the bar?"

"That's the one thing I am certain of."

"It makes me nervous. Do you think you might be endangering Benjamin?" she quietly asked.

"The thought wakes me up at night, Selby. It would be awful if we brought him harm. But from what I've been able to gather, kidnappers usually know what they're doing. If they kill someone when it is clear people are willing to pay, they'll have more difficulty extorting money the next time."

"What if you're dealing with amateurs, Peter? They might not take the long view."

She poured some tea into his cup and then filled her own. "I've hunted the Internet for a newspaper comment about Benjamin being missing. Given his past encounter with a financial scam, I thought he would be newsworthy. But not a line; not even any gossip in the newsroom."

"The longer it's hush-hush the better. If it went public—or so the State Department thinks—a dozen and a half Russians from Brighton Beach alone would show up at Cat's door asking for cash."

Selby gave a quick laugh, reached for another scone but then changed her mind. "Do you think they're watching my house Peter, and that they might try to break in?"

"It crossed my mind. But what good would it do them? If they're professional, you have nothing to worry about; if they're amateurs, they don't know that we're in London. Caitlin could move into a hotel, but I don't think that would stop them from being a little suspicious of you."

"I like a good mystery, Peter, but I never wanted to be part of one," Selby said. Then she finished her tea. "The garden is beautiful," she observed.

~

Koslov made certain there would be no third party taking pictures at their second rendezvous. Slava was to pick them up a few blocks from The Duke, on the northwest corner of Piccadilly and Half Moon Street. Caitlin joined Peter at the hotel and, after a fortifying martini, walked with him to the designated spot. There they waited for forty-five minutes, feeling ridiculous and exposed, wondering if they were being watched, and nervously dismissing random thoughts of being targeted. A cold drizzle forced their decision, and they began to walk slowly back to the hotel, irritated and confused and deeply frustrated.

A small Nissan 4X4 pulled alongside the curb. "Get in," Slava yelled out the driver's window.

Peter held the rear door open for his partner and slid in next to her. "You're late, Slava. Is this how you do business, by treating people like shit," he said intemperately.

"A precaution, Mr. Johnson. I was around," Slava answered as he started to move the car.

Caitlin put her hand on Peter's and cut in, "And where are we going?" she asked without rancor.

"You will see. Do you have the money?"

"I do," she answered.

"And no cameras or listening devices?"

"Just the money," she answered.

"Good," he said with finality.

Koslov was sitting on a bench in the park at Russell Square. To a passerby he would have looked as if he were hugging an old friend when he ran his hands slowly over Caitlin's body, concentrating on her breasts, her waist, and rubbing her ass. Slava put his hand under Peter's jacket, took out the envelope, and stuffed it into his own pocket without counting the money.

"A million, in dollars," Koslov said, "and I will have him delivered to Heathrow in two days. How is that for service?" He gave her a ludicrous smile. Then he chuckled. "We are more efficient than you give us credit for being," he said in his thick accent and took her hand in his.

Caitlin pulled away. She had to work to conceal her surprise. They had predicted a tortured set of meetings, each one bought at an escalated price, and had tried to think through when to put their backs up and refuse to pay more. After a third meeting, she had suggested, but Peter thought the string had to be played out for a longer time. "They are holding all the cards," he had said. "But we have the money," she had argued.

"And how do we know you'll deliver?" she finally asked.

Koslov said something in Russian to Slava that elicited a laugh. "Capitalism is based on trust, is it not?"

"This isn't capitalism. This is extortion," Peter said sharply.

Koslov gave him a knowing sound. Then he repeated the offer.

A manipulative bastard, she thought, and a dead-end. She felt her heart drop. Did he really think that she was that much of a fool? Did he really think she was a grieving spouse who would pay anything to get her husband back? She sat down on the bench and looked to Peter for help.

"Is he in good shape?" Peter asked in an innocent voice.

"I hear he is fine, but who knows for how long. His hosts don't have infinite patience, and your State Department is difficult to deal with. A million is a bargain."

"And where is he?" Caitlin asked.

"Don't be silly," Koslov answered.

He took a cigar from his pocket, walked over to Slava for a light, and then he sat down next to Caitlin. "I don't want to worry you, but he is not in the hands of English gentlemen. His life is worth only what he can be sold for … and quickly."

Slava walked behind the bench and lit a cigarette. "The rain will begin again soon."

"I can come up with the money, Mr. Koslov, although it won't be easy. But you can't expect me to hand it over to you on just your word."

Koslov gave her a fatherly smile. "What else can I do? He is somewhere in the Ukraine. I have to get the money to them before anything will happen. Only then will they take him to Kyiv or L'viv for transport. Do you want me to get a picture or have them cut off a finger so you can run some tests? Time is not a friend."

So now we bargain, she thought. "I won't pay any money until I see him. I want you to get me to the people who are holding him."

"So you can write a story about them?" Koslov snorted. "Don't look that surprised. Google runs on English computers. I know you and Mr. Johnson. He would not be here if you weren't planning on reporting. I am not the criminal. I am a friend trying to help you out. I don't want a story saying I took money from you and didn't deliver. I want to be a hero."

"For a million dollars, you'd be prepared to be called a great many fucking names, and hero isn't one of them," Peter shot back.

"Quiet," Slava shouted in a voice loud enough to carry through the park.

"Will you drive us back, or should we hail a cab?" Caitlin asked quietly, hoping to push the bargaining, but worried that she may have moved too rapidly.

She hadn't.

"What is it that you'd like me to do?" Koslov asked, injecting a bit of charm in his voice.

"I'd like you to get me to the Ukraine and to the people who can get me to my husband. If you can deliver him to Heathrow, you can get me east."

"So I am right. You are after a story and not your husband. We are not so very different, are we?" He reached out and took her hand again. "Let me think. We will meet again. It will cost five thousand British pounds for the next conversation." Then he angled his head and gave her a broad smile. "For a beautiful woman like you, there are ways of lowering the price."

# Chapter 9

Taras stumbled into the path of the old woman, causing her to drop her lantern and its flame to extinguish. He walked away without the slightest hint of an apology. Cursing under her breath, she bent over stiffly, took its handle in her arthritic hand, and held it out to Boyko to be reignited. Silently, but with no obvious sign of annoyance, he struggled with its hot glass, took a long wooden match from his pocket, and relit the wick. The light projected his shadow on the earthen wall.

Ilya looked oblivious to what was going on behind him. He continued to count out American dollars and arrange them in piles on the table. Taras seemed happy with whatever amount was being paid, but Boyko barked something uncomplimentary at the older man. Ilya swung the gun so that its barrel was pointed toward the earthen floor, and, in a low and controlled voice, said something back. Whatever was said caused Boyko's face to redden, and Taras's to turn stern. Ilya reached over and began to pick the money up from the table. Benjamin's heart sank. Anything, he thought, would be better than continuing to be tied to a chair in the damp basement, his body wracked with chills, his sweat-soaked clothes eating into his skin. Taras laid his hand on top of Ilya's and made some crack that caused the older man to laugh. Ilya placed the money back on the table, turned sideways, and said something to Boyko.

"What's happening?" Benjamin asked Ilya as the old lady cut the cord that bound him to the chair. She sliced the line that tied his ankles and helped him stand up.

"What's going on?" Benjamin repeated, his head spinning, his legs unstable.

"I've overpaid for you, that's what is going on," the Russian said, his voice clipped and harsh. "We are going for a little ride. So behave yourself. That's the least you can do."

"To where?" Benjamin asked.

"Behaving is not asking questions, Benjamin Palmer. I'm taking you to a nicer place, better food, and a younger woman. If you don't like the idea, I'll take my money back and they can keep you. It would make them very unhappy, though."

Benjamin gave a tight-lipped nod to acknowledge his subjugation.

Ilya forced his prisoner to lead the way up the stone stairs, through the kitchen, and into the day. The brilliant sunshine stung Benjamin's eyes and caused them to tear. If his hands had been free, he would have shaded his face. Instead, he squinted as Ilya pushed him along the path, and focused his limited sight on the uneven ground to maintain his balance. A couple of times, he gathered enough strength to lift his head and record the place of his imprisonment and its countryside. Images to be remembered, he told himself, if ever there was a chance for retribution.

About a hundred feet from the farmhouse, a tall, thin young man, his long, reddish hair in a pigtail, was leaning against the front fender of a large Toyota Land Cruiser. He answered Ilya's call by stamping out a cigarette and taking Benjamin by the arm. He helped the prisoner into the backseat and got in next to him. Ilya threw his rifle on the left seat and sat behind the wheel on the right, the position you would expect in England or Japan, but not in the Ukraine or Russia.

"Okay," the redhead asked once the car got on its way.

"Okay," Benjamin answered, thankful that this man also spoke English. It was a premature conclusion. The young man came out with a long sentence. When it became evident that Benjamin didn't understand, he repeated it. The second rendering was no more decipherable than the first, so the young man used Ilya as translator.

"He wants to know if they treated you well."

Benjamin was too suspicious to say much. "It was unpleasant," he said quietly.

"His name is Fedya. He's a student in computer science at the Far Eastern University in Vladivostok, and has spent the spring driving this car to the Ukraine for me. He is a good man."

Fedya nodded his head and smiled, but there was no real evidence that he understood what Ilya had said.

The four-wheel drive vehicle, a model Benjamin had never seen in the United States, bounced uncomfortably, heaving now and then as it moved through stagnant pools of muddy water, when its springs fought against the deeply rutted dirt road. Benjamin sat silently, reveling in his liberation but unsettled by new thoughts and fears, hoping against all odds that his two companions were somehow tied to the American embassy or worked for the CIA, that the money they used was given to them by the United States to buy his freedom. If that were so, why were his hands still bound? Why was Fedya sitting next to him in the rear seat if not to guard him? No, he decided, they were probably just another two bandits, the next link in a conspiratorial chain that would lead to years of imprisonment, to torture, to death. And to whom would they hand him off, hooded men with beards who would drag him to yet another Godforsaken spot, a place where there wouldn't even be a haggard old woman to protect him?

He tried to calm his fantasies by turning his attention to the unexpectedly lush countryside, intently examining the rolling fields of tall grass, the shimmer of maturing grains. Now and then, the car would stop to allow a peasant to herd a few cows across the road, or slow down to avoid hitting some strolling farmhands, medieval scythes and rakes resting on their shoulders. It was all new to Benjamin, the landscape, the sunlight, the expressions of the few people they passed on the road. He found it both fascinating and fearful. But he couldn't forget he was a hostage. As they drove through a densely forested area, Benjamin thought of escape, of leaping from the car and racing into the woods. Of hiding in the underbrush until his frustrated captors gave up the hunt. It was a transitory fantasy. How could he manage it with his hands bound? In what language would he appeal for help? All he would accomplish, he reluctantly decided, would be to endanger anyone who tried to help him.

Ilya turned the car onto what looked like a tractor turnoff and parked near the edge of a small brook. The milk-laden cow that was standing in the shallow water lifted its head momentarily and then returned to drinking. Fedya jumped out of the car, unzipping his pants as he strode toward a patch of evergreen trees. Ilya helped Benjamin out of the rear seat, took out a large pocketknife, and cut his prisoner's hands loose. "I shoot straight and run fast," he said with a broad smile. "If you have to take a piss, follow Fedya. Just don't get him wet."

Fedya waited for his prisoner to finish and then escorted him back to the Land Cruiser.

"Feeling good?" the young Russian asked.

"Feeling better," the American answered while rubbing his wrists.

They found Ilya opening a bottle of vodka. "An old Russian custom, Benya, to have a drink and a piece of bread when you pick up a guest at an airport or train station and begin the ride home. It's good for the soul and the spirit, and it keeps the devil at bay." He pulled out three small water glasses from a heavily stained wicker basket and covered the bottom of each with an inch of vodka. He handed the first to Benjamin, the second to Fedya. With his glass held high, Ilya gave a boisterous toast in Russian and emptied his glass in one swallow. An infectious laugh followed. The startled cow moved further up the stream.

Ilya cut a small black bread into three hunks with his pocket knife, and similarly divided a large piece of yellow cheese. He threw a hard-boiled egg to Benjamin and a couple to Fedya. A small saltshaker was passed around.

They sat near a stream, surrounded by growing weeds and drying cow dung, and washed down their meals with rounds of vodka. "Should we milk the cow?" Ilya asked Fedya who answered with a blank look. Ilya seemed to repeat himself in Russian. Fedya laughed and answered by pointing to the bottle of vodka. It was already half empty.

"Beautiful country, isn't it, Mr. Palmer? Dig your hand into the soil, rich and black, full of every farmer's wish. Everything grows here, even beautiful women. Right, Fedya? Barley and wheat, buckwheat, tomatoes, carrots, potatoes, pour effortlessly out of the earth. Further north, near the Carpathians, people produce apples and plums, cherries and berries. No pineapples or coffee or oranges, but we are poor people and hardly miss them."

Ilya stood up and waved to his prisoner to do the same. The vodka had gotten to Benjamin, and he felt a little woozy when he got to his feet.

"See," Ilya began, "all the uses of this land. This part saved for the cow, off in the distance winter wheat, and over there," he pointed to fields brimming with color, "sunflowers and corn."

"It is lush," Benjamin said in an uncomfortably loud voice.

"But dig down a little, my American, just below the surface, and what will you find? Don't answer. You do not know. No one knows. Everyone has forgotten. You will find skulls and thighbones, ribs and ankles, children and old men, grandmothers and virgins. The land is composed of Scythians and Goths, Huns and Bulgars, Khazars and Cossacks. But they are far down." He chuckled for a second, and then turned deeply serious. "The top soil is made of Ukrainians and Jews, Germans and Russians, the killers and the killed intermixed for eternity. A nasty place my American, like Gettysburg and Shiloh."

The mention of two American Civil War battles caught Benjamin by surprise. There was more to this bearded Russian than he had imagined, this energetic man of sixty, his BBC English lurking under a thick layer of Russian vowels and consonants, his clothing an odd mixture of Western panache and Eastern carelessness.

"But Gettysburg and Shiloh were contained battles; they didn't cover as much acreage as our killings, and they lasted days. Our murdering went on for centuries.

The worst was when we invaded ourselves, Benya. The "Great Famine," people call it, as if the rain didn't come, and the sun didn't shine. But it was Stalin who kept the grain away from the people, who drove the peasants from the land and into graves. "To establish a perfect world," his minions said. Millions starved to death and dragged away in search of utopia. The history of man, hunting for the right thing with the wrong weapon. Did you know that, Benya?"

"Only from what I read before I flew to Kyiv," Benjamin answered hesitantly, transfixed by the Russian's emotional tone, his vibrating voice, his gestures, and his facial expressions. He was acting out history as if he were a survivor, or a witness, or a remorseful perpetrator, and not like the person he was, someone born long after the events or shortly before them.

Ilya stood in silent attention for a respectful time. Then, surprisingly, he laughed. "Listen to me, and I'm Russian not Ukrainian. I can only imagine how they feel about the Kremlin's crimes against them. People blame Marx for it. They think it a communist crime when it was truly the offense of little men with corrupt minds. Karl Marx would have been smarter than to starve people into submission. The land disguises the horror well, doesn't it? It is beautiful. I'm told it looks like Kansas."

"I wouldn't know. I've never been to Kansas."

"A pity, Benya, a pity. When you get home, maybe you will go to Kansas to see. You can e-mail me about your discovery."

"So you have come to rescue me?" Benjamin asked quickly.

Ilya shrugged his shoulders and tilted his head as if he had not understood the question.

Benjamin continued. "Are you working for the State Department, or the CIA? Did they hire you to rescue me?"

"In due time, Benjamin Palmer, in due time they will be paying for my services to you," he said softly, and then shouted something in Russian to Fedya who had already stored the basket and its remaining contents in the Land Cruiser.

"We trust your intelligence," Ilya said as Fedya walked around the car and got into the passenger seat. "Don't become theatrical on us and make a scene. I don't want to gag you and keep you covered up on the floor."

Benjamin kept silent. Disruptiveness required more energy than he could muster, and far more nerve. Whatever illness had attacked him in the basement seemed to have been miraculously cured, but he felt weary and exhausted.

The hum of the vehicle lulled him into a restless sleep. He only woke when the car came to a complete halt. Gasoline was purchased in the center of a small village that straddled both sides of a minor river. On the eastern bank stood what Benjamin thought was a small whitewashed school building and a tall, weathered Orthodox church, its rough-sawed timbers placed vertically, its roof terraced in pagoda style; its green colored cupolas anchored iron crosses. On both banks of the river, the unevenly sized blocks were sparsely covered with randomly distributed single story houses, each set on an extensive lot. Cows and chickens roamed within the fenced plots, competing for space with vegetable gardens and patches of corn and sunflowers. An old woman, her head covered with a red and black scarf, looked at the Land Cruiser suspiciously; three young boys, who seemed to be arguing over a tricycle, ran up to the vehicle when Ilya pulled up to the nondescript store. Four modest-sized gasoline storage tanks stood along its eastern wall. Fedya kept his eyes on Benjamin while Ilya negotiated for a few pails of gas. After filling his tank with what looked like an oversized watering can, the Russian purchased a few pieces of candy inside the two-story building and distributed them among the curious and happy children.

They drove for a few more hours before settling down for the night in a small, whitewashed farmhouse, with a dramatically sloped thatched roof. Ilya got a long and tight hug from Galina, a middle-aged woman whose dyed hair looked more orange than red. She kissed Fedya on both cheeks, and nodded to Benjamin, before setting the table with a beet soup and boiled potatoes, and a plate of boiled pork sausages. Fedya and Benjamin shared a double bed in a mosquito-ridden back room, the prisoner's hands and feet once again bound. "Do you have to?" Benjamin asked. Fedya didn't answer. Ilya carried a half-filled bottle of vodka into

Galina's bedroom. His eyes were swollen and his facial skin sagged when they breakfasted in the morning.

The sun was beginning to kiss the horizon when they arrived at the tiny hamlet where Ilya planned to hide his prisoner. A young woman was walking out of the woods, wild flowers in her hand.

~

Peter opened his eyes when he heard Selby step out of the bathroom, her hair wrapped in a blue towel, her body hidden by the white, sexless bathrobe that The Duke offered its patrons. They had met three times since they had taken tea at the Duke—breakfast at Sotheby's cafe on New Bond Street, lunch at Ball Brothers St James's to share a luscious chocolate sponge pudding topped with vanilla ice cream, and one brilliant French dinner that Selby prepared for him and Caitlin. Selby had successfully kept their conversations to the impersonal, no matter how he hinted at other topics, her growing interest in Greek cuisines and theater criticism, Peter's teaching, the protracted maneuvering of Koslov, and Slava's shiftiness. By the time he invited her to once again lunch with him at his hotel, Peter had given up any hope of rekindling their romance. She had given no sign of wanting to restore the past, no hint that she still found him attractive, no intimation that they could ever be more than holiday friends.

When he opened the door of his suite, Peter fought his instincts, and instead of wrapping her in his arms, he kissed her on the cheek. He looked over her shoulder as she studied the room service menu. After they placed their order, he sat on the small upholstered chair in the sitting area and allowed her the comfort of the couch. But the moment after Peter tipped the waiter for delivering the food, they made love, and they made love again before they touched their desserts and drank the lukewarm tea. Peter told himself that the past had asserted its power, and they were the lovers they had been, the same people who existed before their retreat from each other. Her skin was as warm, her muscles as tight, her motions arousing in their predictability. And yet, he could not recall ever feeling so much comfort in her arms, so much joy in her physical responsiveness, in her sighs and laughter, in her outbursts. He felt foolishly romantic and outrageously besotted. When Selby rolled out of bed to shower, he dressed slowly and lay down on the bed, his mind full of plans for their next meetings, a trip to Prague, a week in Northern Italy, a winter vacation in San Francisco.

"So you've dressed," Selby said, feigning disappointment.

"I'm not growing younger."

"You'd fool me."

Peter smiled. "If you insist," he said. He began to unbutton his shirt.

She broke out in laughter. "I'm exhausted, and you know it. I'm out of practice."

"I hadn't noticed," he quibbled, but avoided exploring the subject. He wanted to believe she had no lover during the interregnum, certainly no one serious. He wanted them to have been barren years, time filled with only thoughts of him. He knew enough not to ask her, not to invite reality and disappointment. He had known a number of women during the intervening years, old lovers who looked forward to sharing a nostalgic ski trip or a weekend in Manhattan, and new acquaintances, women who he expected would be more than momentary distractions. Mostly they were black women, lawyers who worked in large firms, college professors he had met at conferences, attractive and smart, assured of their sexuality, happy in their independence. They turned out to be too much like he had once been, ambitious, striving, unsure of their successes, always having to prove their worth. Selby was different. She was comfortable with herself, her social status guaranteed by her ancestors, her success procured by an Oxford first, and her physical appeal secured by an excellent figure and a charming, expressive face. She had one failure, she didn't know she was loveable.

He watched as she took the towel off her head and used it vigorously to dry her hair. Now and then, he caught her looking at his reflection in the bureau's mirror. What did she see? Was she living a transitory moment with a past lover, a trip into what was and what might have been? Was she trying to show him what he had given up? Or was she attempting to push aside his stupidity by acting as if he had never wounded her?

"A penny for your thoughts," she said.

"Shouldn't you be saying 'a pence for your thoughts'?"

"You Americanized me."

"I hope not."

She hung the towel around her neck and sat on the bed next to him. He lifted her hand and kissed it.

"Why did you abandon me?" she asked in a soft voice, her tone without malice or accusation. She could have been asking a chef why he hadn't put more pepper in the stew.

"Abandon is a strong word."

"It's an honest word."

Peter chuckled in defense. The question had too many answers.

She didn't wait for him to reply. "Did we just run out the string, the magic gone, the sex ordinary, expected?"

He walked over to the window and looked across the narrow street. An elderly gentleman was glancing at an historical plaque that he and Selby used to joke about. It announced that Chopin had visited the modest brick townhouse shortly before he played his last concert in London. Selby jokingly assumed that it was to use the loo. It didn't matter. The owners of the house wanted it to be exceptional. Vanity, all is vanity, he thought.

"Nothing was ever ordinary between us, not the sex, not the friendship. I was falling deeper and deeper in love with you, and I couldn't bring myself to admit it," Peter said while still looking out the window.

"A likely story," she shot back.

Her glibness irritated him. "If you don't want to listen to the answer, you shouldn't have asked the question."

"It was a mean question, Peter. I apologize. This has been a wonderful afternoon. I shouldn't have risked spoiling it."

She picked up her clothes and pocketbook and went into the bathroom. When she reappeared, she was back in a conservative dress that cut below her knees and her makeup was restored.

"How about a drink?" she suggested.

They took a table that looked out on the Zen garden. The late afternoon sun cast shadows behind the large rocks that anchored the desert landscape, darkening sections of the otherwise shimmering waves of sand. Peter ordered a glass of Chablis for her and a nonalcoholic beer for himself.

"Beautiful," Selby said looking out the window and holding the glass in her hand.

"I felt we were at a juncture, Selby. I had to go back, and you had your work here. We tried the long distance calls, a weekend here, a weekend in New York. But it wasn't working. Not for me. I wanted you all the time or not at all. I couldn't stand being alone, not when I knew you wanted me."

"Ha!" she exclaimed after turning her face toward him, her cheeks tight, her mouth in a scowl. "And when were you going to tell me? Did I say I wouldn't move to America? Did you ever give me a chance to think about it? You can make up a better story than that."

"I'm being honest."

"*Merde.*"

His hand quivered as he raised the glass to his mouth. Some of the non-alcoholic beer spilled on his fingers. He had to concentrate to take a drink.

"I'm sorry, Peter. I promised myself not to go there, that I'd behave as if nothing sour had happened between us. I'd act as if this was an afternoon assignation that held no meaning beyond itself."

"But it does, Selby, it is full of meaning."

"Then tell me the truth. Did you think I'd say no? Did you think I'd shudder at the thought of moving halfway across the world to marry a black man? I tried to convince myself that it was something outside of both of us that drove you away, some fear of prejudice, or commitment, some racial thing that I didn't understand, that you didn't explain to me. I didn't want to believe that you had tired of me after only a year." She reached over and took his hand. Then, acting as if she wanted to lighten the moment, she smiled. "If we had known each other for three years it would have been more reasonable. But one year! I thought I had more staying power than that."

"We knew each other for five years and had been involved for 18 months."

"So you had enough."

"I didn't want to be a black man with a white wife, Selby. I didn't want to reject my people, to look as if black women weren't good enough for me. I didn't want to be the black man exhibiting his manliness by squiring a white trophy wife."

Selby looked as if someone had knocked her back into the chair. She gasped for breath and began to tear. He picked up his glass with two hands and took a long sip.

"Wow," she exclaimed, "that is right from the shoulder. You couldn't see yourself with a white woman ... at least not in America. Over here it was all right, but not there, is that what you're telling me?"

"It's not that simple."

"So explain. Don't you respect me enough to think I can understand?"

"I don't understand it fully myself."

"Is it prejudice or politics, Peter? I'm not white people. I'm a woman who loved you."

"It's psychological, not political."

"Maybe it's about time you grew up."

He didn't answer.

"Twenty years ago, you might have been right. The world has gotten wiser, Peter. We are permitted to love each other."

He looked pathetic, his head hanging over his glass, desperate that she not hold on to her anger, not after the brilliance of the afternoon, not after he had again found her.

She backed off. "There I go again, trying to make a case for myself. I must sound like a desperate aging woman who thinks you are her final chance." She had a chuckle in her voice. She could always read his mood, he thought.

"You sound like a woman I could love, Selby. I wouldn't want you to be any other way."

"Except maybe black."

The thought tickled him. "But with a serious English accent," he said. He reached for her hand, but she pulled back. "Please," he said, but she did not relent.

"It's late Peter. You might want to wave for the check," she suggested, and began to get out of her chair.

"Please," he appealed. "Don't rush off. Not yet."

She stopped herself and sat back down. "Why Peter, to hear another sociological reason for your dumping me? I deserve better than that. It was something between us, not the history of the world that drove you away."

Her face was flushed when she slid off her chair, grabbed her umbrella and pocketbook, and fled the restaurant.

She had crossed Piccadilly and reached the corner of Old Bond Street when he caught up to her. "Let's not end it this way," he pleaded. "Please, Selby, this is too important to walk away from."

He expected her to be crying when she turned around, but her expression was stoic and distant. "I don't want it to end this way either, but do we have a choice?"

Peter hailed a taxi. She gave the cabby her address. He threw down the meter. Then they sat silently, looking out their respective windows. Now and then, he squeezed her hand; she tapped her fingers against his palm. "Come in for a minute," she said when the taxi pulled up to her door. "Caitlin is away for the evening."

But Selby was wrong. Caitlin was coming down the stairs when the front door opened. She looked surprised when she saw them together, but something else was on her mind. "Koslov is ready to meet us," she shouted to Peter.

~

To Caitlin, it was all bewildering, the clandestine meetings, the clothed language, the unrelenting mistrust, the long periods of time between meetings with Koslov. Peter seemed more comfortable with it all, she jealously thought. He was more at ease with people she found intolerable, people who lived in the shadows of society, people whose facial expressions and vocabularies were designed to mislead, whose assurances were intended to swindle. Peter had tried to convince her that it was all a carefully orchestrated game. At each step, there would be another person inserted into the process and another palm to grease, with the cost of progress escalating as they inched closer to their quarry. He warned her that their resolve to bargain would be weakened by each little success, that their own obsession with triumphing would blind them to the bloodsucking of their enablers. She didn't buy all his arguments. She didn't believe that Koslov was omniscient; she didn't believe that Benjamin's kidnappers were free of folly and confusion. There were limits to her tolerance, she told herself, limits to how much money she would shell out, to how many sexual overtures she would stomach. And yet, Peter was right in at least one way, her boundaries kept shifting. Each forward movement increased her enthusiasm. Each intrigue deepened her resolve to complete the venture. It was an irresistible story, an estranged wife risking her life to rescue her husband, a woman faithful to her vows however difficult the marriage. She imagined the networks and cable producers competing for the documentary. She daydreamed about publishers chasing after her for a book. She delighted in the thought of being Benjamin's liberator.

Georgi Koslov pushed his flabby face in her direction. "Beautiful, isn't it. I wanted a Rolls Royce, but Slava's heart was for a big Mercedes. What could I do? He does the driving."

"Germans are better engineers," Slava said over his shoulder. He was sitting on the right, one gloved hand on the wooden steering wheel, his dirty-blond hair slicked back, the unfolded collar of his shirt pressed against his muscular neck.

"Pay attention to the driving," Koslov bellowed as he put his hand on Caitlin's thigh. She gently removed it.

The S 600 smelled new, its leather seats unsoiled, its burled walnut interior sleek and shiny under the streetlights. "A hundred and fifty thousand dollar car," Peter had whispered in her ear, "give or take the price of a bottle of vodka." It was after midnight, the damp air warm, and London's streets beginning to empty. They had planned, or so Caitlin thought, to meet in a small Pakistani restaurant near Baker Street at 9:00 p.m. By 10:00, Peter ordered dinner for both of them. The restaurant closed at 11:00. Slava was standing across the street, smoking a cigarette.

"The same old game?" Peter asked.

Slava didn't bother to answer. He waved to them to follow him as he walked along a half-dozen streets before turning down a narrow, dimly lit alley. The Mercedes was parked in a driveway.

"Mr. Johnson," Slava said in a thick Slavic accent. "Please," he added as he motioned to Peter to put his hands on the silver car and spread his legs. It looked like a scene from a third rate movie as the chauffeur searched for any hidden instrument, a wire, a recorder, a small camera.

Koslov got out of the back seat and asked Caitlin to take the same position. He ran his hand over her back and around her waist. He started at her ankles and ran his hands to her thighs. "Is this necessary?" she asked bitterly. "I get no pleasure from it," he answered in his deep voice, but she knew it was a lie. He danced his fingers over her crotch. "Enough," she bitterly said. He chuckled.

Koslov bowed slightly when he opened the rear door of the Mercedes and let her slide in ahead of him.

Peter twisted in his seat. "Where to now?" he asked Koslov.

"We will just drive around. Did you bring the payment?"

"In cash?" Slava added loudly.

"Exactly as you instructed," Peter answered. "An envelope full of pound notes—five thousand, to be exact."

"I told you we should have asked for more," Slava said. "Five thousand pays for the gas."

"There is another five thousand if you let us film you," Caitlin said impulsively. "All you are giving us is a couple of names. That's not very much."

Koslov pressed his hand on her knee. "When you come back with your husband, Caitlin, then I will be happy to be filmed alongside both of you. We will all be smiling."

# Chapter 10

There was a time when Ilya found comfort in the architecture of Kyiv's municipal building. The huge structure represented strength and authority, its height majestic, its formidable entryway, a symbol of secular empowerment. But since the collapse of the Soviet empire, everything about the building struck him as unnervingly large and overdone, purposely designed to diminish the individual, to make people feel small and trivial, impotent in front of the collective will, insignificant to history. The massive stone exterior projected power, not grace, force and not tenderness; its immense offices, with their twenty-four foot ceilings and elongated windows, served only the egos of their occupants, the little bureaucrats who sat behind large desks, men of little vision, of no ideals, absent knowledge, absent decency.

The Russian slowly made his way up the enormous and dimly lit concrete staircase to the third floor, keeping his head down, carefully measuring the uneven steps with his eyes so as not to stumble. He practiced smiling. He tried to think of something warm and ingratiating to say. He was sorry he was there. He hoped that his headache would ease.

An unsmiling young man, his thin, short body outfitted in an ill-fitting and poorly made black suit, greeted Ilya as he made his way along the balcony that circled the stairwell. "Ilya Alexeevich?" he asked.

"Yes," Ilya responded blandly.

"You have an appointment to see the deputy mayor?"

"That's my understanding."

"Yes, yes, that's what I've been told. He is running a little behind schedule. Would you be so kind as to take a seat," the young man said courteously, and pointed to the stone bench that stood against the wall.

How long will it be this time, Ilya asked himself, a half-hour? An hour?

He looked at his watch, leaned his head against the wall, and quickly began to doze.

A young woman had to shake his shoulder to wake him. She gave him a broad smile and a quick laugh. "Have we left you out here that long?" she said.

Ilya looked at his watch. An hour and fifteen minutes had gone by. "No more than usual," he answered.

"The deputy mayor is able to see you now."

He followed her through the large oak doors, passed through the windowless outer office where the skinny young man was seated in front of a computer screen, and through the open door that led to the inner office. She closed the heavy wooden door behind her.

Ilya stood silently before the large desk, waiting for the deputy mayor to look up, to acknowledge him with a phrase or a smile. It was an old game, Ilya knew, this making a visitor wait, an obvious vaudeville routine played out with undue seriousness, all to prove the superiority of the man behind the desk, to make certain that his guest recognized his own insignificance. Catherine the Great must have done the same, Ilya thought, and Czar Nicholas II. That was as good a reason as any for the Bolsheviks to shoot him.

A minute or more went by before the deputy mayor took off his reading spectacles and looked up.

"What have you done now, Ilya Alexeevich?"

"It is good to see you Pavlov Karpenko, good indeed. You are looking well."

"Why shouldn't I. I have enough to eat, enough to drink, and beautiful women to adore me."

"I have nothing but a steam bath and cheap vodka," Ilya answered with a laugh.

"And you expect me to believe that, my old friend? I can see the money bulging in your pockets," Pavlov said with a chuckle. "Would you like some coffee, Ilya, or perhaps a little Cognac? I have a real Cognac. An offering from a French businessman who mistakenly believes I will lower my prices for a case or two. It is good, Ilya."

"How can I refuse?" Ilya said.

"Come, let's sit together on the couch."

Pavlov rose quickly, took his jacket off the back of his leather chair, and put it on. He was forty-five years old, of medium height, with a head of radiant white hair that curled around his neck and over his ears. There was nothing particularly handsome about him, not his thin nose or thick lips, not his deep-set brown eyes or his narrow chin, and yet, his features demanded attention. His eyebrows were ever in motion, and the downward twist at the edges of his mouth constantly changed shape. He moved with athletic prowess, quickly, his steps silent, his stomach taut, and his shoulders square. As Pavlov stood in front of the window, he unconsciously moved his weight from one leg to another. If Pavlov could sell his metabolism to overweight women, he would be worth a fortune, Ilya thought.

The young woman who had been leaning her attractive body against the closed door did not need any direction. She opened the side panel of a highly polished walnut buffet, a style made popular in 1930 Berlin, and took out a bottle and two glasses.

Pavlov took Ilya by the elbow and led him to the couch, but he didn't sit down next to him. He walked around the large upholstered chair he normally used and made his way to one of the large windows that looked out on downtown Kyiv. The woman placed the bottle on a coffee table and filled the small glasses. She left one for Ilya and brought the other to Pavlov.

"Cheers," the deputy mayor said after turning toward Ilya. He emptied his glass. Ilya did the same. "Another," Pavlov said to the young woman.

When the second drink was downed, Pavlov resumed his stance and peered out the window. "What trouble have you caused me, Ilya?"

"I don't know what you mean."

"Come, Comrade. I have no patience for a dance. The American Embassy is looking for a missing financier. The government is upset. Moscow is curious. I suspect you are holding him."

"Why do you think it's me, Pavlov? You know I'm a smuggler, not a kidnapper."

"For two reasons, friend. First, you are here. Second, the person who contacted the Americans spoke with an English accent. I didn't need to know more. So, Ilya, tell me more," Pavlov said.

Ilya turned toward the woman. "We are not alone," he said.

"Don't worry, my Ilya. What you can say to me you can say to her. She knows all my secrets."

Ilya was surprised. Pavlov had a taste for pretty young women, usually twenty years his junior, always a blond, or a redhead, always with a perfect body. They tended to wear short skirts and heavy layers of facial powder, their lips thickly covered with bright red gloss, their intense perfumes failing to camouflage the missed bath. Ilya had always thought there was something pathetic about them, as if they knew that no matter what they did they couldn't avoid eventually looking like their mothers, their large breasts sagging, their hips wide, their skin yellow. Pavlov had never invited one of them into a business conversation. They had never shared in the secrets of his craft.

Now that Ilya examined the young woman with greater interest, he realized she was different than the women who usually surrounded Pavlov. Whatever elixir she rubbed on her skin made its glow look natural, its porcelain beauty without flaw. Tall for a Ukrainian, perhaps 5'8", her long hair more amber than yellow. She was wearing a floral cotton sheath that cut below her knees and hugged her modest hips. The dress's skirt waved appealingly as she approached the table, when she poured the Cognac. But there was nothing servile in her movements, no false smile to suggest that she enjoyed waiting on men.

The young woman nodded at Ilya. An almost indiscernible smile came to her lips. Interesting, Ilya thought as he reexamined the simple but classic styled dress and the high heel shoes. They were not manufactured in Rostov-on-Don, he decided. Pavlov's tastes had improved.

"May I introduce Anna Baranova, my assistant. She knows all my business. So, Professor Alexeevich, what have you done to bring me headaches?"

"What are you blaming me for," Ilya laughed. "Did I make it rain? Did I cause a bear to break into your dacha? Did the breakfast I brought cause you indigestion?"

"The indigestion comes close," Pavlov said curtly. "You have a prisoner, my friends in London tell me, a rich American you're planning to exchange for a long-legged movie star or, given your advanced age, a big bag of money."

"I'm not that old," Ilya replied. He turned to Anna and winked. She didn't bother to notice.

Pavlov was not in a humorous mood. "Is it true, Ilya? Have you sunk so low as to become a kidnapper?"

"It was very accidental. I rescued the man, but now that I have him, why not make a little money? We could both use some. That is what has brought me here, to talk to you about him. I came to Kyiv as quickly as I could to tell you what I am up to."

"Of course, you have," Pavlov said in an insultingly sweet tone, "after you called the American Embassy a dozen times and decided you needed help."

"That is a gross exaggeration. I always knew I'd need your help."

Anna left her post guarding the door and sat on the far corner of the couch. "Is Benjamin Palmer well?" she asked in perfect Russian.

Ilya struggled to keep annoyance from showing on his face. Pavlov was ahead of him once again, he thought. This skinny nonentity, this brownnosed bureaucrat who knew nothing of Chekov or Dostoyevsky, who had mastered only graft and corruption, was getting ready to outsmart him. He felt his stomach turn. "He is well. He is even happy. I have left him alone with a beautiful woman. He will speak only good of us when he gets home."

"I'm sure," Pavlov said sarcastically. "Did you really think I wouldn't know what you are up to, Ilya? Did you think you could accomplish a ransom transaction without me?"

Ilya refilled his glass and offered the bottle to Pavlov. "We have worked together too long for you to think that of me. We are partners. I always calculated your share."

Pavlov pushed his glass toward Ilya. The older man poured in some Cognac.

"How much have you been offered, Ilya?" he asked before downing the drink.

"Nothing yet, but he can easily be worth two million dollars. That's not a bad price."

"And my share?" Pavlov asked.

"Fifty percent, Pavlov, of course. I'll cover expenses from my half."

"And why don't I just take it all?"

Because I know where he is, Ilya thought, but as tempting as it was, he kept the thought to himself. "We are partners, Pavlov."

"Smuggling diamonds from Yakutia are one thing, selling Americans is another, Ilya Alexeevich."

"A million dollars is a million dollars. You can buy a great deal of French Cognac with a million dollars."

"Even more with two million." Pavlov walked behind his desk and stood beside the leather chair. He played with a metallic paperweight. He flipped the calendar; he took a silver letter opener from its velvet case and used its point to clean his nails. Unexpectedly, he broke into laughter. "For an old drunk you look very good, Ilya, very good. My back hurts. My knees don't listen to me. My heart is full of misery, but you, you grow younger. How long has it been, twenty years now that we know each other?

"Closer to fifteen, I believe."

"It might as well be a hundred. We were on our knees when we met. Do you remember how the old people lined up outside the airport terminal, the last of their meager possessions scattered over wobbly tables, everything for sale for a dollar bill or a dozen Yen, a dried fish here, a samovar there, a belt, a pair of shoes, your dead grandmother's best dress. And the Americans, 'we are here to help you.'" The last phrase was said in thickly accented English.

"Of course I remember. How could anyone forget? And now we are both capitalists. I buy and sell diamonds. You buy and sell politicians. And we both avoid taxes."

Pavlov broke into laughter. "Shall we take our guest out for dinner tonight?" he asked Anna.

~

It was as beautiful a day as Benjamin could recall, the sun gloriously bright, the sky dotted with small white clouds. The resplendent air was cooled by a light breeze blowing in from the Carpathian Mountains, and perfumed by aromas rising out of the recently harvested wheat fields and the layer of pine needles that coated the forest floor. After a quick lunch and two shots of vodka, Ilya had taken off for Kyiv, his finely tailored gray wool suit in need of pressing, his blue shirt's collar unbuttoned, a red tie folded into an inside jacket pocket. Marya had packed a basket with bread, goat cheese, early tomatoes, and two bottles of vodka, and placed it in the back of the blue Chevrolet Niva Fedya had arrived in the night before, a small 4x4 SUV capable of handling Ukraine's poor roads. After a full-throated argument, Fedya surrendered his cause and let Ilya do the driving to Kyiv. "It's for you I'm going," Ilya said to Benjamin. "Someday soon you'll be coming along. After I get the money, you know."

There was no reason to take Ilya's words seriously. The Russian had made similar assertions in the past, predictions that Benjamin's imprisonment was soon to end, that it wouldn't be long before the payoff, before liberation. Yet, Ilya's brief comment inexplicably lifted his prisoner's spirits. Benjamin waved as the car pulled away, a broad smile on his face. The weather, he thought, as he recognized his cheerfulness.

The outdoors called to them. Marya went to work in the garden, her hair hanging over her shoulders and along her cheeks. Near the edge of the cabin that the sun never reached, Benjamin dug up several worms, and then strolled down to the river, Ilya's old fishing rod over his shoulder, an empty pail swinging from his hand. He returned three hours later with two small perch and a decent sized catfish.

"Success?" Marya yelled out as she saw him coming through the forest.

"Three fish, Marya, one large enough for a meal. But you should have seen the one that got away."

"I should have," she said walking toward Benjamin. She looked at the three fish still clinging to life in a small pail. "Good," she pronounced, "they will make a good meal for the two of us." She tucked her hand under his elbow. "A perfect day," she sang, "If only the bugs would go away."

"They, too, have reason to celebrate."

"Sometimes you are too kind, Benya," she laughed and pulled the pail away from him. "You sit and let me cook."

He sat on the wooden steps, closing his eyes and letting the late afternoon sun warm his face. He was beginning to doze when Marya suggested they eat outside. She carried the cast-iron skillet to the table, its hot handle wrapped in a pale blue kitchen towel. "We have some white wine from Georgia. It is not very cold, but it will be tasty."

Marya talked about the garden while they ate. She told him how her mother knew the names of all the plants and trees that grew about their home in Khabarovsk, how her father would fish in the Amur River, and how they never ate his catch for fear of pollution. Benjamin told her he had never fished before being brought to the cabin. "See, even captivity can teach us a new pleasure," she said whimsically.

"Tell me more about Khabarovsk," he said after they had washed down the fish and black bread with the last of the wine.

"Oh, I will repeat myself. I'm sure I've shared all I know over these last weeks," she replied. She picked up the skillet and prepared to carry it into the cabin. "Have you ever seen a more beautiful sky?" she asked while standing next to the table. The edges of her dark hair curled beneath a multicolored bandana, and her blouse was unbuttoned deep enough to reveal the splendor of her breasts. Threadbare jeans hugged her hips. "How would you describe the sky in English, cobalt and violet?"

"Exactly," he said, although they were not the words that would have jumped into his mind, "a romantic cobalt and violet."

She gave out a low sigh and turned away. Benjamin followed her into the cabin, his hands empty.

Marya was leaning over the sink when he reached her. "How about cleaning off the table," she said in a soft and undemanding voice.

"It will wait," Benjamin answered. He put his arms around her waist. He rubbed his face in her hair and kissed her neck. When she turned to him, he held her head softly in his hands and kissed her tenderly.

"Let me go down to the river and wash," she said quietly. "I will be back."

The slanted rays of sunlight covered her bed and tinted the room yellow. He undressed slowly, throwing his clothes over a small chair on which she had placed a few books, and settled under a thin cover, thinking that he should have done this a long time ago, imagining that she would come back smelling of the river, covered only by her open blouse. He could feel the smile on his face.

"So you found your way," she said in an off-key voice, suggesting to Benjamin that he had been presumptuous and should have waited for a clear invitation before taking over her bed.

He thought his haste was something to apologize for, but said nothing as he watched her unbutton her blouse and remove her white brassiere, as he watched her gracefully step out of her jeans and slide off a flesh colored panty. She was breathtakingly beautiful, her skin bathing in the hushed sunlight, her breasts large and firm, her strong legs calling to him.

She turned her back to him when she slid under the cover, her body pleading for him to go slowly, to be sensitive and affectionate. It didn't work. All the studied principles of foreplay fell before his passion. Forgotten were the tender words, the accumulating caresses, the dance of his fingers between her thighs, the stimulating embrace of their lips. She chuckled when he turned her over unceremoniously, giving permission to his desire, forgiving his haste. She raised her legs, her body wet and ready. He penetrated her forcefully, shocked by his exuberance. All his pent up desires burst in a single stroke, his semen erupting into her with the first feel of her moist warmth. He closed his eyes and heard himself add wordless sounds to his ejaculation. Unhappiness covered her face. She tilted her head to the side in disappointment, and even in the dim light, he could see her eyes moisten.

He lay in her embarrassed by his adolescent sexuality. "I'm sorry," he said in apology. "I just wanted you so much."

Marya could not bring herself to look at him. She sank her body deeper into the thin mattress and pushed her cheek against the pillow.

He could not leave her that way, unsatisfied, dissolute, all the expectations of their first encounter made false by his lust. He rested his weight on his elbows as her legs relaxed, but instead of wilting, his erection was inflamed by his desire to please her. He began again to move within her, this time permitting the rhythms of her body to design his motions. She turned her face and opened her moist eyes. She kissed his shoulder and his chest and tightened the grip of her legs. At first, she came to him with small vibrations and breathy sighs that helped design his movements. Then, he ran his hand over her thighs, and kissed her lips between her quiet exaltations, hoping that he could cause her to erupt, that he could get her to come to him with the strength and power with which he had first burst into her. In a crowning gift, her body made volcanic movements and air rushed from her mouth. When he eased himself away, her eyes were gently closed, and her skin was vibrant.

After the sun had set and the bedroom had grown dark, Benjamin made love to her again. He tasted her lips and felt the softness of her breasts against his chest. He kissed her closed eyes; he smelled the sweetness of her hair. He felt that life was a gift and that he was safe.

In the morning, she brought him wild flowers from the forest. He wanted to take her again, but there was something in her smile, in her tone, in the way she moved her body that told him to wait. He loved her enough to listen.

They walked to the spot where the stream ran slow and deep. "I hope the children don't catch us," Marya said as she lifted the thin cotton dress over her head and uncovered her naked body. "I would never stop blushing."

"I'll keep my ears open," Benjamin offered.

"Ha," she laughed. "I will fill your ears with better sounds."

She cautiously made her way over the rocks and through the weeds that lined the bank, and sank her body into the cold water. A Russian expletive came out of her shivering body. "Aren't you going to join me?" she asked.

"It's cold."

"That's the idea. I expect you to keep me warm."

"Things will never be the same, will they?" she asked after they had dried off and put their clothes on.

"Yes, never the same," he said, but he didn't know what he meant.

# Chapter 11

The British Airline's 747 landed smoothly at Borispol Airport, some forty kilometers outside of Kyiv. It had been an easy flight, the security line at Heathrow blissfully short, the takeoff only a half-hour late, the clouds light, and the winds calm.

Peter dozed most of the way, intermittently daydreaming about Selby, wondering when he would see her next, and hoping that it would matter. Caitlin sat in the adjoining business class seat, scribbling notes about the trip in a spiral-backed notebook, planning to send her observations back to the States over what the hotel had promised would be readily available Internet connections.

They were following every one of Koslov's suggestions, and the tourist advice offered by a secondhand copy of Fodor's *Moscow, St. Petersburg, Kyiv*, and the Lonely Planet's *Ukraine Travel Guide*. Leave on Tuesday and stay at the Dnipro Hotel, Koslov had instructed. "If all goes well, you will need three tickets for your return, so don't buy roundtrip. It may take time. Don't set a departure date. And remember to leave your electronic equipment in London. Let me assure you, no one you will want to meet in Kyiv will want pictures taken. If you don't want to listen to me, it will all be stolen."

"Fuck it," Peter said.

"I prefer women," Koslov said, his voice devoid of laughter. "My contacts know you are reporters. I told them this was a personal mission—her husband and your friend. They are suspicious enough of you two. So don't fuck around. You want to get hit by a car crossing Khreshchatick, carry your television camera, Peter. The hospitals in Kyiv are not as good as the ones in London."

Caitlin's face dropped. She took a deep breath before questioning the Russian further. "We won't film anyone who does not want to be filmed. If we have the equipment, at least we'll have a chance to convince them we mean no harm."

Slava burst into laughter.

"I don't think anything is funny," Caitlin spit out.

Koslov remarked, "You are fighting centuries of secret police and decades of wiretapping, of phony photographs. Don't think you can convince them, but if you do—and I don't put anything past a beautiful woman—there is enough Japanese video equipment in Kyiv to do whatever you want. If you bring your own, it will be confiscated at customs, I can assure you. And when your interrogation is over, you will be happy to get on the next plane back to London."

Peter thought that Koslov was bluffing, but there was no reason to argue with him. Caitlin and he could decide what to do on their own. "Who do we see in Kyiv?" he asked.

Slava laughed again. He reeked of scotch.

"You will be contacted at the hotel by a woman named Anna Baranova. She will tell you what to do."

"And the money? Are we expected to fly with money belts full of cash?" Caitlin asked sarcastically.

"A nice idea, but not very practical. Your girlfriend, why can't you use her as your London contact? When you settle things in Kyiv, let her know. They will tell you how to transfer payments, and you will tell her."

"Girlfriend?" Peter said.

"Come, my black American. Why all this innocence? The woman whose house Caitlin is using, is she not Caitlin's friend?"

So maybe there were limits to Koslov's knowledge, Peter thought but was unconvinced. "We didn't want to involve her," he said.

"Then wear the money belts," Koslov snapped impatiently.

Selby's stoic veneer broke when they pleaded with her to work with them. Her face turned red and her voice jumped an octave. "So you want me to be a money launderer?"

"Money is the cleanest part of this whole operation," Peter mused.

"So I won't be accused of money laundering. I'll only be accused of funneling money to terrorists."

"I don't think they're on any terror alert list, Selby," Caitlin said to mollify her. "The State Department would have told me."

"They don't even know who is holding Benjamin. How could they tell you anything?" Selby argued.

"Pathetic, aren't we," Peter said. "We never expected this to be easy, but we clearly didn't think it through. Without our equipment, the chance of a documentary is totally in the hands of those we will be paying off. We never wanted to involve you, Selby. Believe me. Maybe it's time to pull the plug?"

Caitlin looked heartbroken. She lifted the teacup but couldn't bring herself to drink.

Selby walked by the fireplace three times before settling in a corner of her living room. She glanced over the art hanging on the fireplace wall before her eyes settled on a two hundred year old engraving by William Blake, *Satan Smiting Job with Boils*. She ran a hand through her hair and then crossed her arms in defiance.

"You know Peter, you may yet keep me writing about food, but instead of evaluating prestigious restaurants, I'll be reviewing prison cooking."

No one laughed.

Caitlin put her pen away and tightened her seatbelt when the plane began to descend. She pressed Peter's arm when she leaned into the window to get her first view of Ukraine. Below her were countless rectangular fields burgeoning with summer crops, their boundaries set by variations in color, by slender roads and narrow streams. She caught sight of a farmhouse, a tractor, a car making its way along a rural road, and finally the buildings of the airport. The plane bounced when it landed, and stumbled along the runway as it crossed breaks and potholes in the cement. It passed parked aircrafts manufactured, Caitlin suspected, during the years of Soviet power—Ilyushin passenger airliners, jets produced by Yakovlev, and medium range Topevs—planes now flown by Lot and Aeroflot, by Ukraine International Airlines and Bulgaria Air, by AeroSvit. How different and foreign it all felt. It made her shiver.

For no explainable reason, she expected they would be met at the terminal by someone in authority, an official who could move them quickly through customs, who would have a black limousine waiting by the airport's exit. But they were unheralded arrivals, forced to move through the long lines anonymously. They failed to make sense of the erratic signage and found themselves in a swarm of people holding Ukrainian passports. A middle-aged Ukrainian woman, her hair dyed a circus-red, pointed and poked until they understood their mistake and moved into a crowd of foreign passport holders. Forty-five minutes later they found themselves in the baggage reclaim area. The nightmare became worse. Suitcases, trunks, and duffle bags had been thrown off the airport's carousels to make room for the next flight's luggage, and were now haphazardly strewn all over the floor. Peter immediately sighted his bag. Caitlin's was uncovered twenty frustrating minutes later.

They took a guidebook's advice and headed for Terminal B's taxi kiosk to avoid hiring an extortionist as their driver. An hour later, they booked into the hotel.

There was no message waiting for them at the front desk.

~

Anna Baranova escorted Ilya down the three flights of stairs, her high heels clicking on the uneven cement steps of the municipal building. "It was good to finally meet you," she said as they faced each other on the street. "Pavlov has told me many stories about you. All of them now seem true." She smiled graciously and touched his arm. "Until this evening," she said before turning around and going inside.

Pavlov was sitting on the couch, a glass of carbonated water in his hand when she returned to his office. "Well, what do you think?" he asked before she had sat down.

"A charming rogue, your Ilya. Not very wise, but in good shape for his age. If he shaved off that beard, he might even be handsome."

"You know that's not what I meant."

"And you know what I think. Benjamin Palmer is worth much more to you than he is to Ilya. A million dollars, you could make that every month."

"There are risks, Anna Baranova, great risks."

"No greater than a satellite falling on your head."

Pavlov rose from the couch and began to pace the large office, his cheeks tense, his thick eyebrows pulled down. Anna took his place on the couch, picked up the glass he was using, and mixed a thimble's worth of Cognac with the remaining water. When she finished the drink, she picked up the pack of unfiltered Gauloises that was on the table and lit a cigarette.

"You don't have to decide today, Pavlov. Let's dine with Ilya tonight and talk about it tomorrow. I think we can get him to tell us where he is hiding Palmer."

"Perhaps, but he is not as much of a fool as you think. We have known each other a long time. Mistrust is inevitable."

"It is made to order, Pavlov, made to order. A chance like this doesn't come along very often, if ever. An American financier, convicted in his own country, free only because he betrayed his friends, he comes to the Ukraine to do mischief, to do us serious injury, and you catch him, you drag him before a tribunal, you give interviews to the press, you become a courageous anticorruption candidate, a fighter against foreign rogues, against Westerners out to steal Ukraine's birthright, to piss on our people," she said breathlessly, and then, began to titter at her own performance. "I should have become a movie star," she laughed. "I do get carried away. But think about it, Pavlov. You would be the man of the hour, of the decade. Every office in the nation would be opened to you—elected, appointed, it wouldn't matter."

"Ilya has many friends, Anna, in Kyiv, in Moscow, even in London. He may not look it, but he is respected even when people laugh at him. He has been generous to many."

"If he is as smart as you think, he will go along with us. How could he not?"

"He's not like us Anna; he still believes in Marx and Lenin."

"He is a crook, a gun runner, a jewelry smuggler."

"He thinks he's a modern Oleksa Dovbush, returned to the Carpathians after 300 years. He steals from the rich and gives to the poor. He thinks purity of motives makes him honest."

"He's a Russian from Moscow, not a mountain Hutsul. Remind him of that Pavlov."

~

Built within the medieval vaults of a church destroyed during the Second World War, the restaurant was a warren of small, irregular rooms. A miscellany of tapestries, photographs and roughly carved wooden icons covered the uneven plastered walls. Strings of low wattage incandescent bulbs supplied the dim light. Ilya got there after dark. A small band was playing somewhere out of his line of sight, its music hooking around the cavern's twists and turns, loud and distorted. Anna and Pavlov were sitting at a small corner table, half-hidden in darkness. Pavlov was wearing the same suit he had on when they had met in his office, but Anna had changed into a simple but stunning black dress, with a deep V-cut neckline, and a single strand of pearls. Her long blond hair was combed into a beehive designed for a bride.

They were drinking wine and nibbling at pickled mushrooms and cheese crusted pastries. A third glass was on the table. Ilya poured himself a drink.

"Deafening," Ilya complained.

"Less likely for us to be overheard," Pavlov said.

"And I like the liveliness," Anna injected.

Ilya downed the wine, waved to the formally dressed waiter, and ordered carbonated water and a bottle of Ukrainian vodka. As an afterthought, he asked for a menu.

The vodka arrived first. He poured some for his company and one for himself. "To your health," he said. He leaned his head back and emptied the small glass.

Ilya had looked forward to sharing a multicourse meal with his hosts, but their appetites turned out to be meager compared to his. Anna ordered a mayonnaise based salad composed of carrots and peas, diced roast beef, and hardboiled eggs. Pavlov asked only for a bowl of borscht and Ukrainian white bread. The thought of eating so little made Ilya feel even hungrier. He could never bring himself to bypass borscht although he knew its ingredients varied from restaurant to restaurant and from day to day, so he seconded Pavlov's order, and added a plate of boiled dumplings filled with potatoes and pork and topped with fried onions. It promised an acceptable level of heartburn.

"They're here," Anna announced after taking a zip of vodka.

"Good," Pavlov said. "When did they arrive?"

"Late this afternoon, as we expected."

Ilya paid little attention to his companions' exchange. They seemed to be referring to people who held no importance to him.

"They arranged for separate accommodations," Anna continued. "The African is staying in a single room; the woman is renting a small suite. Maybe they want to appear innocent? What do you think, Ilya?"

The Russian looked up from his borscht. "Think about what?"

"Palmer's rescuers," Anna answered.

She was playing him, Ilya realized, acting as if he knew something of which he was ignorant. A most obnoxious way of asserting authority, he thought, a game played by short people to look tall. Slowly, he took another spoonful of soup.

"Do you know if they're a couple?" she asked.

"You have lost me, Anna Baranova. I don't know who you are talking about."

Pavlov gave out a boisterous laugh. "Let me explain," he said after catching his breath. "Benjamin Palmer's wife landed in Kyiv a couple of hours ago. She has a companion with her, a black man named Peter Johnson. She is a television reporter, and, according to my London contact, thinks she can make a hit movie about her husband's disappearance and his rescue. The black man is a professor of film and television. Anna thinks they fuck one another. I do not care, but I made sure they left their cameras in England. If you want to be photographed, Ilya, I can lend them some equipment."

Ilya felt like a fool. He had thought Pavlov would work with him, contacting the American Embassy, seeking an exchange of prisoner for cash, fully content with his share of the spoils. It was clear now, as he had begun to suspect in Pavlov's office, that he, Ilya Alexeevich, was being manipulated into laboring for this corrupt bastard, that it was Pavlov the prick, the man who filled his bank accounts with thick slices of other people's earnings, who was going to be in charge. "Where are they staying? I can contact them tonight," Ilya asked, knowing full well that he would not be told.

Anna presented her most charming smile. "Let them cook for a while. You understand, a little time will soften them up."

Pavlov laughed again, but this time it was softer. "Ilya, we should divide the work. We will negotiate with the Americans; you prepare the prisoner for an exchange. Is he here in Kyiv?"

"He's being moved around by an associate. If I held him in one place for too long a time, neighbors would become suspicious."

Ilya watched Pavlov's expression alter. The half-drunk comrade disappeared, replaced by a shrewd business negotiator who knew it was not the time to press for a final agreement. "Good," Pavlov said. "The authorities don't want to give the event publicity. We need to build tourism. The Americans won't say anything. They don't want to look impotent. If he is not here, you will need to bring him to Kyiv. The final steps will take place rapidly."

Ilya took another drink but didn't empty his glass. He was determined to keep his wits.

Anna filled Pavlov's four-ounce glass halfway up and then prepared her own drink. "Pavlov tells me that you think you're Oleksa Dovbush," she said sweetly, and acted as if they were sharing a secret by leaning close to him. "You are a hero who steals from the rich so you can give to the poor."

Ilya didn't laugh. "I don't believe in reincarnation. I am no hero." He paused for a lengthy moment, and pointedly added, "I give even more to the rich."

Pavlov slapped the table and broke into laughter. "Did I ever tell you how I met Ilya, Anna? We met in Vladivostok a couple of years after the empire collapsed. Gloomy days. Gloomy days." His face soured when he realized his glass was empty. Anna poured in two thimbles full of vodka. "A couple of American senators were on a 'we're here to help you trip,' flying in on a small jet the government had allowed to enter our air space. If their wives weren't with them, I'd have thought they had come to get laid. They certainly didn't understand what was going on. And Ilya, do you remember Ilya, when they asked if we needed medical supplies for our children? 'No,' you all insisted like a Cossack chorus, 'we have all the medicines we need.' And you, your voice was as loud as anyone's. I sat with the underlings in the back row wanting to ring your neck. 'What medicines?' I wanted to shout."

"Pride, comrade, pride. How could we bring ourselves to admit that we were poor, to act like beggars, petitioners?"

"And the sick paid the price."

"Don't they always," Ilya answered, annoyed that once again Pavlov had reminded him of a time when he had grown small, when the price of his distrust and arrogance was paid for by the sick. "It was a stupid meeting. None of us knew what we were doing. The Americans thought I was a little businessman wanting to learn how to open a coffee shop or improve a bakery. I had 10,000 workers to employ, 10,000 impoverished families rested on my soul. How could you expect us to admit to having been beaten by America, beaten by our own corruption, a victim of universal greed?"

"But we fooled them, Ilya. They never suspected that they were meeting with military leaders made unemployed by the economic deceptions of Moscow. How little the Americans understood. Are we really dumber than they are? It's hard to imagine." Bitterness dripped from Pavlov's voice.

"History doesn't tell us that victory goes to the wiser; it instructs us that victory goes to the powerful," Ilya answered. He clicked Pavlov's glass with his own. How tired Pavlov looks, Ilya thought, far beyond his forty-five years, his eyelids heavy, his face drooping. Half a bottle of vodka and he had become an old man, lamenting the disappearance of the future he had once had, unable to shake the shame of his present success. No, no, Ilya told himself, swiftly realizing that he was pushing his own thoughts into Pavlov's mind. It was Ilya who was embarrassed by being a thief, Ilya who had lost a glorious future, Ilya who had once believed that Russia promised the world something special, something great. Pavlov was too simple a human being to understand the present even as he owned it. And Anna, poor Anna, she was too young to know about noble dreams.

"And we made fools of ourselves," Ilya said. "Remember when I suggested that the Ford motor company take over my plant and design the product, and bring in the machinery, and train my workers, and we would split the profits. The idea turned them white. How little I knew about capitalism. Split the profit? Why? All we brought to the table was broken down machinery and a drunken labor force. They didn't know how to answer. Then I made it worse by threatening that if they didn't help, I would go to the Japanese. They must have been thinking, 'go to the Japanese, please.' I don't know how they kept from laughing."

Anna's head was turned away from the table. She was not interested in history. She was listening to music imported from the West.

~

Anna used her cell phone to contact their driver while Pavlov slipped some cash into the opened hand of the waiter. There was never any thought of paying a bill, Ilya realized, bothered by this ability of power to consume without cost. Perhaps he was just jealous, full of regret that he no longer commanded supplicants, that he no longer held a position that commanded bribes. He tried to forgive Pavlov's minor offense and the waiter's complicity, momentarily recalling the young Pavlov he had met so many years before in Vladivostok, an energetic idealist, a firm believer in mankind's equality. And what was he now … turned by history and political ambition into an ugly bureaucrat? But Ilya couldn't deny Pavlov's transgressions. It was not something he had ever done, this pissing down, this extraction of privilege that leads to more privilege, this simple underground injustice that seeps into the drinking water and contaminates the blood and guts of a whole people.

Ilya didn't ask for a bill. It was easier that way. They would just think him a fool or a holier-than-thou showoff.

The engine of a white limousine turned on and its bright lights blinked twice when Pavlov and Anna exited the restaurant, Ilya following close behind. The car made a sharp U-turn and jumped onto the edge of the wide sidewalk directly in front of Pavlov. The uniformed chauffeur jumped out, opened the front door for Anna, and the rear for the deputy mayor and his guest.

Ilya was barely seated before the car pulled away. "A new toy?" he asked Pavlov.

"An expensive toy, Comrade. I was sick of black cars. That color should be saved for hearses and widows and flatulent commissars. Anna should travel in white, don't you think, pure and beautiful like a snowfall in the Carpathians?"

"So it is Anna's car," Ilya observed knowing it wasn't true.

Anna laughed first. Pavlov quickly followed, but his laugh was fueled more by alcohol than humor.

"He wants to be different, Ilya," Anna said, twisting her body so she could look at the passengers riding in the back of the car. "He is not like the nameless bureaucrats and moguls who ride around in long black cars with shaded windows. Black is the color of corruption. When they see Pavlov's white car roll down the avenue, the people know it is Deputy Mayor Pavlov Karpenko, an honest man."

"And do they believe it?" Ilya asked sarcastically.

Anna turned her head away as if the question had insulted her. "If you would spend more time in Kyiv than you do in the Carpathians, you would know the high regard the public has for its deputy mayor."

Pavlov pushed his body forward and leaned his head against the back of the seat. He closed his eyes and began to snore. Ilya sat silently. He looked out the side window as the car drove by blocks of large boxy office buildings and Soviet era apartment complexes. His chest felt heavy, and the bitter taste of bile filled his mouth. Indigestion, he decided, but he didn't think it was caused by the wine or vodka or the rich fatty food. His body was used to excess. No, he realized, it was the beautiful Anna Baranova who irritated his innards, it was the ignorant Pavlov, Ruler of the Hour, who made his stomach turn. Loved by the people, Anna had implied. How could he not feel sick? Maybe a white limousine could camouflage the darkness of corruption and convey to those desperate to believe that its occupant stole less than other officials did. Who knew? Or, perhaps, it only announced to the people that Pavlov was wise enough to realize that corruption was something of which to be ashamed? That alone would make him popular.

The car headed downhill and drove along a narrow street close to the Dnieper River. The chauffeur parked by an undistinguished apartment house and helped Pavlov out of the car and into the building.

"He's lived here a long time," Ilya observed in an attempt to make small talk.

Anna Baranova turned around to see him before she answered. "But he has a larger apartment, higher up, with a much better view. His wife is very happy with it."

The darkness stole her radiance and made her look like other women, Ilya thought. But he knew she was not ordinary. "Is it the same wife?" he asked, a bit of mischief in his voice.

"It is the same wife. He has only had one."

"Is she still as jealous about his secretaries as she used to be?"

"I wouldn't know, Ilya. I don't have that type of relationship with him," Anna answered emphatically.

Ilya was disappointed that the chauffeur quickly returned. Teasing Anna had eased his indigestion. But he didn't buy the "I don't have that type of relationship with him." How could his wife not be jealous? Or was she just happy to have him pawing someone else?

Ten minutes later, they parked alongside Anna Baranova's apartment building. The chauffeur opened the door but didn't walk her into the concrete block building.

Ilya accepted the driver's invitation to sit in the front seat. It was still warm.

"On the other side of the river?" the chauffeur asked in Russian.

"Yes, the other side, near the Lisova metro station."

"That far out."

"I'm a poor man," Ilya answered.

The chauffeur let out a shallow laugh. He was in his early fifties, Ilya decided. A square faced, stocky man, his gray hair protruding below his leather cap. He had looked very comfortable, almost graceful, when he had eased Pavlov from the car, when he opened the door for Anna and tipped his cap. Ilya couldn't help thinking he was more secret police and bodyguard than chauffeur. He studied the chauffeur's open jacket to see if he was carrying a firearm. None was apparent.

"How long have you worked for the deputy mayor?" Ilya asked. He spoke in Ukrainian, suspecting that the driver was from the region.

He was right. "For two years, almost three," the driver answered in Ukrainian. Then he let out a quick laugh. "What made you think I was Ukrainian?"

"I didn't think it would look good for the deputy mayor to be driven around by a Russian or a Ukrainian whose first language was Russian. It was not a difficult guess."

"And you most probably have guessed that I'm not simply a chauffeur," he said with a degree of pride in his voice.

"I assumed you were more. A bodyguard, certainly, no deputy mayor would travel without one. But I also wonder if you are secret police."

The chauffeur let out a laugh and flicked the headlights off and on although there was no oncoming vehicle. "I'm a bodyguard, nothing more and nothing less."

"Have you been asked to keep track of my comings and goings?"

"Don't be too suspicious. You will begin to sound paranoid, Ilya Alexeevich."

"In our world, the paranoids live longer than the others, and usually better."

"I'm not paid enough to argue," the chauffeur said.

Ilya was tempted to play the expected game, to ask the driver's name and where he lived, to inquire about his family, to discover what political future he saw for Pavlov. He knew the answers to his questions would be unreliable, but he would have to act as if he believed them. And so the evening would end, Ilya thought, with pretense covering pretense, like a child's card game, the chauffeur suspecting that he was not believed, and the Russian feeling angry with himself for acting unsuspecting and naive. No, Ilya was too tired to play that game. But he could not pass an opportunity to needle Pavlov's protector.

"What should I call you?" the Russian asked.

"Hedeon is my name."

"Hedeon, the destroyer of trees," the Russian commented. "You might have found a different profession if your parents had named you Krystiyan, a follower of Christ."

"Hedeon is as good a name as any other. Fate is not altered by names."

"Anna Baranova is very beautiful, is she not?" Ilya asked.

"She is pretty enough."

"Pavlov always had good taste in women. How long has she been his mistress?" Ilya tried to make the question sound as if it had grown out of their casual conversation, but he didn't think he had pulled it off.

"Don't jump to conclusions my Russian friend. Deputy Mayor Karpenko would enjoy your assumption, he expects people to jump to that conclusion, and Anna would not be bothered by it, but their reactions would not make it true."

"Are you trying to convince me they're not fucking each other?" Ilya asked with a laugh.

"I'm not trying to convince you of anything. I drive them to their apartment houses, not to their bedrooms. We're close to the Lisova station. Your address?"

Of his three apartments, this was Ilya's favorite, smaller than the ones in St. Petersburg and Yakutsk, a low rent hideaway surrounded by the Spartan homes of pensioners and teachers, hospital workers and bus drivers. His neighbors didn't ask questions. They knew him only as a part-time occupant who had the apartment cleaned once a month and remembered to tip the building manager.

Fedya was fast asleep on the living room couch, his clothes thrown over the one sitting chair, his shoes in the middle of the floor. Ilya turned on the lamp and struck the couch's arm with his fist. "Fuck," he yelled as Fedya opened his eyes.

When the water came to a boil, Ilya used a single Lipton bag to prepare two glasses of tea. Fedya stumbled into the small kitchen in his underwear.

"I have work for you, Fedya, important work. I want you to find two Americans, Benjamin Palmer's wife and an African."

~

Anna quietly entered the small apartment, dropped her bag on the kitchen table, and took a bottle of Cognac from the wooden cabinet above the small refrigerator. She picked up a small glass from the sink, held it up to the ceiling light, turned on the water, and rinsed it.

"Is that you?" Vika called from the bedroom. "Is that you?"

"No, it's Vladimir Putin and Barack Obama. We came up for a nightcap. Care to join us?"

Anna listened as Vika turned over in their bed and gave a loud yawn. She watched her lover stumble barefoot into the kitchen, her short dyed red hair in disarray, her large breasts spilling out of a thin, white nightgown.

"You seem in a disgustingly happy mood?" Vika said in a loud, sleepy voice. She dropped down on one of the four wooden chairs that surrounded the Formica topped kitchen table, her generous hips covering most of the seat. "It must have been a successful night."

"I'm drunk, so I'm happy. I want to stay drunk. Would you like a glass of brandy? It's free."

"It will keep me up all night."

"And it will put me to sleep. So let me drink alone. I don't want to dream about your pacing the floor."

Anna filled two glasses, knowing that her companion would insist on one. Vika enthusiastically drank the brandy before Anna put the bottle down.

"A good evening?" Vika asked.

"It was very much as I expected, two men rattling on about the past, getting drunker by the minute. Ilya Alexeevich is an interesting man, charismatic and clever, with an athletic build and physical presence. He makes Pavlov look like a functionary. But as the evening went on, he began to look tired and old. He doesn't even suspect what Pavlov is up to."

"So he will be cooperative?" Vika asked.

"What choice does he have? We hold all the cards."

"But he holds the American," Vika maintained. "Surely that's a card you need."

"There are three Americans, Palmer, his wife, and the African. I've been thinking, Vika, how many of them do we need to make Pavlov a hero? All he has to do is arrest the two Americans who are in Kyiv and claim they were part of a criminal conspiracy. Their leader is Benjamin Palmer, a convicted financial felon. Their purpose, to defraud Ukrainian businesses. Before anyone could question his evidence, a deal could be struck with the American State Department to extradite the two of them. Pavlov would come off as an anticorruption champion, a fighter for honesty, for free markets free of manipulation."

Vika poured herself another drink and added some brandy to Anna's glass. She was fully engaged, as Anna knew she would be. "And what of Benjamin Palmer?" Vika eventually asked.

"Unimportant. Oh, it would make better headlines if we got hold of the three of them. 'Benjamin Palmer, Notorious American Financial Criminal Captured,' one could read, or 'Deputy Mayor Pavlov Karpenko Thwarts Financial Conspiracy.' And best of all, no Ukrainian would be involved. He would not have to accuse anyone. He would make no new enemies. Those who are jealous of him would become even more jealous, but no new person would be in the bushes waiting for him."

"What of Ilya, Anna? Wouldn't he become an enemy? Wouldn't he feel cheated? Wouldn't he want to wait in the bushes?"

"Ilya is yesterday. He has friends but no troops. But Pavlov will be kind. He'll pay him off. Think of all the money Pavlov can extract if he becomes mayor, more as president or prime minister. Ilya is looking for a million dollars. And he'd be happy with half. Chicken shit. We'll make tens of millions … maybe a billion or two."

Vika picked up her glass, but finding it was empty put it down with a thud. She looked disappointed, but not disappointed enough to pour another drink. "And what does Pavlov think of all this?" she asked.

Anna yawned loudly, her eyes half-closed. "Pavlov will think whatever I want him to think. He still has no idea how close he is to riches."

"And you."

"And me, my dear Vika. What do you think of buying an apartment in London, maybe Paris? Of course, Florence or Venice might not be bad."

Vika gave out a generous laugh, got up from her seat, picked up the two empty glasses, and placed them in the sink. Using her long fingers like a comb, she ran them through her hair. The nipples of her large breasts looked as though they were ready to break through her nightgown. "I am happy here, but I've always dreamed of visiting Italy," she said quietly. "But let's not crack our eggs too soon."

Vika lay on her back in the middle of the double bed, holding Anna's head between her breasts and her thin body between her thighs. She ran the palms of her hands over Anna's small breasts and kissed her hair. But as her fingers began to move between her lover's legs, she felt Anna's body relax, and her breathing settle down. Vika reached toward the bottom of the bed to grab hold of a soft woolen blanket and pulled it up to Anna's neck. "Goodnight," she whispered, and closed her eyes.

~

With its window shades down and drapes drawn tight, Ilya's apartment was totally dark when the sputtering sounds of city traffic woke him. If it weren't for a full bladder, he would have pressed a pillow over his head and struggled to return to sleep. But bodily functions forced him to get out of bed and make his way to the windowless bathroom. He noticed the couch was empty and remembered the mission he had given to Fedya. What does it matter? he thought.

Sleep had come rapidly, but it proved short and shallow. He kept waking, unhappily reliving his meetings with Pavlov and Anna Baranova, interpreting and reinterpreting their every word, trying to give meaning to a wave of the hand, to a secretive smirk, to signs of glee, to their obvious sense of triumph. Plot after plot entered his mind. He was certain they were out to cheat him, to steal Benjamin Palmer, to bargain with the Americans for sums Ilya could not imagine, to fuck each other under silk sheets, pouring Champagne into crystal stemware, toasting Ilya the gullible, Ilya the ignoramus.

What would it matter if Fedya located the Americans? How could Palmer's wife and the African be persuaded to deal with Ilya the Russian nothing and not Pavlov the Ukrainian big shot? They'd have to be stupid to think he had the power to get Benjamin out of the country; that he and not the deputy mayor and his blond whore conducted this opera. Hedeon would be watching everything he did, and there would be another Hedeon guarding the Americans. The noose was too tight, he told himself, with a laugh. Forget the millions and settle for a case of vodka or good French wine.

It wasn't the loss of money that caught in Ilya's craw; it was the idea of a victorious Pavlov. He abhorred the deputy mayor, a man molded by Stalin, not by Lenin or Marx, an apparatchik without ideology, without a utopian vision, without a commitment to anything larger than his cock. Corruption produced him. Greed fueled his body. All he knew was how to steal and how to fuck. How could Ilya the philosopher, Ilya the idealist, Ilya, humane and skilled, learned and wise, how could he lose to a man who was born in a swamp, who sucks the blood of farmers and workers, who … ? He halted his thoughts. He had no words with which to describe his revulsion. He wanted to piss on Pavlov's head and shit in his mouth.

Ilya opened the tall cabinet that stood next to the old refrigerator and pulled down a quarter-filled bottle of vodka from it highest shelf. He drank the bottle dry and went back to bed. His underclothes were damp from sweat, and his mouth foul tasting when he finally got up. It was again night, and his protégé was standing in the kitchen.

"Would you like a drink, Ilya?" Fedya asked, an open bottle of beer in his hand.

"Beer is not a drink. It is a dessert."

"You look dreadful," Fedya noted.

"Do you have absolutely no respect for your elders?"

The younger man walked into the small living room, and sat down where he had slept the night before, on the upholstered gray couch. "I had no luck today. No one had seen them. No one even heard that someone else had seen an American woman and an American African. I'm exhausted."

"At least you have a reason. I'm exhausted, and I slept all day."

Ilya's tone caused Fedya to drop any attempt at humor. "Worried?" he asked softly.

"We are dealing with detestable people. I have to figure out a way to defeat them."

# Chapter 12

Peter woke early on his first full day in Kyiv, exhilarated by being in a city he had never seen, excited to have begun the next leg of the journey. He took a long shower and shaved a couple days' worth of stubble from his face before wandering down to the hotel's lobby. The first floor bar was already open, but he didn't see anyone in it, neither customer nor bartender. A single clerk was behind the reception desk, sitting on a tall stool and reading a newspaper. His hangdog expression made the American think he had been there all night.

"I don't think we should both be away from the hotel at the same time," Caitlin said.

Peter put down his cup of coffee. "What do you suggest?"

"One of us should be in the hotel at all times. I worry that someone will come to see us, and if one of us is not around, a day or two will pass by with nothing happening."

"We have the money. I don't think they'll play games. They're not going to delay contacting us simply because they don't reach us on the first try."

"Why tempt fate, Peter? They will try to contact us soon."

"Or they're going to test us, Caitlin, by playing a waiting game. They have no more reason to trust us than we have to trust them. We may have to be patient."

"Our cameras are in London. We don't even have a tape recorder. What is there to distrust?"

Peter didn't bother to answer. He finished his coffee, thinking for a moment that he might ask for another, but he had consumed more caffeine than he ordinarily did and decided just to move his chair further from the table and pour more of the bottled water into his glass. They were eating in the Dnipro Restaurant on the second floor of the hotel, working through the buffet breakfast. It was advertised as offering "70 dishes and delicacies," and although Peter had not counted what was available, he didn't think the advertisement was far off the mark. Caitlin had filled her plate sensibly, sticking with white toast and fried eggs, but he had ventured to the Ukrainian dishes and stuffed himself with breakfast hash—a mixture of fried eggs, bacon, and kielbasa—and paprika-covered fried potatoes. It was more than enough calories for the day, he thought, and enough cholesterol for a lifetime. He needed to hit the bathroom and go for a long walk.

"I told the concierge that we were dining here just in case a message came in this morning," Caitlin said, forgetting that she had told him this before they had sat down. "And, if one of us is out, calls should be forwarded to whoever is still here. Doesn't that seem reasonable?"

"It can make for a very boring stay."

"We're not here as tourists, Peter. I'm not even curious about Kyiv. I just want to get Benjamin out of here. We can spend our time working on the script. Since we will have to rely on reenactments and actors, we can invent the dialogue and choose the locations. We might even be able to come back after we've gotten Benjamin and video scenes in Kyiv. We certainly will be able to shoot on location in London. If you want to go outside, why don't you look around and storyboard sections of Kyiv?"

"Without a script, that would be hard to do," Peter said as he watched Caitlin's pale-white complexion subtly darken. He suspected that nothing would deter her, not the lack of equipment, not their shadowy interlocutors—nothing except, perhaps, the possibility of hurting her husband. That seemed to be her only boundary. He saw in her his younger self, the inveterate photojournalist, callously underestimating risks, unabashedly self-confident, purposefully blind to the possibility of failure.

"I'll work on the London script," Caitlin continued as if she didn't hear his comment. "But I will need some help from you on the scene in which you are followed by Slava. We could draw some strong distinctions between London and Kyiv by the careful use of architectural differences, don't you think?"

"I can script shots of London that emphasize the secular, the 21$^{st}$ century city, and Kyiv, as different, nonwestern, part medieval, part Soviet," Peter offered, feigning enthusiasm.

"Exactly!"

"But it would be an oversimplification."

She laughed gently. "You've been in the academy too long. We want a drama, not an historical discourse."

"Maybe we can achieve both."

"The mystery of Eastern Europe has to come through," Caitlin insisted.

Peter tried not to sound cynical. "Narrow streets and ancient monasteries?"

"Perfect," she responded.

Peter watched Caitlin finish her coffee and wipe her face with a cloth napkin. He could tell why the television camera loved her, her sharp features balanced and symmetrical, her lips faintly animated, and her blue eyes announcing her emotions. He watched her glance around the room and wave to the waiter, her hanging pearl earrings just visible under her shoulder length blond hair. He had gotten to like her in the way you would like an overly energetic and determined sibling, her smothering self-confidence in constant battle with self-doubt. He felt momentarily sorry for her as he recalled his own burning ambition, the long sleepless nights he had spent imagining fame, the depressing days when he believed his labor had twisted gold into straw. But there was a deep difference between her present and his past, he decided, even after recognizing that his memories of himself had been bleached by time. She was creating a story about herself; he had chased stories about others. Modern times, he told himself, as they left the restaurant, the reporter as celebrity, the television anchor as hero, the documentarian as autobiographer. He felt out-of-fashion and old.

~

Ilya had been gone three days, three long and glorious days, the afternoons warm, the evenings cool, the bedroom full of quiet murmurings and unanticipated feelings. Marya and Benjamin had spent the hours knit together in the cabin, holding hands on the bank of the river, watching the sunset and the moonrise. "Teenager!" she exclaimed one afternoon when he tried to have her in the woods. "Adolescent!" she laughed when he stopped her from dressing one morning. "Are you really that old?" she asked after she had woken him in the middle of the night and he only longed for sleep.

When they woke on the fourth morning, she invited him to forage through the forest's undergrowth for wild flowers and berries, to hunt for the night's gift of mushrooms. But he was unwilling to give up the comfort of her pillow. He watched as she fixed her brassiere, as she put on her pants, as she slipped into a woolen sweater to fend off the morning's cool air. It reminded him of the early days of his courtship, Caitlin standing near the bed in his small apartment, running a bath towel along her thighs, across her back, over her chest. A model's body designed by Victoria's Secret, he had thought, statuesque, her ass a perfect apple, her breasts firm. Marya's anatomy was different, it came from the genes of people who stored fat, whose muscles pulled plows, who built log cabins and cut firewood. It challenged fashion's current concept of beauty. If he had bumped into her at a Washington bar or conference, at a friend's wedding or an office picnic, he probably wouldn't have given her a second glance. He would have searched for someone who looked like Caitlin. There would have been no cautious flirting, no attempts to elicit a laugh or a look, no exchange of e-mail addresses or telephone numbers. Still, she was a beautiful woman, with a large open face and deep-brown eyes, her smile overwhelming. Only a severely imperfect vision would be blind to her radiance.

He turned on his back and closed his eyes, wondering why this sudden need to compare Marya to Caitlin, to use his wife's measurements to judge his lover. He pictured Marya walking by the river, shouting a word of cheer to the children, asking them if they had some chicken eggs to exchange for tea leaves, if the cow was offering them more than the usual amount of milk. It was not the differences in their bodies that made him restless; it was the differences in the sex that he wanted to understand. Is that what men do who have no work, spend endless hours bewildered by their erections? The thought made him laugh. It wasn't his cock that puzzled him, he decided. The biology was easy; it was the psychology that was perplexing.

Loving Caitlin had been easy. She attracted him in every way a woman attracts a man, physically beautiful, buoyant, and optimistic. Where he thought himself reserved, she practiced being outgoing; where he thought himself as smart, she knew she was exceptional. He was ambitious, as all men he knew were ambitious. But Caitlin was driven. When she slept, she dreamed of celebrity. When she worked, she was obsessed with perfection. It was her energy that propelled the marriage, her enthusiasms that got him moving in the morning, which got him laid at night.

Lying in Marya's bed, the soft pillow warm against his cheek, Benjamin decided that he had always been overly influenced by his companions. He followed Caitlin in bed, he followed his colleagues into financial manipulation and larceny. And Caitlin, whom did she follow? What guideposts did she read as she went through life? Just asking the question confused him. It was evident, he thought, she was following her desires. But desires don't spring from the ether, they are inherited from parents, they are learned from Hollywood movies and cable television. Her ambition came from the water supply. It came out of McDonald's hamburgers and Neiman Marcus catalogs.

He turned onto his back, angry at his wife, thinking she had forced him into this wilderness, that she had let him fall apart. He stared at the wood-beamed ceiling, wondering where Marya was and what was keeping her so long. He wanted her to distract him from his thinking, to turn his mind and body outward. Lovemaking with Caitlin was as easy as loving her. After all the years of their coupling, he still found her body riveting, her sensuality irresistible. There were no whips or chains, no late-night pornography. Her body was open and ready, and her desire for him constant. So why did he find Marya so much more satisfying? Was it because Marya offered him the illusion of safety during an unwanted and frightening period in his life? Or was it that Caitlin had failed to protect him when he had the life he wanted?

He heard Marya fussing around in the outer room. "Would you hurry up and get in here," he shouted. "I'm ready to explode."

"Well, we wouldn't want that to happen," she said as she entered the bedroom. Other words followed, but they were muffled by the woolen sweater as she lifted it above her head.

Naked, the forest's fragrance playing delicately on her warm skin, she lay next to him, her breasts against his arm, her head resting over his heart. She moved one leg over his so that the warmth between her legs touched his thigh. She placed her hand over his crotch but did not play with him. He did not push coitus. He wanted to make love differently, to share the warmth of her body, to luxuriate in the simple pleasure of being together. Benjamin kissed her forehead and slowly ran his hand over her back. She moved even closer.

Caitlin was an impatient lover, but independent, innovative, uninhibited. A dozen nightgowns hung in her closet; bikini panties and lacy bras filled her bureau's drawers. And yet … .

He pushed his thoughts away. Why did he need to compare? Why couldn't he just enjoy the pleasure Marya offered? Was there no way to be satisfied except by believing he had traded up, that what he now had improved upon what he had before? He pushed his head down and kissed Marya's bust. Caitlin's breasts were smaller, compelling miniatures, he had thought, their nipples easily erected and magnificently responsive. He never felt deprived, not by her breasts, not by her hands, her mouth, nor the laughter in her voice. They were tools she had mastered, instruments designed to attract, to entice, to make him boil. But when they had climaxed, the sex was over. It was like drinking a first-growth Bordeaux without a lingering aftertaste. There was no tender residue, no postcoital conversation, no fingers playing over his body, no appeal for him to touch her tenderly.

Marya twisted around until her soft rump fit comfortably against his groin, her back against his chest. He kissed her on the neck and wrapped his arm about her breasts.

"Do you mind, Marya? You've worn me out. I seem too tired to make love to you," he said.

She kissed his hand. "I thought that's what we were doing, Benya, making love. You don't have to fuck to make love. Even Americans should know that."

~

The buffet had lost its luster by the time they took their third breakfast at the Dnipro. The coffee was bad, the bread tasteless, the eggs over fried. Caitlin had spent the previous mornings working on her script, the afternoons napping or going for a short walk if Peter had returned to the hotel. She still talked about finding Benjamin, about the structure and content of the documentary, but there was less certainty in her voice and far less fervor. Once, after consuming a couple of glasses of white wine, she admitted to Peter that her faith in their mission was faltering.

In contrast, Peter was surprised to find himself enjoying Kyiv, relishing the time to wander by himself, to think of Selby, to try to understand why he had left her, to wish that she was with him—two experienced tourists, seeking out the city's museums, its historical buildings, its religious landmarks. He replaced the digital camera he had left in London with a sketchbook, his photographic lenses with a half-dozen sharpened pencils. To project Kyiv's timelessness and elicit a sense of mystery, he sketched its medieval cathedrals, its narrow streets, and its celebratory monuments. Capturing the city's contemporary society and its social structure proved more complex. It was easy to sketch the poverty of the subway riders, and it took only a little more effort to give expression to the exaggerated affluence of those who drove new German sedans and Japanese SUVs. But his attempts to capture the aspirations of the people, the expectations of the young, the tarnished hopes of the middle-aged and elderly, never felt satisfactory. He illustrated young women with attractive legs, their makeup heavier than that applied in America, their skirts shorter, their high heel shoes ungraceful. The nouveau riche appeared in Italian cut suits or sculpted silk dresses, usually entering an upscale hotel. The impoverished sat outside churches, tin pans on their laps, appealing to visitors with their hands. But none of his drawings, he felt, made visual what he was after, the emotional cost of tarnished hope. Ukrainian freedom had brought dreams and expectations. Now there was reality.

Caitlin finished her second cup of coffee. "Where to today?" she asked.

"I was thinking of staying in and letting you enjoy the morning breeze. It would do you good."

The furrows in her brow deepened. "Do I look that dejected?"

"You certainly don't look happy." He tilted his head to one side to emphasize the observation.

"You don't have to be that honest, Peter," Caitlin responded. She forced herself to giggle.

"Some fresh air would do you good."

She pushed her coffee cup and its saucer away. "I'd rather wait until this afternoon. I just have this feeling, Peter; it is going to be today."

"A woman's premonition?" he asked ironically.

"And if I'm right, you'll have to wipe that grin off your face."

"Happily," Peter concluded. He pushed his chair back from the table and prepared to get up.

"And your plans for the day?" she asked quickly.

"Well, I thought I'd be more successful and persuade you to get out. But having failed, I want to go back to the museum of the Great Patriotic War. I feel the need to remember a more glorious time, a time when Ukrainians would have been embarrassed by kidnappings and ransom."

"Was there ever such a time?" she asked.

~

She said goodbye to Peter outside the elevator doors, then settled down behind the desk in her outer room. She began to look over what she had drafted the previous evening, but, unexpectedly, her eyes filled with tears. A futile charade, she thought. The words on the page would never be used, the scenes she imagined would never be shot. Koslov was a fraud, she decided, out to make a quick dollar by leading her on and offering nothing but a wild goose chase in exchange. As for Peter, she felt like a fool for dragging him into all this, for misusing his friendship, for fashioning a witness to her naïveté. What should she do now? To return to the States would be defeatist, but what choice did she have? To wait in Kyiv would be useless and embarssing. It could be months or years before Benjamin was released, or his body was found. Or worse, the story could end without resolution, with his disappearance and her pointless search being the first and last chapters of the saga. If she weren't soon contacted, she said to herself without defining soon, she would be in touch with the American Embassy. She'd contact Hocking. She would ask for advice. Should she wait for Benjamin's release in Kyiv? "You'll be there for the rest of your life," she could hear Hocking say.

Caitlin turned over her pad and went into the bedroom. She pulled the cover over her body to fight the chills that had begun to overtake it, she covered her face with a pillow to dull her thinking. She was sorry she hadn't taken Peter up on his offer to let her play tourist. She was sorry she wasn't in sunlight. She was sorry ... for everything.

It was only after the phone rang that Caitlin realized she had fallen asleep. A heavily accented woman's voice was on the other end of the line.

"I'm Anna Baranova. You are expecting a call from me?"

"Anna Baranova," Caitlin said as she threw off the blanket and swung her legs over the side of the bed. "Yes, Yes, I've been waiting for your call."

"Good."

"Do you know where Benjamin is?" Caitlin blurted out, tossing aside her resolve to feign reserve, her plan to try to take control of the situation by moving slowly. Shit, she thought, after recklessly asking about her husband.

"We have time for that," the stranger said. "I am in the hotel. Meet me in the European Bar on the lobby floor."

If Peter were around, she would have invited Anna up to the suite, but in his absence, meeting in a public space struck her as being safer. "It will take me a few minutes to get down there."

"I will order a drink."

"How will I recognize you?"

"I am very pretty," the young voice said in a thick accent.

~

Fedya noticed him on the third day, standing a hundred yards from the gigantic statue, Motherland, a sketchpad in his hand and his short graying hair glistening in the sunlight. It was easy to spot him, the color of his skin alone separated him from the other tourists preparing to enter the National Museum of the Great Patriotic War, but so did his handsome sports jacket, his pressed pants, and his tan leather shoes. Even his bearing was different, the Russian thought, his shoulders back, his head, high at first, but then bent down as his pencil struck paper.

Fedya had carefully planned his search, determined to move from hotel to hotel until he found the visitors. He talked only to people he felt were unlikely to report his questioning to the authorities—a maid, a bartender, a busboy, a porter—asking them if they had seen his American "friends," a white woman and a black man. He started with the upscale hotels, the Opera, the Premier Palace, the Hyatt and worked his way down to more affordable lodgings, to the likes of the Dnipro, the Riviera, and the Rus. But after two fruitless days, he had exhausted his list of places that were likely to attract Americans and was losing confidence in his approach. It was then that he saw the African. "Luck," he said, to himself. "Foolish luck."

The Russian watched as the American flipped to a new page in his sketchbook and looked around the vast grounds of the monument. When the American turned in his direction, Fedya ducked behind one of the dozens of World War II tanks that stood in historic salute on the cement grounds. When he again looked out, the American was momentarily hidden from his vision by a small group of Japanese tourists, their omnipresent cameras equipped with long lenses.

Fedya had hoped to follow the American back to his hotel, but as the minutes accumulated, he felt unequipped for the role, his ponytail too long and too unusual to go unnoticed, his worn jeans and faded polo shirt out of place. To avoid detection, he would have to hang back, but hesitation was an invitation to lose sight of his target, and there was no guarantee that the man was planning to return to his hotel without making a stop here or meeting someone there. No, he had to do something bold, he decided, something risky but clever.

To avoid looking like a mugger, Fedya waited until the American was standing next to other people before he approached. He held a pack of Marlboro cigarettes in his hand.

"Do you have a light," he asked in a thick accent.

The American looked confused. Fedya put a cigarette in his mouth and mimed it being lit.

"No," the American said, "I have no matches."

"Would you like a guide to show you around?" Fedya asked. When he saw that he was not understood, he tried again, this time speaking more slowly and enunciating each syllable.

The American smiled. "No, but thank you."

"How about a girl? Would you like a nice Ukrainian beauty?"

The American began to turn away.

"Benjamin Palmer," Fedya whispered. "Would you like Benjamin Palmer?"

# Chapter 13

Caitlin quickly applied some powder and lipstick, brushed her hair, and put on a dark blue pants suit. She studied her reflection in the bedroom bureau's mirror, straightened out the collar of her off-white blouse, and fastened the single button of her jacket. The image was right, she felt, businesslike yet feminine.

Two young men with Germanic accents were arguing with the attractive dark-haired woman who was standing behind the registration desk when Caitlin entered the lobby. It was almost noon.

Only men were in the bar when Caitlin entered. One was sitting by himself, rapidly typing on a wireless device; three others were gathered in a booth, deep in conversation.

She turned around to see if she might have missed Anna sitting in the lobby, but no woman other than the clerk was in sight. Now what, she thought. Had she spent so much time dressing that her contact had gotten nervous and left? Or was this just another Koslov style gambit and Anna was watching from some corner, delaying her appearance to emphasize the drama of the moment?

Caitlin sat at a small table near the bar's entrance and ordered a glass of white wine. She would give Baranova fifteen minutes, maybe a half-hour, but no more. They both had cards to play. Anna might be holding her husband, but she had the money. They needed each other. She looked at her watch when the wine came, feeling uneasy and very much alone. She looked at it again after she had taken a couple of sips and prepared to be humiliated.

She heard the kitchen door swing open behind her, and, in a moment, a foreign voice with a foreign accent came over her shoulder. "May I join you?" the voice asked.

Anna hadn't misinformed. Even her unsmiling face was attractive. Her large eyes dramatized by a touch of mascara, her pert nose slightly turned up, her large forehead sparsely covered with mobile amber bangs. "Ms. Baranova?" Caitlin said.

The slight young woman reached out to shake hands. "Anna Baranova," she said. "Please excuse my lateness. The traffic, you know, it gets worse every day."

"I thought you had called from the hotel."

Anna smiled before pulling out a chair and sitting down. She looked at what Caitlin was drinking and ordered a glass of white wine for herself. "It comes from Georgia, you know. They make good white wine—drinkable, you would say, right? The red wine is not so good. I prefer the French."

Anna took off a navy, one-button wool blazer and threw it over the third chair. Her red sheath dress would have been at home in the window of a Manhattan boutique, Caitlin thought. The delicately cut neckline revealed Anna's porcelain flesh and evidenced her thinness.

"You're a reporter, I hear. What newspaper?"

"I'm not a print reporter, at least not recently. I work on television."

"Ah," Anna said, "that was something I always wanted to do, be a television star."

"I'm far from a star."

"Do you think my face would look good on television? I take nice photographs."

"You have an attractive facial structure and lovely skin. You'd be perfect," Caitlin said. How long would this go on, she thought, this feeling each other out?

"The man you are traveling with, Peter Johnson. I was expecting to meet him."

"He's touring the city. He'll be back any minute."

"He's a reporter as well?"

"He once was, but he has been teaching journalism recently."

"Is he a friend of your husband?"

"No. They've never even met," Caitlin said.

She watched as Anna Baranova finished her wine and looked around for the waiter. "Another?" she asked Caitlin. When the American shook off the suggestion, Anna raised one finger and pointed to her glass.

"Then why is he here?" the young Ukrainian asked.

Caitlin kept a bland expression. She had expected that people who did not know them would think she and Peter were romantically involved. Proclaiming innocence, she decided, would only make them more curious, so she decided to let people think what they wished. "I asked him to come along and help me find my husband. We are old friends."

Anna's angelic face hardened. "Koslov said you were planning to make a film of your search, for television or the movies," she said crisply.

"We were going to make a documentary, but Koslov suggested we give that up. It would lower our chances of finding Benjamin."

"And why did your husband come to Ukraine?"

"I'm not certain. We are separated and hadn't kept close contact with one another recently."

"And still you came all this way to find him. Don't you find that strange?"

Caitlin shrugged her shoulders. "He is still important to me, Anna. Our separation has not destroyed our concern for one another."

"And what had he planned to do when he got here?"

"He mentioned visiting a city, Peczenizyn. I'm not sure why."

Anna seemed ready to say something when Caitlin caught sight of Peter standing in the lobby, and abruptly got up from her seat and waved to him.

"Peter Johnson, this is Anna Baranova."

He reached out to take her hand. "A pleasure," he said.

Anna removed her blazer from the third seat and laid it across her lap. "Will you join us?" she said while pointing to her glass.

"Just water, thank you."

In a voice loud enough to carry across the room, Anna said something in Ukrainian to the barman who had just poured her drink. Moments later, a waiter delivered an unopened bottle of sparkling water and three empty glasses. He ceremoniously opened the bottle.

"Did you have a good morning?" Anna asked after tasting her wine.

"I spent the entire morning at the monument that celebrates your victory in the Great Patriotic War. I hadn't realized how vast it was. I could have spent a whole day without difficulty."

"It is worth a full week. You should go back then," Anna suggested. "It is a magnificent place. Perhaps Caitlin will join you?"

Peter nodded agreement, lifted his glass, and said, "So we finally meet. Have you two made arrangements to free Benjamin?"

"We are just introducing ourselves," Anna said curtly.

"So I haven't missed anything?"

There was something odd in Peter's voice, but Caitlin couldn't quite make it out. An unexpected circumspection, she thought, or maybe suspicion. And he was not smiling. "We haven't gotten to that topic," Caitlin said.

"So what have you been talking about? The weather?"

"I don't do business with people until I know them clearly," Anna said. "I'm sure you understand."

"All I understand is that we've been waiting for three days for you to make contact. I don't think that's a good way to begin to bargain," Peter argued.

Caitlin's head snapped back. Rudeness was not something she had expected from him. She hoped that he knew what he was doing.

"So you're a businessman, Mr. Johnson. What business brings you to Kyiv?"

"I'm a professor, not a businessman. I'm here to get Benjamin Palmer home."

"And what business brought him to Kyiv?" Anna continued.

"He came as a tourist and was kidnapped," Caitlin answered, unable to keep her growing annoyance from registering in her voice.

"Koslov must have told you the full story, Anna. I don't understand what you are up to," Peter added.

"It should be evident, Mr. Johnson. I'm trying to find out what you are up to."

Caitlin's patience had worn thin. She blurted out, "I want to get my husband back and I'm willing to pay. We're not working for the State Department. We're not CIA."

"I never thought you were. But there are always other considerations."

"I don't understand," Caitlin said.

Anna Baranova did not clarify her comment. She finished her glass of wine and began to move out of her chair.

"Who are you? We've told you about ourselves, but we know nothing about you," Peter asked.

"I work for the deputy mayor. I will arrange for you to meet him. Do not worry. I am a careful worker. I move slowly, but I move with preciseness."

She rose and put on her designer blazer. When the Americans got up to say goodbye, she shook her head quickly, her hair jostling, and gave them a broad smile. "Enjoy the city. I will leave a message at the hotel. We will meet in his office, tomorrow afternoon if possible. So do not wait. I will be in touch."

"And what is the deputy mayor's name?" Caitlin asked.

"Pavlov Karpenko. He will know what is best to do."

~

They stood behind their chairs and watched Anna Baranova walk out of the bar and into the hotel's lobby. Her slim figured grace and red dress caught the attention of the man at the bar.

A lunchtime crowd had begun to fill the tables. Most of the customers were Ukrainian, Peter concluded, government officials and businessmen having lunch on somebody else's tab. It was an ungracious thought, he knew, but that didn't make it false.

Peter lifted his glass of water without sitting down, drank it dry, and thought of how good it would feel to have some scotch. He ran his eyes over the crowd to see if there was anyone studying them. The men eyeing Caitlin seemed only interested in the salacious, but he didn't want to take any chances. "Let's get out of here," he said, "and go somewhere private."

"We can order lunch in my room."

"I think we might be better off outside," Peter said, his voice insistent.

"Do you think our rooms are bugged?"

"Most probably not, but when you don't know, why risk it?"

Thick clouds had come down the Dnieper River and the air smelled of coming rain. Peter tucked his hand under Caitlin's elbow as they made their way toward the river. In case they were being watched, he took the precaution of smiling as if he had nothing of importance to say. "Anna is not the only person to contact us today, Caitlin. Give out a laugh now and again as I tell you about my meeting this morning. Fedya is his name. He claims to work for the person who is holding Benjamin."

Caitlin let out a short chuckle. "Was he believable?"

"Compared to Anna Baranova, he was a fountain of knowledge."

Peter described how Fedya had contacted him at the Monument to the Great Patriotic War, and how they had strolled along the embankment of the Dnieper River. "His English was very basic, but I think I understood most of what he was trying to tell me. He knew that we were waiting to be contacted by Baranova, and told me that she worked for the deputy mayor. He told me they were not holding Benjamin and didn't know where he was. He suggested we should be cautious with her and be sure not to tell her we had been contacted by someone else. If we did, the deal would blow up."

"Was he threatening?" Caitlin asked. She was unmasked, her expression and tone of voice projecting her anxiety.

Peter, too, could not continue the charade. His smile disappeared, and his face turned thoughtful. "He said it in a very factual way, but there was a clear implication that more than one party was involved and that we had to deal with both if we were to accomplish our mission."

"How are we expected to deal with two interests and their not knowing of one another?"

"They know of each other, but only one of them knows we are in touch with both."

Caitlin stopped walking and waited for Peter to face her. "That bit of information doesn't make me happy." Her chuckle evidenced nervousness, not gaiety. Her eyes moistened. "We don't even know if he's alive. We're being jerked around."

"Fedya claimed he saw Benjamin three or four days ago, right before he and his boss headed off for Kyiv. He said Benjamin was in very good shape, his spirits high, and his humor intact."

"And you believe him?" she said accusatorily.

"I can assure you, when you meet him you will trust him. If he isn't honest, he's one of the world's best con men."

"And how do you know he's not working with Anna? That he's seen Benjamin? That his boss isn't fictional?"

Peter stepped back to study his companion. Frustration covered her face, her thin lips closed, her eyes unfocused, and her skin sallow.

"It's gotten ridiculous. When do we admit that enough is enough, pack our things, and go home?" Caitlin said.

"Today is what we've been waiting for Cat. We've been contacted. We are in the game. Why would you want to quit now?"

"I don't want to argue. I want to cry."

He walked a few paces behind her as they made their way back to the hotel, wondering what had precipitated this unexpected breakdown, questioning if it would last for a day or an hour, if it was only psychological or was biology involved. He felt like a male chauvinist thinking it was her period, and shook the thought loose by adding up the number of reasons she had for feeling frustrated.

When she stopped at a red light, he took her arm.

Caitlin immediately began to talk. "Anna is a horror, oozing sex like a viper, playing us like we were paper dolls. She didn't tell us one thing, not one. Instead of our questioning her, she drilled us. And you're fictional Fedya, did he show you a picture of Benjamin?"

"I don't know, Caitlin, I've never seen Benjamin, or pictures of him."

Caitlin stopped short and grabbed his arm. "Show me."

"He took me through some images on a digital camera's LCD. He didn't have hard copies and didn't want to make any. The man had a full beard and was wearing what looked like Soviet fatigues. A couple of shots were of him alone, standing next to a big SUV. One image was of him and Fedya. There were woods in the background. Was it Benjamin? I'm not sure even you could tell. The beard hid a great deal of his face."

"I could tell," Caitlin said. She continued to walk toward the hotel, this time with a little more determination.

They walked silently up the inclined street for a few blocks. Peter took her elbow again when the traffic stopped them, hoping that his touch would communicate his empathy, would tell her that he understood her frustration, her anxiety. He wanted her old mood to return, the optimistic, unrealistic attitude that he had so often found irritating. He wanted her to be certain again that she'd prevail, convinced that she would succeed. This was not the time for her to turn defeatist.

"I'm hungry," she said, as if surprised by her observation. "We haven't eaten since breakfast."

"And then you ate very little," Peter observed, alerted to the possibility of a change in her mood.

Caitlin stopped walking. Peter watched as the blue of her eyes grew lighter, and her face was conquered by a smile.

"Is this your oblique way of telling me I'm too skinny?"

"You have a perfect figure."

"But not as perfect as Anna Baranova's figure?" she replied with a snicker.

# Chapter 14

"Two hours," Marya predicted. "It is only 100 kilometers away, but the roads are unpredictable, Benya."

She did the driving, sitting high in the Toyota Land Cruiser, looking every bit the woman in command, independent, strong, handsome. She brushed Benjamin's hand aside when he ran it over her bare thigh. She chided him when he reached over and teased her breast, when he kissed her on the cheek. He played with the radio, now and again locating a station that played popular music, mostly sung in Ukrainian, but every so often, an American rock group came on the air. He didn't recognize any of the tunes or the performers, but he enjoyed hearing the vowels of his people, the consonants that flowed over American airways. For reasons he did not explore, he felt at home, sitting next to a woman he wanted, looking out over a land, at least at the beginning of the trip, which had become familiar.

Before long, they left the broad expanse of the rolling prairie and entered the narrow foothills of the Eastern Carpathian Mountains, the foliage lush and dark-green, the abundant streams and rivers no longer at their crest, yet still full of churning water. At one turn of the road, he was reminded of the Berkshire Mountains in Massachusetts, the hills small and close together, the underbrush undisturbed, but then they drove over a rise and he thought of the Catskills in New York, the round topped peaks of its mountains, its wide fertile valleys.

"Where are we," he asked as they drove through a small hamlet of a dozen houses or so.

"I don't know its name, if it has one. We are entering Hutsul country, you know, the land of Oleksa Dovbush."

"The illustrious Ukrainian Robin Hood."

"No other."

"Are we getting near Peczenizyn?" he asked expectantly.

"I'm sorry Benya. We are not going near Peczenizyn. We are heading for a small village, not a city. Ilya forbade me from taking you to cities. He's even worried about this trip."

"Is he afraid I'll escape?"

"He's afraid that someone more ruthless than he will steal you for ransom. That's his fear."

"Or is that a story he wants you to tell me so that I won't try to run away?"

He watched as her expression turned dour. "Do you feel compelled to try to escape?"

"Not from you, Marya. But I don't want to remain a prisoner. You can understand that. I want to be free. I want to touch base with the people who must be concerned by my disappearance."

"And get away from Ilya and me?"

He didn't know how to answer. There was no simple truth. Yes, he wanted to get away. How could he not? But he was glad she was in his life.

"Do we get serious or do we just drive to the wedding and dance our hearts out?" he asked.

"It is too late not to be serious," she said. There was leeway in her voice.

"I came to Ukraine to give living a larger purpose, Marya, not to be kidnapped. On the good days, I love waking up in the forest. I love the river. I love to hear the voices of the children mix with the chirping of the birds. Most of all I love you. But not all days are good."

He had not said that before, that he loved her, and now that the words had slipped off his tongue, he wondered if it were true. Was Marya more to him than a temporary shelter? Had he reached for a romantic word to prevent a depressing conversation? He noticed the smile on her face and relaxed.

"You love having sex with me," she said with a fabricated snarl.

"I tolerate the sex out of love for you. Celibacy would be much easier to handle. It puts less pressure on the back."

Her spontaneous laugh was full-throated and contagious. Benjamin couldn't help but laugh in turn.

"To many it would be idyllic. The earth is beautiful this time of year. We have enough to eat. We have as much work as we choose. We have the river. We have each other. We could build a little cabin for Ilya and tell him to visit only when invited."

"There is not much chance of that," she interrupted.

"But it is not something that I chose, Marya. It has been forced upon me, and no matter how good, it is alien, it is wrong. I have a duty to my previous life. If I am to alter it, I have to do it on my own terms. Do you understand? People are only happy when they make their own choices."

"I wonder," she said as she turned the wheel to avoid a muddy depression in the road. "Maybe we are all happier when there is little choice, when we have to live with what is before us."

"We'll never know, will we? We were raised to believe there are choices. It may guarantee discontent, but it is our inheritance."

"What would you choose, Benya, if everything were in front of you, if no one would be hurt by your decision, if you could start with a blank page and write in whatever you wanted?"

Benjamin looked out on the lush countryside, the sun halfway to its zenith, and light-gray clouds blowing in from the west. A turtle was standing by the side of the road, its large head stuck into the air, and a small falcon was silently riding the wind. They were unburdened by the illusion of choice, he thought, unburdened by a compulsion to find joy. "I don't know, Marya. I don't know what I'd choose. I'd like a penthouse in Manhattan. I'd like you to be happy living with me; with two children who were guaranteed admission into Harvard, and a dog that knew how to use a toilet."

"That's asking for a great deal."

"I'd be willing to bargain away the dog," Benjamin said in a serious voice.

"And would you be willing to bargain away me?"

"Well, that would depend on the size of the penthouse," he answered.

"Nasty," she said without humor.

"The question itself wasn't very kind," Benjamin said. "But let me put the same question to you, "If you could choose the rest of your life, what would you want?"

"That's easy. I'd want three healthy children, a husband devoted only to me and my offspring, and a job that paid enough so that he could do the housework. And I'd want to feel appreciated at work."

"But no penthouse?"

"I can't imagine what one would be like. Here we are," she exclaimed, and pointed out of the front window toward the small village they were approaching. "We are just on time."

Benjamin leaned over to read the car's clock, pausing for a second to kiss Marya on the shoulder. It was 11:00 a.m., Eastern European Summer Time.

A cold rain had begun to fall minutes before Marya pulled over to the side of the road. She parked close to a fenced yard full of chickens. "This is the groom's parents' house," Marya said as she wrapped a bright red and blue kerchief around her head and tied it under her neck. "I do have an extra scarf, if you would like to keep your hair dry?" she said while they were still sitting in the car. "Or would you prefer to use the umbrella I have in the back?"

He was hoping it would be a large black umbrella, the type you still see on the streets of London, one that makes a fashion statement when it is closed. But it was a compact pale-blue umbrella, designed to be folded into a woman's carrying bag, its slender handle made for a small hand.

They crossed the small overgrown field that separated the house from the road, stomping one behind the other to the vibrant Ukrainian folk music that was coming from behind the house.

Marya took Benya's hand as they merged into the crowd that was walking along the side door of the house, and she joined the company in the singing of a Ukrainian wedding round, its lilting words full of good cheer. Once in the backyard, the guests gathered around a row of tables covered with trays of small cakes, breads, and cookies, and poured themselves drinks from opened bottles of vodka. A handsome young man dressed in a cream-colored suit silenced the crowd by offering a toast. He made a long-winded statement in Ukrainian, drank half of the liquid in his glass, and threw the rest over his shoulder. People cheered and followed his lead, drinking vodka and throwing some over their shoulders with little thought that people might be standing behind them. Many of the women were holding small umbrellas over their heads to shelter their stylized hairdos from the rain. Protection from the vodka was a side benefit. The men stood around bareheaded, their suit jackets absorbing the light rainfall, their hair wet. Benjamin closed his umbrella and made his way to the table. He handed a drink to Marya. He poured a short one for himself, swallowed most of it, and threw the rest over his shoulder. Marya's laugh caught the attention of a stout and gray-haired older man whose cream-colored attire matched that of the young toast maker. He immediately screamed her name and pushed past the few people in front of him to get to her. He was a good five inches shorter than Marya, and stood on his toes when he wrapped his arms around her and gave her a long tight hug. When he finally let go, he kissed her on one cheek and then the other.

Benjamin couldn't understand what the stranger was saying when Marya brought him over to shake hands with "the American," but the remark made her blush. "And who am I meeting?" Benjamin asked as his hand was being squeezed.

"This is the father of the groom, and a very good and important friend of Ilya."

"Ilya," the older man said, pulled Benjamin's shoulders down and kissed the American on both cheeks. Then he said, according to Marya's translation, "Are you planning to get married today or just make babies?"

"He didn't really ask that, did he?" Benjamin said after the father of the groom had moved into the crowd.

"He's been in the vodka since sunrise. What do you think he asked you? Do you like the weather?"

"Since sunrise? Will he make it through the day?"

"Everyone will take a long afternoon nap before the evening reception. He'll be fine. His wife will make sure of that."

"Is that when he thinks we are going to make babies?"

Marya didn't bother to dignify the comment with a laugh.

The members of the band, who had been sitting on a bench next to the back of the house, slowly got to their feet and began to lead the crowd out of the backyard. A short, elderly violinist, decked out in a two-tone fedora, led the group. Close behind him were the four other members of the combo, a tall, balding saxophonist, a jovial accordionist, a percussionist whose brightly decorated instrument reminded Benjamin of the drums carried by circus clowns, and, finally, a tall, hefty man banging away on the hammer dulcimer that hung awkwardly from his neck and rested on his ample stomach. Whatever they were playing was well known to the guests who sang as they walked to the bride's house where, according to Marya, the groom was to ask his fiancé's parents for permission to marry her.

When the groom, surrounded by a number of men his age, approached the house, a short and rotund middle-aged woman, dressed in a white lacy wedding dress, jumped out of the front door. The crowd went into hysterics.

"So?" Benjamin said to Marya, assuming his question was evident.

"She's the fake bride. An old tradition, Benya. A friend of the family, or a relative, I imagine. If there are any evil spirits around, they will latch on to her, and by the time they find out their mistake, it will be too late. The marriage will have been consummated."

"Well, that part I understand."

"I'm sure you do."

The crowd moved into the tight interior of the bride's home where a long table offered a feast of breads, cold meats, and varieties of potato salad. Opened bottles of Russian brandy and Ukrainian vodka stood between the plates and breadbaskets. Those who could, found seats, the others, including Benjamin and Marya, ate standing up. The band continued to play cheerful songs written for joyous celebrations, its members now and then imbibing on a drink offered by one of the guests.

The bride, dressed in a light-blue suit, its jacket tight around her thin waist, its slimming skirt cut below her knees, arrived with her parents. The mother, whose figure could compete with her daughter's, wore a similar outfit, its cloth not as fine, its color a degree darker. The bride looked pale and stunned; her mother, in sharp contrast, looked exceptionally cheerful, her cheeks bursting with color, her large blue eyes darting back and forth as she welcomed guests to the party.

The bride's father waved the band into temporary silence, lifted a glass of clear liquid, made what Benjamin assumed was a toast, swallowed half of the beverage, and threw the rest over his shoulder, dampening the heads of a couple of children who were moving behind him. Tall and thin, with broad shoulders and an open face, he looked uncomfortable in a gray, poorly tailored suit. He filled his glass again, and swallowed it dry. He was built for denims, Benjamin thought, with a rake over his shoulder and mud-coated boots on his feet.

The band began to play again. Some of the guests sang, others concentrated on the vodka and food.

Benjamin washed down a piece of black bread with a shot of vodka, took a glass of beer from a woman who seemed to be offering drinks to anyone in reach, and followed it up with a shot of brandy. It was far more drink than he was used to. His brain began to fog; his balance became uncertain. He began to move around the other guests, hoping to make his way outside for some fresh air. But before he had made much progress, Marya elbowed her way next to him, pulled at his sleeve, handed him a small glass of vodka, and kissed his cheek. "Keep looking at me," she said in an unexpectedly grave voice, her face flushed. "And smile as if you're happy to be talking to me. I think we are being watched. An overweight middle-aged man, wearing a heavy brown suit and a dark-blue shirt, has been keeping his eyes on us. He looks out of place. No one is talking to him."

"I hadn't noticed him."

"Don't look for him and don't go outside. In a few minutes, we will all be leaving for the church and the marriage ceremony. Let's keep in the middle of the crowd. If he comes close, don't talk. Speaking English is not going to help."

Benjamin placed the drink on the table, surprised by the panic in Marya's voice. Did she think he would forget his promise and foolishly seek somebody's help, or was she afraid that a curious guest would try to uncover who he was and what he was doing there? He nervously squeezed himself into a vacated spot on a table's wooden bench, and, to blend into the company, put a couple of slices of sausage on a thick piece of white bread. As he bit into his open sandwich, he searched his surroundings. There was no mistaking Marya's suspect. He stood apart, his short hair, the thick gold jewelry hanging from his neck, distinguished him from the others. He was holding a cell phone up to his face and pointing it at Benjamin.

Benjamin quickly looked away, thinking that central casting couldn't have selected a more evident looking hood. He took another bite of his sandwich and focused his eyes on the bride and groom who were seated on the other side of the table and a little to his left. The groom was feeding her a piece of cake, smiling broadly, his skin darkened by an alcoholic flush. She seemed only slightly more relaxed than when Benjamin first saw her, sitting stiffly, her mouth wide open, and her eyes shut.

Someone shouted in Ukrainian, and the guests began a cheerful song. The groom responded by kissing his bride, her mouth still full of cake. They had to kiss a second time before the company ended the chant and slowly begin to exit the house and head for the church.

By the time the last guest made it halfway up the path that led away from the groom's home, Marya was walking alongside Benjamin. Unanswerable questions muddled his thinking. Who had sent this man? Was he on a mission for the State Department? Was he in the employ of the CIA? Or was he working for Ukraine, and trying to rescue a kidnapped American and end what could be an international embarrassment?

"What do you expect me to do?" Benjamin asked Marya.

"I expect you to do nothing foolish. He is not here to help you, Benjamin. Of that I can assure you."

He didn't believe her. She couldn't possibly know enough to be so certain. Her judgment was clouded by fear, he decided. Fear that her prisoner would break away, that Ilya would be angered, that both of them would end up being punished for holding him hostage. But he was sober enough to know that his thoughts were polluted by optimism, filled with an unproven promise that rescuers had finally found him, that there were people in this crowd who could initiate his travel home.

Marya's grip grew tighter. Her bottom lip quivered, and her complexion lost color.

He wanted to pull away from her, to run to this outlandishly dressed middle-aged man and shout, "I'm Benjamin Palmer. I'm Benjamin Palmer." He had begun to pull Marya's fingers from his forearm when a young man in a gray waterproof jacket jumped in front of him. "American?" the wild-haired young man asked in a thick Slavic accent, his eyes in a squint. "American?" he repeated.

Marya began to shout at the stranger. A stream of words, rapid and thick, poured out of her mouth, silencing Benjamin and causing the young man to take a step back. But it did not stop him. "American," he yelled in a voice that carried through the crowd. "American," he said again with no hint of a question mark.

Benjamin could see the burly middle-aged man break quickly through the swarm of celebrants, his overweight frame moving ungracefully over the uneven pebbled path.

Marya continued to shout, but now she forcefully projected her voice over the intruder's head and to the crowd. Whatever she was saying was getting to the young stranger. His large face turned a deep red; his eyes grew even angrier. He slapped her across the face, forcing her to let go of Benjamin and stumble to her left. When she regained her balance, he struck her again.

Thoughts of escape were blown away with each slap. Benjamin lurched at the younger man, throwing his shoulder into his stomach and knocking him a few steps backward. But the assailant kept his balance and lunged at Benjamin, driving one fist into his stomach and the other into the side of his head. Benjamin's knees buckled. His face hit the weed-covered turf; his ears filled with alien voices and unfathomable words. He heard, or so he thought, the middle-aged man bark out orders and the younger man yell something in return. Marya began to scream. The band, which had never stopped playing wedding tunes, had turned around and was now coming closer, their ever-louder music turning militaristic. By the time Benjamin raised his head high enough to see what was going on, four men had pinned his assailant to the ground, and a larger group had surrounded the middle-aged man and was forcing him to retreat. An elderly woman was threatening the younger man with her umbrella, while an old man waved a walking stick over his head like a Cossack and shouted curses into the air. Only the hammer dulcimer was being played. No one sang.

Benjamin struggled to regain his balance as Marya helped him to his feet. His body shook; he gasped for air.

"Come," Marya demanded. "We must make it to the car."

The groom's father put his arm under Benjamin's and helped him into the back seat of the Land Cruiser, then he jumped into the driver's seat and Marya handed him the key. He drove around a bend in the road and over a hill before pulling onto a half-hidden road that cut into a wheat field. He drove toward an assortment of farm buildings, their gray wooden exteriors bleached by the sun and stained by rain, and into a dilapidated barn. There, he parked next to a Lada station wagon. He exchanged a few words with Marya and handed her the keys to the smaller car. She and Benjamin immediately drove off.

"Cell phone service is not perfect from the Carpathians," Marya said. "But we think, whoever they are, took cell phone photographs of us and of the Toyota. That's why we have a new car. Ilya will eventually get the Toyota back … or maybe not. It is not an immediate worry."

"Who were they?" he asked.

"I don't know."

"But the wedding guests seemed to know. Why else would they have ganged up on them?"

"They were reminders of the past, Benya, of secret police and party thugs. They know Ilya. To them, you and I are friends of Ilya. They didn't need other reasons."

He sat silently looking over the countryside, but his mood prevented him from seeing its beauty. Dull pains ran down his back and his head throbbed. He ran a finger in front of his face to test his vision. He blinked his eyes to see if he was overly sensitive to light. There was no evident sign of a concussion. His jaw worked. His teeth were still in place. Time alone would handle the swollen lip, the bruised cheeks.

"I thought I was going to lose you, Benjamin. I pictured you mistaking their intentions and running off with them thinking you were being rescued. No one rescues anyone anymore. Not here, not in Ukraine or in Russia. Not anywhere, I expect. They would have used you for their own ends. We have all become buyers and sellers, Benya, or stealers and sellers, or inheritors and sellers."

He would never know, he realized, as he dismissed her cynicism. In a perfect world, there would have been more refined rescuers, people dressed by Brooks Brothers, who spoke Ivy League English, and wore lapel pins that tied them to the State Department, or the American Embassy, or the European Union, or the United Nations. But he would have been ecstatic to be liberated by goons in overalls, with shit on their boots and tobacco between their teeth. It was the wanting him back that was important, proof that his disappearance had meant something to someone, that he was of some importance. Perhaps Marya was right in thinking they were just another pair of rogues, and he should be thankful that the wedding party had helped him escape harsh treatment and further enslavement. But he couldn't bring himself to thoroughly believe her.

Marya emitted a Russian phrase, her facial muscles taut, her eyes riveted on what was in front of the station wagon.

"And what did that mean?" Benjamin asked.

Marya laughed. "It was an expression of relief. We are away and safe. It was also an expression of personal need. I have to pee. Soon!"

Her physical need broke his mood and turned him to thinking about her. "How are you?" he asked. "He slapped you hard."

"My face is fine. It's my bladder that is complaining."

She pulled the Lada off the paved road and parked on the edge of a recently harvested field. Mounds of drying hay were off in the distance. "Don't look," she demanded as she walked quickly away.

"Of course not," he answered. "I'm a gentleman."

She faced away from him when she lifted her skirt, pulled down her panties, and squatted. He looked only long enough to implant the image in his memory, and then he forced himself to turn away. She was his love, he realized, this foreign woman, awkwardly crouching over the flat land, her body shyly turned away from him, the sun making her dark hair glisten. He wanted to be angry with her, to be furious that she might have prevented his liberation, to be bitter about her complicity in his captivity, but deeper feelings prevented his outrage.

He began to laugh as she walked toward him.

"You looked," she accused.

"Just for a second."

"And when you have to go, I'll not stop. You'll have to wet your pants."

"Now that's a serious threat," he said, suspecting that she could never bring herself to carry it off, if not for his comfort, then for the benefit of the car.

She cooed something in Russian, her voice full of tender vibrations, and fought against smiling. He held her tight against his body and, despite the pain from his wounded lips, gave her a long and lingering kiss.

"Thank you for protecting me," she said.

"I wasn't very effective."

"It cost you to help me. I know that. We may never know who they were. They would have taken you away from me, but I doubt if they would have taken you to a better place."

Milton's famous phrase, "it is better to rule in Hell than serve in Heaven," jumped into Benjamin's mind. He converted it into meaning "it is better to be free in Hell than a captive in Heaven," but when he looked at Marya's profile, he knew he was wrong.

"You will be free soon, Benya. Ilya would not be in Kyiv if he weren't certain he could make arrangements for you. You will be free to make your own choices. I will miss you, but life is full of losses."

When they got back in the car, he wanted to say something reassuring, words that predicted a continuation and not an end to their love affair. But hope without reality is a lie, he decided, and sat silently.

"And if Ilya's mission fails, I will persuade him to get you home. It is a promise," she said.

Benjamin slumped in his seat and wondered what would happen next.

# Chapter 15

Pavlov did not look up from the majestic mahogany desk when Peter and Caitlin entered his office. He kept his head bowed, his eyes peering over a leather-bound document, one temple of his wireframe eyeglasses stuck between his clenched teeth, the spectacle's thin lenses swinging awkwardly below his chin. His posture didn't change when his guests sat down on the large upholstered couch that hugged the wall to his right. He didn't seem to notice when they refused Anna's offer of hot tea or coffee.

"Yes," he finally said to Anna as she stood at attention in front of his desk.

"They are here," she answered.

"Good, I'll be with them in a minute," he muttered as if his guests were in another room. He flipped to the next page.

Anna moved the large wooden chair that stood at one end of the couch so that she could look directly at the Americans. "Are you certain you do not want something to drink?" she asked, her amber eyes—dim under the somber lights of the bar—moving from Caitlin to Peter, then back again.

"A bottle of water, please," Caitlin said. "That would be nice."

Anna used her cell phone. "It will be here in a minute," she said after giving instructions in Ukrainian to whoever answered her call.

Peter watched the deputy mayor underline a sentence, turn the folder slightly, and make a note in a margin. Then he turned to the next page. It was a practiced performance designed to show his importance, to emphasize the responsibilities of his office, to make his visitors thankful for every moment he graciously spends on their concerns. Peter was not surprised by this bureaucratic theater, but he was surprised that the Ukrainians had spoken to each other in English, a thickly accented classroom English, but English nonetheless. Was it to make Caitlin and him feel comfortable, or was it to keep the conversation out of the understanding of less linguistically able political adversaries? "No conversation should be considered private," Peter had once been told before covering a story in the Soviet Union. He had not forgotten the advice.

Pavlov closed the leather folder. "So we finally meet," he said, leaning back into his chair and twirling his eyeglasses in his right hand. "How long have you been in Kyiv?"

"This is the fifth day," Caitlin said, her voice pitched higher than normal.

"And in the Ukraine?" the deputy mayor continued.

"We flew into Kyiv. We haven't been anywhere else in your country," she answered.

"And you?" he said, addressing Peter.

"We've been traveling together. Hasn't Anna or Koslov filled you in?"

Pavlov's facial muscles tightened. He slowly rose out of his chair and walked to the front of his desk. After carelessly pushing aside some papers, he perched himself on its rich mahogany surface and looked down on his guests. "Anna Baranova tells me you are a professor, Mr. Johnson. Do you teach about Ukraine?"

"I teach journalism, with a concentration in television coverage and documentaries."

"And are you planning to make a documentary in Ukraine?"

"Why are we doing this?" Caitlin snapped. "You know why we are here. I want to make arrangements to get my husband back."

"Two journalists sneaking around Ukraine, claiming to be looking for a missing husband, with no interest in telling a story ... why would you expect me to believe such a story?"

Caitlin's answer was cut short by a soft knock on the office door. Before anyone could say anything, the young man who had welcomed the Americans into the building quietly entered Pavlov's office with four glasses and two opened bottles of sparkling water. He placed them on the coffee table in front of the couch. Anna said, "thank you" in English. The young man smiled, walked backward for a few paces before turning around, and left without saying a word. Peter thought he noticed him dip his head in obeisance.

"Why else would we be here?" Peter said as Anna poured water into his glass, annoyed that Pavlov was acting like Anna had during their interview in the hotel, asking them questions that seemed to have no purpose. "If you don't know where Benjamin Palmer is, or have no way of helping him get released, just tell us. We can go home. There is nothing keeping us here. No journalism. No television show."

"Have you been in touch with your embassy?" Pavlov asked.

"Not since we've been here," Caitlin said.

"See what I mean? You claim to have a husband who came to Ukraine to visit Peczenizyn, in Hutsul country."

Peter quickly interrupted him. "So you have been in touch with Koslov?"

"I've been in touch with your embassy. Your ambassador has kept me informed ever since the first ransom call was placed. If you had been in touch with them, you'd know that."

"I didn't think it would help my husband get free if we told the embassy what we were doing or whom we were asking for help," Caitlin said.

"So they don't know Koslov sent you to Anna Baranova?" Pavlov asked.

"No," Caitlin replied.

"I wouldn't worry. Your embassy knows how to keep secrets," Pavlov said. His face turned sour.

"I'm prepared to pay handsomely for my husband's release. You just have to tell me how."

Pavlov looked at his watch. He pointed to the tray and Anna carried a glass of water to him. They exchanged some words in Ukrainian.

"The deputy mayor has some important matters to attend to. He wants me to apologize for him, but you will have to come back tomorrow. In the meantime, I suggest that you stay in Kyiv. The hotel will hold on to your passports until this affair is over. And please leave your cell phones with them as well."

"Are you forcibly detaining us in Kyiv?" Peter asked. There was an astonished inflection in his voice, as if the question itself came out of a second rate movie about the Soviet Union, with commissars in tight uniforms threatening tourists who had mistakenly walked into a government building, or had taken pictures while their bus passed an industrial plant. He couldn't bring himself to believe this was happening, and he couldn't help but be alarmed.

"We are just being cautious, Mr. Johnson. Forcible would mean handcuffs and leg irons," Pavlov said. He twisted around and smashed his half-smoked cigarette into a large crystal ashtray. It was already full of butts.

~

"Fucking bastards," Caitlin said as soon as they exited the municipal building. She repeated the expletives as they crossed a wide boulevard and began to scurry through downtown Kyiv. She repeated them again when they finally sat at a table on the outdoor patio of a small restaurant and ordered tea and open-faced sausage sandwiches.

She hated the way she felt, anxious and angry and deeply frightened, her security vanished, her sense of control stolen. She loathed Pavlov. She had felt violated as his eyes undressed her when they first met; she felt assaulted when he incriminated her in some bizarre crime she couldn't even imagine. When he smashed his cigarette out, she imagined it burning through her skin. And Anna, what was she to make of her? Pavlov's whore, she decided, brainless and empty minded. She reached into her handbag for the cell phone she had rented at Boryspil International Airport and placed it on the table before the waiter had taken their order.

"And whom do you plan to call, if the phone still works, the White House?" Peter said sarcastically.

"I don't deserve that."

He closed his eyes for a moment. When he opened them again, they were kinder.

"You don't. We don't. What a hell of a morning. Do you understand what's going on?"

"We were being threatened, that's all I know. I want to think it's a game they're playing to get me to pay more, but I just don't know," Caitlin said.

"I have the feeling they're playing for time, that they don't know where Benjamin is being held. They're trying to find out and want us to stay in place until they do. If he's alive and they can get hold of him, they'll sell him to us. If he's dead, or if they can't find him, they'll figure out some other way of extracting money from us."

The hot tea came first, the sandwiches shortly afterwards. Peter finished his, but Caitlin had no appetite. She ended up offering Peter most of her meal. He accepted.

"We are different," she began. "When I'm under stress, my digestive system shuts down. Your appetite increases."

"That my downfall. I'm an addictive personality. That's why I can't drink. The more I feel I need one, or would enjoy one, the greater my desire to have one after another. I have no off button."

"If this morning's meeting didn't drive you to drink, I think you're pretty safe."

"I was thinking the same thing, Caitlin. But it did drive me to want a drink … many drinks. That concerns me more right now than whether or not we are being threatened. I don't want those bastards to push me off the wagon."

She suddenly realized how self-absorbed she had been, that she had not for a moment concerned herself about Peter. "I'm sorry," she said.

"About what?"

"About placing you in a difficult position. Perhaps it was a mistake to ask you to come along? If this morning was any clue, it's going to get worse."

She watched as he looked down at the table, as he ran his hand over his chin, as he took a deep breath and held it for five seconds. "You have enough to be concerned about without worrying about my drinking. Put that out of your mind, please. It will make it much easier to stay sober if you're not crowding over me."

She picked up the cell phone, ran her thumb over the keyboard, and put it down again. "I think we should call the American Embassy, just to let them know we are in Kyiv. Maybe they can set up a contact we can call each day, so if anything happens to us, they'll realize something is up. Do you think that's reasonable?"

"Let's leave it for now. It would be premature to blow the whistle on Pavlov, and I don't want them to know about Fedya."

"Fedya, of course, your lurking Russian. Maybe he can explain what is going on?" Caitlin said without conviction.

# Chapter 16

Abramowitz entered his dream. He was sitting on the side of the bed, his old eyes cried red, his swollen lips pale. "I didn't want this for you, Benjamin. I wanted only health and happiness. I wanted you to discover a soil so rich with experience that you could plant a new life, a land that would grow you tall enough to touch Heaven and talk to God. You must be very angry with me."

Benjamin saw himself lying in bed, a rough gray blanket pulled up to his neck. Clean-shaven, his fair hair cut short, he looked as he did when he first met Abramowitz almost a year before. "I am angry, bitterly angry, but at myself for being taken in by an old fool. How could I have been so dumb as to believe a half-demented ruin with a faded photograph, with stories about a dead world? I was an idiot to listen to you."

Abramowitz defended himself. "I told only the truth." He took a handkerchief from his vest pocket and patted his eyes.

"Truth, you say. Truth. What was true? That I come from this land? That there is goodness in the world?"

Abramowitz tried to find Benjamin's hand under the blanket, but Benjamin moved it away.

"Be angry at me," Abramowitz said softly. "You needed a quest. I gave you the wrong one. I am at fault. I've always believed that if I could reverse the movement of the earth and have it go around the sun in the other direction, I could get back to a better time. I would find myself in a better place. But I can't move the earth."

"And life was always bitter, Abramowitz. It was never better. It was never worth more than the scum on the riverbank."

Tears ran down Abramowitz's cheek. "I failed you, Benjamin. You don't have to roll time back. My mistake was not explaining to you that life is always good, as much in the present as in the past."

"Death is the only peace."

Marya broke into Benjamin's dream, her hands on his shoulders, and her long hair brushing his face. "Benya, are you alright? Who are you talking to?"

It took him a moment to shake the sleep from his mind. "A dream, that's all. Was I making noise?"

"You were talking in your sleep, but I couldn't make out about what." She was speaking softly, her face hidden in the darkness.

Benjamin turned to one side. "Go back to sleep. I'm sorry I woke you."

"I wasn't sleeping well."

"Did I keep you awake?"

"No, it was the two men at the wedding. I can't get them out of my mind. They frightened me. They made me remember that we are all in hiding. I try to push that out of my mind. I prefer to imagine that we are on our honeymoon, settled in a deep forest, protected from people's misdeeds. I forget you are a captive. I forget that I am holding you against your will. I remember only that I love you."

Rolling the word love around his mind, he struggled to find the tranquility Abramowitz had stolen. He turned his head toward her, brushed her hair away from her face, and tenderly kissed her lips.

"I am frightened, Benya. We haven't heard from Ilya. The men have seen us. I feel as if a chapter is over. I feel as if an unhappy section of this story is ready to begin."

He tightened his grip and kissed her again. "Sleep," he finally said. "Try to sleep." After he let go of her, he turned on his stomach and sank his head into the down pillow.

Marya massaged his shoulders and rubbed the small of his back. She kissed him on the neck and rolled the muscles of his thighs. When he turned over, she bent her knees and took him into her body. Then they slept.

The sun was still low in the horizon when Marya jumped out of bed and raced into the outer room, her movement pulling Benjamin out of a deep, dreamless sleep. When he heard her speaking in Russian in the other room, he became alarmed. He thought someone else might be in the cabin, someone from the wedding, someone who had come to get him. He listened intensely for sounds of an intruder while silently making his way out of bed. Nervously, he moved out of the bedroom.

But there was no intruder. Marya was standing in the other room, her naked body bronzed by the light, a cell phone against her ear. For a moment, he wondered if she had placed the call, but her nakedness made him realize that he had slept through the phone's ring. He began to ask whom she was talking to, but her frown quickly silenced him. So he stood in the doorway, noticing that she closed her eyes when she listened and that she opened them wide and paced the floor when she spoke. When he saw her shiver, he pulled the blanket from the bed and threw it over her shoulders.

"Fedya," Marya said before she folded the phone. "Fedya was calling from Kyiv." She pulled out a kitchen chair and sat down, looking unexpectedly forlorn, the gray blanket wrapped around her. "Things are more complicated than they expected. Fedya was calling from a roof a couple of buildings away from Ilya's apartment. They're afraid their telephone calls are being tracked by a truck parked outside of Ilya's place. I told him about our experience at the wedding. He was going to tell Ilya. He told me that your wife and a black American were in Kyiv looking for you. That Pavlov was on to their presence."

"My wife and a black American, that's impossible," Benjamin proclaimed.

"Impossible or not, Fedya says it's true. He has made contact with your wife's companion." There was a sense of loss in Marya's voice.

Benjamin was sitting across the table from her looking totally confused. "I'm surprised, that's all. I wouldn't think she cared enough to look for me. There must be some other reason for her coming? Or it isn't her. Believe me. But who is Pavlov?"

"I don't know much about him, but he is Ilya's contact with the west, the person who could help pick up the ransom and get you home. But now that your wife is in Kyiv, things have become more difficult." Marya flipped open the phone and then closed it again. "She must love you very much to have come this far to help you?"

"I doubt if she's in Ukraine, Marya. There must be some mistake. If she is here, it is more likely out of guilt than love. We both feel we've done the other an injustice. Her feelings would not be for a lover or a husband. She'd be looking for a brother or a dear cousin."

Marya looked as if she were trying to believe him, but failing.

~

Isolation suffocated Ilya. Drinking alone depressed him. Silence frightened him. He longed for conversation, for drunken laughter, for upstairs brothels and backroom whores. For a couple days, he sat on the couch where Fedya slept, guzzling the bottle of vodka he had opened at noon and drinking it dry by midnight. He would stare into the dimly lit living room, his eyes vacant, his mind buzzing with random thoughts, with political equations, with visions of revenge. Drinking slowly enough, Ilya would think, to keep him from getting drunk, but fast enough to keep his demons at bay. This day he could not wait for noon. He broke fast with vodka.

Fedya had left early in the morning, leaving Ilya alone and causing him once again to feel like a Russian fool. He saw himself as under house arrest, waiting for a reprieve from Deputy Mayor Pavlov, hoping his comrade would visit him with news of the Americans. He spent the long hours arguing with history, with Stalin's paranoia, with Brezhnev's obstinacy, with Gorbachev's abandonment, with Putin's recidivism. Camus was wrong, he decided, passing years do not make revolutionaries into heretics. Time transformed them into opportunists and survivors, into shrewd little people who permitted themselves every sin. True revolutionaries are boiled for their ideology, stoned by the greedy, shot by the selfish, buried by the petty. But that would not happen to him, not to Ilya Alexeevich Petrov, the son of an honored general, the child of a Bolshoi ballerina. No, he was not going to die an oppressor; he was not going to end his life as a heretic. He was a believer. He believed in Mother Russia, he believed people were capable of rising above themselves, that human nature wasn't permanently poisoned by avarice, that men and women were capable of charity and justice and love. He loved his beliefs. He'd do anything not to lose them.

Ilya was drunk when Fedya returned to the apartment. He staggered to the door.

"It worked," the young man announced. "You were right, he did return to the Great War monument. He threw his head back when he noticed me, an awkward gesture which he repeated a couple times. A signal for me to look behind him and catch sight of the man who was following him, a man in his forties in a bad fitting suit, a character from an old American movie about the KGB. It was comical."

"A drink?" Ilya asked.

Fedya was noticeably surprised by Ilya's interruption. He followed the old man into the kitchen. "Are you sober enough to listen to me?" Fedya asked.

"Don't worry about how much I drink, worry about how little you do," Ilya shouted angrily. But as suddenly as his temper flared, it disappeared. He gave out a raucous laugh and reached into the small refrigerator. "Here, take this beer. So, tell me how it worked."

"The American weaved through the outdoor display of military hardware, slowly moving this way and that. The shadow followed him. I followed the shadow. The American cut swiftly behind a tank, and then he disappeared behind the Battle of the Dnieper monument. He looked like a black James Bond. I watched as his shadow struggled to find him. KGB finally made a telephone call, and, it looked like he was instructed to go somewhere else. I, too, had lost sight of the American. But I hung around until he reappeared next to me. We sat in my car talking, but I couldn't understand what he was trying to tell me. I'm parked a few blocks away. What shall I do?"

~

Peter had tried to keep track of his location, but simply recalling the names of the streets they drove down was beyond him. The few signs he noticed were in Cyrillic, sets of strange scribbles that wouldn't stick to his memory. House numbers seemed non-existent. All he knew was that they were somewhere on the other side of the Dnieper

River, parked in front of identical looking concrete and brick apartment houses. There were few cars parked on the street, fewer still driving past him. Small cars, Peter noted, designed by Germans and Italians, but built in Russia and Ukraine, cars driven by solitary men in their thirties who seemed not to notice Fedya's vehicle. Missing were the BMWs and Mercedes he had seen on the prosperous side of the river. There were no blonds sitting in passenger seats and no chauffeurs. Out of the rear window, he watched a small, scraggly dog chase a bitch in heat, but the comedy of it didn't lift his spirits. Somberly, he tried to recall the route Fedya had taken when he walked away from the car. It didn't really matter, he knew, without an address, an apartment number, a name. He looked around to see if there was a telephone booth, a church, or a shop that he could run to if things turned sour, if the car was surrounded by teenage muggers, if Pavlov's security forces broke through the windows of the locked car and attempted to drag him from his seat. There was no evident sanctuary.

Peter closed his eyes. Pavlov was the reason he had stupidly driven off with someone he didn't know and could hardly understand, Pavlov and Anna Baranova, questioning Caitlin and him as if they were criminals, as if they were the culprits. To Pavlov there were no unknown kidnappers, no pirates who were asking for bounty, for blood money. There were only Peter and Caitlin, Caitlin and Peter. So he voluntarily got in a car with someone who claimed to hold Palmer. He felt stupid. He cursed ever going to Ukraine. Expletives had begun to leave his mouth when he heard a fist come crashing down on the hood of the car. Fedya signaled for him to open the door.

He followed Fedya into one of the indistinguishable apartment structures and climbed to its often-patched tar and gravel flat roof. To prevent their being seen from the street, they crouched as low as mobility allowed them and made their way to the edge of the building. They swung over a ledge and onto an adjoining rooftop, and then to a third. In the hallway two flights down, Peter found himself standing in front of an old Russian holding an empty glass in his hand.

"Ilya Alexeevich," he declared. "You must be Peter Johnson. I've been looking forward to meeting you."

They gathered around the small kitchen table. Fedya said something in Russian to Ilya and began to fumble in the refrigerator. Ilya poured a small glass of vodka and handed it to his guest. Peter didn't try to resist the drink. He took hold of the vodka and gulped it down. It burned his mouth and esophagus. Ilya moved to refill the glass, but Peter covered it with his hand. "Bastard," he muttered under his breath, cursing himself more than cursing the Russian. But why not? How much worse off would he be if he got drunk? He was ready to surrender to his addiction and have another drink when Fedya placed a plate of cheese and sliced ham on the table, along with a wicker basket filled with slices of black bread. He followed up with three small plates, each of them chipped.

"Thank you," Peter said, but Fedya was already turning to the stove to boil water for tea.

"You must be hungry, my American," Ilya said. "Anxiety always makes me hungry." He put some cheese and ham on a piece of bread and placed it on the plate in front of Peter. "Are you surprised that I speak English so well?"

"I hadn't thought about it."

"And with an English accent," Ilya continued. "I was lucky enough to study engineering in England many years ago as a graduate student. Two years in Edinburgh and one in London. I've always wanted to go back—to visit not to live."

Peter strained to listen beneath the thick Russian accent. He could hear only hints of England. "And now, are you still doing engineering?"

Ilya let out an uproarious laugh. "Time is short. Let's put our cards on the table. You and Benjamin Palmer's wife are in Kyiv to ransom him home. I have him in my possession. When I get the money, you can have him back in 24 hours."

"And why should I believe you? I'd hand you the money and most probably never see the next day."

Ilya tipped his chair back on its rear legs, his eyes focused on the African American, his hands gripping the stained edge of the wooden table. After a long pause, he laughed quietly and smiled. "Whatever happened to trust, Mr. Johnson? Don't I have an honest face?"

Wanting to exhibit strength rather than weakness, Peter answered quickly, "I can't see very much of it under that beard."

Ilya didn't laugh. "Fedya showed you some pictures. If that isn't enough, what can I tell you? His wife, who you are traveling with, is named Caitlin McCoy. Benya describes her as skinny with small tits, but very pretty, long blond hair, the perfect television face. She is a television news anchor. She is ambitious to a fault. Celebrity is her goal, and she doesn't seem to care how. Am I right so far?"

"Much of that you could have gotten with a Google search," Peter answered.

"But not all of it, Peter Johnson, not all of it. Benya is a felon. His crime seems rather inconsequential to me, but he helped cause the demise of a company by starting a Wall Street whispering campaign that its bankruptcy was imminent. He avoided jail by ratting on his colleagues."

"Again, Mr. Alexeevich, you could have gotten all of this from Google," Peter said sternly. He had to resist easily trusting the Russian, he told himself.

"Alexeevich is my patronymic, not my family name. Just call me Ilya. When you met with Pavlov, was his mistress around?"

"If you mean Anna Baranova, she was there. But I didn't know she was his mistress."

"Wasn't it evident?" Ilya asked, surprised that the black American didn't jump to that conclusion.

"I'm not naïve, Ilya. Common prejudice would have you assume that any pretty woman called assistant to a Ukrainian bureaucrat is really a mistress. They work their way up on their backs," Peter argued, irritated by what he saw was the Russian's bigotry, and expecting that his bigotry was vast enough to envelope any descendent of Africans.

"Not just Ukrainian bureaucrats, my friend. Common prejudice is not always wrong." Ilya gestured to Peter with the top of the vodka bottle to see if he wanted another drink. Peter turned over his glass. "Tea?" the Russian asked.

"Yes, I'd like some tea."

"Good, take some more bread and ham. You can wash it down with the hot tea." Ilya turned his head around and yelled, "Fedya."

The young Russian quickly brought glasses, the kettle, and Lipton tea bags to the table.

"Was there something in Anna's behavior that made you think she was not Pavlov's mistress, something I missed seeing?"

"Whether she is or she isn't is not of much importance, is it?" Peter answered, puzzled by Ilya's interest in Pavlov's sex life and suspecting it came out of a competitive battle between the two men that had little to do with Benjamin Palmer and kidnapping.

"Perhaps, but just to satisfy an old man's curiosity, was there something that kept you from jumping to the conclusion 98% of us would reach?"

To give himself time to think, Peter picked up the slice of bread Ilya had prepared for him. But before he took a bite, he said, "I've seen her twice. Each time she seemed more interested in Caitlin than in me, her eyes almost undressing my companion. And then there was Pavlov. He kept looking at her for confirmation. Was he asking the right question? Was he coming off hard enough? Maybe a mistress can have that much control, but in my experience, withholding sex is just as potent, maybe more so. The complications are fewer. But you know them better than I do. If they live together, well, that would underscore your suspicion."

Ilya couldn't hold back. He let out an uproarious laugh and poured himself another drink. "They don't live together, but a lesbian? What a loss." He pointed a few Russian sentences to Fedya who began to laugh.

Ilya took the glass of vodka to his lips, threw his head back, and emptied it dry. "What did Pavlov tell you? Did he talk about the money?"

"He treated us like criminals, like nefarious characters who had come to Kyiv to do damage. The world was turned upside down. We were guilty, although I don't know of what. We weren't seeking to save Benjamin Palmer; we had come to Kyiv to join him. To prove he had Benjamin, he showed us some pictures that were taken of him at a wedding."

Ilya again tipped his chair back on its rear legs. "Could you recognize him with a full beard and long hair?" he asked.

Peter returned Ilya's smile, realizing the Russian was again trying to prove that he knew where the captive was. "Caitlin recognized him. I don't know Palmer."

"Was there a woman in the picture, a head shorter than Benya, with flowing dark hair and beautiful dark eyes?"

"There seemed to be a woman with him."

"Do you think I could have discovered that on Google?"

"For all I know, you and Pavlov are in this together," Peter uttered.

Ilya didn't react to the comment. "Did he talk to you about money, Mr. Johnson?" Ilya continued. "Did he give you a number?"

Maybe another drink, Peter thought, to keep him alert and focused. He moved his arm toward the bottle, but stopped himself, realizing how ridiculous the thought that drink would keep his mind clear. He knew what it was to be a drunk. He didn't want to face it again, certainly not when he was going to have to deal with this Russian and with Pavlov. Peter watched as Ilya straightened out his chair and leaned across the table. "He just took our passports, and our cell phones," the American said.

His chair scraped against the floor as Ilya pushed it back. "Anything else?"

"We were told not to try to leave Kyiv."

"And the American Embassy, did he tell you to stay away?"

"No. He showed no concern about that."

"Interesting," Ilya said. Then, as if it would help him to understand, he rubbed his beard. "That is important information, Mr. Johnson, more important than you could know. Are you sure he was unconcerned about your touching base with your embassy?"

"He just about invited us to make the call, and let us hold on to our cell phones long enough to make contact with our country's representatives."

The old man leaned back in his chair and, under his breath, let out a stream of Russian. To Peter, it sounded like a parade of expletives.

Ilya looked like someone who had just had an epiphany when he got out of his seat, took Fedya by the arm, and walked him into the living room. Peter could only hear small snippets of their conversation, and those he could hear he could not understand. He was amused that they had bothered to move into the adjoining room. His unfamiliarity with their language should have been evident. Ilya was not a person to take chances, Peter thought. But as the minutes passed, he grew increasingly uncomfortable sitting alone in the kitchen, his companions plotting God knew what in the other room. He looked at the bottle of vodka, angered that he had taken a drink, angered further that he wanted another. He had been off the sauce for two years. He was desperate not to go back. He got up from the chair and poured the once boiling water into his tea glass.

Peter heard the front door of the apartment open and close. He was still standing when Ilya returned to the kitchen. The Russian pulled out one of the wooden chairs, sat down, and watched Peter finish his tea and return to his seat. "Fedya will be back in a couple of minutes, Peter. He will let you off close to the hotel. You then will have a number of choices. You can tell Pavlov of this meeting. He will call and curse me out, but he will respect me if only for finding you. You can remain silent and wait to hear from Fedya. It makes little difference to me, but it will make a great deal of difference to you and to Caitlin."

"I don't understand," Peter said.

"We don't trust each other. I don't know why I expected it to be different. Old age, I imagine. I thought Benjamin would be worth a great deal of money to me, but when I couldn't make a deal with your State Department and had to use Pavlov, the plot got away from me. I'm an honest businessman, Peter, trying to eke out a living in a corrupt world. I bought Benya from the people who kidnapped him. I wanted an honest middleman's profit. Pavlov has his own desires. He wants power and the torrents of money that power can extract. He doesn't want to be a middleman.

Benjamin Palmer would help him get what he wants, but he can do almost as well with you and Mrs. McCoy." Ilya gave a small smile and rubbed his beard. "Is she Mrs. McCoy or Ms. McCoy? I can't keep track. Once she would have been happy to be Mrs. Palmer."

"Ms. McCoy, I imagine, but I've never talked to her about it. It's rather beside the point, isn't it? I still don't know what you are trying to tell me?"

"Fedya is contacting the woman you saw in the photograph of Benya. He will instruct her to prepare to bring Palmer to me. Pavlov has outmaneuvered me."

"So you'll be handing him over to the deputy mayor?"

"That will depend on you, Peter. If you remain silent, something far better might happen."

# Chapter 17

Rain was beating down on the thatched roof of the cabin when Benjamin woke from a long afternoon nap. The thick fog that had kept light from seeping into the cabin during the morning was still impenetrable, keeping the bedroom dark and damp. Automatically, without thought or memory, he rolled over to touch Marya, but the bed was empty. He raised his head to listen for sounds of her—the movement of a chair, the opening of the stove, the humming of a folksong—but there was only silence.

He found her outside, harvesting squash from her garden. She had draped Ilya's long raincoat over her head and shoulders to keep off the rain. "It feels like autumn," she said. "A cold front must be moving through the Carpathians. It is still too soon for the first frost, but the weather is hard to predict. Summer will hang on for a while, and then, after a cold snap, summer will fight back, at least for a few days. You have a name for that season, don't you?"

"Indian summer," Benjamin said.

"Indian summer," she repeated with a chuckle. "Now I remember. I wonder where that name comes from. It does have a nice sound."

Carefully avoiding stepping on any of the vegetables, Benjamin made his way through the garden to be closer to Marya. When she looked up, he noticed that her eyes were swollen. He took a half step back, puzzled by her unexpected appearance. "Have you been crying?" he asked.

"It's nothing," Marya answered. She averted her eyes.

"If it caused you to cry it's not 'nothing.'"

"I'm a romantic, Benya. I hate to see the summer end. I hate to think of my beautiful garden being buried under snow. And I don't like seeing you get soaked by the rain. Go inside," she insisted.

Benjamin put his arms around her, but his action did not give her comfort. She began to sob into his shoulder. He gently pushed her back and cupped a hand under her chin so that he could look into her eyes. "Fedya called again, didn't he? Is that what all this is about?"

"You know me too well," Marya answered before breaking away from him. "Let's talk about it over a glass of tea."

He had expected that if the time ever came when freedom was within reach, his fervent desire to be liberated would rub against the peacefulness of his prison, against Marya's love and Ilya's laughter. But now that he could taste the end of his captivity, he felt relieved and joyous. The nightmare is over, he told himself, the nightmare is over. As he followed her into the cabin, her head and body hidden by Ilya's heavy raincoat, he knew that nightmare was not the right word, and wondered if dream might be better. What was coming to an end was not something lurid but something surreal, and the surreal, too, had to be escaped.

He watched as Marya prepared the tea, as she put some cakes on a plate and brought them to the table. For a brief moment, he felt as if he was abandoning her, and accused himself of repaying her warmth and affection with desertion. But he buried those ideas by believing that her sadness would be transitory, that her tears would quickly dry, that she would be glad for him. And if his deep feelings for her were more than the product of desperate loneliness and dependence, if they were built on an inexplicable affinity, he could find her again. He wasn't dying. He was being reborn.

As she filled his glass, her body quivered. Her eyes avoided his as she sat down, as she silently drank her tea. He was full of questions that her gloom did not allow him to ask: Was he to be taken back to Kyiv? Was Caitlin and her companion on their way to the cabin to take him home? He would have liked that. As for how much Caitlin was going to pay Ilya, he decided it could never be too much.

His patience ran out. "So what did Fedya tell you?" he asked firmly.

"He conveyed some instructions from Ilya. Ilya wants us to leave tomorrow morning for L'viv. Once there—we can make it in 24 hours if you share the driving—we are to contact someone named Bohdan Karmalyuk. He lives near the airport. He can hide us for a couple of days if he needs to."

Benjamin interrupted her rapid flow of words. "Hide us?" he asked. "What is all that about?"

"Fedya wasn't very informative. 'Ilya has things to work out,' is what he told me. Ilya is not worried about people finding this cabin, but he wants us to be somewhere that allows us to travel fast. Karmalyuk is a pilot and has a small plane at his disposal."

Benjamin's euphoria disappeared. "Shit" he shouted and hit the table with his hand. "Will this never end?"

Marya looked into her tea glass to avoid seeing the dejection in his face.

"Was there more, Marya? Is my wife resisting the amount being asked? Is Ilya getting greedy? He always rants against greediness, but he's not immune from the disease."

"Ilya wants you to shave your beard so you look as if you belong in a large city, and he wants me to cut my hair or dye it that awful red color you see around the country. Both would be best."

"Fuck Ilya," Benjamin exploded, "Fuck the bastard."

"It's for your safety, Benya."

"Or is to ensure that he gets his blood money?"

Marya spread her hands on the table in absolution. "Benya, my love, please listen to me" she began, her soft and solemn voice like that of a distraught mother delivering an unwanted message, "it is no longer a matter of money, at least not your money. Pavlov has other plans, political plans, plans that he can pull off without you. Pavlov has your wife and her friend. He will claim that they are not here to find you, but to join you in some crime against the Ukrainian people. That he refused to be corrupted by them and by you. He will use the story to become mayor or president. It will make more money for him than you could ever pay."

For a moment, he was confused. But she didn't have to repeat herself. Benjamin understood as much as he needed to. He pulled himself out of the chair, threw his glass at the cast-iron stove, and stomped out into the cold rain.

~

Peter went straight to Caitlin's room as soon as he got back to the hotel. He placed a finger over his lips to silence her when she opened the door.

The signal altered what she was going to say to him. "How was the sightseeing?" came out of her mouth rather than the "Where the fuck were you?" he expected.

"Kyiv is a beautiful city, Caitlin. I'm sorry you didn't come with me. If I hadn't gotten hungry, I'd still be out there. Would you like to join me for dinner?"

"I could use a walk before dinner. Could you hold out long enough for us to find a place we haven't eaten in before?" she said, sensing their need for privacy.

Caitlin put on some lipstick, ran a brush through her hair, and threw on a lined raincoat. As they walked through the reception area, Peter noticed the man in the gray-flannel suit who had followed him around the monument. Peter nodded in his direction as if they were comfortable associates. "Our shadow," he informed Caitlin. A porter opened the hotel's front door for the Americans, and continued to hold it open for the man in the ill-fitting suit.

They walked quickly, trying to make certain that their shadow was too far away to hear or record what they were saying.

"What do you make of it?" she asked after Peter had filled her in on his conversation with Ilya.

"I trust him more than I do Anna and her Pavlov. If it was an act, it was a good one. But what do we have to lose? If Pavlov learns of my meeting, I can plead ignorance. How could he expect me to know who to deal with? He didn't trust me, why should I have trusted him?"

A break in the traffic let them quickly cut across the street, leaving the man following them on the opposite side of the highway, impatiently shifting from one foot to the other. "Let's wait for him," Peter insisted. "I'd like him to think he just lost sight of me this morning and that I didn't purposefully slip away from him."

"I don't think Pavlov is predictable, nor Anna Baranova," Caitlin said as they waited for a pause in the traffic. "Let's go with your gut and wait to hear from your Russian friends. If Pavlov is furnishing a jail cell for us, he'll move us into it with or without the excuse of a clandestine meeting on the other side of the Dnieper."

"Is that what you think he's doing?" Peter asked.

"He's taken our passports and cell phones."

"But we're still free to move around. The guy behind us is just a tail. We could ask protection from the American Embassy," Peter suggested, his tone serious, his look weary.

Caitlin stopped walking and turned around to face her colleague. "Are you arguing against yourself just to make sure I want to go along? It's nice of you, Peter, but I just don't want to give up, at least not yet." She paused for a minute and looked as if she might kiss him on a cheek. "I've really gotten you into a mess, Peter. I am sorry I involved you, but I am very glad that you're here."

Before Peter could answer, the man in the gray woolen suit nearly bumped into him.

# Chapter 18

Ilya watched Fedya move his finger over the map of Kyiv, first seeking the fastest route from Ilya's apartment to the Dnipro Hotel, then running his finger from the Dnipro Hotel to the street where Pavlov lived, then searching for an exit from the city and a road west. Ilya rubbed his beard, picked up the bottle of beer Fedya had been drinking, and, to the younger man's amusement, took a swallow.

"The beer is rotten," Ilya said stridently.

"Your taste buds are too old to enjoy it," Fedya suggested without looking up from the map.

Ilya had convinced himself that the dangers were few and the risks small, but still, looking at Fedya's open face, his light blue eyes, his wiry frame, he couldn't avoid feeling queasy about endangering the lives of others in his plot to get even with Pavlov. Was it youth, Ilya wondered, that enabled his young associate to dismiss the venture's perils? Or was Fedya truly outraged by corruption, and deeply intolerant of the Pavlovs of the world? Ilya had asked Fedya if he felt misused, if he was volunteering to do something he didn't want to do out of loyalty and friendship. The younger man had answered by bending down and kissing Ilya on his forehead, and saying something about being mature enough to make up his own mind.

Whatever his comrade's motive, Ilya felt blessed by the young man's loyalty. He knew, however, that his plan required more than the two of them. At least one other person would be needed, someone to work aside Fedya, someone strong and reliable and fearless. An incorruptible former communist party member was Ilya's first choice, someone from the old days who continued to hate public sleaze. If he were in London, he would have used a directory or an internet search engine to locate the telephone numbers or e-mail addresses of old comrades, but in Kyiv, all he could do was recall the blocks they lived on and the apartments they occupied. It meant going into the city, exposed to informants and secret police, and knocking on doors. But he had no choice.

Ilya brought his young comrade into his thinking, chuckling when he realized that Fedya was not the only one who could use an additional pair of hands. He too could use an assistant, although that person's task would not be physically demanding. If he could find one person to help, he could find two, he decided, although it would not be simple.

Fedya led the older Russian over the rooftops, down a stairway, and onto the street, turning around periodically to make sure his comrade was keeping up, smiling broadly when Ilya fell behind, and looking surprised when Ilya said something about his being excited. But Fedya's patience became noticeably short when Ilya's search for old comrades took them into sections of the city the older Russian only vaguely remembered.

Yakiv's girlfriend opened the door to the one bedroom flat where she lived with two teenage daughters only to inform Ilya that his friend had found life in Kyiv too difficult and moved to Brooklyn to join his brother. "He sends me a check every month. It's much more reliable than a state pension," she said with pride. Vasily's place proved to be the easiest to find, close to the river, in a pre-Stalinist single-family house that had long ago been divided into seven apartments. An elderly neighbor told Ilya that Vasily's liver had given into alcohol, and that his son now occupied the place. Ilya wanted to wait for the son to return from work so that he could extend his condolences, but the hour was growing late, and there was no certainty that condolences would be welcome. You just never know about children, Ilya thought, while speculating that the son might be a possible candidate for the operation. He could always come back if he found no one else.

The last person Ilya could think of was Oleksander, a muscular Ukrainian with a sharp tongue who had worked with him in the eastern provinces of the Soviet Union.

Ilya had knocked three times and was beginning to turn back when her voice came through the door. "Yes," she said, "What do you want?"

"I'm looking for Oleksander Chemenko. Is this still his apartment?"

"Why, may I ask, are you looking for my father? If he owes you money, you are unlucky. If he got your daughter pregnant, congratulations."

"I am an old friend of your father's. I want nothing but his good health," Ilya answered.

"All of his old friends are dead," the voice came back, but it had softened.

"I am still breathing."

"And do you still have a name?"

He paused for a moment, wondering if he might be giving his name to someone who did favors for the government, who made a habit of reporting visitors looking for her Bolshevik parent. He kicked himself for his thought. Things are not that bad, he told himself. "Ilya, Ilya Alexeevich Petrov."

She turned the lock. "Ilya Alexeevich?" she said as she opened the door just wide enough to see him. "Ilya

Alexeevich Petrov, hiding behind a beard," she continued, and swung the door wide open. "Do you remember me?"

She was in her early forties, Ilya thought, although he knew he wasn't very good at judging age, a short, muscular woman, her large brown eyes set close to her nose, her long auburn hair in need of a shampoo. "There is a lot of your father in you," he said, struggling to remember her name.

She let out a deep-throated laugh. "Kolyna Chemenko," she reminded him, "the loyal daughter."

She put glasses of tea and sliced honey cake on the small table that hugged the wall in the living room. "I first met you in Vladivostok, almost twenty-five years ago. My father was working for you then. When you'd keep him in the shop late, he'd come home and curse out your limitless dedication. I don't remember what he was doing, something about repairing submarines, I think. But underneath the curses, he had great respect for you."

"That's nice to hear, even if I know you are saying it out of politeness."

"I've never been accused of holding my tongue, Ilya Alexeevich. No, my father loved you. And I remember having a crush on you. I was preparing for entrance exams to Moscow State University, and you helped me with algebra and English. I can't believe you don't remember that?"

"I remember helping Olexsander's daughter, but you have changed. You wore your hair short, I remember, and"

Kolyna cut him off. "And my face was thinner, and my skin unwrinkled."

"You were beautiful then, and you are beautiful now. I find your longer hair more becoming."

"I was on the wrestling team. I couldn't afford long hair."

"Yes, like your father, you were a wrestler."

"But not as good."

"And you wanted to be a doctor," he recalled with pride.

"I am. I'm a cardiac surgeon. I know, I know, you'd think I would be living in a larger place, but this is big enough for me, and I really can't afford much more. My clients are poor people. When my father visits, he sleeps in the bedroom, and I sleep on the couch over there." She didn't bother to point it out. "We fight each other for the bathroom. He will be terribly sorry to have missed you."

"Even if he cursed out his old boss?" Ilya said pointedly, still bristling at the thought of being disliked by one of his employees.

She looked surprised. "He dedicated one of his poetry collections to you, did you know that? He titled it, *The Last Believer*, a collection of patriotic odes to working people and communal responsibilities, full of old-fashioned notions and nostalgic beliefs."

"To me?" Ilya asked. He wanted to hear her repeat the news.

"Dedicated to you and titled for you. He thinks of you as the last believer, other than himself and his daughter, that is."

His heartbeat jumped, and his chest tightened, and he felt his eyes water. Silly he told himself, but it didn't feel silly. It was wonderful. "Do you have a copy that I can see?"

"It was never published. Editors didn't want to accept the political risk, and he didn't have the money to print it himself. He wrote in Russian thinking he'd find a larger audience, and manuscript copies can be found in Moscow, he tells me. He reads from it in nightclubs and bars, and collects the rubles that people throw at him."

"*The Last Believer*, I like that," Ilya said. "But I think there are others, Kolyna, young and old, angry people who want the world to be better, who believe it can be better."

"Then you know more than I do, Ilya. Our dreams only live in the old, and even they don't truly believe they will come true. Do you still believe, Ilya Alexeevich, do you really still believe?"

He leaned back in his chair and let out a boisterous laugh. It took him a minute to catch his breath.

"I didn't think my question was funny," she said. She was not smiling.

"I am the last believer. It is easier when I am drunk, but I even manage it when I am sober."

Kolyna left the table and made her way into the narrow kitchen. He heard her run some water and open and close the refrigerator. "I have little to serve you, Ilya, other than bread and cheese, but nothing hot."

"How about a drink?"

"I'm sorry. All I have is tea and cold water."

"Don't be sorry. I've already intruded on your goodness."

She stood in the kitchen doorway wiping her hands with a small towel. "You didn't just drop in, Ilya, you had a mission. What did you want from my father?"

"It is complicated, Kolyna, complicated. It would have been good to see him even if he couldn't help."

"If it is criminal, Ilya, I can't help you. If it is something else, I may be of some assistance. If not me, I know lots of other people."

He trusted her. She was Olexsander's daughter. She was a doctor to the poor. She lived like a factory worker. And he had no one else to turn to. "It's political and not criminal, but political things sometimes require laws to be broken."

She quickly broke into his words. "I don't want to hear what you're planning. Not knowing can be protective. Just tell me what resources you need."

"I need two people. A fighter, someone quick and strong, who knows how to avoid a physical confrontation as well as how to win one, and I could use a messenger. I also need a car, not something fancy, but a reliable vehicle that can blend with other cars on the road."

"Will they need to drive very far?"

"Only the fighter, and not very far if things go well."

"For how many days?"

"For tomorrow night, but if things are delayed, they may have to be ready to assist me until the plan is completed."

She played with the ends of her long curly hair. "You are not giving me much time, Ilya. But I know a couple of women who might fit the bill."

"Women?" he blurted out. "I don't think I made myself clear."

"You don't know the women. I coached both of them. They are very good wrestlers. And they read Gogol."

~

Marya and Benjamin stayed away from each other for most of the afternoon. She swept the cabin floor and dusted the furniture and windowsills, her face drawn, her head bowed. She scrubbed the top of the stove and returned the tableware to its drawer. She inspected the pots and pans—washing those that failed scrutiny—and returned them to the shelves above the kitchen sink. The utensils that might be needed for dinner and breakfast were placed on the wooden table.

Benya threw on Ilya's oilskin poncho and made his way through the wet undergrowth of the forest. The heavy rains of the previous days had swollen the river, raising it high against its banks and covering the rocks that had enabled him to walk from one bank to the other. He was hoping to find the children at the water's edge. A final farewell, he thought, not by word but by look, by an exchange of smiles that would cement their images into his memory and his face into their imaginations. It was a selfish quest, he knew. There was no chance of him forgetting them, but he feared that he would be a passing memory, a fleeting encounter lost among the myriad experiences of their youth. He wanted them to remember that he was there, that they were important to him. He wanted a permanent place in their lives.

The landscape was empty and silent. He leaned against the broad willow tree, surprised that he was feeling sorry for himself. Much of him was desperate to get home. He yearned to hear his language on the airwaves, to look into the storefronts on Connecticut Avenue, to walk by the Capitol and lunch on hamburgers and French fries and a cold glass of beer. He wanted to tell people about his adventure, and he wanted to find a career. Above all else, he wanted to demonstrate to the world that he was more than a survivor, that his ordeals—in the US and in Ukraine—had made him a person of substance and growing value. He wanted again to be somebody.

Still, there was this river, this paradise, this simple world. As artificial as he knew it was, he could not deny its appeal, its beauty, its offer of boundless love. "L'viv," he said out loud, and silently asked, and where from there?

Marya made a hot soup for supper, a light broth in which she mixed potatoes, onions, and lentils. Mixing ground beef with milk and onions, she rolled meatballs on the wooden cutting block and fried them on a flat pan. Benjamin opened a bottle of Georgian red wine, and they clicked their glasses.

"To your freedom," Marya toasted.

"To my love," Benjamin answered.

"It will be hard living here without you," she said, her eyes holding fast to his.

He didn't answer. He didn't know what to say. Nothing seemed real, not his captivity, not his love, not the possibility of going home.

When the first bottle of wine was finished, Benjamin opened a second. They finished it as the meal ended.

Marya, her complexion darkened by drink, brought a Soviet era map of Ukraine to the table. It was printed on plastic coated paper, its surface covered with palm prints and coffee stains, its folds cracked. She moved the plates away and spread the map out in front of Benjamin. He made way for her to stand beside him.

"We need to figure a route to L'viv. Fedya wants us to be careful, but I'm not sure how to do that. The major roads have more police patrols, but using back roads will expose us for a longer period of time."

"I don't know enough to help you," Benjamin said as he began to study the map. It was littered with dots and circles, with countless, overlapping Cyrillic names of towns and villages and cities. Multicolored veins ran over the vast expanse of the country depicting roads and highways, rivers, and railways. His unfamiliarity with the country and the language made it a bewildering document. He tried to locate Kyiv and find L'viv by the size of the lettering and the prominence of the circled mark.

"Kyiv?" he asked pointing to the most prominent label on the map.

"Good," Marya said like a proud teacher. Then she placed her finger on lettering of almost equal size. "And this is L'viv."

"And where are we now?" he asked eagerly, expecting to finally place the hamlet where he had spent the last three months.

Marya placed her forefinger down on the map. "We are in the *Ivano-Frankivsk Oblast*, east of the Carpathians and west of Kolomyja."

"But where exactly? What's the name of this village?"

"Marya let out a light, gay laugh. "We are too small to be on the map and too insignificant to have an official name. Everyone calls it differently."

Benjamin leaned over the table. Their bodies touched. "Don't tease, Marya. I want to know how I will be able to find you."

"I think we will drive toward Kolomyja, then turn north until we get to the highway that connects to L'viv. We could make the trip in one day, but I don't want to get there after dark, so we should spend the night in Kalush. I have a school friend who is living there. She will not ask any questions."

"But wouldn't it be safer driving at night?"

"Maybe driving at night would be safer in America, but not in Ukraine. I'm unfamiliar with the route. If the police don't get us, the drunken drivers or the dilapidated roads would finish us off."

"But what if we get a flat or we're stopped for going too fast or missing a stop sign? What do we do then?"

Marya burst into a substantial laugh. Benjamin heard no element of tension in her full-throated expression, no evidence that the night held the same unavoidable sadness for her as it did for him. Was it the drink, or did she not love him as much as he thought she did? How mixed his feelings, he realized.

"Half of you is still in America," Marya said. "If we are stopped for a traffic violation, which is very unlikely in Ukraine, I'll open my wallet. If we get a flat, you will change the tire. If something more serious happens to the car, we will be in trouble."

"Will you introduce me as a mute cousin?"

"I hadn't thought of that," she said, the words catching in a giggle. "I've thought of other ways of concealing your identity. One was to have you lie on the back seat, a blanket keeping you warm. I'd tell people you have tuberculosis, and I was driving you to a clinic in L'viv. That would keep people on their guard, but if you got out of the car, you'd look much too healthy, and they'd get suspicious. I could, of course, keep you in the back covered by rags. How does that strike you?"

Benjamin was not sharing her humor. "Very uncomfortably," he said, "but this is too serious to joke about."

She put on a serious face. "I think I have found an answer. I will describe myself as a tour guide and you as a Jewish traveler looking for his ancestral village. It is not unusual. Many descendants of Jews come to Ukraine to discover the villages of their ancestors. You will need a new name, however. The police will be looking for a Benjamin Palmer."

"And it doesn't sound Jewish, does it?" he answered, surprised by her suggestion, but thinking the subterfuge might just work.

"Every name sounds Jewish if that is what you are listening for," she answered. She turned back to the map. "What will we call you?"

"What would you think of my using the name Martin Abramowitz? It is the name of a Jew who was born in Peczenizyn."

"The man who suggested you visit his hometown. It would work. I could say we had just come from Peczenizyn and were returning to L'viv where you will catch a plane home."

"And if they ask for my passport, what do we do then?"

"You had to leave it at your hotel in L'viv—the Leopolis. It's the place I'd like to stay if I had the money. We might have to pay higher bribes because you are staying at such a fancy place, but we will manage." She squeezed his hand and kissed him on the cheek. "I won't let anything happen to you, Benya, not if I can prevent it."

~

Gusts of wind burst against the cabin, and pellets of hail broke against the cabin's windows. They stood together in the bedroom's chilly air, her naked breasts pressing against his bare chest, his arms tightly around her waist, their pelvises teasing each other. He kissed the lids of her closed eyes; he kissed her neck, her forehead, her chin. He nibbled on her earlobe and cupped his hand under her breast to raise it to his mouth. He could recall no greater passion than he felt at that moment, not for Caitlin, not for the nubile women he knew when he was young and adventurous. He didn't want to rush. It was a last meal, a last taste of adventure, a moment to be savored for a lifetime.

He found her passion as deep as his, her body as animated, her love as demanding. Exhausted, they fell asleep in each other's arms. When they woke they made love more tenderly. She began to cry after she came. He kissed the tears from her face.

They would leave for Kalush in the morning.

# Chapter 19

Fedya was going to have enough difficulty handling Pavlov and the driver, Ilya reasoned, without having to contend with Anna Baranova, but it took him a while to think of a way of insuring that she would not be in the car when the deputy mayor was driven home. It turned out to be simple. He realized that Anna was unlikely to accept an ordinary invitation for an evening drink, but an invitation to join him at the Dnipro Hotel where the Americans were staying might be difficult for her to reject. Mischievous, he thought with some glee, to use his knowledge of where the Americans were staying to entrap her. She would tell Pavlov, of course, but he would tell her to go ahead and learn whatever she could. "Lust is more likely to get Ilya to talk than vodka," he would tell her. The idea made Ilya laugh. What could be better than using the Americans to lure her to a drink? It would not only get her out of Fedya's way, it would teach her that Ilya Alexeevich was not going to play impotent before her Pavlov, that behind his gray beard and wrinkled skin wasn't an old drunk, a stupid, unrepentant Bolshevik, but a clever and virile man, a resourceful rogue and bastard who knew how to accomplish his ends, who had to be taken seriously.

Laughter was Anna Baranova's first refuge when he phoned her to arrange the date, but after a long pause, she offered to meet him at the Premier Palace Hotel. Having made his point, he had no reason to negotiate. Ironic, he thought, after they hung up, how the prospect of buying Anna a drink had swelled his pride.

Anna was suitably late, ten minutes, perhaps fifteen. She had dressed differently than she had for their meeting in the cabaret. Gone was the blatant display of sexuality, replaced by a well-tailored blue skirt that covered her knees and a white blouse buttoned up to the neck. Her long hair flowed over her back. Her amber eyes glowed under the interior light. To Ilya, she looked even more appealing than she had in the more revealing outfit. The power of mystery, he thought.

"Have you been here before?" Anna asked after Ilya pulled out a chair so she could sit down.

"It is my first time, Anna. I'm a poor man. Is this a favorite of yours?"

"It has the best Japanese food in the city, perhaps the best in all Ukraine. Do you like Japanese food, Ilya?"

"The very thought revolts me. Only carrots and vodka should be consumed raw."

"Pavlov calls you a peasant. I think you revel in the honor. I know different, Ilya. I know different." She looked around for the waiter, moved her body toward her companion, and crossed her legs. "Their Japanese cuisine is world-renowned. It is of the quality you find in Moscow and London. The same owners, I've been told."

"Raw fish has never been high on my list of culinary delights," Ilya said, his thirst growing by the minute.

"They do serve other things, my friend," Anna said with a slight laugh. "So you've never eaten here?"

"Anna Baranova, when you get to know me you will realize that I only lie about big things, like being a peasant, but not small things like the restaurants I choose to eat in. But if the cost of having dinner with you is having raw fish, it would be a small price. I would pay much more to be seen in public with such a beautiful woman."

"Thank you," she said, "I do take that as a compliment."

She looked away from Ilya when the waiter approached and ordered an overpriced glass of French Chardonnay and the Sushi menu. Ilya asked for a bottle of Guinness Stout.

"I'm not very hungry, Ilya, but I would like a snack. I'm sure the waiter can find something for you. But beer and not vodka … you'll lose your peasant persona."

"I can't resist being reminded of my days in England. Vodka is all over, but not many places I frequent carry imported beers. In London, of course, I would have ordered a pint and it would have come from a tap and not a bottle."

"Pavlov told me you studied in England for a number of years. Is that what you plan to do with the money you get for Benjamin Palmer, return to London?"

"I've given it a lot of thought, but that was when I expected it to be a great deal of money," he answered. He worked to keep the laughter out of his voice.

"And why do you think it will be less?" she asked, a wry smile on her face.

Before he could answer, the waiter placed the wine on the marble-topped table. He filled Ilya's glass halfway up. Ilya used Anna's preoccupation with the menu to take a quick glance at his watch. It was after nine. It would be dark out, he thought, and wondered if Fedya was being successful.

Anna ordered two pieces each of tuna, baby octopus, and shrimp sushi. Ilya stayed with his beer. "You didn't answer my question, Ilya. Why do you think there will be less money now?"

"I'm a realist, Anna Baranova. Since the Americans came to town, Benjamin Palmer's value has gone down. Whatever Pavlov wants, he can get from those two. If he extracts money from them as well, he'll throw me a tip and not a payment."

"You exaggerate —" Anna began, but Ilya cut her off.

"But you, you are in a position to make things right."

She moved her body further back into the seat and lifted the Chardonnay to her lips.

"I know Pavlov. He would listen to you. Convince him to put his political ambitions on temporary hold. He will have other opportunities to become a public hero.

"Politics is always risky, Anna Baranova. You know that. Cash in a Swiss bank account is far more guaranteed. Pavlov has competitors. They lie all around. They are most probably watching us right now. Maybe they have a microphone hidden in the crystal chandelier that's hanging over our heads." He picked up his glass to give her time to digest his thoughts.

"You have been reading too many English spy novels," she said.

He had anticipated a better actress, Ilya mused before he continued. "We can make a clean deal for at least $2 million, Anna. Benjamin Palmer has told me so. Pavlov can bury a million wherever he hides his money. I will give you half of what I get. Just think Anna, what half a million can do for you. You and your lover could move anywhere in the world."

"My lover?" Anna broke in. "And what makes you think I have a lover?"

"You are too beautiful not to have, your skin has too much of a glow, your walk has a bounce in it."

"You Russians, you always think it takes a man to make a women attractive," she said, a tad of relief in her voice.

She thanked the waiter when he put down the attractive plate of sushi. "Would you like a piece?" she asked Ilya.

He brushed off the suggestion with the motion of his head, touched the waiter's arm, and ordered another beer. Anna polished off her wine and handed the empty glass to the waiter for a refill.

"I don't know if your lover is a man or a woman or a horse." He watched her face turn hard and suspected that Peter was right about her sexuality. "It is unimportant. There may be no lover at all. Half a million would go further without a lover."

She reached down and picked up the tuna covered rice with her fingers. "I'm not good with chopsticks," she said while chewing.

When the tuna was safely swallowed, she shifted her body so he could see her cross her legs. "And when would I collect my money, Ilya, after you have taken off for London or Vladivostok? Will you send it by mail or by private messenger? And will it be in dollars or Euros or hryvnia?"

Ilya let out a boisterous laugh. "Details, Anna Baranova, small details. All that can be worked out, but the US dollar is the money the Americans will be using, I expect. It is a trustworthy currency."

He watched as she ate some octopus, trying to read her body language, to see if her eyes had turned inward and she was giving his offer some thought. He saw nothing helpful. "I don't know what your plans are, Anna. I expect you see Pavlov as mayor, or president, or prime minister. But there are others with their eyes on those jobs. The odds are against his success. He has challengers. He has enemies. Nothing is certain in politics, but $500.000 is security."

She shifted her body so that she could look straight into his face. "Nothing is certain, Ilya. I'm not even certain you have Benjamin Palmer. Maybe you have him, and maybe he is buried somewhere in the Carpathians."

"You've received pictures of him since I've been in Kyiv. You know he's alive and healthy."

"And you have done your homework. But how do I know you can deliver him? Someone else may be in charge."

"We need to have some trust," Ilya said.

"Why don't you bring Palmer to Kyiv? I could meet him and then we can talk."

"And you and Pavlov can steal him from me and divide the money between the two of you."

"Trust, Ilya, we need some trust. I'm certain you could work out the details," she said with a smile.

Anna Baranova did not linger. She finished the second glass of chardonnay, told Ilya that he'd be hearing from them, not just her, and left him alone with his Guinness Stout. When the wall clock read 9:40, he left the restaurant, and slipped the doorman a roll of hryvnia to get him a cab. It was an unexpectedly large tip, he realized, but superstition had taken hold and he tried to believe that this minor redistribution of wealth would buy him luck. Things had to break perfectly if he were going to outwit the cunning and corrupt.

He directed the cabbie to drive a mile north, and then demanded that the driver backtrack a few blocks. Once the cabbie had driven off, Ilya got into the Chevrolet Niva and proceeded to Maydan Nezaleshnosti.

# Chapter 20

Most of Kyiv was foreign to Fedya. He knew how to get to Ilya's apartment and could make his way to the major tourist attractions with relative assurance, but the rest of the city was a haze, nothing but blocks of buildings held together by potholed streets and trolley tracks. But Veronika had given him no choice but to use the underground to get to the other side of the Dnipro River. "I'll pick you up in front of the Swedish Embassy at 9:00 p.m.," she said in a deep and firm voice. "I'll be in a red Skoda Octavia, the hatchback. You can't miss it. The front fender is dented, and the right side needs to be repainted."

It was raining when Fedya got out of the subway. He pushed up the collar of his black leather jacket, pulled down his Lenin style leather cap, and watched a red Skoda slow down not far from him. But as Fedya moved toward it, the driver accelerated and pulled away. He had met Veronika that afternoon, in a sordid bar not far from Ilya's apartment, but darkness made it impossible for him to recognize the passing car's driver. Still, he looked around to see if there was something that could have chased her away. The street was empty. The car came by again, but this time it didn't slow down. He was ready to break his silence and use his cell phone to reach Ilya when the car appeared for the third time. It pulled to the curb.

"Why all this driving around?" Fedya asked testily after he had jumped in the vehicle. "Did you enjoy seeing me get wet?"

"I was just making sure it was you. It is dark out. I expect you sound pleasanter when you are dry."

Fedya shook the water off his cap and rolled down his collar. As the windshield wiper struggled to keep up with the storm, the glare from the oncoming cars stung his eyes. He felt the inner pocket of his jacket, took out the gun and turned it slowly around in his hands before replacing it. Then he put a hand in a side pocket to feel for the handcuffs Ilya had given him, and for the kerchief he was to use as a gag. He was nervous. He had never carried a gun; he had never placed a cloth in someone's mouth. Ilya had given him rudimentary lessons on both pistol and gag, but Fedya hoped he could avoid putting them into practice.

"Are we on schedule?" he asked.

"We are fine. I know where we are going. I know how to get there and how to get away. I know where we go next. I'm not an amateur, Fedya."

"And I am—is that what you're saying?"

"Don't shoot anyone, Fedya, that's all I ask. I've never been involved in a shooting. I want to avoid it if I can."

She had the voice of a larger woman, a contralto who might appear in a Rimsky-Korsakov opera. It was the first thing he noted about her, this deep voice. It was only after she had stood up to leave the tavern where they had surreptitiously met that he noticed other attributes, the athletic figure, the dark hair cut shorter than was in style, the broad shoulders. "Kolyna says you need some discreet help," she had said to Ilya and Fedya after picking up a bottle of beer at the bar. "Tell me what you need?" And Ilya had answered, "I didn't think you would be so beautiful."

She parked the Skoda on a dark side street, settled back in her seat, and asked Fedya for a cigarette. For the next hour they lit cigarette after cigarette, preventing with cupped hands the flames of their matches from reflecting in the car's windows. They talked about the weather, about political corruption, about the lack of jobs in Kyiv, about anything that was not personal or revelatory. As the minutes passed, he found it more and more difficult not to flirt. The young man in him wanted to know everything about her, about the wrestling title Kolyna mentioned to Ilya, about her father's political career and his assassination, about the way she smiled and her hips moved, about the way her legs might wrap around his body. But he couldn't allow himself to feel young; he had to feel joyless, he had to be focused. At another time and place, he told himself, he would have gotten her to smile and laugh. He wondered if he would ever see her after that night.

As soon as she saw the large car turn the corner, Veronika started the Skoda's engine. When the white limousine pulled along the curb in front of Pavlov's apartment house, she pulled her car into the middle of the street and abruptly stopped, the engine still running. Then she and Fedya jumped out of the vehicle and began to throw obscenities at each other. In slurred voices, their bodies precariously balanced, they hurled indictments of sexual perversions and physical abuse. As she faked stumbling forward, she threw her pocketbook at Fedya. He scooped it up and threw it back. With her eyes concentrated on the chauffeur's movements, she failed to avoid it hitting her thigh.

Fedya continued to swear and gesticulate, but Veronika fell silent. She turned her back on the young Russian to insure that what was planned was true, and there were only two occupants in the limousine. But she had to wait for the chauffeur to open his door and the interior light to go on before she could be certain. Seeing only Pavlov and driver, she allowed herself a deep breath and watched as Hedeon slowly pulled his body from its seat and made his way to his passenger's door. She moved closer to the red Skoda when the chauffeur leaned into the opened window to speak to Pavlov. She got into her car when Hedeon opened the rear door of the limousine, and she shifted into first gear when the two men stood on the street laughing at Fedya's antics.

Hedeon and Pavlov were halfway up the front steps to the apartment house when a black Chevrolet Aveo, its bright lights blazing, came to a rapid halt behind the Skoda, its horn blasting, its driver yelling out his window. Veronika slowly moved her car so that the intruder could drive away; then she accelerated and smashed the front bumper of the white limousine.

Hedeon quickly pushed Pavlov into a crouch and put his body in front of the deputy mayor. He reached behind his jacket and pulled out a large revolver, his eyes darting from Fedya to the limousine and then back to Fedya. With both hands on his gun, he pointed it at the Skoda and slowly made his way down the steps.

"Don't shoot, don't shoot," Veronika yelled in Ukrainian as she stepped out of the Skoda and onto the sidewalk, her blouse half unbuttoned, her mini skirt too tight to be concealing a weapon. Hedeon kept the revolver pointed at her as she put her hands over her head and threw out her breasts.

"Down, down," the chauffeur yelled.

Veronika went down on her knees.

"Fucking bitch," Hedeon yelled. "Are you out of your mind?" He yanked open the driver's door and quickly examined the interior of the Skoda. He looked up to see Fedya still waving his arms over his head but no longer making a sound.

Hedeon yelled at the young man. "Down, you fucking bastard, get your fucking body on the road."

Fedya hesitated for a moment, but as Hedeon raised his gun, he began to go down on his knees. Veronika shouted at the chauffeur as she sprang up. When he turned his head in her direction, she grabbed hold of his gun arm, flipped him over her leg and onto his back, and kicked the weapon out of his hand. Hedeon seized her ankle and pulled her down. He was struggling to get up when she kicked him in the neck with her free foot, the two-inch heel of her shoe cracking into his air pipe. When he got on all fours, she chopped the back of his neck with the side of her hand. Hedeon lay motionless on the sidewalk.

Pavlov looked in shock. He hesitantly moved down a couple of steps to help Hedeon, then changed his mind. He jerked around and headed for the front door. It was too late. Fedya raced up the stairs, the small revolver in his hand. He motioned to Pavlov to be silent, and then pushed him down the stairs and toward the Skoda. Fedya put the handcuffs on the deputy mayor, pushed him into the back seat, and sat down next to him.

"You'll never get away with this," Pavlov said.

Fedya pointed the gun at him and took out the kerchief. Pavlov muttered a series of curses, and then a prayer. Then Pavlov opened his mouth, and Fedya carefully inserted the gag.

~

Hedeon lay on the cobbled street, his head throbbing and stabbing pains running from his neck down his back. He lifted his head just high enough to see the red car speed around the next corner, but then he lost focus and the street began to swim. Images of city traffic entered his mind, and he imagined hearing a running engine and squealing wheels. In a haze, he pulled himself to the sidewalk for safety and lay on the cold cement in disbelief. Images of the young woman in the short skirt rolled before his eyes and his ears filled with the strange man's curses. "Fuck," he said out loud and forced himself to all fours. "Fuck," he said again when his body fought against his wishes, and all he had the strength to do was sit on the sidewalk, his legs stretched out in front of him.

He was determined to sound professional when he dialed Anna's number, but as her phone rang over and over again, his emotional turmoil returned. "Pavlov has been kidnapped," he shouted into the cell phone.

"Hedeon?" Anna asked.

"They've kidnapped Pavlov. I tried to protect him, but they got him."

"Who are they?" she screamed.

"I don't know. I never saw them before. And they said nothing. What should we do?"

"Is this a drunken joke," she asked, her breathing labored.

"I am not a prankster, Anna Baranova. And I wouldn't joke about something so serious."

"Are you certain he's been kidnapped?" she asked.

Hedeon couldn't believe she could be so stupid. "Anna Baranova, think. Pavlov has been abducted. We need to do something."

"Tell me, tell me exactly what happened."

Embarrassing as he found it, he described the entire episode, the car crash, his immediate concern, his foolish belief that he was witnessing a lovers' drunken argument, and the unexpected martial arts expertise of the woman. "And now what?" he concluded.

"And now we think. Come over to my apartment. By the time you've gotten here, maybe we will have thought of something," Anna answered.

Hedeon heard no shred of confidence in her voice.

~

Anna Baranova turned the small glass upside down and watched the remaining vodka trickle down the kitchen drain. She shouted a series of Russian expletives, realizing for the first time that the meeting with Ilya, the wine and sushi, the awkward attempt to bribe her, were part of a well thought out scheme. So the target was Pavlov, she told herself, another captive, but for what purpose?

"No one will pay for him," she said to Vika. "Who does Ilya think will buy him back? The mayor? The Party? Ilya is smarter than that. He knows that they are competitors and not friends. They'll be planning trysts to the Black Sea while they carry Pavlov's casket. Everything's fucked up Vika, everything. I have no money. Pavlov's wife doesn't know where he has hidden his wealth. And everyone else is an enemy."

"Why don't you call in the security forces or have Hedeon speak to them?" Vika asked.

"And if they found Pavlov, what would they do, shoot him and blame it on the Americans, on Ilya?" she said, her hands pulling at her hair, her amber eyes raging. "Maybe worse, they would accuse him of plotting with corrupt Americans to rob Ukraine. Pavlov's strength is with the people, Vika, with his popular appeal. But the people have no power. Can you imagine me standing on a soapbox and appealing to people to pay the ransom?"

Vika poured herself another drink. "You draw such a dark scene, Anna. There must be something you can do? Pavlov has friends. He has an entourage."

"They'd sell him for an hour with a second-rate whore," Anna said in a harsh, gravelly voice, and continued to pace the kitchen, her arms flailing in the air, her hands in constant motion. "I don't know what to do, Vika. I want to bang my head against the wall until an idea rattles loose."

The cell phone went off before Vika could speak. Anna grabbed it off the table.

"What, Hedeon, what now?"

"The Americans are gone," he said in Ukrainian.

"What do you mean 'gone'?"

"They slipped by my man and got into a small SUV. That was the last he saw of them."

"Did he recognize the driver?"

"It was too dark, and he was too far away."

"Fuck," Anna said vehemently. "Where are you now?"

"I'll be at your place in a few minutes."

She hung up without another word and slumped onto a kitchen chair. She put her head in her hands and began to mumble. Vika walked over to her lover and rubbed her shoulders. "And what now?" she gently asked.

"The Americans are trying to get out of Ukraine. They have no passport; they have no car. Ilya must have left the restaurant and gotten to them. He will know how to smuggle them out of the country. They will be happy to pay him a lot of money. Is that why he took Pavlov, to help in the movement of money?"

"Perhaps," Vika said before kissing Anna on the head. "But maybe he isn't after money. Perhaps he only wants to taunt Pavlov. You describe Ilya as an old bull. Capturing Pavlov keeps him at the head of the herd, his cock still swollen, his balls aching with desire."

"He's after money, Vika, not cunt. I'm certain of that. He talks like an idealist, but he is just a man."

"You are most probably right," Vika answered, but there was no sincerity in her voice. She pulled out a chair, slugged down the remaining vodka in her glass, and sat close to her friend. But just as she settled down, Hedeon rapped on the apartment's door.

Anna jumped out of her seat. "It's about time," she shouted after opening the door. She struck him on the chest with the side of a fist. "How the fuck did you let this happen?"

Vika tried to take the chill out of the air by inviting Hedeon to the table and offering him a small glass of vodka.

When she brought out black bread and cheese, Anna glowered at her. "Enough," she said. "We have business to attend to. Tell me Hedeon, what happened."

He emptied the glass in two gulps and began a detailed description of everything that had transpired down to the clothing that was worn, the color of the kidnappers' hair, the car they drove, the unanticipated judo throw. When he was finished, Anna asked him to repeat it all, acting as if there was a crucial fact that repetition would reveal, some seemingly minor observation that would lead her to a next step. He looked for another drink, but Anna put her hand over his glass. He repeated what he had said, but his tone had changed, there was less emotion behind his words and more calculation. When Anna asked him to repeat the story for a third time, he bristled. His back straightened. His eyes grew hard.

"Enough," he said, repeating Anna's word with the intensity she had used when she prevented Vika from serving him. "Repeating the events will not change them. It will not return Pavlov. We need to get the security forces involved."

Anna tried to sweeten her tone. "Who are you thinking of, Hedeon? Pavlov's anticorruption statements have not made him a hero to the security forces. They take his charges personally. Do you know of a group that would be loyal to him, people who would not add their own mischief to the search?"

"Let me think on it, Anna Baranova. Let me think on it. By morning, I will know."

She rang Hedeon's cell phone early in the morning. He did not answer. When she called five minutes later, it just rang and rang. A half hour later, the line was dead.

"Where do you think he is?" Vika asked.

"Bastard," Anna shouted. "I think he has contacted his old friends, and the security forces are now involved, Vika. Fucking Hedeon is making certain he has his next job."

# Chapter 21

Earlier in the evening, Peter had checked his watch before taking the elevator up to the 12<sup>th</sup> floor of the Dnipro Hotel. It was 7:00 p.m. He wasn't late.

"Meet me in the Panorama Bar in fifteen minutes. It's in your hotel. I will be wearing a long gray raincoat and holding a rain hat in my left hand. I am very tall and am considered attractive," a soft female voice had said.

"And who are you?"

"Raisa."

"That's not what I mean. What are we meeting about?" he remembered asking lightheartedly, thinking she was a call girl fishing for a lonely business traveler.

"Telephones have ears, Palmer," she said quietly. Then she hung up.

The name Palmer rang in his ears long after the phone went dead. He wanted to call Caitlin or knock on her door, but telephones did have ears, and so did light fixtures, and bedside radios. So he combed his hair, put on shoes and a jacket, and headed upstairs alone.

The evening dinner crowd was first beginning to gather, but already the tables that lined the restaurant's large windows were occupied. He walked back to the elevators and leaned against the wall, wishing that Raisa, or whatever her real name was, would arrive soon. After a slow ten minutes, an attendant tapped him on the arm and said something in Ukrainian he didn't understand. But he followed the young man into the restaurant and to a small table near a window. He glanced over to the entrance now and then, but filled the time looking out the window and watching the incessant rainfall fragment the lights of the city into brilliant splinters. He imagined the taste of scotch but took hold of himself and ordered a borscht and tea, thinking that some opaque trick was being played by Pavlov or Ilya or Anna Baranova. But to what end? He didn't have a clue. He imagined Selby throwing her cloth coat over the back of the table's other chair and asking him to marry her. How wonderful it would have been to have her there, watching the night, sharing the rain, declining dessert so they could race more quickly to their bed.

A tall, elegant woman, about thirty years old, was standing by his table when he shook the daydream from his head, her long sleek coat soaked, and a rain hat in her left hand.

"May I join you?" she asked in a thick, Slavic accent.

Peter stood up and helped her off with her coat. She put it over the back of the chair and carefully placed her hat on the table. He pulled a chair out for her.

"Thank you," she said without a smile, her long dress waving gracefully as she sat down. She glanced at the neighboring tables and put a finger against her lips.

"I've already ordered. Would you like something?"

"Some white wine, please," she said as a waiter brought Peter his borscht and tea.

"A beautiful view," she said as she looked out on the city.

"It is a beautiful city."

"From this height, I expect all cities are beautiful. She ran her fingers through her raven hair. Long silver earrings reflected the overhead light. "My hair is still damp from the rain. I should have combed it up. The hat would have protected all of it."

"It is wet tonight."

"Kyiv in the fall is always wet."

"Where did you learn English," the American asked after her wine had arrived. "Did you live abroad?"

"I studied to be a translator at the International University in Magadan, and had a six month exchange at the University of Alaska in Anchorage."

"Do you work as a translator?"

"Now and then, but mostly then. There are few English-speaking business people in Kyiv. I'd make more money with German. I do lead tourist groups in the spring and summer. They tip well."

"And where would you take me?" Peter said, expecting that if anyone in earshot spoke English, or if there was a microphone hidden under the table, he would sound hopefully flirtatious.

Raisa recognized the game. "For a handsome man like you, there are many places to go. Do you like to dance?" She moved the hat closer to him, tipping it slightly so that he could see the envelope underneath.

Peter slipped his hand under the hat and palmed the paper. She had folded the envelope in half. He waited for her drink to arrive before tasting his borscht and drinking some tea. They chatted for a few minutes, and then he excused himself and went to the men's room.

The note was printed by a bold hand on a half sheet of course paper and put in a stained, unsealed envelope. "Timing is everything. Leave the hotel at 10:00 p.m. When you exit the revolving doors make a right. Walk along Khreschatyk Boulevard until you reach the entrance to the metro stop Maydan Nezaleshnosti. Hang around the entrance until a

Niva SUV pulls up. It is blue. Jump in quickly. It will get you to Palmer." There was no signature, but he assumed it was written by Ilya.

"I'd love to go dancing," he said when he got back to his seat. "But I don't have a car, and I don't particularly like to take a cab at night. The city can be dangerous, I hear."

She lifted the glass to her lips and finished the wine, her eyes never leaving his. "It can be very dangerous, particularly for foreigners who come out of fancy hotels. But from the little I know, Peter, and I know a great deal, sometimes it can be more dangerous not to go to the dance. The planet never stops turning."

He needed something more from her. They were being paranoid, he thought. Who would be listening, certainly not the mature man sitting to their right who was intent on getting a young blond drunk, or the two gentlemen across from them who were speaking German? But then he remembered that he had not chosen the table himself, and wondered if his sitting at it had been orchestrated by someone who knew there was a hidden microphone.

"I have some telephone messages to answer, so it would be best if I could meet you later. I'll have the hotel get me a cab." Peter took his pen out of an inside pocket of his jacket and began to doodle on a napkin. "What was the address again?"

While she uttered something in Ukrainian, he wrote down Ilya and turned it toward her. She nodded before getting up from the chair.

"Do you have to go?" he asked as he helped Raisa on with her coat.

She turned around and hugged him. "Fedya," she murmured into his ear. "A young man with a red ponytail."

After she left, he sat back down, finished his tea, and called for the bill. He left the borscht.

Caitlin was working on the script when he knocked on the door. His voice gave her little choice. "Let's go for a walk," he said, his eyes wide open, his facial muscles tight. "Bring your umbrella. It's wet out there," he added as he unfolded the note for her to read.

The man in the shabby gray suit was nowhere to be seen. But a thin man in a herringbone sport jacket looked annoyed when he saw them come out of the elevator. He quickly put on a black raincoat and followed them out the door.

"Is he behind us?" Caitlin asked after they had walked half a block.

"He's keeping his distance, but he's there."

"Shit," Caitlin exclaimed, "this is getting more than tiresome. Let's slow down so we can talk. I don't see why you trust this note. I think we're going to be kidnapped just like Benjamin. That we'll be held for ransom or end up buried in a mud pond. I don't like any of this."

"And if we sit around and let Pavlov and Anna design our future, would that make you feel safer?"

She stopped walking and looked down the street at the man who was following them. He was a distance off. "Yes, I would feel safer. At least we met Pavlov in his office. We met him in daylight. This is shit, Peter, this spy on spy crap."

"There isn't enough time to convince you, Caitlin. You just have to trust my judgment. If you had met Fedya and Ilya and Raisa, you'd understand. We can split. I'll get into the car, and you can go back to the hotel."

"That's crazy," she said, "and then I'll have two men for whom I feel responsible."

She bristled when the small blue SUV pulled up beside them, but she got into the vehicle.

"Welcome to the future," Ilya said after his passengers slid quickly onto the rear seats. He stepped on the accelerator and entered the nighttime traffic.

Out the rear window, Peter saw the thin man who was following them begin to run after the car, but after half a block, he gave up.

Peter waited until he could no longer see the man who was pursuing them before he asked, "Where are we going?"

"We are leaving the city to meet up with Fedya, and then we will travel to meet Benya."

"Benya?" Caitlin asked.

"We call your husband Benya. It is his familiar name. Benjamin is much too foreign."

She leaned forward before she spoke, her hand braced against Ilya's seat. "And who are 'we?'" she asked, sounding deeply suspicious.

"We are the people who have cared for him during the last three months," Ilya answered, his voice calm, his head facing forward.

"And why should I trust 'we?'" Caitlin spit out.

Ilya turned up a side street before he abruptly pulled to the curb and stopped. He flicked on the car's interior light and turned to the back seat.

"I can't force you to ride with me. I don't have a gun. I have no ropes to tie you. I have no gags to put in your mouths. I need you to work with me. If you are not willing to do that, I will drive you back to the hotel. You will be under constant surveillance. If Pavlov doesn't find Palmer, and he won't, he will arrest the two of you. He will say you came to the country not to find your husband but to help him swindle Ukrainian businessmen. He well say you are international criminals. He will be forced to let you go by your State Department and Ukraine's need for American support, but it will be only after he has convinced the public that he is incorruptible, that he is the champion of the people. Then he will run for mayor, or president."

"And how do you know all this, Ilya? Can you read his mind?" Peter asked.

"I make intelligent deductions. Think, Peter. What is he up to? He takes your passports; he takes your cell phones. He makes certain you are always watched. Do you think he is planning a birthday party?"

"So you are being altruistic and rescuing us from Pavlov. Is that your story?" Caitlin said sarcastically.

"Get out, get out," the Russian shouted.

"You kidnapped my husband, and now you are asking us to trust you. You ask us to think. What do you expect us to think?"

Ilya's shoulders slumped forward, and he wiped his forehead. His tone modulated. "I'm not a kidnapper. I'm an honorable smuggler. I buy, and I sell. I help people make money and live better by going around a corrupt government. I don't steal. I don't murder. But I am human. I cannot always resist the crowd. I can't always stand against the currents of the time. Your husband was taken off the streets of Kyiv by two hoodlums. When I rescued him from them, the opportunity to make money overwhelmed me. I became greedy. I became a capitalist. I became an opportunist. What more can I say? But I never hurt Benya. He is well. And foolish as it sounds, I think of him as a friend."

Moments passed. Ilya watched his passengers lean back in their seats and look at each other. Each seemed to be waiting for the other to say something. Peter broke the silence. "So you think you're offering us a Hobson's choice. We either go with you or are left exactly where we are. But what would happen if we got away and told Pavlov that you attempted to abduct us? Are you willing to live with that?"

"Go, my Americans. Run to Pavlov. Tell him I tried to turn you against him. What do you expect—a first-class ticket on British Airways? Are you that naive?"

"Naive might be staying in this car?" Caitlin said.

"We don't have time for an intellectual debate, Mrs. Palmer. We shit, or we get off the pot. Isn't that an American expression?"

She leaned forward in her seat until her face was only inches from Ilya's head. "Nothing about this is intellectual, let me assure you. Intelligence didn't bring us to Ukraine. And it seems that intelligence won't get us out. Peter trusts you, and I trust Peter. You have your passengers," Caitlin said in the voice of a news anchor, certain and secure.

As Ilya pulled into a crowded thoroughfare, Caitlin pushed further back into her seat. "First Selby and now him. You'll always be a sucker for an English accent, even one smeared with Russian," she said to Peter.

"My English is perfect," Ilya intruded.

"Of course it is," Caitlin said.

Peter listened for a hint of acceptance in her voice, but he found none. So she knows about Selby, he thought.

~

That evening in Kalush, Oksana greeted Marya with a bear hug and kissed her on both cheeks, tears pouring down her face. She was a short, heavyset woman, about the same age as Marya, Benjamin guessed, but she looked more worn and burdened, her long dress made of dark-green cloth, her dull brown hair combed back into a bun. The bright red kerchief she wore around her neck made her skin look sickly.

Oksana took her school friend by the hand and led her to the window to look at her in the light. They spoke in Russian, short and friendly phrases punctuated by smiles and laughter.

"My friend, Benya," Marya said in English. "He's an American."

When Oksana's arm reached out to him, Benjamin thought she wanted to shake his hand. Instead, she put her palm on the back of his hand and led him next to Marya and near the window. Noticing the spots on his face where he had nicked himself using Ilya's old straight razor, she said something to Marya and disappeared into the kitchen. She returned with a bottle of vodka and a clean cloth, dabbed the cloth with the alcoholic drink, and washed the thin scabs on his face.

"Thank you," he said.

She replied with a broad smile.

They sat in the small living room drinking tea, and eating butter cookies coated with apricot jam. He listened to the two women talk, watching their facial expressions change from gaiety to sadness, from surprise to resignation.

Oksana picked up a cookie and looked at Benya suspiciously. She asked Marya a question in Russian.

"She wants to know if you came to Ukraine on a romantic tour in order to find a wife," Marya translated.

"Is she available?"

"She thought that I might be your selection. But if you'd like, I can introduce you in a different way."

Marya said something in Russian. Oksana laughed so hard her eyes watered. She looked at him and blushed.

"I told her you had an English libido and a castrate's balls."

"No you didn't," he said uncertainly.

"I told her you were desperate to seduce me, and I was ready to give in. Your balls may be small, but you have a good heart. She would still like to know why you came to Ukraine."

"Tell her what we agreed on, Marya, that I came to Ukraine to find my roots."

"I hate to deceive her."

"The truth would involve her."

He listened to the Russian, thinking he might recognize a word or two—Peczenizyn or Jew or Washington—that would lead back to the story Marya had concocted. But he found the language too dense, and all he could do was watch the two friends talk to each other.

Oksana, a soulful expression on her face, took his hand and led him out to the narrow balcony. Below them, not more than two hundred yards from the wooden fence that surrounded the apartment complex, was an old cemetery, its heartlessly damaged tombstones separated by barren pieces of land that had once hosted other shrines to other dead. It was a sad, deserted place, Benjamin thought, empty of trees or bushes or memory.

Oksana said something in Russian, and Benjamin turned to Marya for a translation. "It's all that remains of a large Jewish cemetery," Marya said. "The last burial was in 1940."

Benjamin wondered what his old friend would think as he recalled Abramowitz's photograph of his fellow yeshiva students, and he wondered if there was a fossilized cemetery in Peczenizyn where Abramowitz's classmates and ancestors stirred.

"There is supposed to be a mass grave somewhere around here, but no one knows where," Marya continued.

"Or admits to knowing where," Benjamin said.

Marya moved closer to him and took his hand. "It is not easy to admit to evil, Benya."

He threw her comment off. He didn't want silence to be excused. "Has she ever been to Peczenizyn?" he asked.

The women exchanged a few sentences before Marya answered the question. "She has driven through the town but not more than that. It is not a very prosperous place."

"Does it have a Jewish cemetery?" he asked, and impatiently waited for Marya to translate his question into Russian, and then translate the answer into English.

"She doesn't know," Marya said.

He drifted back to the restaurant in Dupont Circle and imagined sitting tenderly with Abramowitz, a glass of tea on the table in front of his friend.

"And what did you see of my people?" the old man asked him.

"Not much, I'm afraid. I was locked away for most of the trip and saw very little of the country. There was an abandoned cemetery in Kalush," he heard himself answer.

"Five hundred years of history, and what is left, some worn tombstones adorned in a language none of the local people can read."

"Even history perishes, Martin."

"Perhaps it does, but I hope not. Remember when I told you about the last phrase on my grandfather's tombstone, 'May his soul be tied to the knot of life.' Perhaps all those souls are tied to the knot of life?" Abramowitz said. Then he quietly added, "I'd like to think so."

Benjamin forced his mind back to the present. He slowly ran his eyes over the cemetery, spending a moment on each headstone to show respect, to offer condolence, to remember a people cruelly erased from this land. A wound upon the world, he thought, but was immediately dissatisfied with his observation, annoyed that he couldn't think of something more telling, something profound. The dead have a claim on us. We owe them something, something more than a respectful glance, a sorrowful countenance, a tear. We owe them more than merging companies and selling short, more than buying stocks and trading bonds, more than a Swiss bank account and diamond studs. Like a dull knife, the use of the pronoun "we" tore at him. It was self-exculpating. It trivialized his emotions. He owed them something more, he, not we—but he didn't know what. "To lead a good life," Martin Abramowitz would say, but what did that mean for Benjamin Palmer? The question made him dizzy.

"Oksana would like to know if you are ready for dinner," he heard Marya call out from the living room.

~

The lights of Kyiv lay far behind them when Ilya parked the SUV behind an abandoned roadside restaurant and turned off its headlights. Immediately, the interior lights of another car, about a hundred yards away, went on.

"Stay in the car. I will leave the keys," the Russian said over his shoulder. "If anything goes wrong, drive due west and try to cross over the Polish border. It is your best hope. But I expect to be back in a couple of minutes."

"Now that's what I call an exit line," Peter said after Ilya slammed the driver's door behind him. "Drive to Poland. And how in the world would we do that?"

Caitlin gave a mirthless laugh. "It does get us to want him to return, doesn't it? Do you think Benjamin could be in that car?"

"I wish I did. It would be a great way to end the night. But I think more will be demanded of us. I don't think you'll get to your husband until you've paid an exorbitant ransom."

"I'd be happy to pay it," Caitlin said in a convincing voice.

Peter rolled down his window to see better, but without the SUV's headlights, the parking area was black. He saw nothing. "This is ridiculous," he said to Caitlin as his impulsiveness got the best of him. He threw open the car door to step out. Ilya's voice stopped him short.

"We will be a little crowded," the Russian said. "Let the woman sit in the front next to me. Pavlov will sit between you and Fedya."

"Pavlov?" Peter shouted.

"The deputy mayor is our guest. He's a little unhappy right now. You may have to cheer him up."

The car's interior light illuminated the faces of the additional passengers. Pavlov's hands were bound behind him, a gag in his mouth. Fedya was close behind him.

"What the hell is going on?" Caitlin asked.

"Just move to the front seat," Ilya commanded. "We are in for a long ride. I will have time to explain it to you."

She did Ilya's bidding, but waited for Pavlov to be unceremoniously pushed into the rear seat, and Fedya to slide in next to him.

"Hello, Benya's wife" Fedya said once he was seated.

Ilya started the engine and turned on the headlights. The driver of the other car did the same and followed the SUV out of the parking lot. Ilya turned west. The driver of the red car beeped its horn and turned east, the direction from which they had come.

Pavlov's body shifted with the movement of the car, leaning against Fedya when the car swung left, leaning against Peter when the terrain tilted the car in the other direction. But he struggled to keep his face toward Peter, and pleaded with him with movements of his head and shrugs of his shoulders.

"Do we have to keep him trussed up, Ilya? Can't we make him a little more comfortable and get rid of the gag?" Peter asked. "We don't have to torture him."

"So you think this is torture. You should only know what he had in store for you. He would have put you in a solitary cell shared only by roaches and rodents, with no light and little air, your life constantly threatened, your whereabouts unknown by anyone who could plead your cause. This is paradise. Good company. A comfortable automobile. A beautiful woman to look at."

"I don't think having your hands bound behind you, and a gag in your mouth is exactly paradise," Peter argued. "I didn't get into this car to be a murderer."

"Who said anything about murder?" Ilya bellowed. "Pavlov is an old comrade of mine. I only want to murder him half the time."

Peter wasn't in the mood for humor. He reached behind Pavlov's head and began to untie the gag, but Fedya forcefully stopped him.

"Oh, my American," Ilya said as he pulled to the side of the road. "Does this bother you?" he asked Caitlin.

"I think Peter is right. We don't have to be barbarians," she answered, but she sounded uncertain.

Ilya let out an unruly laugh. "Perhaps you are right. We could just shoot him and leave his body on the side of the road."

"Please," Caitlin said.

"And are you planning to shoot us as well?" Peter asked.

Ilya got out of the car and Fedya followed him. The younger Russian pulled Pavlov from the back seat and Ilya took out the gag. A torrent of Russian invectives poured out of the deputy mayor, his voice growing in volume and harshness as anger exploded in his throat. Ilya glared back but remained silent. Then he lifted the gag in front of Pavlov's face and said something quietly. The captive fell silent.

Fedya redid the handcuffs so that Pavlov could keep his hands on his lap, and the three of them got back into the car.

"Is that better, Peter?" Ilya asked after pulling back onto the road.

"Do you really plan to kill him?" Peter asked.

"Only if he does something stupid, but with some luck, he will go back to Kyiv, back to his desk, and back to his corruption. I have only one plan, to bring Caitlin back to her husband and get all of you out of Ukraine."

"And what about you?" Caitlin asked. "What will happen to you?"

Ilya turned to look at Caitlin. There was no smile on his face. "It is very kind of you to ask," he said. "If all goes well, I will be a happy man.

# Chapter 22

For breakfast, Oksana emptied her refrigerator and pantry of all foods she thought might please Benjamin and Marya, hard cheese and boiled eggs, black bread and butter, two kinds of herring, an assortment of small chocolate candies, and a variety of homemade cookies. She poured some Russian Cognac into each of their teas and toasted her guests.

Marya continued her role as a translator. "Oksana would like us to stay longer. We could use the apartment and travel through the Carpathians. This is a most beautiful country. We are poor, but we have the sun and the moon. Fishing is good; hunting, they tell her, is even better. She would like you to go home and tell people what a lovely place is Ukraine, how friendly the people, how hospitable. They have good wine and good vodka, and handsome children."

He thanked Oksana profusely and promised he would tell his friends and neighbors only good things about the country.

Oksana's eyes watered when she spoke to Marya.

"What did she say?" Benjamin asked.

"She said that this was a tease, that old friends need to spend more than a few hours with each other. She is sorry that you insisted on sleeping on the couch, and that we didn't take the double bed and make love to each other. She would not have been embarrassed."

"Did you tell her we were lovers?"

"I didn't have to tell her, Benya. She can see."

Oksana hugged him when they were ready to leave. She hugged Marya more tightly. Then Oksana stepped back, crossed herself, and said a prayer.

After they got into the car, Marya said, "I find goodbyes difficult, and can't help but wonder if we will ever see each other again. I wish I could believe, as Oksana does, that God is good."

~

L'viv's small airport was located a few miles outside the city, in a residential neighborhood of small houses and large gardens. Nothing about it spoke modernity. Its weathered concrete runways showed deep cracks and irregular dips; its prefabricated, metal hangers, of which there were few, looked, even at a distance, dirty and worn.

From the parked car, they watched a three-engine jet passenger plane descend and bounce on the runway. As they got out of the car, they saw a ground crew—four men and one woman—push a mobile staircase across a patch of grass and toward the plane's passenger door. By the time they got to the terminal building, passengers were exiting the aircraft.

"Do you think we'll be flying out on that type of plane?" Benjamin speculated.

"I don't think we will be on something that large. Our contact owns the plane. I expect it will be very basic."

"With an engine or a rubber band?"

"Don't worry, it will be a good Ukrainian rubber band," she answered.

All contemporary trappings were absent from L'viv's airport terminal. There were no electronic bulletin boards, no coffee shop or restaurant, and no information booth. Missing, too, were the counters and luggage handling facilities that Benjamin had once considered ubiquitous. If there was a public bathroom serving the main waiting room, it wasn't evident.

"Rather basic, isn't it," he said to Marya.

"What do you mean?" she replied.

"This airport has none of the features of a modern terminal."

"L'viv is a small city."

"Not that small."

Marya began to laugh. "Is this what life with you would be, arguments about travel conveniences?"

"We'd find other things to argue about," he answered, "like how many eggs one should eat in a week and if herring is healthy, and whether we should name the children after George Washington or Vladimir Lenin."

When Marya didn't laugh, he realized that his going on about a shared future was not funny, and he kicked himself for being insensitive. "I'm sorry," he said.

"And so am I."

They sat silently on one of the few wooden benches scattered around the terminal, their hips touching, her arm entwined in his, their hands merged. Eventually, she asked, "Are you nervous?"

He was too deep into himself to understand the question, so she had to repeat herself.

"Nervous, expectant, worried, all those things, Marya. Not knowing is uncomfortable. Where am I going? Who is going to take me?"

The expression on her face told him it was not the answer she wanted. So he tried again, wanting to be honest but painless. He didn't know if it was possible. "I'm a jumble of feelings. I can't order them. I'm excited, Marya, and nervous. I'm afraid and elated. I want to get moving, but I want you with me. The thought of saying goodbye to you makes me shiver. I want a guarantee that we will see each other again, not in decades but in months or weeks. I need to believe that we will have the chance to be together."

"Only heartbreak is guaranteed," she said. Her voice so low that he could hardly hear her.

"Don't do this, Marya. Don't fill our last hours with sadness. They are going to be difficult enough."

She put her hand under his chin and turned his face toward her. "And how do I turn my feelings off, my dear Benya? I'm a Russian peasant from Magadan and Khabarovsk and Vladivostok. To smother my emotion is to smother my soul."

He brought her hand to his mouth and then let it rest on his lap. There was nothing he could say to lift her spirits, at least nothing believable. He stared into the distance, and imagined himself back in his small Washington apartment. He pictured himself riding the building's elevator surrounded by the aspiring young, the men clean-shaven, the women nubile, their clothing conservative, their briefcases stuffed, their lives empty of kidnappings, of imprisonment, of nighttime with Marya, of the children who lived across the stream. He wondered what life would be like without Marya's smile, without the comfort of her body, without her laughter. He fantasized about having dinner on the patio of the Greek restaurant with Abramowitz. Marya was sitting between them. "Benjamin tells me your mother was a Bolshevik," Abramowitz says. "Does it show?" Marya asks, annoyed that Benjamin was saying things about her that she would not have immediately shared. "Yes," answers Abramowitz, "it shows. You are very beautiful."

A young boy's voice interrupted Benjamin's daydreaming. He couldn't have been much over six and was bouncing nervously from one foot to the other as if in desperate need of a bathroom. "Marya?" he asked.

"I'm Marya," she said with a large smile, delight written over her face.

The young boy said something in Ukrainian, but turned around before she could answer, and quickly ran across the room to grab the extended hand of a young woman.

Marya waved, but the woman just turned away and began to walk toward a door.

"What did he say?" Benjamin asked.

Marya looked exasperated. "One word, 'wait,'"

Benjamin stretched out his long legs. "A secret message delivered by a child? This cloak and dagger stuff is getting tiresome, Marya. Wait for what, the moon to appear?"

"Maybe not that long," she said, her eyes on a tall, lanky man, with a full head of curly gray hair.

The stranger said a few words in Russian to Marya before holding out his hand to help her up from her seat. She motioned to Benjamin to stay put and walked a few yards away with the stranger. They exchanged a few sentences before returning to the bench.

"I'm Bohdan Karmalyuk, but Americans call me Dan." The Ukrainian smiled with a closed mouth. "Ilya told me you would have a full beard and an unruly head of hair. That's why the caution. I gave the boy and his mother enough money for a box of chocolates."

"Marya thought it would be wise for me to look like an American tourist."

"A Jew looking for his homeland, Marya Ivanova told me. Peczenizyn—isn't it? Not many people come to seek out that town. But some Jews have full beards," Bohdan said cautiously.

"I didn't think I would be convincing masquerading as a Hasid," Benjamin answered.

Marya laughed nervously. Bohdan's bright, hazel eyes stayed focused on the American's face. It made Benjamin uneasy.

"Do you know the city of Peczenizyn?" Benjamin asked.

"I don't go there very often."

"But it has an airport?" Benjamin questioned.

"My plane doesn't need an airport. Do you speak Russian?"

"No," Benjamin said.

"How about Ukrainian?"

"English is all I know. I don't have an ear for languages."

In Russian, the pilot said something sharp to Marya. Her eyes seemed to flame when she argued back. He looked at Benjamin for a long time, and then spoke again to the woman.

"What? What?" Benjamin asked. His voice was loud enough to cause a distant head to turn in their direction.

"Nothing," Marya answered. "He is still unconvinced that we are who we say we are."

"Does he want more money? Is that it?"

Bohdan stretched his head back and glared at the American. "Do not insult me," he spit out. "My ear is very good for languages." He turned toward Marya. "Make the call," he insisted.

Marya used her cell phone, but got no answer. "He's asleep or is out of range. I will try him again."

"And what should we do until then, fly to Peczenizyn?" Bohdan said. The edges of his mouth curled after he finished the sentence. Benjamin couldn't tell if it was a smile or gas.

"Maybe your phone would have better luck," Marya said. Her black hair unfurled as she shook her head.

Bohdan dialed the number. No one answered. "Have you killed him?" he asked with a straight face.

"Would you try to kill a Russian from Vladivostok?" Marya said.

"Ilya is from Moscow," Bohden corrected, his voice tense. "Are you from Vladivostok?"

"You are right, he was born in Moscow. I was raised in Khabarovsk. For a while, I lived in Vladivostok. That's where I met Ilya. He was a friend of my mother. She came from Magadan. Perhaps he told you about her."

Bohdan pulled down his heavy gray eyebrows and squinted at her. "Was your mother a guard or a prisoner?" he asked.

"There were never any guards in my family. But does it matter? We were all victims of the same corrupt regime were we not?" Marya answered.

The Ukrainian's mouth opened, and he let out a quick laugh. If there were any teeth left, Benjamin didn't see them. "You have a woman's voice but a mind like Ilya's."

"I take that as a compliment, Bohdan Karmalyuk. Do you want us to stay here while you try to reach Ilya? Or should we leave with you and try to reach Ilya together?"

Bohdan turned toward the exit and motioned to them to follow. A Carpatair Saab 2000 was beginning its approach as the swinging door closed behind them. "Beautiful, isn't it?" Bohdan said. He didn't wait for an answer. "My plane is even more beautiful, you will see. It can take off and land anywhere, anywhere."

Low-lying clouds had rolled in from the east by the time Marya and Benjamin followed Bohdan out of the terminal building. They turned the landscape gray and put a chill in the air. Benjamin turned around after they had walked a distance to examine the structure they had just left. The facade of the two-story building seemed out of place. Its Roman columns looked worn and dingy; its walls had no character. But it was unlike most of the structures designed under Stalin, buildings without souls, buildings that made no statement, which had no dreams. Architecture smothered by ideology, a story in itself. Someone at least was trying for distinction when the airport terminal was built, Benjamin thought. If there was any manmade beauty in this city, and he had read that there was much, none of it was visible from its airport. Even the gravel in the parking lot looked abandoned.

"You will drive," Bohdan began to say, but he stopped short when he heard the engine of an automobile start. He quickly glanced at the silver Lada that was parked by the terminal building, trying to look as if he hadn't noticed the vehicle. He said something in Russian to Marya, his head turned away from the distant car.

"Act as if we are asking him for directions, Benya," Marya ordered crisply, her hand blocking her mouth.

"What's going on?" Benjamin asked.

Marya turned to Bohdan but spoke to the American. "He thinks the people in the silver car are looking for us. He wants them to think we are not together, that we are just asking him for directions. Did you notice the car when we were driving here?"

Benya motioned with his hand and looked toward the exit of the parking lot as if he were trying to understand some driving directions. "I didn't notice anyone following us. Is he certain?"

"He's just concerned," Marya said. She shrugged her shoulders, looked at Bohdan, and began to speak in Russian.

Whatever she said, Bohdan answered at length, and then turned around and reentered the terminal.

"Come," Marya said, "let's go to the car. I'll tell you where to go once we've gotten on our way."

Bohdan's suspicion was warranted. In the rearview mirror, Benjamin watched the silver Lada. Its driver did nothing to avoid detection. If another vehicle slipped between the two cars, the Lada would pick up speed and swerve through the oncoming lane to keep sight of its prey. When Benjamin stopped for a red light, the Lada pulled up within inches of his rear bumper. Two men were seated in the front seats; it was impossible to see if others were sitting behind them.

"Should I try to lose them?" Benjamin asked.

"How? We don't know the streets. We don't know the city. It would just give them the pleasure of a race we cannot win. But Bohdan has a scheme."

"Which is?"

"We are to head downtown and find an Armenian restaurant called Kilikia. He said it's located in a tiny alley off Virimenska. We are to eat inside, let a half-hour go by, and then slip out its rear door. He will be there with a car."

"Do we at least pay the bill?" Benjamin asked sarcastically.

"The owner will know what is going on, Benya. Bohdan will have been in touch with him."

"And you trust Bohdan?"

"What choice do we have? He could have sold us out at the terminal. He could have just abandoned us to our trackers."

"Maybe he has," Benjamin said.

"Then trust me," she said.

He did not answer. His thoughts mimicked her comments. What choice did he have? But he didn't say it out loud. He watched her shift the angle of her head to read street signs, her long black hair covering her shoulders, the tip of her tongue every now and then poking through her slightly opened mouth. How could he not trust her? He loved her.

As they approached the city, the road became more congested, full of small, older cars, and Soviet era trucks. Heavy exhaust fumes entered their car, irritating his nose and turning his stomach. The silver car was still in the rearview mirror, its driver undeterred by the growing traffic.

The route took them out of the distant suburbs and into a hodgepodge of a city, a place lost in the 1960's, where factory smokestacks still spewed out dark particles, and covered concrete buildings and stucco siding with smut. The coal burning debris impregnated the entire environment. Even the air was ashen, Benjamin decided. But then his thinking jumped, and he became concerned that these observations were too simple, too superficial. He was allowing his mood to color what he was seeing. What waste, this negative thinking, he mused, and drove himself to play tourist. He searched the streets for glimmers of beauty, for hints of the 19th century, imagining how L'viv must have looked before it was invaded by vans and automobiles, before it was full of boxy high-rise structures. He tried to visualize the city as it must have been when people rode in horse drawn wagons and walked long distances on the cobbled streets and bricked sidewalks. But he found it a futile search. He would remember L'viv, if he lived to remember it at all, as a dark and cheerless place.

~

Bohdan was parked on the narrow street that ran behind the restaurant.

"You don't have to rush," he said when Benjamin banged open the sliding door of the white van. "They just picked up a couple sandwiches and a couple of bottles of beer. They won't remember what they're supposed to be doing for at least a half-hour."

Bohdan drove slowly over the bumpy cobblestone streets, heading back toward the airport, a lighted cigarette between his fingers or his lips, a Lenin style cap pulled low on his forehead. He gave a loud yawn when he found himself stuck behind a double-car trolley, its electric engines fueled from overhead wires. He belched when a huge truck hurdled out of a half-hidden driveway and forced him to slam on the brakes.

Marya's impatience was palpable. Her knee pulsed; her fingers twisted little curls in her raven hair.

"Relax," Benjamin instructed, "The traffic won't allow them to go any faster than we do."

"Bohdan seems to be relaxed enough for all of us. He is worried about our identities, but he doesn't seem at all concerned about the people following us. I'm beginning to question my trust."

Benjamin steadied her knee with his hand before speaking to Bohdan. "Who do you think they are?" he asked.

Bohdan answered with a Ukrainian phrase which Benjamin couldn't catch. "I didn't quite get that," the American said.

"The Ukrainian Security Service," Marya said.

"Secret police under a new label," Bohdan added.

"You seem pretty relaxed about them," Benjamin said.

"I don't fear them. They need me. I bring them products from Poland and the Czech Republic, sometimes from Germany."

"You're a smuggler," Benjamin said.

"I'm an international businessman," Bohdan corrected. Then he laughed.

"But why would they be after us? To rescue Benjamin?" Marya asked.

"I don't know why they are interested in you, but they have never been accused of putting rescue work at the top of their agenda. I reached Ilya while you were in the restaurant. He didn't tell me very much. He said I would have more than one American to get out of the country. Once again, he promised no pay, only appreciation. But if money should eventually come along, he would not be a cheapskate."

Marya uncrossed her legs and leaned forward. "Are you sure there will be more than one American?" she asked in Russian.

Bohdan answered in the same language. "That's what Ilya said. Perhaps he was doing it to make me more interested, but he referred to more than one, I am certain."

"Of course," she continued in her native language. She would meet them, then, the wife and the African. The thought depressed her. She wondered if she should translate what had just been said to ease Benjamin's curiosity, but decided to lie. "I told Bohdan it was good that he had such a large plane."

The van moved more rapidly when they got out of the inner city and onto streets lined with Cold War era residential buildings. They moved even more quickly through the less densely populated outskirts of the city where small, newly constructed houses were sprinkled among the older homes of agricultural workers. Bohdan parked on a commercial street, the ground floors of the two and three story brick buildings designed for small retail shops. They climbed the wooden staircase that ran along the back of one of the buildings, and entered the third floor apartment through its narrow kitchen. The flat smelled of dust and stale smoke.

"I'm not used to visitors," Bohdan said over his shoulder as he walked into the living room. "But the roof won't leak, and you will be safe. I will go down and pick up something to eat. There is already enough to drink."

"I could use a little vodka," Benjamin said, "and I'm sure Marya wouldn't mind a drink. It's been a pressured day."

"I don't think I have any vodka," Bohdan said with great pride. "I have some single malt scotch and good Kentucky bourbon, and a nice Cognac, from France and not Georgia. I have cigars from Cuba and cigarettes from America. But vodka, I don't carry vodka." He opened a bedroom door and pointed to the cases of whisky and boxes of cigarettes and cigars he had smuggled into the

Ukraine. "The other bedroom is less crowded. It has one narrow bed, but there is a couch in the living room."

"And where will you sleep?" Benjamin asked.

"Do not worry. I will not sleep on the street. Make yourself at home. I will pick you up after Ilya has arrived. But first I will pick up some food."

~

Through the partially opened front door, Bohdan handed Marya a thin plastic bag of breads and sliced meats and four triangular cardboard containers of Kefir.

"Sleep well, tomorrow will be an interesting day," he said before going down the concrete steps that led out to the street.

"What are you doing?" she yelled out to Benjamin as she distributed the groceries between the kitchen table and the refrigerator.

"They have hot water, Marya, very hot, and they have one of those large Russian bathtubs."

"Is that an invitation?" she shouted back as she unbuttoned her blouse and made her way to her lover.

The mechanics of lovemaking cruelly tested their flexibility. Her neck strained against the rim of the tub as she opened herself to him. His head hit the wall when he tried to enter her. Her knees rebelled when she went on all fours to welcome him from behind. His back screamed when she attempted to come on top of him. They burst into laughter at their failure and ended up with her sitting between his legs— her face pointed away from his—while he lathered her back with a fine French soap, and washed her hair with a perfumed shampoo.

Their bodies were still damp when they made love on the rough woolen blanket that covered the slender bed. She surprised herself by coming before he had fully entered her, and by coming again before he reached climax, and again when she felt his body explode within her. They opened a bottle of Oban single malt, cutting it with bottled water, and washed down the pork sausage Marya had fried. Then they made love again. But it was different the second time, her mind more active, her body less honest. She couldn't drive away the knowledge that he was going away, that this might be their last night together. She was going to be robbed of his voice, of his laughter, of his touch. She was going to have to live without his hands telling her she was desirable, without a passion that convinced her she was beautiful. If only she was better, she thought, if only she could find a sexual mystery—a twist of the body, a use of a hand, a movement of a tongue—which would overwhelm his dreams of departing, which would erase the memories of his previous life.

There was no physical act that would keep him in Ukraine, she knew. It almost made her glad. She didn't want his staying to depend on sex; she wanted him to stay because their souls sang the same song. And yet, what wouldn't she give to find a nostrum, an elixir, a shamanistic spell that would keep him in her arms? And what was she going to do after he deserted her? Would she go back to Ilya's cabin in the Carpathians? Would she return to Moscow or live in Kyiv? Would she be driven to put her picture up on the internet: Marya, 29; 175cm; 60kg; single? She turned away from Benjamin so that he would not wake to her sobbing.

When he wanted her in the morning, she moved away from him. "This day will be hard enough," she told him. "Making love to you would make the pain deeper."

Benjamin kissed her on the neck while she lit the gas stove. She pressed her buttocks into his groin but then pulled back. He kissed her again.

"I love you," he said softly.

"I know. But it doesn't help," she said.

# Chapter 23

The sun had broken over the horizon, and the eastern sky was aflame when Fedya took over the driving. He drove faster than Ilya had, stepping heavily on the accelerator when the road accommodated speed, and liberally applying the brakes where stretches of pavement had given way under the pressure of time and weather. When they drove through small villages and towns, Peter pulled a light blanket up to Pavlov's neck to conceal the handcuffs, and Ilya pushed the pistol against his captive's ribs to keep him quiet. But most of the trip took them through a vast hilly countryside, the trees hinting of autumn, the fields being harvested.

It was dusk when they entered the cabin where Benjamin had been held. Peter lit the fire while Caitlin helped Ilya cut some cheese and ham and black bread. The older Russian opened a couple of bottles of vodka, and they all drank, Pavlov most of all, as the cabin grew warm.

"This is where I held your husband," Ilya said in his heavily accented English after they sat down at the table to eat. "It's not bad. There are no bars on the window. There are no chains attached to the walls. We fed him well. He had all he wanted to drink."

"And who are the 'we' you refer to?" she asked.

"Marya and I. Fedya sometimes," Ilya answered as he cut a slice of black bread and handed it to Caitlin.

Fedya, who looked as if he was struggling to follow the conversation, broke into a supportive chuckle. Pavlov continued to frown. Vodka had depressed him. His complexion had grown ruddier during the long evening, and his expression more forbidding.

Drink had gotten to all of them, Peter observed. Ilya's laugh was louder and less predictable. Fedya had difficulty keeping his eyes open. Even Caitlin, who had drunk far less than the Russians, had begun to slouch and slur her words. He tried to imagine what was going on in Pavlov's brain, but all he could do was project how he would react to being held prisoner, to being handcuffed and forced to hold a shot glass with two hands. He was surprised by how easy he was finding it to stay away from drink. He felt at once superior to the others, proud of his ability to remain lucid. But part of him envied his companions' capacity to delay their drinking until the dark hours of the day. He had never mastered compartmentalizing time. Drink was desirable in the morning, by lunchtime it was irresistible.

"Is Benjamin well?" Peter heard Caitlin ask in a high-pitched voice. It pulled him out of his thoughts.

"Marya didn't indicate that anything was wrong with him when we last spoke, so I assume he is fine. Will you be happy to see him?"

"Of course," she answered, looking insulted. "He's my husband. I came all this way to rescue him."

"Foolish of me," Ilya continued. "Of course you will be happy to see him. But you are separated. You can understand why I ask."

"No, I don't understand. Do you think I would have come all this way if I didn't want to see him?"

Ilya slid his body off the couch and sat next to Pavlov. A layer of sadness coated the Russian's voice, and his accent grew stronger. "The deputy mayor and I know of such things, wives and husbands, lost and found. But what we know is about Slavic women. They stick by their thieves. They joined them in the Gulag; they waited for them outside Lubyanka Prison."

Peter couldn't contain himself. He broke into laughter. "For every wife who waited outside of Lubyanka, I'll give you twenty who ran home to their lovers."

Ilya squinted. His face turned red. But he hesitated before speaking—his head on Pavlov's shoulder, his vodka glass empty. "See, my black American, the price of sobriety. A drunk can design the world in which he lives. If he likes the darkness, he can choose to swim in a cesspool, forever bumping into huge turds, and skinny men, and diseased sluts. Or he can go swimming on a sunny Mediterranean beach, forever bedding shapely and lustful women. But sober, what does he see? Reality, he sees reality. What a terrible price for not drinking."

Pavlov stomped his feet on the floor and, in Ukrainian or Russian, Peter didn't know which, fiercely broke into the conversation, his voice in a roar, his eyes aflame. Ilya bounded up from his seat and shouted back with equal venom. Pavlov pulled his head back and spit at the Russian, but his saliva dropped short of its mark.

When Ilya raised his arm, Peter was certain he was going to strike his prisoner, but the old Bolshevik quickly took hold of himself. He lowered his arm and patted Pavlov on the side of his head. It was not a love tap, but it wasn't meant to do damage.

"Hypocrite," Pavlov yelled in English, "a fucking, cock-sucking, Russian hypocrite."

"Do you think the Americans will save you?" Ilya asked, the volume of his voice turned up, the drunken slur disappeared. "You want to curse me in English so they'll think less of me. But they know you, Pavlov. You can't deceive them. They've seen your type. Ukraine doesn't have a monopoly on criminals."

"But you, Ilya, you made me a criminal. Have you told them that part of the story?"

Pavlov struggled to say more, but anger constricted his throat and he began to cough violently. He raised his cuffed hands to his mouth and tried to regain his breath, but his coughing fit continued.

Ilya poured some vodka into Pavlov's glass. "Take a sip," he said in an empathetic voice. "Go on," he said after Pavlov had calmed down. "If telling lies about me makes you choke, you may want to stay quiet. But if not, spit it out, Comrade. I have nothing to fear."

"You made me what I am, Ilya," Pavlov charged, "you, the second generation of Lenin, the heir of a general who defended Stalingrad, who captured Berlin. You inherited the world's great power, half of Europe and most of Asia. What did you leave me, Ilya? What was my inheritance from you, polluted rivers, polluted minds, polluted politics? If I'm a corrupt bastard, who are you, Ilya? The fucking father of corruption, that's who."

"So you blame me for your becoming a shit. Precious, Pavlov, you are very precious. I am not your father; I am your conscience. Listen Comrade, I carry my shame quietly, but I carry it. But you, you have no shame, no moral bearing, no sense of right and wrong.'

"And this is right?" Pavlov asked, and raised his handcuffed hands over his head, the vodka glass squeezed between them.

Ilya broke into Russian. Vile sounding words spit out of his mouth, abhorrent sentences, one upon the other, poured over his captive. Ilya grabbed the glass from Pavlov's hands and shattered it against the stone oven. Pavlov was not intimidated. He argued back, flinging coarse and harsh words into his captor's ears.

Peter intently observed the brutal argument, his eyes darting from the Russian to the Ukrainian and back again, wishing he understood their language, craving a way to measure their arguments, despairing that all he could do was sense their bitterness and anger and hatred.

Peter looked at Caitlin and shrugged his shoulders. "They have a private battle," he said. "I doubt if we will ever fully understand it."

"Fascinating, Peter, isn't it, Ilya's inability to relinquish utopian dreams? If only we could catch it on camera."

~

Ilya allocated the sleeping spaces. He kept Pavlov close to him by pulling the cot Benjamin had used alongside his own and tying the deputy mayor's feet to its frame. Fedya was relegated to the floor, his pallet made of spare blankets. The inner room was saved for Caitlin and Peter.

Fedya lit the kerosene lamp, broke into a knowing grin, and left the Americans alone.

"I don't think Selby would appreciate this sleeping arrangement," Caitlin said, her voice tuned by the vodka.

"What do you mean about Selby?"

"Oh, Peter. I'd have to be deaf and blind not to know what's been going on."

The revelation was not unexpected, but it still caught him off guard. At first he began to deny the affair, but he stopped himself, realizing that a large part of him wanted her to know, wanted everyone to know that he and Selby were important to one another. He ended his aborted sentence with a chuckle.

"It is something out of a 1930s comedy with Clark Gable and Claudette Colbert. Would you prefer I slept on the floor?" Peter said after a prolonged silence.

"That would take the fun out of it, Peter. But if you don't find me attractive … ."

For a moment, he thought she was serious, but the mischievous smile on her face put him at ease. Caitlin had drunk less than the others had, but more than she was used to handling, Peter observed, suspecting that drink was good for her. Her complexion had grown darker, her television diction less precise, her smile more frequent.

"Choose your side," he said.

They kept their clothes on when they curled into Marya's bed. They tried to prevent their bodies from touching, but the bed was too narrow, and Peter could feel her ass press against his.

"You got a hard bottom," he commented as he shifted his body.

"Don't press your luck or you will end up on the floor."

He reached over to the bureau and turned down the kerosene lamp. The room filled with a yellow glow.

He turned on his back. "This is crazy, isn't it, locked away with three drunken Slavs, not knowing where we are, where we are going?"

She turned toward him so that she wouldn't have to raise her voice. "Are you frightened?"

"I was, Cat. When Pavlov took our passports, I was frightened. When Ilya shoved Pavlov into the car, I felt we were all doomed. But now, I think I'm just too dumb to be frightened. I can't understand what Ilya is doing. I want to dislike him, to distrust him, to be angry, but he is so disarming. Take his joking about my not drinking, how can I dismiss him as a hoodlum, as a gangster? But you, are you frightened?"

"I've been scared. I've worried about being gang raped, about being tortured, about getting maimed or being killed. I fear we will never find Benjamin. I worry that our search will make his life worse. That it will cause his death. But mostly I try to go with the flow, praying that fate will be kind, that there is a purpose to our travels. I know it sounds foolish, Peter, but I'm again the Catholic schoolgirl sitting with her hands on the desk, believing in a merciful God."

"That's not foolish. I've said prayers of my own, and I don't believe in God. I don't believe that right wins or that justice prevails, and yet I've prayed that we will be allowed to survive."

"Recently, I've buried my fear under thoughts of the story we would tell, of the documentary we would make. I wish I could get Ilya on film. I wish I had Pavlov in his office and Anna Baranova at the bar. How could something dreadful happen to me with so much left to do?" Caitlin said. She punctuated her optimistic observation with a laugh.

"How could it?" he chuckled.

She snuggled closer to him and laid her head on his chest. "Selby is a very lucky woman."

"I'd like her to think so."

~

The sun had yet to rise above the horizon, but the indirect light of the coming dawn was bright enough for Peter to find the outhouse and see the trees of the surrounding forest. He used the latrine as quickly as possible, hurried away from the wooden structure when he was done, and pushed the putrid stench from his senses by gulping chunks of chilly air. They had arrived after dark, and it was only now that he saw the steep pitch of the cabin's thatched roof, its vertical wooden plank construction, the whitewashed exterior that looked shabby in the dim morning light. Peter walked slowly around the structure annoyed that he had abandoned his sketchpad and pencils in the Dnipro hotel. He tried to compensate by memorizing what he was seeing, the shape of the front door, the number of windows, the smoke coming out of the chimney. There must once have been a fence, he thought, that outlined the boundaries of the extensive garden that lay in front of the house, and the backyard where pigs and chickens, he imagined, were once raised. He wished he knew how old it was, how many families had lived in it, how many children had been born within its walls. He looked around to see if there was a graveyard. None was apparent.

When children's voices came out of the forest, Peter pulled his attention away from the cabin and walked slowly into the woods. Soon, he began to worry about getting lost and questioned how the children would respond to the sudden appearance of a stranger, a black man no less. Reluctantly, he turned around and headed back. The horizon was a brilliant red when he got to the door. He sat on a wooden step, his feet planted on the ground. There was an important story here, he thought, in this isolated old-world cottage, where the light came from kerosene lamps and the heat from a wood burning stove, a story that would begin with a kidnapping, and then. He wished he could predict the outcome. He looked forward to finding Benjamin, to learning about what he had endured, to discovering what he had learned. He asked out loud, "And now Benjamin Palmer, what are you going to do with the rest of your life?" The sound of his own voice alerted him to his circumstance. He was embarrassed to be talking to himself, and wondered if anyone in the cabin had heard him.

But as he realized that everyone was still asleep, he also realized that the question was not for Benjamin Palmer. What have you learned, Peter Johnson? What do you know now that you didn't know before you left for Kyiv? It was not a frivolous question, he realized, sitting outside in the morning cold, and watching the sun begin to bathe the earth in light. But his answers were disappointing shibboleths: life is fragile; life is precious; there are bad people in the world. There had to be something more. He was lost in a foreign land, among people he did not understand, without any control over his life, over his movements. He was, like Benjamin Palmer, a prisoner. So what did he know that he didn't know before? Oh, he had collected all the things that tourists collect, sights and sounds, the tastes of a new cuisine, the architecture of a new city, the beauty of an unknown countryside. He had a new chapter for his memoirs; he had tales to exaggerate. And yet, in the confusion of his thoughts, he knew he had gained more than sights and sounds and smells. There were new feelings and new desires. There were emotions he couldn't draw or photograph. He walked faster than he had on his college's campus; he laughed more frequently. His smile was less automatic and more real, he breathed more deeply, he saw more clearly. After years of routine, he was doing things that were new. He was an actor and a witness. He was on the battlefield. What was he going to do if he survived? What could he do to keep up the pace and feel so alive? Snippets of ideas rushed so quickly into his mind that he couldn't grab hold of them. He would have held onto and explored these new visions, and was pained to let them go, but he heard the door of the cabin open behind him and had to move aside to let Fedya race by.

# Chapter 24

It was raining when Marya prepared eggs and sausage for breakfast, made a pot of coffee, and set two places at the table. But when they sat down together, sadness erased her appetite, and the thought of eating made her feel queasy. She drank some black coffee before leaving Benjamin to eat alone, and tried to lose herself in the warmth of a hot bath, in the creamy suds from the bar of fragrant French soap, in the American shampoo.

"You should take a bath," she said to Benjamin after she had dressed. "Bohdan's smuggled soap won't take off your skin and the shampoo will make your hair feel like silk."

"Am I that dirty?" he asked.

"Dirty enough."

"How about scrubbing my back," he suggested.

"You will have to get used to doing that by yourself," she answered, realizing only after the words had left her mouth that there was a wife and perhaps a mistress who might be more than ready to help him bathe, who would be happy to share his bed, who would make him better breakfasts and better coffee. She realized how little she knew about him, about the place where he lived, about his boyhood, his education, his taste in theater, in restaurants, in women. She wondered if he could dance, if he sang in the shower, if he kept his clothes neat—simple things, she realized—things she would have learned if she had met him in Moscow or in Vladivostok, if they had met at school, if they had been children together. So why did she love him so? Why couldn't she imagine life without him? She would survive. She was strong and independent. He was not going to rob her of anything real; he was only stealing fantasies and daydreams.

"Make love to me," she said when he came out of the bath wrapped in two white towels.

Bohdan's call came later than they expected, about 2:00 in the afternoon. He picked them up at 3:00.

Marya sat next to the Ukrainian when they drove to his landing strip. They took a circuitous route, part the road to L'viv's airport, part country lanes she had never seen. It was a long trip, providing more time than she wanted to imagine saying goodbye to Benya, to picture him flying off to his past. She fantasized that he would change his mind and race back to her. For a moment, she almost believed he would. Was his wife as beautiful as he had said? Was the African her lover? Marya's eyes began to tear when they sped by L'viv's airport. She gained control over her emotions when they weaved their way into the Carpathian Mountains.

Ilya was standing outside the barn that Bohdan used to shelter his Antonov An-2 biplane when they pulled up in the white van. "You keep getting younger and younger, Bohdan," he shouted in English as the pilot lowered the driver's window. "If you don't begin to drink more you're going to damn yourself to live forever." He broke into a roaring laugh as he swung the door open and pulled Bohdan out of the van. The old friends hugged each other tightly, leaned back and kissed each other on both cheeks, and then hugged each other again.

"Bastard," Bohdan trumpeted, "and what trouble have you gotten me into now?" He, too, spoke in English, as if using a less familiar language added weight to the moment.

"I will make you a hero, Comrade, despite yourself. Have you taken good care of my friends?"

"I have been the perfect host," Bohdan insisted. "They've been dining on Champagne and venison."

"Come, Marya, come," Ilya said. "Has Benya been behaving himself?"

He didn't wait for an answer. "We have some company. They are in the back of the hanger and waiting for you impatiently."

"The other Americans?" Marya asked.

Ilya didn't answer. He turned his attention to Bohdan. "Is your wife ready to fly?"

"If you are referring to my Antonov, of course. It is always in condition to fly. If I feed it enough fuel, it takes good care of me."

"Just like a wife," Ilya said.

"Better. She doesn't complain when I don't come home at night," Bohdan said, his voice playful.

When Ilya finished laughing, Bohdan asked, "How many passengers will I have?"

"I expect there will be three," Ilya answered in English. Then he switched to Russian.

Benjamin turned to Marya for a translation, but she motioned to him to wait and continued to listen to the conversation. Her heart fell when she heard Ilya tell of his capturing Pavlov.

Ilya didn't wait for Marya to translate his words. He enjoyed telling the tale himself. "It is a long story, Benya. I will make it quick. My attempt to ransom you back to America was thwarted by Kyiv's deputy mayor. He had his own agenda and was in a position to hold hostage your wife and her African friend. So I smuggled them out of Kyiv."

"I don't understand," Benjamin said, his mind racing to catch up to Ilya's words. "Are they the other passengers?"

He was going to ask more about the African American, but realized it would have been out of place.

"You didn't want to fly alone, did you?" Ilya asked. "But I also brought the deputy mayor. He was less willing to come along, and I don't think he will want to fly out with you."

"You're crazy, Ilya," Marya exclaimed. "No wonder the secret police followed us."

Ilya looked startled. "Secret police?" he questioned.

Bohdan answered in Russian.

Ilya stopped walking and put his head in his hands. "I didn't think this would happen. Pavlov's strength is in Kyiv. In the rest of the country, he is very suspect. I wonder if they're out to save him or kill him." Ilya looked ready to say more, but silenced himself when he saw Caitlin come out of the barn.

Caitlin abruptly stopped walking. She shaded her eyes from the sunlight.

"See, Mrs. Palmer, I keep my promises," Ilya shouted toward her.

Caitlin looked dumbstruck, standing by the open door, her mouth partly opened, waiting for her husband to come to her. Marya watched as Caitlin pounded Benjamin's chest with her fists, as she ran her fingers through his hair, as she pressed her head into his shoulder, her body trembling. He put his arms around her and embraced her. He murmured something only Caitlin could hear, but she continued to cry.

Marya turned away from the couple, and looked over the farmland that Bohdan used as an airstrip.

"Come, let's go inside to see the others," Ilya said to her tenderly. He grabbed Bohdan's arm and pulled him along. "Give them a few minutes to reunite. She's come a long way to find him."

Ilya's attempt at empathy failed. His sorrowful face seemed artificial, his grimace an attempt to mask the pleasure he was taking in his victory over Pavlov. Marya wanted him to project her sorrow, to look as if he was going to miss Benya as much as she was, she wanted him to admit just how much he had enjoyed the American's company, their arguments about collectivism and capitalism, about the meaning and purpose of life.

"You will miss him, Ilya," she insisted. "You will miss him as much as I will."

"Of course, I'll miss him, and I'll miss the money he should have brought. I'll miss the apartment I was going to buy in Moscow, I'll miss our visit to the Riviera, and I'll miss showing you London. But we are doing something good. We are doing what is right. I rescued him from his kidnappers. I kept him out of Pavlov's clutches. We taught him about life. Feel good Marya, we are doing something good. How often does life give us a chance to do something good?"

She couldn't bring herself to feel that anything was right. Nothing, she felt, was good.

"It is almost over," Ilya continued.

She nodded, her eyes unfocused, the corners of her mouth turned down.

"Are you worried about the secret police?" he asked.

She hesitated for a moment, giving him a quick smile. "In part, but we didn't see anyone following us into the mountains." She looked into Ilya's eyes and patted his arm nervously. "It is a bittersweet day, isn't it? I feel like I am losing a lifelong friend. I feel glad for him, but for me, there are other feelings."

Ilya's voice turned compassionate. "He has become a friend. It's hard to admit that we held him against his will."

Marya looked away.

"Have you fallen in love with him?" Ilya asked.

"That is a very strong word," she answered.

"There is room in the plane for more than three passengers. Bohdan would not refuse you."

"He's outside hugging his wife, Ilya. There is nothing more to say."

She took her hand off his arm, gave an insincere smile, and quickly walked ahead of her companion. She stopped next to the plane. "Can it fly," Marya asked as she looked up at the biplane, its fuselage and wings painted a dull orange, the four blades of its huge propeller painted blue, their tips yellow.

Ilya let out a sharp laugh, and waited for Bohdan to catch up with them. "Marya wants to know if it can fly," he said.

The pilot looked insulted by the question, "Do I look like a suicide," Bohdan said. "My Annushka is perfect. I would not take off if it wasn't." He patted its tail and gave Marya a toothless smile. "You have never seen one before, have you?"

"I've seen biplanes, but not as large as this one," Marya answered. She tilted her head and looked toward the top of the plane.

"Don't start with him, Marya, he will talk about this plane until your ears fall off," Ilya said without wit.

"Only if she is interested," the pilot insisted.

"And I am," Marya broke in.

"Only because she is gracious," was Ilya's comment.

Marya stamped her foot.

"This is among the last built in the Ukraine, but not the last built. The Chinese and Poles have manufactured them. It was used by the North Korean military for parachute missions. It was built for a rugged countryside. It can take off and land in people's backyards or on a frozen mountainside."

"Mountainside?" Marya queried in jest.

"Sometimes I exaggerate," answered Bohdan.

Marya watched Ilya's old comrade's complexion brighten, his body grow more erect, his closed mouth smile become more frequent. The plane was his bride, his mistress, his first and last love. It was an emotional investment she could not understand. Falling in love with a mechanical object was a part of life that had eluded her. She was invested in people and not things. And people could disappoint. They could unintentionally hurt.

Fedya took Marya in his arms when she entered the backroom where the others were waiting. He kissed her on her forehead like an older brother and smiled broadly. "Come, let me introduce you to our other guests," he said in Russian. "This is Peter Johnson, from America. He came to the Ukraine to find Benya. The mean looking man over there is Kyiv's deputy mayor. He came today to wish the Americans a safe journey home."

~

The silver Lada glistened ominously in the distance. Benjamin sighted it first, looking over Caitlin's shoulder, her hand tightly gripping his arm, her eyes fastened to his face.

"They're back," he whispered to her as if the occupants of the car might hear him.

It took her a moment to realize she had lost his attention. "Who is back?" she asked.

"The secret police. We have to warn the others."

As she turned to see what had grabbed his attention, he put his arm around her and directed her toward the hanger.

"How many cars?" Bohdan asked.

"Just the one," Benjamin answered.

"Fuck," Bohdan exclaimed. "Is it moving toward us?"

"They seem to be watching us from the top of the hill and not moving," Benjamin answered, deepening his tone to camouflage how dispirited he suddenly felt, how certain that everything was going to fall apart. He pictured himself in the backseat of a secret service sedan, his arms shackled, his head forced between his knees.

Bohdan made certain everyone could hear him. "They're waiting for others, Ilya. They won't try to stop us without help. They're agents and not military, and they're not suicidal. Help is most probably already on the way, armed help, with AK-47s and helmets. What do you want to do, Ilya? Quick. You don't have time to think."

"What choice do we have?" the old Russian asked, his complexion darkening, his gray eyes suspicious of the question.

"We can give them the Americans," Bohdan shot back.

"That won't satisfy them, comrade. You know that. They will want all of us. They'd make a political circus of the deputy mayor of Kyiv. There is an arrest warrant out for Marya in Vladivostok, and for a case of vodka, maybe just for a bottle, they would laughingly send her back. Fedya and I will be detained for as long as it takes for our friends to empty their pockets to buy us free. But you, Bohdan, they need you to bring them silk underwear and bottled perfume. So it is up to you, comrade. Do we do what we came to do, or do we let the bastards win?"

Bohdan's laugh sent a chill through Benjamin. Nothing seemed funny.

"You could always get me into trouble, Ilya. You know me too well. There is never any fun in letting bastards win, is there?" He broke into a nervous laugh before going on. "If they kill us, let's at least hope we're laughing, Ilya." With opened hands, Bohdan slapped Ilya's biceps, and then he wrapped his arms around his compatriot and kissed his cheek.

"Help me get the plane ready," the pilot yelled to Peter and Fedya in a raspy voice. Then he quickly ducked under the plane and moved from one wheel to the other in a squat, pulling aside the large wooden blocks that held the craft in place. "Push on the wings. It's light, so make sure to keep it straight. We'll move it back a few yards and partially close the hanger doors so they can't see us start the engine. Ilya, you take care of fucking Pavlov."

Pushing him with the butt of the gun, Ilya moved Pavlov in front of the plane and out the huge barn doors. When he thought the occupants of the silver car could see him, the Russian waved the old rifle over his head, daring them to come get him.

"Friends?" he asked Pavlov sarcastically.

Pavlov shrunk back, his arms swinging, his face red with rage. "Is that all you have, Ilya, this rusty old gun. A lot of good it will do you. They'll kill us both. I have no friends in the secret police. My friends are in the army."

Pavlov twisted around until the barrel in the gun was pressing against his chest. "Wave the fucking rifle over your head, Ilya, and hope they think it's an AK-47."

"Stay in front of me," Ilya yelled.

"Fuck you, comrade," Pavlov exclaimed and began to run toward the hanger.

Ilya waved the rifle over his head, hoping no one in the car had a long-range scope. He could hear Bohdan screaming commands at Caitlin and Marya, and shouting expletives at Peter and Fedya. He had stopped using English and was shouting at them in Ukrainian.

Pavlov began to help close the hanger's doors. "I have friends, Ilya," he yelled. "If you kill me they'll hunt you down."

Ilya didn't listen. He was looking beyond the Lada at the two large SUVs that were pulling alongside the small car. "Bohdan!" he yelled.

"Fuck," Bohdan said. "Listen, Ilya" Bohdan demanded, his voice echoing through the hollow barn. "If there are only three cars, we will give them three objects to chase. After you've helped open the hanger's doors, throw Pavlov into your car, Ilya, and drive toward them. Before you get too close, run over the field to get away. Fedya, you drive my van with Marya." The young Russian was unprepared when Bohdan threw his keys to him. They ended up on the dirt floor. "Take good care of my van," Bohdan said with an exaggerated snarl. "I will want it back. You should drive on the road but in the opposite direction and race away from the bastards."

"So you will sacrifice the old for the young," Pavlov shouted.

"Maybe we should shoot you now and let them fuck your body," Bohdan shouted. "Will you be able to handle him?" he asked Ilya.

"I have my rifle, and I'll take Fedya's pistol," the Russian said.

Bohdan poked his head through the narrow space between the two hanger doors. "Fuck," he said under his breath. He balled his right hand into a fist and beat it against the wooden door. "Fedya, Marya, bring the cars out front, but then come back. I'll need you to help open the doors so I can take off. I'll signal when by waving my hand. Then I'll shoot out of the barn like a cannonball." He turned from Russian to English. "You Americans, get into the plane." He paused for a moment, and then, almost to assure himself, he added, "There is no time for a pre-flight check, but it's the world's most reliable craft."

Benjamin helped Caitlin climb into the plane, waved goodbye to Ilya and looked around to find Marya. But she had already run through the barn's rear door and was on her way to the van. Slowly he climbed into a rear seat, wishing in vain that Marya would appear, that he could throw her a kiss, that they could smile at each other.

"Go in good health, Ilya, and with God's blessings," Bohdan shouted before climbing into the cockpit and disappearing into his seat.

The huge engine started with a roar, blowing dust and dirt behind it, and making the old barn rattle. The noise was overwhelming. Benjamin covered his ears and watched Fedya hand the pistol to Ilya and kiss the old Russian three times, once on one cheek and twice on the other. Then he struggled once again to catch sight of Marya, but he failed to see her.

The engine roared. The plane quivered. Bohdan waved his hand, and the hanger doors slowly opened. With frightening speed, the Antonov lurched out of its shelter, raced over the scraggly grass, and onto the bumpy dirt airstrip.

~

Benjamin twisted in his seat to see what was happening behind him, but all he could make out were four racing bodies and two stationary cars. When he straightened out to look through the windshield, he could see the threatening security forces speeding toward the biplane.

Benjamin braced his hands against the back of the threadbare seat in which Caitlin was sitting and pressed his feet solidly to the floor. Peter was sitting next to him, his head between his legs, his hands covering his ears.

It was all happening too fast, Benjamin thought, with time moving so quickly that it seemed to be standing still. Prayer had replaced thought when he had pressed his body against the An-2 to move it into position, as he scrambled over the wing and into the fuselage. He had only waved goodbye to Ilya; he had no chance to kiss Marya, to whisper into her ear. Too fast, he thought, life moves too fast. He had dreamed of holding Marya one more time; he had imagined a last toast with Ilya, some utopian wish about the universe miraculously healing. He looked down to the ground to see what his friends were doing, but the plane's distance from them was too great to learn anything. He tapped Bohdan's shoulder and motioned for him to circle over the airfield so that they could decipher what was happening. Bohdan didn't respond. Instead, he took the Antonov higher and higher. When the biplane eventually leveled off, the world of the Ukraine looked like a topographical map, and the jagged Carpathian Mountains were beautiful.

# Chapter 25

Abramowitz's blue eyes were fixed on Benjamin. "And what happened after you took off from L'viv."

"Nothing dramatic happened. The rest is pretty uninspiring."

"Try me," Abramowitz urged.

They were eating in a small French restaurant on Wisconsin Avenue, sitting at a table for two, and washing down their dinners of braised lamb and beef Burgundy with a moderately priced Saint Emilion. Some of the trees still had their autumn leaves, but the night was cold and wet, and few people had come out to dine. With the tables around them empty, their enjoyment of one another was undiluted.

"Bohdan landed at a large farm outside of Sibiu, Romania. The airstrip was owned by a business associate who drove us into the city. We stayed there for three days waiting for Bohdan to hear some news from Ukraine. That was when he got the call from Ilya. He and Marya were back at the hamlet where they had kept me. Fedya was on his way back to Vladivostok."

"And the deputy mayor? Did Ilya leave him in a ditch on the side of the road?" Abramowitz asked, leaning forward in his chair, the bags under his eyes looking heavier than they had earlier in the evening.

"Would you have done that?" a surprised Benjamin asked.

"Oh, I would have thought about it, but I couldn't have brought myself to do it."

"Ilya would have acted the same way. I think that's the funniest part of the story, Martin. Ilya and the deputy mayor concocted some story that allowed Pavlov to return to Kyiv as a hero. A brave Pavlov risked his welfare to rescue an American who was being held captive not far from Kolomyja, and whose wife had come to Ukraine to find him. They need each other, the Russian and the Ukrainian, Ilya to continue smuggling, Pavlov to continue to get his cut."

Abramowitz couldn't keep himself from laughing. "I should have predicted that, Benjamin. Nothing is new. But won't Caitlin's documentary unveil the truth?"

"I doubt if Pavlov is worried. He'll just claim that it's an American fabrication. But I think she will be careful. Offending Pavlov would just about cancel any future reporting from the Ukraine. That's not something Caitlin would sacrifice."

"So the truth will never get out," Abramowitz observed with a sad smile. "It's an old story. So, tell me my friend, what happened after Sibiu?"

"We took a train to Bucharest. Once there, our embassy handled the details. New passports were issued; flight arrangements made. Caitlin flew right home, but I stayed in London for a couple of weeks. I didn't want to get caught up in Caitlin's plans. I used the time to heal. I took in some theater, visited most of London's more celebrated museums, and ate at fine restaurants. Peter's friend Selby knew the best places. She reviews restaurants for *The Times*. They liked bringing me along. I had a couple of suits made for me, and half a dozen shirts. They were pricey, but since no ransom had to be paid, I felt wealthy, and I thought I deserved a birthday gift. One doesn't get reborn very often in life."

Abramowitz settled back in his chair, his smile revealing his yellow teeth. "You deserved to treat yourself, Benjamin. Maybe we should celebrate your rebirth right now. Can I treat you to another bottle of wine?"

"How about a glass of Cognac?" Benjamin suggested.

"Even better," Abramowitz said.

They had seen each other once since Benjamin's return to Washington, but he had found it an uncomfortable meeting. The restaurant had been full of young and exuberant patrons whose presence caused a shyness to fall between the two men, overcoming their past intimacies, their multiple conversations. This time it was different. They were again friends.

"It is very good to see you, Benjamin. I thought my stories about Peczenizyn had driven you to a premature death. That your body lay with my ancestors in some unidentified grave where no one who loved you could come to pray for your soul." Abramowitz took out a bright white handkerchief and wiped his eyes. "See, I even put a new handkerchief in my pocket to have dinner with you. I knew I would cry."

"Oh, I cursed you for sending me off to that forlorn land, but only on the bad days. I do need to thank you for visiting Caitlin. If you hadn't gone to see my wife, I may never have made it back."

"Or you may have come back sooner. A little poorer in money and with fewer good stories, but it might have been a safer journey."

"One of life's dilemmas, we never will know what might have been. But I am here now, and that's what counts."

"Caitlin is a very beautiful woman," Abramowitz said after he had sipped some Cognac.

"That she is, very beautiful. She gets more beautiful with each passing year, but she continually worries about losing her looks. There is no talking her out of her fear. The price of being attractive, I imagine."

"It is not something I've had to worry about," the old man laughed. "I see that she's back anchoring the news. Her co-host interviewed her about your rescue, but it was a short interview. She said something about the documentary that will be aired later, the film about her search for you. I expect you will be in it."

"She'll be interviewing me. She continues to work on the documentary with Peter Johnson. He's preparing to go back to Ukraine and has been in contact with Pavlov. He's still living in London with Selby. But it's Caitlin's story that will be told and not mine."

"A pity. Your story is so dramatic."

"Perhaps, Martin, perhaps," Benjamin said as his thoughts shifted elsewhere. "We're going to be divorced. We thought of trying again, but we both realized that it was a romantic notion brought on by my captivity and her coming to rescue me. She has done very well without me, and I wanted to push forward."

"I'm sorry, Benjamin. It must be unsettling."

"It's a joint decision. But it is still difficult. We failed each other. There is no way to avoid feeling bereft, but we both know that our marriage is the past."

Abramowitz's face turned somber. "And what is your future?"

"That's why I am having dinner with you. I thought you could come up with some suggestions," Benjamin said with a comic nod of his head.

They bowed their glasses toward each other and sipped their Cognacs.

"Is your journey over?" Abramowitz asked, his eyes squinted, his forehead wrinkled.

"What do you mean?"

"You will need time to digest the experiences you have had, that's all. There must be many unsettled remembrances."

"Part of me is still there, Martin, in the hamlet, in Kyiv, at the landing strip in L'viv. When you laugh, you remind me of Ilya, when you speak, your accent is much like his even though your English doesn't remind me of London. You would have liked him. He's an old fashioned Russian intellectual, full of emotion packed theories."

"You liked him, no?"

"It was impossible not to."

"And Marya, did you fall in love with her?"

"I was a prisoner. I relied upon her for my very life. How could I not love her? But was it the romantic love that fills the dreams of young men? I'll never know. It's another example of life's dilemmas. She does pop into my mind at the least expected moments. I imagine seeing her in a crowded subway car; I call out her name when she suddenly appears in a theater, at a restaurant, as I shop at Whole Foods. She invades my dreams, Martin, looking more lovely each time, but unhappy, lonely. Sometimes she is pregnant or holding an infant."

"It could be true, you know. You did lie with her."

"We were careful, Martin. I practiced withdrawal when she thought she might be ovulating. It increased my regard for the pill. But sometimes in the middle of the night, I like to think that somewhere in this world there will be someone who has my chin, my nose, the color of my eyes, and her warmth, her wisdom, her humanity."

"Do you think of trying to find her? You are going to be single again."

"I have, Martin, but I don't even know where I was being held, let alone where she might be living now. No, I am the one who is easy to find. If she wanted or needed me, it would be easy for her to locate me. But she belongs to Russia, and I belong here. It's hard to imagine either of us changing enough to bring us together."

"Was it the romantic love that fills young men's dreams? It's an interesting way to put it. Old men dream of love, too. The young do not have a monopoly on wanting lives to cherish." Abramowitz leaned forward and pushed his eyeglasses further up on his nose. "If you were Adam looking for Eve, you might decide to hunt for Marya."

Benjamin wanted to end the subject. Marya, too, he had decided, would become part of his past. "You think too much of me, Martin. I am not that adventurous or creative. It is interesting that you mention Adam and Eve. Ilya thought that the Bible's creation story was wrongly interpreted. God didn't chase Adam and Eve from the Garden. God took their weakness as a sign of his failure and not their wickedness. So he fled from the Garden of Eden and left mankind to fend for itself. 'Look around,' Ilya would say, 'look at the mountains and the streams, the trees and flowers, the sunrise and sunset, look at Marya, and then tell me this is not the Garden of Eden.'"

"To an old Bolshevik, the world can be made perfect. I once shared that dream, Benjamin, but the years have taught me differently."

"Ilya was more than that, Martin. He had no faith in the old way. There were too many Pavlovs in the world. He thought America suffered the same future. Puny and greedy men were burrowing under our society just as they had tunneled under his dreams. America will have to abandon the road it is on, Ilya insisted, and be driven— kicking and screaming—to search for a new way. If Ilya had faith in anything, it was in the search. Ultimately, mankind will find a balance. If a balance proved eternally elusive, Ilya believed, the search itself would offer a balm to the righteous."

"So he, too, was looking for Eve."

"What is this fascination with Eve all about?"

Abramowitz let out a deep sigh before continuing. "It's nice to hear you speak of yourself as a young man looking for romantic love. That was missing in your conversations before you left."

"Part of me feels young, the part that escaped back into life. I'm even planning to look for a job. I was pretty good at what I did."

"Before you got caught, you mean."

"Now that is being naughty."

Abramowitz tried to cover a yawn.

"How about having dinner with me next week, same time, and same place?" Benjamin asked.

"This place is a little too fancy and expensive for me. How about meeting at our Greek hangout?"

"Our old place would be fine. It just shows how difficult it is to be reborn.

"My bank paid my rent automatically, so all I had to do was unlock the door and wipe off the dust, and I was back home. Former colleagues are trying to find me a new position. I piss in the same toilet; I drink at the same Starbucks. At times, I find it very depressing, Martin. The experience should have forced a more fundamental change in me. I should be looking at the world from a different angle. I should be thinking in ways I never thought before."

In a familiar movement, Abramowitz reached across the table and squeezed Benjamin's arm. A grandfatherly expression covered his face. "You never did get to Peczenizyn, did you?"

Benjamin laughed. "And if I had gotten to Peczenizyn, all my problems would be solved, Martin? Is that what you are suggesting?"

The old man's hand squeezed harder. It punctuated what was going to be said. "Peczenizyn was never an end, my Benjamin. It was always a beginning, a humble place from which to begin. We should all take on new ventures with humility."

"For all I know, Martin, I could have been in Peczenizyn. Ilya was afraid to tell me precisely where the hamlet was. It was his secret retreat, and he didn't want to risk its location. And Marya was loyal to him. But when we were preparing to go to L'viv, Marya told me that the hamlet was east of Kolomyja, and so is Peczenizyn."

"Peczenizyn is very close to Kolomyja, but so are many other towns and villages, Benjamin. I'd hate to think that my village was your prison."

Benjamin's laugh was barely audible. "That would be the final irony," he said. "But—it occurs to me now—it would be just like Ilya to live near Peczenizyn, the birthplace of Oleksa Dovbush, the Ukrainian rebel. He did think of himself as a modern day Robin Hood."

~

A year had passed since his disastrous trip, yet here he was again, taking off from Dulles International on a Delta flight to Europe. Again, he was scheduled to occupy a seat on a Ukrainian Boeing 737 headed for Kyiv. At first, Abramowitz had tried to talk him out of it. "Phooey on Peczenizyn," he would say whenever Benjamin mentioned the trip. "Do you miss being beaten? Do you miss being jailed? You can get those things in Washington. You don't have to fly halfway around the world," Abramowitz preached. As Benjamin's resolve grew, Abramowitz's concerns deepened. "It is a large country, Benjamin, a very large country. People get lost. People want to be lost. What will you do if you don't find Marya? What will you do if you discover that she has become a stranger to you, or that she had buried her memories of you so deep that they cannot be awakened?"

"And if I don't try, Martin, what will I do then?"

Benjamin accepted a glass of sparkling wine from an attractive middle-aged steward with a sweet smile. He pulled a tray up from the arm of his seat and pulled a small notebook from his shirt pocket. He planned to write down the plans for the trip—land at Boryspil, meet Peter and Selby at the Grand Hyatt and book in, meet with Pavlov—but the uncertainty surrounding the rest of the trip weighed upon him. In the end, he left the page blank. There was no way to plot the journey. Peter and Selby were in Kyiv documenting his captivity and his rescue. Pavlov was helping them—hard as that was to believe—expecting, Benjamin mused, to become a hero in the piece, a rescuer of a kidnapped American. The deputy mayor had promised to protect Benjamin from the evils of his first trip to Ukraine, and expected to shake the American's hand shortly after his arrival. If Pavlov told him where Ilya was living, he would try to get to the Russian. From Ilya, he would learn how to reach Marya. If Pavlov didn't know where Ilya was, or wouldn't tell, he would travel with Selby and Peter to Kolomyja and from there to Peczenizyn. Then they would travel to Kalush to find Marya's friend, and finally to L'viv where they would try to locate Bohdan and discover the field from which the biplane took off. Peter was hoping to replicate the final chapter of Benjamin's escape, the plane taking off, the flight over the Carpathians. "Fewer bullets and more landscape," he had said.

Benjamin closed his eyes and ran through the alphabet to recall Oksana's name. He tried to picture Marya's friend's face; he searched his memory to remember Bohdan's features. He was certain he would find Marya. The world was not that big.

He finished the glass of wine. It was better than he had expected, decently cold and not overbearingly sweet. He waved to the smiling steward for a refill, leaned back in his chair, and watched an Air France gracefully land on the tarmac.

He had not waited for lightning to strike or hung around waiting for an epiphany. He had done all the things he could think of to grasp hold of life. Google had proved the enemy of his job search. No firm dared offer him a principal's job while countless articles about his indictment and conviction roamed the internet, but he had become a well-paid unnamed consultant, and had worked on two mergers and a buyout in the last few months, separating those executives who had talent and vision from those who only knew the words, suggesting to his clients who to retain and who to let go. He had taken a two-bedroom apartment further up Connecticut Avenue in one of the "best address" apartment buildings, and had a balcony that overlooked the National Cathedral and the green trees of Rock Creek Park.

He had even tried dating, inviting accomplished and interesting women to dine at upscale restaurants. There was rarely a second date and never a third. He felt distant from them and—repulsive as it was to him—somehow superior. It wasn't what the women were that drove him away; it was their empty spaces. They had never seen the river or heard the voices of the children. They had never been to Magadan. They had never had a husband whose avarice had made them fugitives. And Ilya's pronouncements and lamentations didn't ring in their ears.

But what did he expect? His dates knew only the world in which they thrived. They didn't suspect that ambition could be separated from avarice, that aspiration and greed need not be synonymous. Ilya would have laughed at him for dreaming it would be otherwise. He had gone back to what he knew, doing what he had done, in a city that heralded success, that applauded accumulation. "Oh, Benya," Ilya had once said, "I will send you back to America, but your return will only be physical. This land has changed you. My words are in your mind; Marya's beauty will dance in your memory."

Ilya was right, Benjamin thought as he emptied the second glass. He could no longer be content in the universe he knew before Kyiv. Washington was too spoiled, too rich, and too insular. He had begun to feel imprisoned by its streets and shackled by his desk. He had begun to imagine that his apartment was a lonely cell.

Benjamin looked around to see if he could catch the steward's eye. A third drink would be welcome. She waved him off with a broad smile and a shake of her head.

Caitlin had driven him to the airport and kissed him goodbye. "Be careful," she had said, "you are important to me." He found the words comforting, a recognition that they had grown into friends, that they were fond of each other. He had seen her often during the intervening months, joining her for dinner or catching a concert at the Kennedy Center. He had even escorted her to political fundraisers, events at which she would often leave him talking to an attractive colleague of hers so she could walk a distance away to have an "off-the-record" talk with a candidate or a lobbyist. He found the occasions fun, but a bit of envy would creep into him when a senator or congressman gave her a firm handshake. He'd even get a little jealous when a handsome man in a well-tailored suit kissed the side of her face.

"Are you going back for her?" Caitlin had asked when he mentioned the possibility of returning to Ukraine.

"There are lots of reasons," he fumbled.

They were riding along Connecticut Avenue in a cab and heading to the Kennedy Center to hear a string ensemble. The driver kept looking into his rear view mirror, wondering, Benjamin thought, why Caitlin looked so familiar.

"Oh, we can be honest with one another. I'm competitive, Benjamin. I'd like to be the only woman you could love that deeply, but I'm old enough to know better. She is why you want to go back, isn't she?"

"I have to find out just how important she is to me. All I know is that I don't want to forget her, and I don't want her to forget me. I can't imagine a future with her. Where could we live? What would we do? And yet … ."

"But you can't see a future without her," Caitlin said.

"Not yet."

"You are both very lucky, you know, her to be wanted, and you to want someone."

"It doesn't feel very lucky."

Caitlin spoke softly. "You should make the trip. But be safer this time. I don't know if I have the strength to search for you again."

When the driver turned around to accept Benjamin's payment, he said, "You're the lady on television aren't you? Is it alright to tell you how much of a fan I am?"

"It is much more than alright. It is very kind," Caitlin said with a smile.

They stood on the curb watching the cab pull away. "I love being recognized. It's a personality flaw, I know, but it's who I am. You deserve someone better, Benjamin, you deserve someone who wants only to be recognized by you."

"I don't know what to do" Benjamin had said to Abramowitz before deciding to return to Ukraine. "I keep thinking about transcendental questions: Why am I here? How should I live? Unanswerable wonderings, I know, and yet, how can I avoid them? How can any person? I can't even find temporary answers. I can't identify my choices. I drift back to Marya, to the cabin, into the woods. I know she is not the answer. I have no right to burden her with my salvation. I feel that I need her as a fellow explorer. I need her to share the questions and the journey. Do you know what I mean, Martin?"

The old man had rubbed his chin. "Can epiphanies come as questions and not answers, Benjamin? I wonder."

# Chapter 26

Benjamin watched the empty luggage carrier pull away from the plane and turn back to the terminal.

"Fasten your seatbelt," the steward said to him.

He slept over the Atlantic, and picked up a silver and gold plated "Peace Lotus" brooch for Selby and a box of dry Dutch cigars for Peter at the Amsterdam airport. The plane to Kyiv was only half full.

Unexpectedly, they met him outside the customs area at Boryspil. Selby handed him a small bouquet of wild flowers, and Peter smiled broadly.

The next afternoon, Pavlov met them in the doorway of the small conference room that adjoined his office. He welcomed them in English and invited them to sit around the table. There were clean drinking glasses and bottles of water and a plate of chocolate candies. Peter, as requested, had not brought his camera.

Pavlov stood at the end of the table. Anna Baranova was seated to his right. He introduced her to Benjamin as his trusted assistant. She smiled shyly.

"Ilya is a free spirit," the deputy mayor said after lighting a cigar. "He could be in Moscow or Vladivostok, or he may have gone back to Siberia for his diamonds and is living in Yakutsk. I have no way of knowing. But if he pops up in Kyiv, I'll tell him you were looking for him."

"And what of Marya?" Benjamin asked, still too distrustful of the deputy mayor to share Marya's full name with him.

"Marya?" Pavlov repeated with a question mark, and looked over to Anna.

"She was the woman who drove me to L'viv," Benjamin continued.

Pavlov laughed. "It was such a busy day, Mr. Palmer, fighting off the intruders, getting you and Mr. Johnson and your wife safely into the air. I don't remember noticing a woman named Marya. Is she important?"

Before they left his offices, Pavlov invited a photographer in to take their pictures. He placed Benjamin between Anna and himself, Peter next to Anna, Selby next to him. "It is always good to document the meeting of friends," Pavlov said. There was no irony in his voice.

They left for Kolomyja early the next morning. Selby did the driving while Peter filmed the rich agricultural countryside with a Sony digital camcorder, its microphone protruding over its telescopic lens. Every so often, Selby would slow down so Peter could capture a horse-drawn wagon, its bed filled with hay, and a wrinkled, kerchief-covered wife sitting on the straw. Once they stopped in a small town so that Peter could film a weathered wooden church with its multiple roofs and steeply angled spires. They got to Kolomyja before sundown. Benjamin wanted to go straight on to Peczenizyn—only 7 miles to the west—but Peter insisted that they stay in the larger city where it was more likely to find decent accommodations.

With a little help from a street vendor, they booked into one of Kolomyja's few centrally located hotels. It advertised five bedrooms to rent, a Georgian restaurant, and a fully stocked grocery store. Breakfast was included in the price. Benjamin moved into a small rectangular room, its toilet in a closet-sized room, its bathtub in a larger space. Selby and Peter got a suite with a double bed.

Benjamin spent the night twisting on a narrow bed, his mind too alive with imaginings of Peczenizyn for him sleep. He realized that he was seeing the town through Abramowitz's eyes, a 19th century village, quaint and isolated, with thatched roofed houses, with wooden churches and synagogues, with chickens in the front yards, and cows herded along dirt roads. When the birds began to sing outside his hotel window, he thought they were welcoming the sunrise over Peczenizyn, and he imagined smelling fresh air blowing off the Carpathian Mountains.

Selby and Peter were still asleep when Benjamin slipped out of the hotel to explore the neighborhood. It was daybreak, and the streets would have been empty if not for an old woman who was sweeping the sidewalk in front of a two-story brick building. Using the rising sun as a geographic marker, he ensured his ability to get back to the hotel by keeping track of the number of streets he crossed, the number of corners he turned. Churches were the most distinctive buildings. He looked over a dark-brick Roman Catholic Church, the top of its steeple painted a bright white. He lingered in front of a wooden church, admiring craft and beauty, and wondered if it was really as old as it looked and had miraculously survived two centuries of invading armies, or if it was a recently constructed replica. He turned south when he hit a wide avenue, surprised by the beauty of the city, its many trees still leafless, and tried to imagine how attractive it would be in summer, its 19th century structures surrounded by green spaces, its streets filled with pedestrians.

He was ready to turn back when he saw it. A comical building, shaped like a giant brightly painted Easter egg, about four stories high and proportionately wide. If it weren't for the small white building that supported it on one side, the egg-shaped structure would have looked ready to turn over and roll away. There was no doubt. He had seen the building before. It was dusk. Fedya was doing the driving. He was sitting in the back seat. Ilya was sleeping next to him. It was the second day he was with them, and they were on the way to the cabin. "What is that strange looking building?" he had asked Fedya when they drove by, but the young Russian didn't understand the question and Benjamin was not going to risk waking Ilya. But there it was. There couldn't possibly be two like it.

Peter and Selby were having breakfast by the time he got back to the hotel.

"I've been here before—in Kolomyja," he excitedly announced as he pulled out a chair and prepared to sit down. "I'm certain of it. We were on our way to the cabin."

When Benjamin finished describing the curious building, Peter said, "It's most probably the Pysanka Museum. It houses a vast collection of Easter eggs."

Selby screwed up her face. "How do you know?" she asked Peter.

"It's not because I'm so smart," Peter said with a laugh. "Google Earth. I looked up Kolomyja to find some of its tourist highlights. I am a reporter."

"But I've been here. Doesn't that excite you?"

"You are excited enough for the three of us," Peter answered. "Of course we're excited. How could we not be?" He got out of his chair and put his arm around Benjamin. "I'll settle the bill and begin to move our stuff into the car. You get something to eat. Then we'll push off."

"Do you think Marya is still living there?" Selby asked after Peter had left.

"I doubt it. But one step at a time. There must be people who know her, in Peczenizyn, or here in Kolomyja. A grocer, a butcher, at the post office, someone who knows her or Ilya, and can tell me how to find them."

He was too keyed up to take anything other than tea and bread, but he tried to sound calm and in control of his thoughts when they carried their few pieces of luggage to the car. Inside, he was in turmoil. Finding the cabin was unlikely. It was hidden in the woods. He had seen no neighboring town. He had never heard traffic from a nearby road. But no reality could keep him from being hopeful.

Benjamin studied the countryside as they drove along fields green with winter wheat, as they continued through the foothills of the Carpathians where houses and farmlands mixed on gently sloping land. His eyes hunted for familiar structures, for a building, a bridge, a fork in the road that would remind him of his first trip to the Carpathians. But the houses were no different from the ones he had seen surrounding Kolomyja or in the towns where they had stopped on the ride from Kyiv. The farm structures were utilitarian, the agricultural equipment indistinguishable from the equipment used throughout Ukraine. By the time they had finished the short trip to Peczenizyn, he was losing hope.

The weather turned against them. Heavy clouds were moving rapidly across the sky, graying the landscape with periodic downpours and casting a dreary tone over the town. All the houses in Peczenizyn seemed to have been constructed after the devastation of the Second World War, ordinary structures built for people who couldn't afford to seek architectural beauty. Some of the homes sat on pieces of land large enough to be considered small farms; almost all of the others had yards that could contain a vegetable garden and a chicken coop. But instead of seeming quaint and charming, all Benjamin could see was commonplace. Maybe if the sun was out, Benjamin rationalized, it would look better. But he knew that the sun alone would not bring Abramowitz's imaginings to life. If there was a center to the village other than a recently built church, Benjamin didn't discover it, nor did he find the marketplace that the old man had described, or traces of a study hall, or of a synagogue. Nothing that he saw hinted at his having been there before.

When the clouds began to break up, and the rain turned to drizzle, Peter parked the car on the side of a dirt road that ran by an old Jewish cemetery. Headstones covered the unkempt plots, a few still standing upright, but most of them lying on the ground, broken and worn, and strangled by the wild grass. Time had erased most inscriptions, and the words that could still be read were in Hebrew, a language none of them knew.

Benjamin roamed among the ruins. He wondered how many of Abramowitz's ancestors were buried there, how many of the faces in the photograph Abramowitz had shown him when they first met now lay under this soil. Few he realized. Most of their lives had ended in mass graves, without monuments, without prayers. He found the scene unbearably sad.

Selby and Peter stepped out of the cemetery when they noticed an old man walking down the road and asked him where they could get something to eat. But he knew no English and even hand signals, from the stomach to mouth and back again, did nothing but elicit a tilted smile. A young boy on a tricycle made circles around the three, his face full of questions. The old man eventually pointed in one direction, out of frustration Benjamin thought. The boy rode away.

When Benjamin joined Selby and Peter, they walked in the direction suggested by the old man, but with little expectation. After two turns in the road, they came to an unexpected end, and found themselves looking over the remains of a stone and wooden bridge that had once enabled access to the other side of the churning, narrow river. It looked as if it had been washed away decades ago, destroyed by some flood, or shattered during a war.

The desolate view sparked a long forgotten memory, hazy perhaps, Benjamin thought, but still real. Fedya had stopped abruptly when he realized the bridge was gone. Shouting a Russian phrase or two, he had woken Ilya from a shallow sleep, and seemed to ask the older man—Benjamin remembered thinking at the time—what to do next. They had both sounded unhappy. Benjamin couldn't remember much of what happened next, other than their turning around and traveling for another hour or so before reaching the cabin. Ilya had apologized to Benjamin for their arriving at the cabin at dusk. "If the bridge hadn't been out, we would have saved a lot of time," Benjamin now remembered him as saying. Or was Ilya's comment an imagined moment, a product of hope?

He consciously decided against sharing his memory with his companions. If he was right, it brought them no closer to the cabin. And if he were wrong, he didn't want to mislead them. There were dozens of washed out bridges in this flood prone land. And yet, the smell of the air, the flow of the water, the mountain range that loomed in the far distance—compelled him forward.

"Where are you going?" Peter yelled out.

"I'm just curious," Benjamin shouted back. "Don't worry. I'd like to be alone for a while. It's nothing personal, just a quirk in the stomach. Why don't you and Selby drive back into the town and find something to eat. I'll meet you back here in say two hours. I promise not to get lost."

Peter was hesitant, but Selby seemed to understand Benjamin's mood. She got a reluctant Peter to walk back to the car and told Benjamin that they would not get lost and he shouldn't either.

Benjamin began slowly, hugging the border of the stream, pushing through the undergrowth, brushing aside the twigs and branches, still wet from the morning rain, which blocked his way. But the further he walked the faster he found himself going, resting only for a moment when the forest gave way to an open space, and he could enjoy the warmth of the spring sun. It was no longer drizzling, and a blue sky enfolded the forest. The patterned, white bark of the birch trees, and the sway of the weeping willows, convinced him that he had been there. He dreamed of hearing Ilya's laughter break through the forest; he saw himself catching Marya washing clothes in the stream. With each step, some new imagining came into his mind. The very sound of the river and the music of the birds were familiar. The air smelled of pine needles and Marya. He felt compelled to raise his watch to his ear to test its ticking when it showed that thirty minutes had passed. It seemed like a moment; it seemed like he was just beginning. It was only when he stumbled over a rock that he realized he was tiring. When he tripped over a fallen branch, the contours of the land turned unfamiliar, the trees alien, the river threatening. Had he forgotten the direction of the water's flow? Had wishful thinking robbed his memory? He forced himself to slow down, to look for a stump or a fallen log on which to rest, to find a place where the sun could reach him and raise his spirits. He thought of climbing one of the hills to see if he could get a better view of his surroundings, wondering if height would enable him to find something familiar, a farm, a cut in the stream, a house. But the land did not rise, it rolled, and even if he was adventurous enough to climb a tree, it was unlikely he'd see very far.

Frustration began to gnaw at his mood. Time and distance began to bully. He would have to turn back; he would have to accept his failure.

Then the voices began, so far in the distance that at first he thought he had mistaken the sound of the wind, but then they became clearer and loud enough to cause him to disbelieve his ears. Children's voices, sweet soprano voices, were coming toward him from the other side of the water. He drew in his breath, telling himself to stop, to realize that they could be any group of children. Do not allow your hope to spike, he demanded of himself, but before realizing it, he had stepped into the stream, his feet sinking into the water.

He pulled his shoes from the muddy bank. "Kostya," he yelled out. "Mila," he screamed.

The voices grew silent.

"Dasha," he said at the top of his lungs.

"Benya," the boy's voice rang back. There was no question mark. "Benya," he shouted again as if greeting a dear friend he had seen a couple of days before.

Then a young woman's voice—more cautious and skeptical—came over the water. "Benya?" she asked. "Benya?"

He could see them now, Kostya running through the low grass on the opposite bank, his arms waving in the air, and Dasha huddling next to her older sister as they ran down to the rocky edge of the river.

Benjamin waved back, jumping up and down to be certain they could see him. But he didn't linger. He turned up the path to the cabin, his breathing heavy, his heart racing.

She must have heard the shouting, he thought, when he saw Marya walking toward the river, her dark blue sweater familiar, her long skirt blowing in the light breeze.

"Marya," he called.

Her body froze.

"Marya," he called again.

"Are you crazy?" she shouted up into the air. "Have you gone mad? Are you seeing things?"

She took a few steps back and almost stumbled. Then she turned around and began to race to the cabin, but before she got to the wooden steps she turned again, her face contorted, her arms wrapped across her breasts.

He had dreamed of this moment. He would plant a thousand kisses on her lips, on her forehead, on her cheeks, in her hair. But now that he had found her, they just stood staring at each other, and sobbing.

She reached out and ran her fingers over his brow and along his nose. She put one palm on his neck and tucked the other hand under his chin to lift his face. "You are real, Benya. You are not a ghost."

Marya trembled when he took her into his arms and pressed her warm body against his. She tilted her head back to look at him, and then rubbed her cheek along his, whispering something in Russian into his ear—a prayer, a blessing, a wish—that he couldn't understand. It didn't matter. He knew he could learn.